MYRENNE MAE

Three Coins from a Dead Man's Pocket

REALMS OF SOULS SAGA
BOOK ONE

Diving into these pages you will not only be a reader, but discover your-self as a co-conspirator of the Realms, cheering for our heroes, crying for their losses and encouraging them through their struggles.
(And trust me, you will.)
Thank you, dear readers, supporters, and my very first fans: your encour-aging words have brought this vision to life, especially the authors and friends I found in FanGrrl Romance Recs Authors Corner, you know who you are.
Thank you to my editors at CookieLynn Publishing, Jessica and Suzi. Their challenging critiques and endless emails of encouragement made my first editing experience tough, but educational, and in the end, this story is so so SO much better than it was when I first wrote it.

And, lastly, to my true flame, *mé dáru ardé*:
Every change of heart, new plan of life, or crazy scheme I hatch, you are there. Thank you, *a yah ageré*, from the depths of my soul.

However...

If you love this book feel free to write notes, draw pictures, squiggle lines, arrows, emojis and anything else that makes you happy inside the pages.

If you love this book SO much you just have to share it with someone, please pass it on (and maybe write a note in it for the future reader!)

I'd love to see your doodles, highlights, notes and hear your stories. You can scan the QR code or click HERE

to find all my socials and my newsletter.

(I don't email often: only when I have some really important things to tell you.)

I can't wait to know you more and hear how Ava, Thorben, Tobias and the crew snuck into your heart!

~Maió yah aríla vylá efusar, obúmes.

~May your soul fly freely, friends.

~Myrenne

A note to my readers about the content you will find in this book. Your mental health is valuable, don't let anyone tell you otherwise. In respect to that, here is a short list of what you will find in this book:

- alcohol consumption

- explicit sex scenes

- graphic torture scene (from one mage to another, both adults)

- child being held and a spell cast on her against her will (don't worry, she gets saved)

- group sex scene where someone accidentally gets hurt

- parallels with dissociative identity disorder

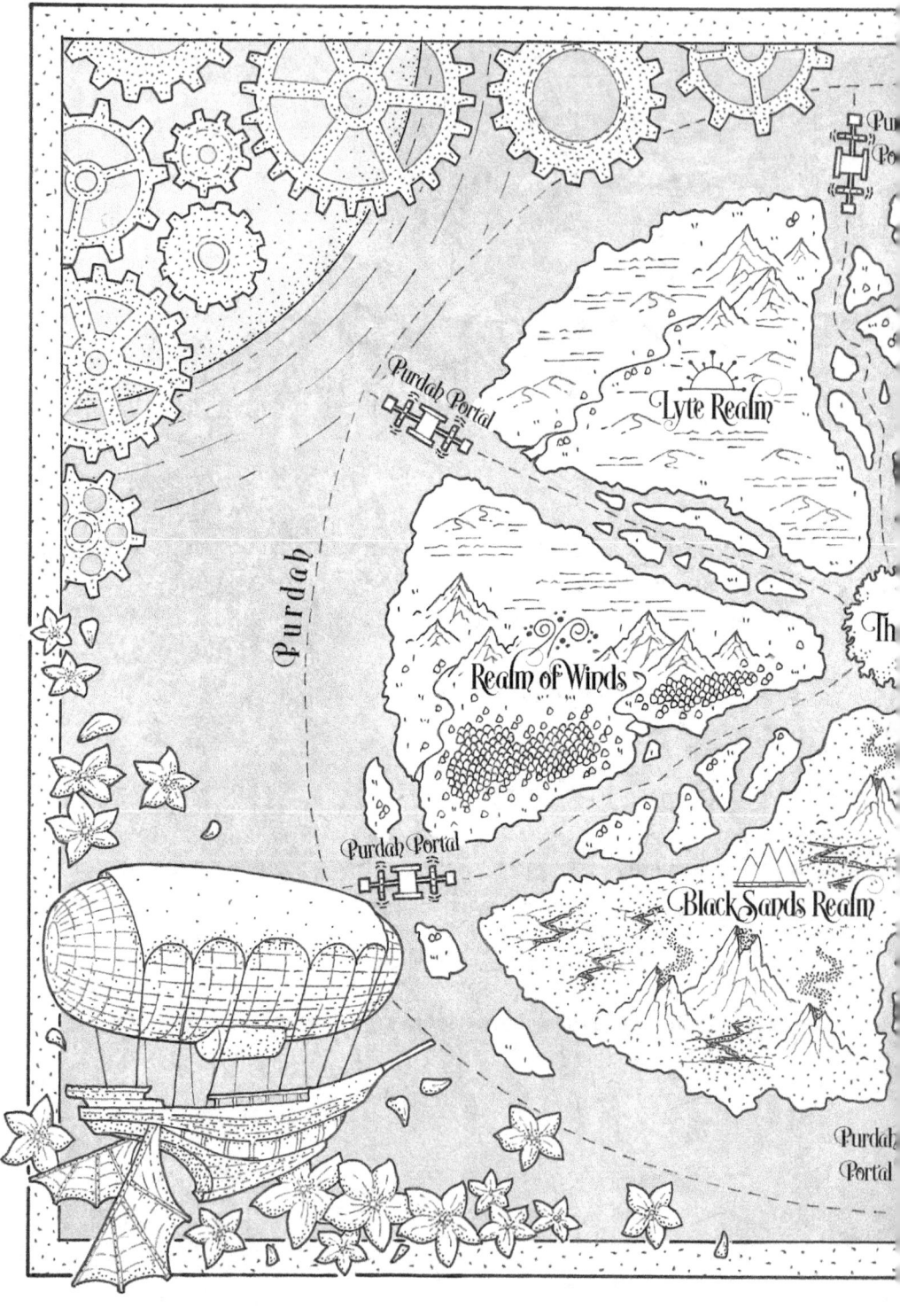

Purdab

Purdah Portal

Lyte Realm

Purdah Portal

Realm of Winds

Th

Purdah Portal

Black Sands Realm

Purdah Portal

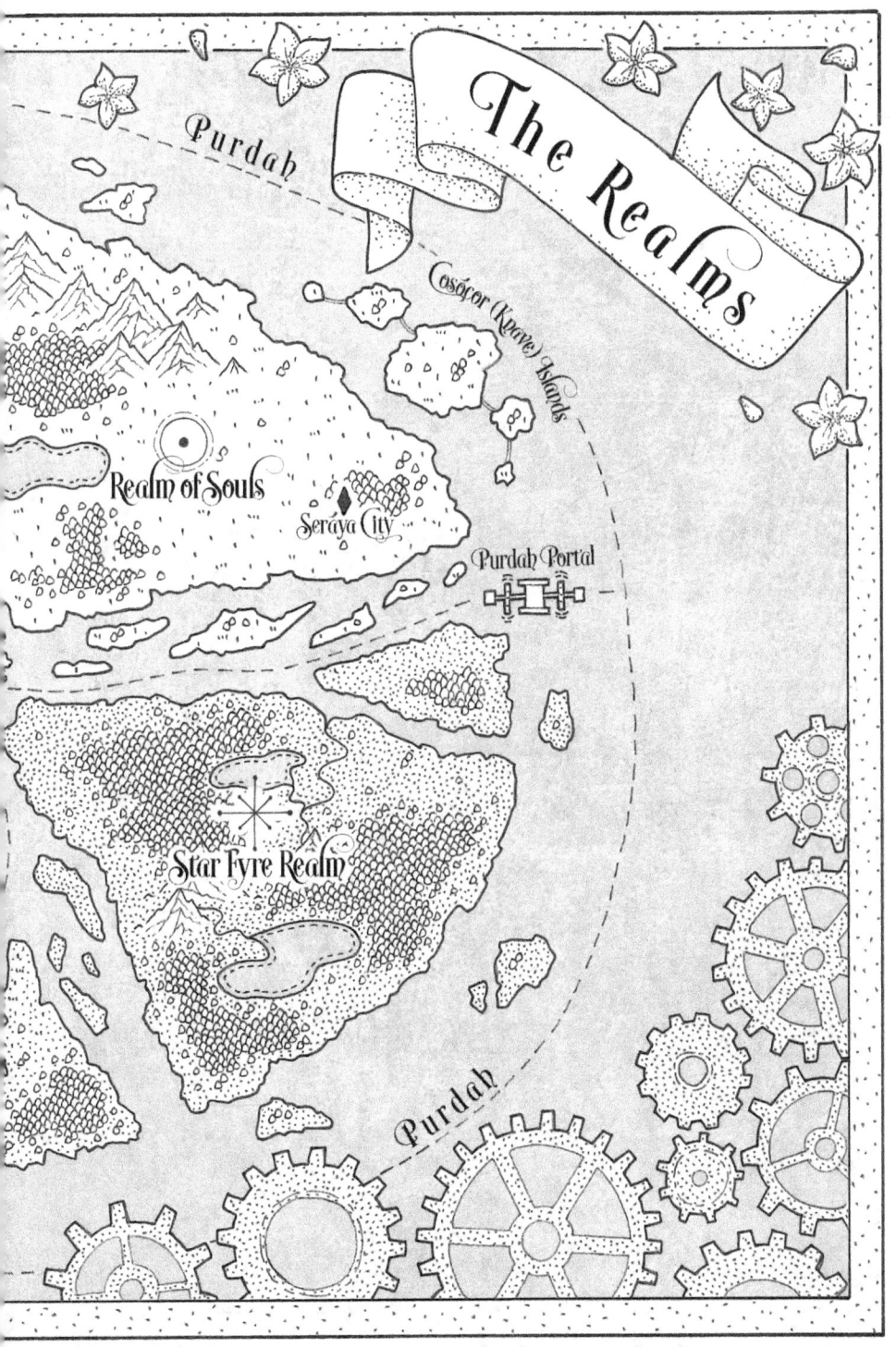

The Realms

Purdah

Cosócor (Knave) Islands

Realm of Souls

Seráya City

Purdah Portal

Star Fyre Realm

Purdah

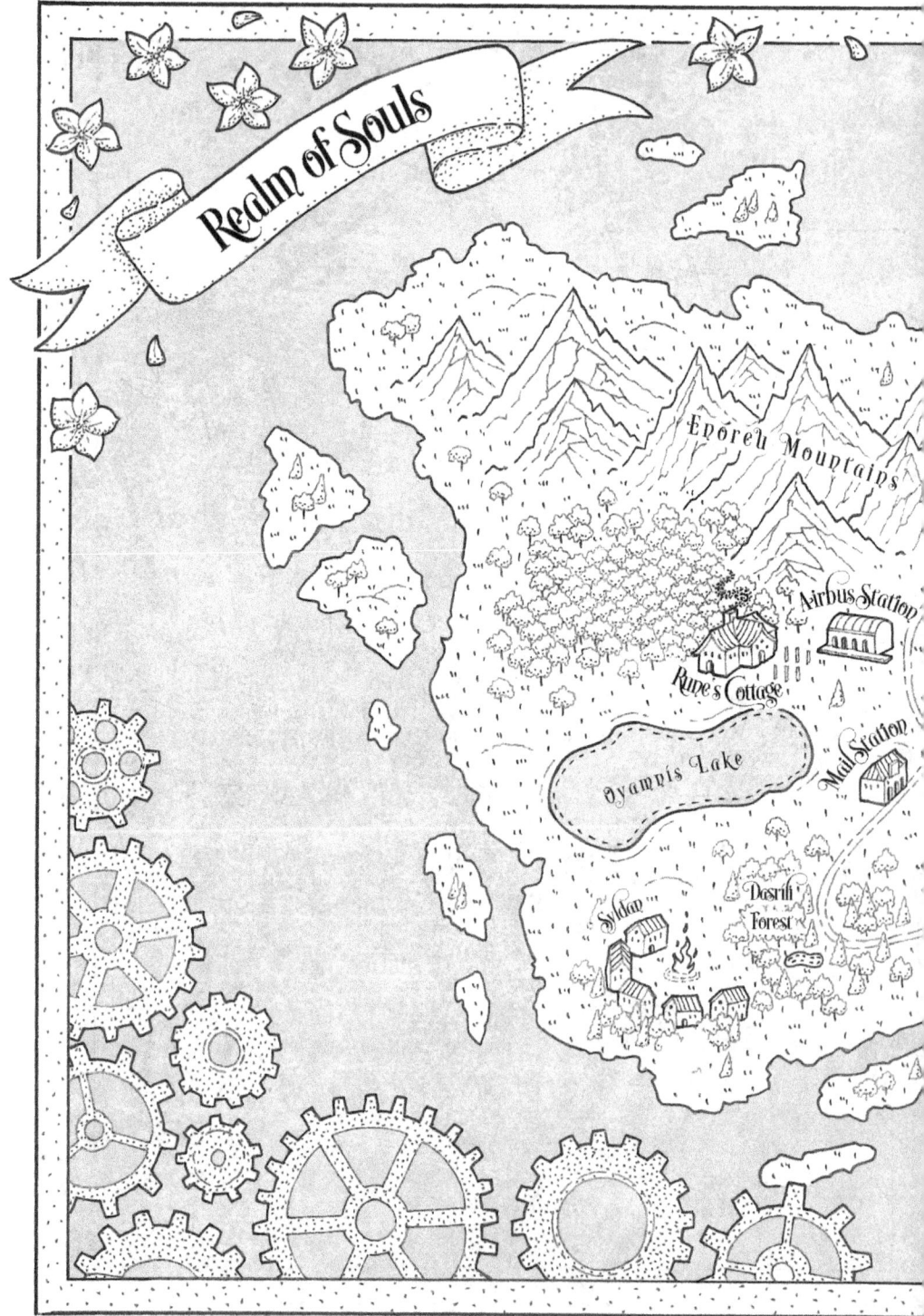

soul/spirit/essence

The very core of a person; the soul houses one's personality, emotions, memories, and magic; transferable to any object or another body

druid/druis

A male or female mage, respectively, who has druidic magic and can see into the liminal level, to find lost souls and guide them to Empyrean

druidic magic

The magic a druid or druis has that allows them to see the liminal level and those inside it, namely souls

phylactery

A small box worn on the arm of a druid or druis. This is where they store items that have been bonded with souls (essentiae)

utility belt

Can be worn by anyone needing it, but druids and druises carry items on hand for collecting souls inside

liminal level/plane

A level of existence between the real world and the afterlife; only souls exist in the liminal plane (well, mostly)

Empyrean

The blessed afterlife; where noble and righteous souls are destined

Tartarean

The cursed afterlife; where evil and corrupt souls are taken

Day of the Five

A holiday in which all realms celebrate the five mages who each bonded with a single realm to save their world from utter destruction.

The Ancient Language of Ili

Ili, the native tongue of the Realms, echoes through the fractured islands, and is now a shadow of what it once was. While some must know it to weave spells and incantations, the everyday tongue has morphed into something else.

The cataclysm that shattered their world and birthed five new realms caused the Ili language to wane, losing its place as the seat of their culture. Now, the language has dwindled to a handful of words and universal phrases, weaving itself into the tapestry of everyday speech.

Throughout the story, ancient Ili words are depicted by italics.

Adorimé **(ah-door-eh-MAY)**

Direct translation is "my daughter" often endearing and respectful

Decorimé **(day-core-eh-MAY)**

Direct translation is "my father" often endearing and respectful

Elehí **(eh-lay-HEE)**

A woman, usually older, a term of respect, as in "my lady"

Essentia(e) **(es-SEN-shee-yah)** plural: **(es-SEN-shee-ay)**

An object(s) that a druid or druis has used to bind a soul until they can guide them to Empyrean (NOTE: souls bound for Tartarean are called by the prince who rules the icy afterlife and are not bonded but are left for him in the liminal plane)

Esprí alúta **(es-PREE ah-LUTE-ah)**

A morning greeting, direct translation is "joyous morning" or "good morning"

Laurimé **(lawr-eh-MAY)**

Direct translation is "my mother" often endearing and respectful

Mé le dar (MAY lay dar)

Direct translation is "my little one"; a term of endearment

Mé talé (MAY ta-LAY)

A term of endearment, direct translation is "my treasure"

Mé veláh (MAY vay-LAH)

A term of endearment, love, or sweet nickname as in "my dear"

Neyá (nay- YAH)

Commonly "no"

Seáh (say-AH)

"Yes" or agreement, commonly used with **llaéh** as a warm welcome greeting

Seáh llaéh (say-AH la-AY)

A common, welcoming greeting; when the entire phrase isn't used, it is typically a cautious greeting

Venúste (ven-OOS-tay)

Adjective to describe someone as handsome, good-looking, sexy as hell, desirable

Vjáme (vuh-HAAM-may)

Exclamation, equal to "holy shit," full of more feeling than saying a plain ol' "shit"

Chapter One

The body plummeted through the labyrinth of steel, its descent a chilling symphony of clangs and scrapes against unforgiving metal. With a final, dull thud, it landed in a cloud of dust at the feet of a druis, hundreds of levels below.

Avalína Llahenór had collected souls from bodies like this before—too many in her thirty years. She dropped to her knees, her heart drumming against her ribs, the dust motes dancing in the dim light. The body lay crumpled in a heap, twitching and contorted, the limbs twisted in unnatural angles.

"Merg," Ava said, gesturing to her friend as she shoved her ebony waves to one shoulder. "Come here."

Mergen's booted footsteps crunched on the gravel. "Souls, Ava, what happened?"

"She must have fallen through the levels." She shook her head, her lips twisting into a grimace. Hurtling through the labyrinth of steel and iron was a horrifying prospect and a guaranteed one-way ticket to oblivion.

Ava pressed her lips together and rolled up the sleeves on her loose white shirt. She brushed the fair hair away from the person's face. A woman stared back—alert, blue eyes, terrified and furious.

Ava's fingers moved with practiced efficiency—years of this work had taught her exactly where to search, how to move quickly without disturbing the dying. She found the woman's utility belt tucked under her shirt and ripped open a pouch. Small metal bars tumbled out, brightly clinking against one another.

Most souls bonded best with an item they were already comfortable with. It was more personal to the soul and made it more willing to accept the bond.

She snagged a bar as warmth spread over her knee—blood, always blood. She'd stopped wearing light colors long ago.

Three Coins from a Dead Man's Pocket

WritingFormatting

BD

Body

"Don't leave me," Ava whispered, though the woman's eyes were already glazing. "Almost ready."

Ava's hand trembled—just for a second—before she steadied it. A hundred bodies, and she still had to force her fingers not to shake.

"Better hurry." Mergen reached for her utility belt. "You don't want her soul to jet off."

Ava nodded absently. If the woman's soul wandered off before she could bond it, she'd spend hours searching the liminal plane—hours she didn't have, not with Rune getting worse. Ava scooted across the gravel, bending low so the woman could see her.

"I'm here," she said. The woman tried to speak, but her jaw was broken, her words incoherent. Tears rolled down her cheek and she let out a small moan. Mergen bent on the other side to take the woman's hand.

"It's alright. I know you are not finished here," Ava whispered. "But you can't do anything with the body you are in. Let me help."

Ava began to sing, and the woman's eyes slowly fluttered closed.

"Follow my voice and the lilt of my song,
There is a new world for you to belong,
You will find hope and the beauty of light,
Come to me, for a safe haven this night."

The woman's soul released, taking flight in an exquisite swirl of lavender and silver. The air instantly filled with the heady aroma of spring hydrangeas and cloves. The woman's spirit folded over on herself and hovered above her body, unsure of what was happening. Ava, her voice barely a whisper, hummed a wordless melody to ease her worries.

The vibrant soul curled toward the bar in Ava's hand and settled herself against the cold, sterile metal. The rod became slightly heavier, the last bit of her spirit nestling inside. Ava stood and sighed, relieved she had been able to bond it. Being lost could be a true death sentence for a wandering soul.

Ava stood, the essentia heavy in her palm—heavier than it should be. A decade of collecting souls, and they still surprised her with their desperate weight, their furious reluctance at being torn from bodies that had failed them. She'd thought the work would become easier. It hadn't.

"How far do you think she fell?" Mergen said quietly, her gaze lifted toward the dim lights filtering from above.

"I'm not sure." Ava studied the woman's body again—the angle of the fall, the pattern of injuries. The woman's hands were shredded, like she'd been gripping something. Or trying to.

"High enough," Ava finally murmured. She unclasped her phylactery and slipped the rod inside with four other essentiae. Five souls so far this week. Twelve the week before. The city was crumbling faster than she could catch the falling.

Ava reached into a pocket on the side of her black cargo pants and snagged a thumb sized beacon. She wound the key on the back. The light blinked steadily—red against gray, urgent against lifeless. Ava clipped it to the lapel of the woman's gray work suit. The gleaners would come, burn what remained, while somewhere someone was waiting for this woman to come home.

"Let's get going." Mergen said.

Nodding, Ava and Mergen continued to the temple, their footsteps crunching on the gravel as they traveled through the oppressive pathways of the swale at the very bottom of Seráya City. It was dark and dirty, the debris from above constantly raining through the cracks. The rail system, only a few levels above, had once been the highest point. Over time, the lowest levels had been built over, the tracks now uneven and in need of repair. Buildings upon buildings were erected over and atop themselves, creating a jigsaw of houses and business complexes that pressed down on the city's lowest inhabitants.

They reached the temple, its broken beauty a light in the darkness of the swale. The temple was over a thousand years old and had once been a building of awe, with tall stone towers and stained-glass windows letting in colored light when the sun shone. Now it was beautifully ruined—pock-marked stone that wore its thousand years like jewelry, humbly buried beneath the city's layers.

Mergen and Ava entered, the screeching door hinges announcing their arrival. The aged stone floor had been freshly swept, the candlelit sconces illuminating Mother Zoya's petite frame in the doorway beyond.

"Avalína, Mergen." Zoya smiled, her almond shaped eyes wrinkling delicately at the corners. Ava had always wondered how old the priestess was but never dared to ask. She had known Zoya her entire life and Zoya and Ava's aunt, Rune, had both loved, raised, and educated her, each in their own way.

"It's good to see you." Zoya approached, her shoes silent on the ancient stones. Her shiny, black hair swung rhythmically in a braid behind her, the rest piled atop her head.

"Seáh llaéh, Mother." Ava and Mergen said in tandem, both bowing their heads. Ava heard Zoya kiss Mergen's forehead as she whispered a blessing. Mergen murmured her thanks, bowed and left.

Ava watched Zoya's toes, just visible in her range of view. She waited, expecting Zoya's blessing, but it didn't come. Ava peeked out from beneath her dark lashes.

Zoya's lips moved with silent words, her eyes closed—praying, always praying something different over Ava than she gave the others. A longer prayer. A more desperate one. Ava had stopped asking why years ago. Some questions had answers that came in their own time, or never came at all.

She drew in a breath and Ava quickly lowered her gaze.

Zoya's hands, cool and fragrant with the scent of jasmine, settled gently on either side of Ava's head. A sigh escaped Ava as the tension in her body melted away, peace filling her as she surrendered to Zoya's comforting touch. "My daughter, it's been a while since you visited. Where have you been?"

"Aunt Rune's been sicker than usual." The words tumbled out. She hadn't planned on dumping her worries on Zoya and unexpected tears welled in her eyes. "Her episodes have been occurring more frequently, sometimes for days at a time. I can't leave the cottage when she's like that."

Last week, Rune had been working in their expansive garden, pulling weeds and planting flowers. Then she'd stopped mid-row, dirt-covered hands frozen, and turned to Ava with eyes that didn't recognize her.

"Run!" Rune had screamed. "Get as far away as you can—they're coming to murder us!"

Three days. Three days of Rune barricading doors, checking windows, sleeping with a knife under her pillow. Three days of Ava talking her aunt down from terror, going without sleep herself, pretending she wasn't terrified that this time, Rune wouldn't come back.

On the fourth day, Rune had woken completely normal, smiling over breakfast as if nothing had happened.

Ava was exhausted in the way that went bone-deep, soul-deep. Each episode was longer than the last. And when Rune came back, she seemed fainter, like a wilted flower left too long in the sun.

Zoya lifted her head, her dark eyes meeting Ava's. They skipped across her face, and Ava wondered what Zoya was thinking.

"I know it is exhausting for you." Zoya let her hands drop to Ava's shoulders, and she squeezed them gently. "What will you do?"

"I'm not sure." Ava rubbed a hand over her face. "She refuses to accept a cadaver." Rune was her only living relative. She didn't remember a father or a mother. Just Rune. And Zoya.

Rune had taught her games in their yard, recipes for phytomedicines, and the ancient language of Ili. They designed their garden themselves, creating a beautiful landscape filled with herbs, topiaries, archways covered in vines, and a small pond with a calming waterfall. When a mirror accidentally broke in the house, Rune gathered the pieces and showed her how to string them together to create a cascade of reflectors that made the entire garden glitter.

And then there were the souls.

While Rune taught her herbs and medicines, Zoya taught her about souls. Souls from all over were naturally drawn to Ava and their serene garden. They would flit through the flowers and Zoya would visit, teaching her about the afterlife, a soul's journey, and the ultimate peace it sought. Zoya had shown her how to speak to the souls and how to collect them for the souls' next phase of life.

When Rune began having episodes, Ava and Zoya had spent countless hours bent over ancient texts, consulting with druids across the Realms, writing letters to temples in distant cities. Every book said the same thing: soul deterioration was irreversible. Every expert offered sympathetic condolences but never cures.

Rune was slipping away like water through cupped hands—slowly, then all at once. And Ava—thirty years old, trained by the best, able to see and speak to souls in ways even other druises couldn't—was powerless to stop it. If Ava couldn't find a way to keep Rune's soul from deteriorating, her spirit would completely evanesce, and Ava would never truly be with her aunt again, not in this life and not in the heavenly afterlife of Empyrean.

"Your aunt is strong, and your souls have always been intertwined," Zoya said, bringing her out of her thoughts. "You'll know how to help her when the time is right."

Ava nodded wearily. "*Seáh ter dáru*," she sighed. The phrase had been one of the first things Rune had taught her in ancient Ili. It meant, 'Let it be true.'

"*Seáh ter dáru*." Zoya's lips lingered against Ava's forehead, a small sigh escaping before she pulled away. Ava prayed Zoya was right. Rune had always been a pillar of strength, her unwavering spirit a source of comfort to those around her. The moments of her lucidness fading and her eyes losing her bright spark scared Ava.

Ava wandered through an archway and into the Passing Room. The sweet citrus tang of orange mingled with the warm spicy aroma of ginger wrapped around her like worn leather—familiar, broken in. Ten years since she'd been a fumbling disciple here, burning her fingers on the embers, crying over her first soul release. She'd been twenty and thought she understood death.

But, over time, she had begun to understand that souls are the truest form of a person, regardless of where they were or what they had bonded with. Souls were life, not a physical body. With the right guidance, souls could be retained for years. They could choose to accept a new body or be set free to their afterlife.

Choosing an alcove, she set her black aviatrix boots to the side, brushed off her pants and removed the leather glove from her left hand. Her knees pressed into the soft padding of the mat as she knelt before the elements. She clicked open her phylactery and withdrew her essentiae: a small cog, a piece of fabric, a box made of paper with a delicate butterfly drawn on top, a notebook, and the metal rod. Each piece was calm and content, except for the metal rod. It thrummed anxiously in her hand.

"I know," Ava whispered. "We'll get you home." Ava breathed deeply and closed her eyes, reaching out with her spirit. If Ava had tumbled through the latticework of beams, she would be upset too. Sighing, Ava dropped the rod back into the little black box. This soul had too much to tell and wasn't ready to move on. She would need to see if there was a cadaver available.

Ava turned her attention to the circular table in front of her. It held an offering basket in which she placed her essentiae, an urn of water, and a small iron bowl filled with embers kept warm by the servants.

Humming, Ava filled the clay bowl with water and set it on the embers. Her eyes drifted shut and she focused on her essentiae. Singing to the souls was Ava's way of sending them to the afterlife in a peaceful manner. Some used spellwork, but for her, a gentle song worked perfectly.

Glowing ribbons of sea green, sapphire blue, bright pink and liquid silver lifted from the items and swirled in the air. The bright pink soul, its essence a delicate blend of vanilla and blooming roses tickled her neck as it weaved its way through her ebony hair.

Ava brought her palms together, touching her thumbs to her forehead. She bowed at the waist, offering respect and honor to the Five and to the souls before her.

"*Maió yah aríla vylá efusar.*" She whispered. The phrase meant 'May your soul fly freely' in ancient Ili and it felt like coming home every time she said it.

The bowl of water shimmered, and Ava glimpsed Empyrean through the ripples—sparkling meadows for miles, a dark sea of the deepest blue and trees dripping with golden leaves. She had asked Mergen once what she thought of it. Mergen had raised an eyebrow and questioned if she had been inhaling too much smoke from a parlous house. After that, Ava hadn't mentioned it again, but simply took pleasure in seeing her souls freed to such a beautiful, inspiring place.

As each soul disappeared into the water, the liquid took on their delicate hues. The last soul, an emerald ribbon streaked with silver, caressed her cheek before sliding away, leaving Ava with the comforting smell of fresh pine.

As the portal shimmered closed, a wave of bittersweet contentment swept through her. She had been an important step in the souls' journeys, and it validated her purpose. Snapping her phylactery closed, she stood and went to see if she could find a cadaver for the soul in the metal bar.

The cadaver benches. Ava walked past them with the same assessing eye she brought to the airship junkyards—what's new, what fits, what will work. Ten years ago, this would have horrified her. Now it was just another task.

On the first bench lay an old woman, her hair in braids flowing over the side of the stone. Her deep copper skin reflected the light and Ava wondered what had happened to her. A strange sense of unease flitted through Ava, and she decided this cadaver wasn't quite right for the angry little soul, so she kept looking.

The second body was a gray-haired man, his face wrinkled and whiskered. Traditional white linen covered him, his face at peace. Definitely not this one either.

"I'll have to try again a different day," she whispered to the soul. The soul gave her a buzzy reply.

Ava gathered her things and met Mergen coming in from the main temple room.

"Are you going to Toby's today, Ava?"

Ava fastened her phylactery, not meeting Mergen's eyes. "Seáh."

Two years of working on her airship at Toby's shop, keeping her face neutral when he smiled, her voice steady when he said her name. She was thirty years old and very, very good at wanting things she couldn't have.

"Want a ride?" Mergen raised her eyebrows. "I've been wanting to try a sky trick I saw one of the aerobatic show planes doing the other day."

Ava's exhaustion lifted—just slightly—at the promise of wind and speed and forgetting, even for a moment, everything she couldn't fix.

"Count me in."

Chapter Two

M ergen and Ava made their way to the stepping lift. Mergen wrenched the steel accordion door open, and they entered.

"How's your airship coming along?" Mergen asked.

The button clicked under her thumb. She grabbed the railing as the box lurched upward, jarring them both. It clacked as it moved, stopping every three levels to slide backward or forward. The ride was rough, but they weren't nearly as unstable as the city's elevators which hung by long cables that were rarely serviced. The stair-like railing that supported the lift kept it from being a death sentence, but it took twice as long to reach the top.

"It still needs a ton of work. But, if I get it running soon, I can travel to the other realms to find a cure for Rune." She had begun refurbishing her zeppelin as a hobby, feeding her fervent, wishful dream of traveling to the volcanic Black Sands Realm, the bright Lyte Realm, or even the colorful barren deserts in the Realm of Winds. But when Rune's episodes began happening more frequently, her adventurous plans quickly turned into a desperate need.

"How's Rune doing?" Mergen asked.

Mud caked the lift floor. She scraped her boot against it. "She's getting worse."

Mergen gave Ava's arm a quick squeeze. "Aw, Ava, I'm sorry. Have you received a reply from the council?"

"Not yet."

Weeks since she'd petitioned the council for travel permits. The Purdah Regulations Office controlled all realm crossings—had for a thousand years, since the Magisterium bound the realms together to keep them from floating into the void. Getting approval could take months. The Black Sands Realm had healing waters. The Realm of Winds had earth medicines her realm didn't. If they'd just approve her, she could search them all.

But bureaucracy moved slower than Rune was fading.

"Why doesn't she take a cadaver? I'm sure Zoya would find her one," Mergen said.

Ava shrugged, the familiar and tiresome argument with Rune instantly springing to mind. "She thinks it won't help, but only make things worse, which I don't understand."

"What did she say when you told her you are looking for a cure?"

"I haven't." The admission made her chest tighten. Perhaps it was selfish, but she didn't want to live without Rune. And if Rune continued to refuse a cadaver, then Ava had to find a way to fix the body she was in.

"What? Why?"

"If I tell her, she will make me stop trying to find one."

"Well, let's hope the council will grant you permission then."

"I should hear from them soon. I do have some new parts I need to install and Toby is going to help me. The minute I get my approval, I'll be ready to go."

Mergen bumped shoulders with her. "Girl, you know Toby would do anything for you."

"Toby is like a brother to me, so stop that." She studied her black boots, disappointment creeping into her chest.

They'd been fifteen when his family moved to the city and they'd been everything to each other—first kiss, first love, first fumbling intimacy in the garden shed. She'd thought it would last forever. It lasted three months after the move.

Fourteen years of barely thinking about him. Then, two years ago her airship needed parts she couldn't find anywhere else. She'd walked in and he'd smiled at her—easy, friendly, sure. Like those three teenage months had never happened.

So she'd smiled back the same way. And she'd been doing it ever since.

Just then, the lift jerked to a halt. The door heaved open, and Flip stood outside— a tall, lanky boy with a dirty cap and even dirtier grin.

"Hello, lovelies."

Mergen's scowl could've snuffed out a flame. "The lift's going up."

"Perfect." Flip wedged himself inside before Mergen could stop him, bringing with him the reek of parlous house smoke and unwashed skin. Ava's eyes watered. She stepped back, pulling Mergen with her.

"A few more levels," Ava murmured to Mergen, who looked ready to shove Flip through the grating.

The lift lurched upward in tense silence, Flip watching them from beneath his cap brim, that oily smile never wavering.

Finally, the lift staggered to a stop. Mergen shot Flip a hostile glance and flung open the door. She stomped out mumbling to herself about people who spent time stuffing their rods in doxy boxes.

Before Ava could escape the lift, Flip placed a firm hand on her arm. "Ava, wait."

His oily smile was gone, his blue eyes steely under his cap. His stench was overwhelming and Ava held her breath. "Your aunt is one of those people who makes herbal medicines and such, seáh?"

She crossed her arms, unsure where this was going. "She's an inyanga if that's what you want to know."

Flip scanned the pier quickly and lowered his voice. "I need a medicine that helps with night terrors and delirious fits. Something with a calming and a...bringing to consciousness effect."

Ava studied his face. He seemed hopeful, desperate even. Who needed it? A lover from the parlous houses? Himself? She almost asked, then decided she didn't want to know.

"Also, I heard about your aunt's sickness," Flip said quietly. Ava's gut twisted. "Temple disciples talk, you know." He smirked. "Knowledge can be valuable to the right person."

Ava's hand moved to her glove—not pulling the tab, just resting there. A reminder. "Are you threatening me, Flip?"

He lifted his hands, the smirk fading. "Souls, no. I'm offering a trade. Listening is a valuable skill—you might want to try it."

Ava glared at him.

"Now, what I haven't heard is if her magic is still functioning."

"She still has her magic." The words came out harsher than intended.

"Good. If you can get me a healing tonic, I could get something for you." He absentmindedly tapped on his phylactery, lifting his eyebrows at her.

A rough laugh escaped her. "I doubt you have anything—"

"I could arrange a meeting," Flip interrupted. "Someone who can travel through the Realms. Someone who might be able to find her a cure."

She had researched all her aunt's books and notes, finding nothing helpful. And fixing her ship was taking longer than expected since she could only work on it when she wasn't taking care of Rune or collecting souls. She was beyond frustrated and was running out of options.

"Who?"

Flip leaned against the wall of the lift and examined his dirty fingernails. "The parlous houses always have interesting visitors. There's a knave belonging to a smuggling ship that frequently drops in. I heard where they are docked. You could speak with the captain and see if he would take your request."

It was close to impossible to get through the barriers unless you were granted a permit. Or you were sneaky enough to avoid them altogether, like the knaves.

"Aren't the knaves...thieves?"

Flip grinned. "Sometimes."

"I would be asking a bunch of criminals to find a cure for my aunt. Would they even do that?"

"For the right price." Flip shoved himself off the wall. "Listen, if that is too dangerous for you, then I'll find someone else to get me a tonic. Plenty of healers around."

Flip let the last thought hang in the air between them. He was right, there were other healers, but none as good as Rune, even in her current state. And if he was asking for Rune's tonic, he wanted the best.

But could she trust criminals? They might take her tonic and disappear. Or worse—use it for something terrible. But if they could help...

"If I get you the medicine, you'll give me the docking coordinates for the knave's ship?"

Flip nodded, his eyes steely.

"Ava." Mergen's footsteps jangled on the iron grating as she returned, her distrustful gaze flickering to Flip. "Everything okay here?"

Flip lifted his eyebrows, waiting for an answer. Ava disliked Flip and the company he kept. But the druid code demanded honesty with their temple kin and she had to trust in that.

"I'll get it," Ava replied. "But you better hold up your end of the bargain."

Flip saluted them with two fingers to his brow, his slippery smile back in place. "See you lovelies later." He rammed the door shut, fingers waggling through the grate as the lift descended.

"He must have some kind of special powers because I don't know a single soul that would want to be closer to him than necessary," Mergen muttered, watching the lift descend. "What did he want anyway?"

"He claimed he knew someone who could get a cure for Rune." If the knaves could help, Rune could be cured in weeks. The council could take months. Flip's offer was dangerous—but waiting might be worse.

Mergen raised an eyebrow. "You believe him?"

"What else can I do, Merg?" Her hands flew up. "I'm sky high in dead ends."

Mergen hmphed. "Just be careful. I don't trust him."

The mainland spread below them—Seráya City's airstreams filled with zeppelins, their sails harnessing the wind. Piers of different heights dotted the horizon, small planes zipping in and out.

Surrounding the city were forests, mountains, and helium mines in the distance. The sun's melon, yellow, and pink rays cast the metropolis in a constant sunset glow, morning being only slightly brighter than evening.

The views from the pier were usually breathtaking—city lights, zeppelins, the constant sunset glow. But today she couldn't focus on any of it. Not with thoughts of Rune and the possibility of a cure.

"There's my baby," Mergen cooed as they approached a small blue turbo prop. Usually, Mergen flew over the main island of their realm, collecting souls from crashes. She unlocked the cockpit and slid it open, revealing a pilot seat with a passenger seat behind it. She grabbed two aviatrix helmets, handing one to Ava.

"What's this trick you saw the pilots doing?"

"They had wing walkers on both sides of the plane." Mergen put her aviatrix helmet on, cramming her brown curls under it. "They did a nose rise, spinning into the clouds before falling—literally, no engine running—out of the sky before they fyred it back up. It was flipping fantastic." Mergen grinned, her face lighting up at the prospect of a new challenge.

Her heart kicked at the thought of free falling. "I hope you aren't going to ask me to wing walk." She shoved her hair beneath her helmet. "And you'll get your engine running in time, right? I don't want to have to get a cadaver just yet."

"Seáh." Mergen waved away her comment. "I have a friend who spell-casted my plane, making it safer than anything they have in the airshows. We'll be fine."

Mergen flopped into the front seat and pulled a lever. The engine sputtered and steam spilled from beneath the wings. The propeller above the cockpit began to spin and the plane lifted away from the dock.

"Ready?" Mergen yelled over the noise.

Ava was eager to feel weightless and have the wind crash into her face. She banged on the back of Mergen's seat, hollering, "Let's go!"

Mergen threw a lever and the plane burst upward, jetting into the clouds. For five minutes, she could forget Rune's declining mind, the council's silence, and the knaves she was about to trust with her aunt's life.

***

"You are beyond crazy, you know that?" Ava laughed and climbed out of the back of the airplane. Her hair was damp with sweat, and she let it loose to float in the high breeze above the city's iron gridwork. "I'm pretty sure my heart stopped."

"You know you love it." Mergen teased.

"I suppose I do."

"Hey, did you see the commodore's ship?"

"Neyá." Ava tugged a scarf from her back pocket and tied it around her head.

"Well, I saw it. And you know who I saw on deck?" Mergen huffed and shoved her helmet into the plane. "Commodore Van Alst."

"Van Alst." Ava wiped her sweaty face. She hadn't seen the commodore in person since she was a child—a distant figure at his ascension ceremony. Rune never spoke about him, but her silence on the subject said more than words.

"He also had the Magisterium on deck with him," Mergen continued. "All of them."

"That's unusual. Maybe he invited them for the Day of the Five?" Ava didn't know much about how the Magisterium operated, and she couldn't remember a time they had convened in the Realm of Souls.

"Give Toby a kiss on the cheek for me, eh?" Mergen winked at her as she climbed back into the plane. She flipped a switch and the engine roared to life. Mergen gave her a quick salute and piloted out of the docking station into the sky traffic.

Give Toby a kiss.

Two years of working on her ship, and her heart still kicked at the thought of seeing him. She'd gotten so good at hiding it, sometimes she almost believed her own performance.

There had been a time during their teenage years that she and Toby had been more than friends. They shared dreams, kisses, and the awkwardness of being each other's first time love.

But when Toby's family moved to the city, their relationship faded. Years later, Ava decided she wanted to refurbish an airship—it might be the only way she could search the Realms for a cure for her aunt. When Ava needed a specific part for the engine, Toby's shop was the obvious choice—he was the best tinker she knew. Two years ago, she'd walked in prepared to keep things professional, and he'd greeted her with the same easy smile he'd always had. Friendly. Brotherly. Safe.

She'd been doing this ever since: showing up when she could work on her zeppelin, keeping her face neutral, and pretending her heart didn't kick when he said her name.

Ava headed toward the shop, footfalls clanging against iron grates, and practiced her smile. The one that said just friends.

Chapter Three

T he shop sat on one of the highest levels in the city, where the wind sang through the gridwork. "Wynstann Assemblies" gleamed above the polished iron door in hammered metal letters.

Ava pushed it open. A light whirring filled the air as gears spun in a hidden cupboard. On a high shelf, a delicate hammer lifted above a rotating metal disc and bounced from tube to tube in a lilting melody. The sound loosened something in her chest, the way it always did. Her shoulders relaxed and she breathed in the scent of oils, grease and polished wood.

Before she could call, the door behind the counter swung open. Toby appeared, magnifying goggles pushed up over his regular glasses, his attention locked on an igniter switch. His teeth caught his lower lip. Grease darkened his knuckles.

Ava had seen this a hundred times—the focused intensity, the unconscious lip bite. It used to make her stomach flip. Now it was just...Toby. Her lifelong friend.

She touched his arm to get his attention. "Hey, Toby."

"Oh. *Seáh llaéh*, Ava." He pushed the magnifier up into his messy brown hair and blinked. "Sorry I didn't see you. I'm trying to get this igniter unstuck."

"It would be easier to tell Old Man Newton to pay for a new one." Dáhlia walked into the room and threw a towel on the counter, her long chestnut curls swaying. "He is so scuffing cheap."

Aamina, Dáhlia's little girl, trailed directly behind her. Her large blue eyes surveyed the room. When she spied Ava, Aamina grinned and skipped over.

"*Seáh llaéh*, Aamina. Have you been helping your mom with her studies?" Ava nudged away Aamina's dark bouncy curls to whisper in her ear. "You know she needs all the help she can get, *seáh*?"

"Ha ha," Dáhlia scoffed. "Mama's good at what she does, right, Aami?"

Aamina looked between her mother and Ava, shifting her weight from one foot to the other. In the end she waved her hand in a "so-so" motion and ran through the door that led to their adjoining apartments.

"Traitor!" Dáhlia yelled after her, and Ava laughed. "I only melted the door a little," Dáhlia explained, waving her hand to the victim door behind her. "And now she thinks I'm a terrible mage. She keeps telling me one day I'll melt the floor and we will all fall into the swale."

Ava's gaze followed where Aamina had disappeared. "Anything yet?" Five years of gurgles and coos and brilliant, expressive eyes—but never words.

"*Neyá*," Dáhlia sighed. "Not a word. I keep thinking today might be the day." Her hands moved in quick signs—the language they'd been learning together. "But she talks plenty with these."

"Do you have a minute before you work on your ship?" Toby asked. He put his glasses on, and one side of his mouth quirked into a smile. "I want to show you something."

"Sure." Ava followed him to a room behind the parts shop. Sunshine streamed through the wide windows. It glinted off cogs, metal bits, and tools while the smell of grease and wood filled the messy, idea inspiring space.

"Come look." Toby gestured with a dirty hand to a large machine sitting on his worktable. His tall frame leaned over it, his hair hanging in his eyes.

"What is it?" Ava circled the machine, taking in the impossible angles, the pressure system that shouldn't work but somehow did. She admired Toby's imagination for new and wonderous things.

He grinned. "It's a soul locating device. It's something I've been working on for a while and I wanted your thoughts before I handed it over. Watch this." Toby wound a crank, and the scent of vanilla and cinnamon wrapped around her—Toby's particular combination of oils and flux. She stepped back, putting the invention between them.

"This machine is designed to make finding lost souls easier for the temple. Especially for the average person who doesn't have any skills for the craft at all," he explained. "Dáhlia helped to create the workings on the inside—which is kind of how the door got melted. There is a pressure system in the back, here."

He snagged her hand and tugged her around to the other side. His hands landed briefly on her waist, positioning her for the best view, then released just as quickly. The touch was practical, efficient—the way he'd guide anyone.

"Here we go." He paused, making sure everything was in its proper place, and pulled a lever. Dark liquid in a glass jar began to slowly empty into a large clear container. The disc below it turned, heating a coil of glass tubing. Gas rose to the top of the canister and slowly, the pistons above it pumped, the gauge on the front spinning wildly.

"This is where it gets interesting!" Toby said over the noise. The pistons chugged rhythmically, setting the wheel into a frenzy. He motioned for her to return to the front of the device, and she scampered back. The needle on the gauge wobbled, trying to decide where to point.

Toby frowned. He moved to the back, his slim fingers adjusting. After a moment, he returned and clapped his hands.

"Ah! It's pointing this way." Toby looked up. His finger was aimed directly at Ava. "I don't understand. It should be pointing in a direction where a soul would be found, not directly at a person." His shoulders sagged. He flipped the switch harder than necessary. "Maybe the calibration isn't accurate."

Ava stared at the machine, thinking. "I have an essentia in my phylactery. Is it sensing that?"

Toby snapped his fingers. "That's probably it. I calibrated it to only detect souls not bonded to a body."

"Toby, how long have you been working on this?"

Toby shrugged. "Almost a year. I've wanted to show you before now, but the person who commissioned the device asked me to not discuss it with anyone until it was finished. Technically...I finished it last night." He grinned.

Toby always did what he wanted, even while following the rules. Clever tinkerer. "Ah, technicalities."

"Seáh," he sighed, and they both laughed.

"Alright," Ava said. "Talk me through it. How did you make it?"

"Dáhlia and I were approached by someone wanting to devise a machine that could detect lost souls," he explained. "I told him you don't simply make something like that. We would need lots of time and resources, not to mention a scientific method for locating a soul on a totally different plane of existence. But the challenge was intriguing, so I told him we would try. And while I was thinking through the process of soul detecting, I thought of you."

"Why?"

"You sense souls differently, seáh?" he asked.

Ava nodded. "My magic is like any other druidic magic. But I can...connect with souls on a deeper level. I hear their thoughts and understand their feelings." She wasn't sure why no one else felt souls like she did, but her gift was special, and she was thankful for it. It meant she could find a lost soul when no one else could, sense when a soul was upset, and understand when it wasn't ready to move on from this life.

"Exactly. Other druidic mages find them by using their magic alone and not an extra sense of knowing like you do. This device mimics basic druidic magic, using its unique frequencies that locate souls. Souls are sentient beings and therefore, they have a chemical makeup. I mean, everything is made of something."

Ava's mind churned with the implications. Anyone could find souls with this? Even people without magic? Her temple had thirty druids and druises—would they need half that? Would they need any?

"In theory, I suppose that would make sense," Ava said slowly, unsure what this revolutionary device would mean for the temples—and those with druidic magic—across the Realms. "But souls are the core of who we are, not the body itself."

"Right." Toby continued. He began to pace, his hands waving as he talked. "I explained we would need the chemical makeup for a soul to even begin this project. I thought after that request, he wouldn't return. But a few days later, he brought me a formula."

"You have a formula for exactly what a soul is made of?" Her eyebrows rose. "That's something I would have never thought about. I only know how it feels to me, in here," she touched her chest. "It's fascinating you can take such an emotional thing and describe it as something so concrete."

"It wasn't easy," Toby took a rag and wiped the device. "The customer wants it delivered this week and he's getting impatient. I don't want to disappoint him."

"I'm sure it will work exactly as you want it to," Ava reassured him. "I think it will change the way we do things at the temple, though."

"Really?"

"Seáh. It will help us rescue more souls and keep them from being lost. That's a victory any day."

Toby nodded, his eyes glued to the machine.

"What's that?" Ava asked, pointing to a symbol pressed into the gauge's console.

Toby smiled proudly, his dimple showing. "That's my official emblem for my shop. Aamina helped me design it. Do you like it?"

A large W with an A inside was carved into the metal for Wynstann Assemblies. An outline of a gear encircled the letters, while a few smaller gears were placed in several sections of the teeth.

"I love it."

"I'm glad," Toby said, his deep brown eyes crinkling at the corners behind his wire rimmed glasses as he smiled. "You want to work on your ship? I got the accelerometer you needed. It's in the cabin."

"You did? A yah ageremé, thank you." Ava patted his arm and slipped past him. She paused at the melted door and turned back. "Oh, I forgot my glad rags. I need to see if I can borrow one of Dáhlia's work suits. And Toby? Your invention really is impressive."

Toby nodded his thanks, his eyes and fingers already back on his invention. Ava went back out to the parts shop just as Dáhlia walked through the door from the attached apartment, her little shadow missing.

"Dáhlia, can I borrow some glad rags? Mine were covered in grease and I had to soak them. I forgot them in the garden tub."

"Sure." Dáhlia waved at the door. "I have a few clean ones hanging up in the closet. Grab what you need. Be quiet, though, I just put Aamina down for a nap."

"Thanks." Ava padded quietly into the apartment. When the twins had purchased the flat, they redesigned it to have the shop and apartments side by side, each with its own entrance from the public walkway, but with an inner door connecting them.

Ava wandered into the common room, her feet tapping quietly on the shiny metal floor. The gathering room housed a woven rug, hues of lavender, peach, and lemon making the space feel fresh. A cozy couch, two bag chairs, and one made of netting hung from the ceiling.

She picked up one of Aamina's books and dropped in a basket. An entire wall of windows overlooked the city, the rise and fall of piers and levels of gridwork dark against the sun's rays.

In Dáhlia's room, she found the selection of glad rags and snagged one. She swapped clothes, buckling her belt around her waist and the phylactery on her arm. The work suit had been worn and washed many times and it was soft against Ava's skin, the smell of clean laundry soap drifting off the fabric. Dáhlia was a bit taller than Ava so she bent to roll up the legs.

She reentered the shop and climbed the iron stairs to the upper pier. Wind whipped her hair as she emerged. Several other ships were tethered along the walkway, waiting for repairs. An orange skybyke with red and gold flames caught her eye, parked in the first pier. The paint—and the large engine—screamed reckless. The kind of person who'd ride through airstreams on nothing but momentum and prayer.

Her airship, *The Spirited Gent*, was at the very end. The zeppelin's balloon was currently deflated, the prow and stern held in place by cantilever beams, so it didn't fall off the dock.

She had purchased *The Spirited Gent* from Old Man Newton who ran the junk yards. The wood was rich sable brown, smooth beneath her palm. When she'd run her hands along the hull, the ship had almost seemed to preen. The worn leather covered wheel hinted at previous adventures, like a sly, sexy smile. Ava had immediately known he was meant for her.

The interior of the cabin had been a wreck and they'd had to gut the entire thing. His helm had been dusty, the knobs and levers begging to be touched. Ava had painstakingly taken him apart piece by piece and was now in the process of putting him back together, albeit slowly.

Once his engine purred with steam, his wood polished and his crème-colored balloon inflated, *The Spirited Gent* would be the sauciest, most intimidating machine in the airstreams.

Ava dumped her clothes on the captain's chair, a puff of dust bursting from the cushion. She waved it away with a cough and noticed her new accelerometer on the control panel.

She grabbed it and climbed below deck to work on the fore engine. Before she could ratchet it together, the ship swayed beneath her.

"What the...?" Ava shimmied out from beneath the engine and peered over the railing to check the iron cantilever beams. They looked intact, thank the Five. What could have possibly caused her ship to rock so hard?

"Did you feel that?" Toby appeared at the gangplank. "Are you okay?"

"I'm fine. I was installing the accelerometer and thought the cantilevers were giving out. What happened?"

"I don't know."

Another tumultuous quake shook the pier, and Ava grabbed hold of the railing to keep from falling. Iron screeched, the levels grinding and straining. Ava's gut clenched. The cantilevers groaned. If they gave way, her ship would shatter against the beams below—and she'd go with it.

The movement ground to a halt and a heavy, thick silence settled around them. Toby and Ava exchanged glances. A crisp crack suddenly split the air. Ava spun. Her eyes widened as a section of the island trembled and slowly tilted downward. It tore away from the main island, dropping huge trees, fields, and homes into the air below. The lake that had been blue and sparkling a moment ago was now emptying into nothingness.

"Rune!" Ava's eyes strained toward the forest, but she couldn't see their cottage from here. How close had the split been to their home? She scrambled toward the gangplank. "I need to go. Now."

Chapter Four

Ava and Toby raced down the walkway, metal clanging under their feet. She threw her things into a bag—phylactery, gloves, the half-eaten sandwich she'd forgotten about. Her throat was tight, her mouth dry as an old chapbook.

"Dáhlia? Where are you?"

"We're here." Dáhlia appeared in the doorway with Aamina slack against her shoulder, half-asleep. "What was that?"

"I'm not sure." He crossed to them, his hand gentle on his niece's head. "Are you alright?"

"We're fine." Dáhlia shifted Aamina's weight. "The sound of the complex shifting was deafening."

Aamina sleepily spoke with her hands, and Dáhlia nodded. "*Seáh*, Aami, it was scary."

Ava flung open the door and shot out. Was the island falling apart? Had something happened to the soul that was bonded with it?

"Ava, where are you going?" Toby asked.

"I have to get to Rune," Ava called over her shoulder.

"Wait. I'll take you." Toby kissed Aamina's head and motioned for Ava to follow him back up to the pier. Ava's chest tightened watching him—the gentle way he touched his niece, the worry creasing his forehead. Toby would make someone a good father someday.

"Be careful," Dáhlia called after them as they ascended the stairs.

Toby led the way to the dock. The orange skybyke sat there, gleaming and improbable.

His. That cocky, beautiful machine was his.

He extended a helmet. "Put this on and let's go." He stretched a pair of goggles over his eyes. He swung a long leg over the seat and flipped the burner switch, igniting the fyre inside. The pistons roared to life. "Hop on! You'll need to use the harness I designed."

That was an understatement. One slip off the hard leather seat and she would fall thousands of feet.

"This is insane," Ava muttered. If she hadn't been so concerned about Rune, the daring ride through the sky would have had her tingling in excitement.

She swung her leg over the seat. Her body pressed against his back—closer than comfortable, but necessary. He pointed to the harness straps. She lifted the them, trying to puzzle out the configuration. Toby hopped off the byke.

"Here, let me—" His hands hesitated near her waist before reaching for the buckles. His fingers worked quickly, professionally, across her middle and shoulders, his touch careful not to linger.

"All set." He patted her knee like she was a secured package. Ava wanted to smack him but instead gave him a sarcastic thumbs up.

She barely grasped his waist before they soared out over the city. Her breath caught—not from fear exactly, but from the sudden freedom of it. They zigzagged through organized airstreams, ships blaring horns when he skimmed too close.

For three heartbeats, she set her worry about Rune aside. Just felt the wind and speed and the solid warmth of his back against her chest.

The guilt crashed back. What kind of person forgot their dying aunt for the thrill of flight?

She peered over his shoulder, searching. Steam train tracks disappeared under the canopy. The forest spread endlessly green.

No cottage. No tiled roof. Nothing.

Her stomach dropped so fast she tasted copper. What if the house had gone over the edge? What if Rune—

"There!" The shout ripped from her throat as she spotted it. A tree was laying over the roof, partially hiding the small house. Relief flooded through her, and her her grip on his waist relaxed.

Toby expertly tilted the byke into a turn, his slim fingers dancing over the switches with practiced ease. Wings deployed, it grumbled and descended, steam hissing as it kissed the wet grass. Ava hastily unbuckled herself, stumbled onto the ground, and vanished into the house.

"Auntie? Auntie, where are you?" Ava ran from room to room. The fallen tree had sent tiles and debris everywhere, crunching beneath Ava's anxious footsteps.

Hearing a mumble, she turned. "Auntie?"

"Avalína?"

"Auntie? I'm coming!" She rushed to the back of the house, toward Rune's bedroom, and skidded to a stop. A tree blocked the bedroom door. Ava desperately pulled on the branches, hissing as the needles pricked her hands and arms. Desperate to get inside, she pulled out the tab on her laser glove and began to burn through the tree trunk.

"Here, let me help." The handsaw appeared in his hands—the one she and Rune kept in the back shed.

He attacked the trunk in steady strokes while she cut through smaller limbs. The smell of burning pine filled the hallway.

"Talk to her." His voice was quiet between breaths. "Keep her mind busy."

Ava stared at him. The saw stilled.

"She's scared," he said simply. "Talk to her."

Oh. She retracted the wire on her glove. "Auntie? Can you hear me?"

"Seáh." Came her aunt's quiet reply.

"What were you doing when the tree fell?" Ava heard a shuffle and could picture her aunt trying to move her hands while she talked.

"I was cataloging our new crop...our new crop of acid flower and I came in here..."

"Why did you go into your room?" Ava's eyes were fixed on the saw as he worked furiously, his wiry frame straining.

"I came to get my catalog journal," Rune said. Ava could hear her take a deep breath, as if explaining had taken a lot of effort.

"Are you hurt?" Ava focused on the noises in Rune's room, trying to decipher what her injuries could be. What if she had a broken leg or arm?

"How much longer?" Ava asked Toby. She bounced on the balls of her feet and leaned over to see how far he had managed to cut through the trunk.

"Almost there," Toby huffed. A loud crack echoed in the room and Toby pulled back. "Got it." He set the saw down and they pulled one side forward enough for Ava to squeeze through.

A large limb had knocked over Rune's thin frame and was pressing her to the floor. Her aunt's long silvery-white hair was tangled in the leaves. Rune's eyes were shut, but she was breathing.

"Auntie, I'm here." Ava hurried over and grasped the bough, the rough bark scraping against her hands. The branch barely moved, determined to keep Rune captive. Ava pulled harder. Suddenly, the weight shifted, and she snuck a look sideways. Toby had come behind her, helping her to push. She threw him a grateful smile.

"Can you hold it?" Ava asked him.

Toby nodded, his lips pressed together in concentration. "For a few minutes at least."

Ava let go and scampered beneath the tree. "Come on. Let's get you out of here." She gently tugged beneath her aunt's arms and Rune moaned. Ava quit tugging. She needed to see where Rune was injured before moving her. Blood seeped from a wound on the back of her aunt's head. Her hands shook.

"Is she alright?" Toby asked.

"She's injured. We need to get her out." Ava pressed her lips together and laced her fingers over Rune's chest. Digging in her heels, she pulled. Ava landed on her behind, her aunt's delicate frame falling on top of her. "Got her!"

Toby released the branch and it fell back with a rustle of leaves. He wiped his face with the back of his hand, smearing soot along his cheek.

"*Seáh llaéh*, Rune." Toby grinned. "Let's get you somewhere more comfortable."

Ava and Toby moved Rune to the common room, sitting her in a plush, lemon colored chair.

"I'm going to get something for her head," Ava whispered. "Can you stay for a minute?"

He nodded and snagged a small stool, settling beside Rune.

In the kitchen, Ava chose several jars of dried herbs. She ground each in a bowl, adding oil. Floral and spicy aromas filled the kitchen. She couldn't do the spellwork her aunt could, but she could at least make the cream for healing.

Toby was holding Rune's hand when Ava returned, murmuring something that made her aunt smile dreamily. He glanced up.

"She keeps calling me Sebastian."

Ava winced. "She talks about him sometimes. I think he must have been someone special a long time ago. Sorry."

"Don't be." He looked back at Rune with surprising gentleness. "She's especially charming when she doesn't realize I'm the one talking to her."

His dimple showed with that half-smile. Ava busied herself with the salve bowl, refusing to examine why watching him hold her aunt's hand made her throat tight.

"Auntie? It's Ava."

"Avalína, *mé veláh*, my dearest. I was telling Sebastian about you." Rune's blue eyes sparkled as she petted his outstretched arm. "She is such a wonderful girl, Sebastian."

Toby smiled fondly at Rune. "I know she is."

The words hung in the air, simple and certain. Ava's hands stilled on the bowl. Did he truly think she was wonderful, or was he simply pacifying her aunt? She couldn't look at him—afraid of what she might find if she did, or worse, what she might not find.

When he finally looked away, she pressed her palm against her chest, willing her traitorous heart to settle. It didn't mean anything.

"Auntie? Will you help me? A friend of mine has hurt her head and I need you to spellcast this ointment please." Ava pressed the bowl into her aunt's hands.

"Of course." Rune's eyes shut, her face relaxing. People and places were always slipping through her memory, but spellcasting and remedies were still there, for now.

Rune murmured an incantation. The salve's hue darkened as the chemical makeup changed. Toby watched in fascination. She wondered if it ever bothered him that Dáhlia was a mage, and he wasn't.

Ava grinned to herself. It had been months since he'd visited, and he would get a tongue lashing once Rune realized he was not her beloved Sebastian.

"There you are, *mé veláh.*" Rune handed her the salve and spotted Toby. Her eyes narrowed, and Ava's grin widened.

"Tobias Wynstann. Where have you been?" Rune grabbed his ear.

"Ow, ow, ow." Toby batted her off and Ava unsuccessfully tried to smother a laugh. "What happened to me being a good boy?"

"You? Well, I suppose you are better than you used to be." Rune let go of Toby's ear. "Why haven't you visited us? It's been ages since I've seen you."

"Sorry, Rune." He shot Ava a dirty look and rubbed his ear. Ava shrugged, the smile stuck on her face. "We've been busy at the shop."

Rune huffed at him, settling in her chair. She eyed him as if she were trying to decide whether she should harass him more. Toby leaned back, out of ear pulling range.

"Auntie, could you hold still, please? I need to put this salve on your head. You bumped it." Ava set a gentle hand on her shoulder. As much as she loved seeing Toby get harassed, Rune still needed to be patched up.

"I did what? Surely not." Rune crossed her arms. "I am fit as a flywheel. I don't need your—ow. What are you doing?"

Ava spread the salve over Rune's head generously, the magic tingling on her fingertips. Slowly, the blood stopped oozing and the skin knitted itself together. She sighed in relief.

"All done." Ava set the bowl on a table. "Does that feel better?"

"Now that you mention it, I suppose it does. How did that happen again? I don't remember."

Ava grabbed another stool and set it beside Rune, completing the small circle.

"There was a tremor." Ava explained. "The city rocked from the force. We aren't sure what happened. We came here first to see if you were alright."

Rune quickly straightened in the chair. "What do you mean a tremor?"

"The island sort of...shook. I was working on my zeppelin at Toby's," Ava said quietly. "At first, I thought the cantilevers had given out. The quake rocked the ship and the entire complex of the city. I could see Oyamnís Lake and a piece of the island fell off the edge and just...disappeared."

Rune's gaze went from Ava to Toby. "Oh no."

Ava stood abruptly. "Toby and I need to see what happened. We'll be right back. Will you be alright by yourself?"

"Of course, I'll be alright." Rune waved her hand, already getting out of her seat. "I need to get some healing tonics ready. There will be injuries. I'll grab my journal and get started." Rune made her way back to her bedroom.

Once outside, Ava's shoulders slumped. "What am I going to do about the house?"

"Let's figure out what happened out there first, then we can make a plan." His hand settled on her shoulder, warm and steady.

"We could walk, you know." She stepped away and gestured to the dirt road. His hand slipped from her shoulder, but the heat lingered. "It's not far."

"I'm guessing the ground will be unstable after the landslide. I don't want to risk falling into a sinkhole." He swung back onto the skybyke. "Besides, flying will be faster and give us a better view."

Ava sighed. Apparently, having her front pressing against his back didn't seem to bother him. Fine. She could make it not bother her either.

"Right." Ava grumbled, shoving her helmet back on. She swung her leg over the seat and flipped the harness onto her shoulders.

"Can you manage the buckles?" Toby asked over his shoulder.

"*Seáh.*" She shoved the buckles into their housings, determined to keep herself away from his dexterous fingers.

"What the hell is this tree doing in my house?" Rune yelled, and Ava paused mid buckle. She probably should have told her aunt about the tree. Toby chuckled, the vibration purring against her. Before Ava could tell him to wait, he roared the byke to life and they lifted into the clouds.

What had once been a pristine, holy lake reflecting the sky was now a desert—beautifully terrible in its devastation. Cracked mud like shattered glass. Marine life dying slowly in shallow puddles that reflected nothing but their own slow end. The forest's new edge was raw and honest, ancient trees clinging by roots that had held for centuries and might not hold another hour.

Something pulled at her spirit—that familiar tugging sensation that meant souls were near. She turned her focus to the liminal plane and nearly gasped.

Hundreds. Maybe thousands. A color-filled haze of spirits drifting aimlessly through the biosphere, lost and searching. They were everywhere, bright and confused, trying to find their way back to bodies that no longer existed.

The weight of them pressed against her chest. All those souls—now drifting without a cadaver.

She wouldn't be able to collect that many by herself. Not even close.

Rune met them outside. Instead of scolding Ava for not telling her about the tree, she enveloped her in a tight hug. Her floral scent wafted on the breeze and Ava relaxed.

"Avalína, what did you see?" Rune leaned back, worry in her eyes. Ava recounted the damage, including the multitudes of souls she sensed drifting through the liminal plane. She wouldn't be able to collect that many by herself.

Rune nodded. "We have work to do. Let's get the supplies." She disappeared into the house.

The skybyke hissed as Toby released the air pressure. Ava jogged over, slid her helmet off, and handed it to him. "Here. I'm going to stay home. Tell Dáhlia I'll return her clothes later."

Toby stored the helmet in a saddlebag. "I'll check in later and see about fixing the house."

"Would you mind sending a message to the temple? I think I'm going to need help." The admission tasted bitter. She always needed help lately, didn't she? Another crisis, another plea for assistance she could barely manage alone.

Toby nodded, pulling his goggles into place. "I'll drive to the mail service station and have them transport a tube."

"A *yah ageremé*, thank you." The words came out smaller than she intended. "For everything. The ride, the rescue, the—" She gestured vaguely at the ruined house, at Rune, at the mess of her life.

"Of course." His response was immediate, automatic. The way he always showed up, reliable as sunrise. Did he ever grow tired of being her convenient hero?

She watched the orange byke disappear toward the city, steam trailing like a farewell. The silence pressed in once he was gone—heavier than it should be, emptier than she wanted to admit.

That saucy orange byke was a damn good way to travel. Maybe she should rethink that zeppelin. Maybe she should rethink a lot of things.

But she wouldn't. She'd go inside, help Rune prepare tonics, guide souls to their rest. She'd keep doing what she'd always done.

She turned toward the house and felt the lie settle in her soul.

Chapter Five

Inside, Rune was mixing healing ointments, potions, and balms for the injured. Ava rushed into her room to change—stripping out of Dáhlia's glad rags and into her own dark trousers, cream shirt, and gray corset. She brushed her hair and wiped the dirt from her face.

Her turquoise eyes stared back from the mirror. The adrenaline from Toby's byke was still singing through her veins, and beneath it—exhaustion so deep her soul ached.

She didn't have time for this.

She slipped on her belt and phylactery. The small metal rod from the soul thrummed angrily in her pocket.

"I promise we will talk later," Ava whispered. She reached to a top shelf and lifted the lid off a clay jar, placing the rod inside for safe keeping.

"Auntie? Are you ready?" Ava walked into the kitchen and found Rune putting her cures into several baskets.

"Almost." Her blue eyes were alight with fyre in a way Ava hadn't seen in months.

"Auntie." Ava paused in the doorway. "What's going on?"

Rune's head snapped up. "What?"

"You're different. You look..." Ava searched for the word. Alive. Awake. Herself again. "What do you know?"

"I know nothing." Rune closed the basket lid with finality.

"Alright then," Ava mumbled, heading to the storage room off the kitchen. She picked her way through boxes and bowls, stuffing her pockets with essentiae—glass spheres, wooden pieces, small cloth bags. Her spirit reverberated with the call of souls, making her skin itch. It wouldn't be enough. She hoped the temple would send help.

"Ready?" Rune was almost bouncing.

They traveled quickly toward the new edge, Ava watching for sinkholes. Her spirit was heavy with the sudden influx of wandering souls.

A glow rose from the horizon—not one color but dozens, swirling together like a stained-glass window shattered mid-flight. The cloud grew as they walked, frenzied and searching.

Ava's steps slowed. Her spirit pulled toward them, answering their call.

"There must be thousands," she whispered, gripping Rune's hand.

"Then, you have a lot of work to do, mé veláh."

"I know." Ava sighed. So many, and none of them ready. The souls swirled around her in agitation, urgent to know where they belonged now that they were free from their forms.

"There are so many." The souls weaved through her hair, her legs. Their fear, anxiety, and worry crashed over her in waves.

How could she possibly bind them all? She hadn't brought nearly enough essentiae, and the Gathering lake had drained dry in the landslide.

Survivors began emerging from the forest, some with wounds from the quake and others walking toward the city to find safety and shelter.

"I'm going to help the injured," Rune said, carefully extracting herself from the press of souls. "Will you be alright?"

Sunlight glittered beyond the tree line—a small pond, barely visible. Not as large as the lake, but it might work.

"I'll be fine." Ava managed a smile. "I'll find you later."

Rune left. Ava focused on the souls and forced herself to relax. She stretched out with her spirit, piquing the souls' interest. As they connected with her, she heard their longings, their hopes, and desires. Her song formed, acknowledging their wishes, but suggesting a new, different path.

Leaving the survivors' murmured conversations behind, Ava moved toward the pond. The souls followed, entranced by her spirit and song. She knelt beside the water and raised her palms to her forehead.

"Ava." Mergen dropped beside her, breathless. "Looks like I got here just in time."

"Thanks for coming."

Side by side, the druises hummed a temple song. The water's surface fluttered, breeze moving through their hair. Ava peered into the murky depths. At first, she thought perhaps the portal wouldn't open.

Then—like a circular curtain drawing back—the beyond came into view. She exhaled in relief.

Mergen and Ava raised their hands to signal to the souls that it was time. Mergen kept humming while Ava brought words to their song. She opened her spirit and invited them to be with her, part of her. To know they were safe.

Your life has ended, a new one begins,
Choose another way.
Let the past go now to see what is next,
Come through, here this day.

The souls stirred. Several wound around her wrists and waist. Others circled over the pond, investigating the portal. She gently urged them on.

The souls' movements shifted—frantic, swirling and zipping. Ava frowned.

"What's going on?" Mergen asked.

Ava sang again, urgency sharpening her words. The innate nature of the souls washed over her—innocence and evil, mixing like oil and water. Ava's words stumbled as the sensation caught in her throat. The innocent souls should be guided to Empyrean, but the corrupted and vile ones—they needed to stay in the liminal plane and wait for the prince of Tartarean's dark, haunting melody, sentencing them to the icy hell in which they belonged.

Suddenly, the souls changed direction. They flooded Ava, spinning her in their midst and streaming through her hair. Coils of all colors raced across her vision, enveloping her in a multitude of scents and emotions, pressing her back.

Ava put out her hands, trying to emanate a calmness she didn't feel. Souls had never reacted this way before. The corrupt ones must be tainting the innocents. Mergen shouted her name, but she was too overcome to respond.

"Wait—" Ava protested, her words caught in the wind of the maelstrom. A bright blue soul paused in front of her face and Ava caught a hint of a briny wind before it spiraled away. The souls forced her back another step and her foot splashed into the pond. Cold muddy water squished between her toes and her heart raced.

The spirits cocooned her inside a cyclone of colors, the wind whipping her hair into her face. A thrust of movement threw Ava off balance. Her hands flung out, searching for anything to keep her from falling into the water. Another frenzied shove erupted from the spirits and Ava tipped, Mergen's shouts fading as she plunged into the pond.

Instead of splashing, Ava fell into a void. Her body was weightless, every worry vanished. She was in her soul's true form—bright turquoise with a streak of silver.

She flitted and reveled in freedom. If she could have giggled in this form, she would have. She glided along grasses, rocks, and flowers, the wind whispering through her being. Trees dripping with golden leaves glinted in the wind. A bright beacon sparkled on the horizon against an emerald sea. She moved toward it.

"Hello, little one." A silky voice, warm as summer honey. "You aren't supposed to be here."

A shimmering silver face smiled down at her—loving, achingly familiar. His body was translucent with a streak of orange. His eyes shone with a bright, kind light that made something in her soul ache with recognition she couldn't name.

He seemed familiar. No—beyond that. Like she'd known him her entire life and, instinctively knew, he was trustworthy. She slid into his palm and settled along his wrist. It felt like coming home.

"There we are," he said, the words tinkling like bells. "Let's get you home before it's too late. As much as I'd love a visit, Empyrean is no place for you right now."

Empyrean? She wasn't ready for the afterlife. Rune needed her. Mergen, Dáhlia, Toby—she couldn't leave them.

"I know, I agree." Sadness colored his voice—ancient and deep. "We will have time together again, you and me. Not yet, but soon enough."

He lifted her, gazing at her with golden eyes that held a thousand years of waiting. "Don't forget about me, Avalína. Even when you can't remember, don't forget."

Then he blew gently against her spirit, and she was falling—

Ava bolted upright in the pond, gasping.

"Ava!" Hands grabbed her arm, hauling her from the water. Mergen's face swam into focus. "What happened?"

"I don't know." They trudged out of the muck, each step sucking at their feet. She swiped at her face, water streaming through her hair. She reached the bank and collapsed, breathing in gulps.

"When you went under that water and didn't come up..." Mergen shook her head and wiped mud from her hands. "I thought I'd lost you. Scariest moment of my life."

The memory rushed back—golden leaves, weightless peace. Had she truly entered Empyrean? She pressed her palm to her stomach. Heaviness settled against her chest, wrong and oppressive after the weightless freedom of her spirit form. That lightness had been intoxicating. Seductive.

The silver being said it wasn't time for her to be there. He was right.

But souls, she wanted to go back.

"I...think I went into Empyrean."

Mergen's eyebrows rose. "What? How?"

Ava shook her head. "I don't know. Have you ever heard of anyone going and coming back?"

"No." Mergen searched the water's surface, as if an answer would be found in its ripples. "Once you are in the afterlife, you are there forever, regardless which one you end up in."

The voice—the silver soul—he knew her. How?

"Whatever happened, let's not do it again." Mergen huffed, wiping her face. "There's no guarantee you'll come back next time."

"Right," Ava muttered, wringing water from her hair. But her soul yearned for the lightness beyond.

"Let's get back to your aunt and you can tell me why there are so many souls out here."

The souls.

"Merg." Her voice came out rough. "Where did they go?"

"They zipped off after dunking you in the water." Mergen shook her head. "Something spooked them."

Ava closed her eyes, pressing her palms to her face. She'd failed to send them to Empyrean. Now they might get lost—wander too long in the liminal plane until they disappeared, their afterlife forfeit.

What could possibly scare souls that badly?

Ava explained the quake to Mergen as they made their way back to the group of villagers.

"Do you think the island breaking off and the erratic behavior of the souls are connected somehow?" Mergen asked.

"I'm not sure," Ava said, spotting Rune. "We should tell Zoya, though."

"Seáh," Mergen agreed. "I'm going to fly over the forest, see if I can find those wayward souls and then I'll go back to the temple."

"Thanks, Merg." Ava gave her a squishy hug and went to help Rune.

"Ava. There you are." Rune waved her over while comforting a woman crying hysterically. The woman's child had gone over the edge during the quake. "My Ava will find her spirit." Rune promised. Sighing, she straightened, giving Ava a once over. "What happened to you? Decide to go for a swim?"

"Something like that," Ava mumbled.

Rune studied her but said nothing else. "I need you to help these people. They've lost loved ones over the edge and are looking for their souls."

She tugged Ava's arm, pulling her aside. Her voice dropped. "Were you able to collect any? Do you think you can reunite them with their families?"

Ava shook her head. The words stuck in her throat. "There were so many. They were upset." Tears welled. "They jetted off into the forest. Mergen went to look for them. I'm staying here in case they return."

Rune nodded. "Their distress is to be expected. They were not ready for their lives to end today."

She patted Ava's hand. "Don't worry. We have some time. For now, will you take these and share them with the wounded?"

Ava accepted the salves and worked her way through the shaken crowd. Their faces were covered with dirt, tears, and blood. An older gentleman sat sobbing. His wife was missing. Ava promised to search for her.

Why had the island fallen apart? The question circled her mind as she walked. Her foot caught on a root and the pots scattered from her hands. She stacked them again and tried a different carrying method. They tumbled from her hands.

"Shaft it." Ava stared at the jars scattered across the ground. *Of course* this was happening today.

A man stood off to the side, arms crossed over his hunter green tunic. He didn't look injured. Maybe he could help.

"Hey," she called.

He didn't react. Just kept watching the crowd like he was observing something behind glass.

"Hello?" She waved her hand.

Still nothing. Was he deaf? She was about to give up when his head turned and his eyes found hers.

He froze. Stared at her like she'd appeared out of thin air.

"Me?" He pointed to himself, his voice shocked.

"*Seáh*, you." Ava knelt beside her pile of jars and motioned him closer. "Will you help me with these?"

"You're talking to me." Not a question this time. Something raw in his voice—disbelief, maybe. Or hope. "You can actually see me."

"Why wouldn't I?" She frowned.

He moved toward her slowly, like he was afraid she might vanish if he approached too quickly. As he got closer, his skin shimmered in the afternoon light—almost translucent in places.

Strange.

"Here." Ava held it out to him. "Take a few of these containers and give them to the wounded, please."

He reached for the jar but paused, his gray-blue eyes taking in her muddy clothes and hair. "Are you...alright?"

Souls, she'd forgotten what she must look like. She tried to tuck her hair under the wet scarf, wiped at her face. Probably making it worse.

"*Seáh*." She gave up. "I'm fine." She stood and held out a small jar. "Here you go."

He accepted it reluctantly, and for a moment they just stared at each other. The silence stretched.

Then—that small, sideways grin. Something in her chest did a strange flip.

He knelt and picked up another jar and glanced at her. She raised her eyebrows.

"Is two all you can muster?"

"Um, no." He grabbed three more quickly, as if to prove something. Hesitantly, he walked over to the closest group of people, set the small pot on the ground near them, and quickly stepped backward. The people kept speaking amongst themselves until one finally noticed the ointment. Calling out to Rune, they thanked her and dipped their fingers into the cream, applying it to their wounds.

For each pot, he did the same—awkward, cautious. Was he not used to people?

But the most interesting thing was his soul. Why did it feel so strange? Ava stretched out her spirit, brushing against the curtain between planes. She shuddered—the sensation bringing back a terrifying memory. She pushed through anyway.

There.

His soul felt sincere, but quiet and muted, as if he were weighed down. He existed, but not fully. Like a part of him was missing. Before she could explore him further, the pressure of the liminal plane crashed over her, and the darkness pulling her under.

She gasped and yanked herself back, stumbling. Her vision swam.

"Whoa—hey." His hand caught her elbow, steadying her. Cold. His touch was cold as winter water.

She looked up at him—really looked. Those gray-blue eyes held something she couldn't name. Loneliness, maybe. Or recognition.

"You can see me," he said quietly. Not a question. A statement of wonder.

"Of course I can see you." Her heart was doing something erratic in her chest. "Why wouldn't I?"

Something flickered across his face—relief so raw it made her throat tight. He released her arm quickly, as if the touch had burned him despite the cold.

"No reason." That sideways grin again, but this time it didn't quite reach his eyes. "You should probably sit down. You look like you're about to fall over."

She should argue and tell him she was fine, that she'd been through worse today. But the way he was looking at her—like she was the first real thing he'd seen in years—made all her carefully constructed walls crack just a little.

"What's your name?" The question came out softer than she intended.

He hesitated, as if he'd forgotten how to answer such a simple question. "Thorben."

"Ava." She offered her hand without thinking.

His eyes dropped to her outstretched palm. For a long moment, he just stared at it. Then, carefully—so carefully, like he was handling something precious—he reached out.

The cold of his skin should have made her pull away. Instead, she found herself holding on.

Chapter Six

The liminal plane had her.

She'd only meant to brush against his soul—just a quick touch to understand what felt so wrong about it. But the darkness pulled, thick and sticky, dragging her under. She tried to surface but couldn't find the edge, couldn't find the light—

"Ava. Ava, can you hear me?"

A voice. Distant but solid. She latched onto it.

"Come back. Back to me."

The dirt beneath her fingers came first. Then the weight of her body. Her eyes were closed, and she forced herself to take long, slow breaths.

When she opened them, she was sitting on the ground. Claw marks scarred the mud where her fingers had dug in. Thorben leaned over her, his face tight with worry.

"Are you alright?" His voice was clearer now, urgent.

"I...*seáh*, I'm fine." She brushed dirt from her hands, heat rising to her cheeks. She'd gotten lost in the liminal plane. In front of him. "I'm sorry."

"Don't be sorry." His smile was strained around the edges. "You gave me a scare."

"I gave myself a scare." Ava stood. "Were you, um, able to pass out the healing balms?"

"*Seáh*." He watched her for a minute, an eyebrow raised. "How—I mean, who—" he said but couldn't quite get out a question. "Are you sure you are alright? You were...not in the Real. For a while."

"How long?"

He hesitated. "A few minutes. Maybe longer."

The weight of that settled between them. A few minutes in the liminal plane could feel like hours. Or days.

"I came back," she said quietly.

An awkward silence stretched. Eventually, he tipped his head toward Rune. "Are you with the inyanga?"

Rune was spellcasting and murmuring comforting words as she applied creams and tonics to the crowd.

"*Seáh*," Ava answered, but then had a terrible thought. What if *he* had been injured and she had made him do work?

"Wait—you're not hurt, are you? Do you need healing?"

She scanned him quickly—no blood, no obvious wounds. Though with those dark clothes, it would be hard to tell.

"I'm fine." He gave her that dazzling smile. "Better than fine, actually."

Something in her chest fluttered.

"*Venúste*," she muttered under her breath. When was the last time she'd noticed a man was attractive? Years, probably. And today of all days—exhausted, grieving, covered in mud—this was when her body decided to wake up?

Inconvenient timing.

The crowd began to disperse—some to salvage what they could, others to find shelter in the city. Ava packed the remaining ointments, her mind on the landslide.

What could have caused such a massive quake?

A tug at her heartsoul. She glanced up at the new edge—pastel colors glinting in the light. Several souls weaved and wavered, lost in confusion.

She set down the basket. She couldn't lose two groups of souls in one day. Families were looking for them.

"So, do you live nearby?" Thorben followed her toward the souls. "I've been all over this island, but I don't think I've ever seen you."

"I live across the lake...well, what used to be the lake." Ava kept walking toward the cliff, watching the souls while staying aware of the odd, attractive man following her. She reached inside her utility belt for the essentiae she had brought. As she neared, the souls became clearer, each of them a different color.

He paused, catching sight of the ribbons of color. "Are those souls?"

She stopped. "You can see them?"

"Sure."

"Are you a druid?"

"Oh, um, no."

"Then how can you see souls?" Ava asked. Did he have some other type of magic allowing him access to the liminal layer?

"I'm not sure." His eyes went distant, lost in memory. "One day I could see them, and I've been able to ever since."

He ran a hand through his hair. The gesture seemed unconscious, like he didn't realize he was doing it. She looked away.

He could see souls in the liminal plane, but he wasn't a druid. What did that mean? Did it correlate with the current state of *his* soul?

In her peripheral vision, a stray soul glinted in the light, reminding her she had work to do. The souls had gathered off the edge of the island, and she refocused, cautiously peering over the edge. The fringe of the island was broken, bits of rocks, trees and roots reaching out, trying desperately to hold onto itself. Nothing was left but mist and dust.

"What in the...?" Ava leaned farther over. The wind blew, forcing her hair back and bringing the smell of sulfur over the brim. "That smells like..."

"Be careful." He moved closer. "The edge is probably unstable."

Was that a cord sticking out? What would a wire be doing in the middle of the island? Ava searched the exposed dirt. There was another one. They were definitely ropes of some kind and looked as though they had been connected.

"What is—" The earth dissolved beneath her feet, stealing her last words. Ava screamed, her body twisting as she desperately searched for something to hold onto. Her fingers found a long root and quickly grabbed hold. Sprinkles of dirt and plants clattered over her, grit landing in her mouth and eyes. Her side burned where it had scraped against the rocks and her hands chaffed on the root.

"I've got you!" Thorben threw himself down and grabbed her wrist. His eyes went wide—surprise, then determination. His grip tightened.

The ledge she held onto gave way. She opened her mouth to scream. Grit rained into her throat, and she searched frantically for another place to hold on to.

"Take my other hand!" He shouted, reaching out. Ava twirled, trying to twist her body into place so she could get a hold of him. Kicking her legs in the opposite direction, she pivoted, snagging both of his hands.

"Look at me." His voice was steady, certain. "I'm not going to let you fall."

She looked. Found those gray-blue eyes holding hers—a promise in them. Ava slowly nodded, too afraid to speak.

"I'm going to pull you up." He hauled her over the edge as if she weighed nothing.

Her feet hit the earth. She lost her balance immediately, stumbling into his chest. His arms caught her, steadying her.

He smelled like mint. And rain.

"Here we go," he murmured walking backward carefully. "Let's get on safer ground."

After several steps, he stopped. She steadied herself, then stepped back. Her hands slipped from his arms.

"Thanks." She coughed, trying to clear the dirt from her throat.

"I've never seen an island break apart like that." He waved at the edge, looking into the emptiness. "Have you?"

"Neyá." She shook her head, wiping her dirty hands on her thighs. It mixed with the water still soaking her pants, creating a muddy smear. Heat crept into her cheeks. She must look like she had crawled out of the swale. Pressing her hair away from her face, she grimaced as the dirt grittily smeared under her fingers.

"I think I saw something on the underside of the island," Ava said, flinging globs of mud on the ground.

Thorben raised his eyebrows. "That so? What was worth leaning over so far to see?"

"There are cords." Ava pointed. "Lots of them."

"What type of cords?"

"Braided ropes or wires...and they were placed every few feet."

His demeanor became thoughtful. "Braided ropes? Like the ones they use on airships?"

Now that he mentioned it, yes. She and Toby had been experimenting with a similar cord for the highly explosive fyre power portion of their prototype engine. If a large amount of combusting material had been wired together and spell cast, it might have enough force to blow an island apart.

"Something with massive power had to have been attached to those wires." She sniffed the air. "It would explain the sulfur smell too."

"What would?"

She paced, her thoughts spinning. "What if someone engineered this? What if the island was meant to collapse?"

"Why would someone do that?"

"I don't know," Ava replied, looking out to the sky. The explosion had been large and damaging. It had to have been someone who knew exactly what they were doing. Who would have enough knowledge and capabilities to make such a thing happen? And why?

"What are you going to do about..." he motioned to the souls circling her. "Them?"

"Oh, I forgot." She pulled several objects from her pockets and sat cross-legged on the ground. Thorben watched, intense fascination on his face.

"You're going to watch?" she asked.

"I like to watch." That teasing grin was back. Her confused look made it drop. "I mean—" He cleared his throat. "I'd like to observe. If you don't mind. Souls usually avoid me."

Interesting. Souls' instincts were sharp when it came to danger. What was it about him they found disturbing?

"Be still and quiet, then," she said.

Ava closed her eyes and sang. The melody soothed the souls, and she opened her hands in offering. The souls wandered toward the collection of items, each choosing one. Thankfully, these souls seemed content. When they had finished bonding, Ava sighed. She hoped she could find their families soon.

"Well? Was it everything you thought it would be?" Ava asked Thorben with a teasing smile.

"It was beautiful to watch." Thorben nodded, his eyes thoughtful. "Thank you for sharing it with me." They both headed back toward Rune, who was working her magic, healing and comforting people.

"The inyanga..." He motioned toward Rune. "How do you know her?"

"She's my aunt."

"Oh." He paused but then said quietly. "It's good you both have magic that can help people." Ava thought she caught a hint of sadness in his voice. "I...don't have much magic, but I can do simple things."

Ava and Thorben watched Rune speak to a patient, each silent with their own thoughts. Ava wondered again how she was going to find a cure. Rune was everything she had. What would she do without her?

"Can I walk you home?" Thorben asked, breaking into her thoughts.

"Don't you have someone to take care of?" She had seen the close-knit group in this small settlement. Surely, he had a family...a wife.

"Not really. My sister and her husband have two girls, but they..." he shrugged and shoved his hands into his pockets. "Well, they keep to themselves, I guess."

"Oh." Ava thought he seemed sad about it. They approached Rune as a patient thanked her and handed her a jar of honey.

"Ava, would you mind taking these things home?" Rune put the jar in a basket. "I'll be right behind you."

"Of course." There were several baskets, all filled to the brim. Ava glanced at Rune—she seemed focused, with no hints of an impending episode. And carrying the baskets by herself might be a bit of a challenge.

Thorben's gaze hadn't left her. He raised an eyebrow—he was still waiting for her answer. She supposed if Rune could accept a gift from a patient, Ava could accept the offer of a handsome man.

"Would you mind helping me carry these?" Ava asked.

Thorben frowned at the pile and then back at her, as if he were contemplating a big decision. After a moment, he said, "Seáh. I can do that. Lead the way."

Ava lifted a basket and Thorben grabbed two. "I'll see you at home, Auntie." Rune waved her away, her focus on another patient.

Between the two of them, they made it in one trip. Ava showed Thorben into the kitchen, where they set the baskets on the table. They returned to the entry way where leaves had blown in from the hole made by the tree in her aunt's room.

"What are you going to do about this tree?" He peered through the doorway into Rune's bedroom, checking the exposed beams.

"I don't know." Heat crept into her cheeks—from embarrassment at her appearance, or from standing this close to him, she wasn't sure. "I have a friend I can ask for help, but he's in the city and won't be able to come for a few days."

Toby would help if she asked. He always did.

Thorben's face suddenly lit. "I can help."

"You can?" His hesitation at carrying the baskets hinted that perhaps he wasn't used to manual labor. "Are you sure?"

"I can absolutely fix this."

"Well...that would be great." Ava smiled. If Thorben could repair her house, she wouldn't have to bother Toby.

Rune bustled in and swept past them into the kitchen. "My realms, girl, you carried the entire haul by yourself."

"I had help," Ava called.

Thorben's gaze dropped to his feet. His face reddened.

"I should go." His voice went quiet. "I'll be back tomorrow morning to help with the roof."

" A *yah ageremé*." She meant it.

He left. The leather pants caught the light with each step. He seemed nice, if strange.

The door clicked closed.

She pressed her palms to her hot cheeks. What was wrong with her today? The island had fallen apart. Souls were lost. Rune was dying.

And all she could think about was whether he'd wear those pants again tomorrow.

Chapter Seven

B efore today, Thorben had abandoned hope. Years of isolation and despair had broken any belief he might have had in restoring his life to what it once was.

But today, she spoke to him.

Then—impossibly—she *touched* him.

He stared at his hands in the fading light. When he'd grabbed her wrist at the cliff's edge, he'd done it on instinct. Ten years of being unable to touch anything, and his body had simply reacted. He'd expected his fingers to pass through her like they did everything else.

Instead, he'd felt her. Solid. Warm. Real.

His grip had faltered in shock before determination kicked in. He'd hauled her up, felt the weight of her body against his chest, smelled mint in her hair—

He pressed his palms against his face.

Ten years. Ten years without touching another person. Without being touched.

And she'd offered her hand at the end like it was nothing. Like he was just a man she'd met, not a ghost haunting the edges of existence.

If she could touch him, if she could see him—maybe she could help him understand what had happened. She was a druis. They dealt with souls, with magic, with the space between life and death.

Maybe she knew about curses.

The thought made his chest tight with something dangerous. Something that felt like hope.

He'd followed her home with his hands full, but it hadn't been with pure intentions. He needed to see where she lived. And understand who she was.

Now, he peered out from the forest, studying the back of the cottage. Their garden was impressive, boasting a wide variety of herbs and flowers, some of which were difficult to cultivate. Whoever tended this knew their craft.

The back door opened and Thorben's gaze cut to the person who stood there.

Ava stepped into the evening light, and Thorben's breath caught. Her black hair absorbed the golden light, curling slightly at the ends. She lifted her face and smiled, and he had to remind himself to why he was there.

Focus. He needed to focus.

The first person to see him in ten years, and she just happened to be a druis. It couldn't be coincidence. Maybe this was another trap—someone sent to make his existence worse. His gut clenched.

He'd trusted before. Been tricked before. The *Shaitán* had taught him that lesson with exquisite cruelty.

But what choice did he have? Ava was the first person to perceive him in a decade. If there was even a chance she could help him, he had to take it.

Even if it meant using her.

Ava stopped in the middle of the garden. She pulled a glove from her back pocket and slid it on. Taking a deep breath, she moved through a series of slow poses—arms stretching, bending, curving. Her movements were fluid, deliberate. Meditative.

Then, she moved.

She whirled—leg kicking out, hands coming together. When she pulled them apart, white-hot light flowed between her palms. The laser wire circled over her head, deadly and graceful, a pirouette of glowing fyre.

She fought invisible opponents, the light cascading around her like a living thing. Pivoting, ducking, striking with lethal precision.

Holy souls. Not only was she a druis—she was a weapon.

Thorben watched, his mind cataloging. The precision of her movements. The control she maintained over the laser. Did she have that same kind of control over her druidic magic? What were her limitations? Would she be able to use her magic on souls that were cursed?

Her aunt appeared—Rune, the inyanga. Ava retracted the laser wire and removed her glove, walking over to help with the garden. A soul wandered into their space, and Ava stopped long enough to guide it gently into an essentia.

She smiled, laughing with her aunt.

Thorben watched the care she took with the soul. The patience. The kindness.

If this was a trap, it was an elaborate one.

But he'd been desperate before, and it had cost him everything. He couldn't afford to be careless again.

Still—what choice did he have?

She was the first person to see him in ten years. The first to touch him. If there was even a chance she could help, he had to take it.

Thorben watched a while longer before heading deeper into the forest. He would stay close and learn everything he could about her.

Tomorrow, he'd fix her roof. Be useful. Helpful. And he'd ask questions. Carefully.

What kind of druis was she, exactly? What did she know about soul magic? Had she ever worked with curses? Could she manipulate soul bonds?

The questions lined up in his mind, neat and orderly. He'd been alone so long he'd forgotten how to have real conversations, but that didn't matter. She seemed kind. Understanding. She'd probably be happy to talk about her abilities.

He reached out with his spirit, searching the forest for answers as he always did. Silence. The same maddening silence that had answered him for ten years. The forest kept its secrets, and his soul remained out of reach—separated from him, underwater somehow, just beyond his grasp.

He needed answers. He needed his soul back. He needed his life back.

And Ava was his first real chance.

He couldn't just ask her outright. He would sound broken, desperate and demanding. If he told her how he ended up this way she might leave him in his misery.

He couldn't chance it.

He kicked a rock. All that mattered was breaking this soul-forsaken curse. She was a means to an end. That's all she needed to be.

He'd push down whatever else he might feel—that lurch in his chest when she smiled, the way his hands still remembered the warmth of hers.

Those feelings didn't matter.

After ten years of having no hope, he wasn't going to lose sight of the only person who could possibly set him free.

Not for anything.

Not even for her.

Chapter Eight

The next day, Ava opened the door to find Thorben dressed for work—the same green shirt and black pants, but now with a utility belt and leather vest. Dark circles shadowed the skin beneath his eyes. Had he slept at all?

"*Seáh llaéh*," Thorben greeted her, a hesitant smile on his lips. His dark wavy hair was pulled back at the nape of his neck, showing a small amount of stubble on his cheeks.

"*Seáh llaéh*," Ava mumbled, stepping back to allow him entry. Her teacup warmed her palms as she studied him. Something about his eagerness felt off—like he'd been waiting outside her door since dawn.

"Where is your lovely aunt this morning?" he asked, eyeing the hall.

"In the garden reading. She'll be out there for a while. She likes the first rays of the sun best."

"Perfect." His grin widened in a way that didn't quite reach his eyes. "Shall we get started?"

Ava led the way to Rune's room. The previous night, she and Rune slept outside in the gazebo they had built, a fyre's light flickering over them. Rune entertained her with stories, her descriptions so vivid, Ava wondered how true they really were.

Tools clattered to the floor as Thorben set down his box. He pulled out a hammer and slid the hard, wooden handle through his hands, which looked rough to the touch.

"Ah, what are you going to do first?" she asked, pretending to study the tree instead of his hands.

Thorben motioned for her to follow him. "Well, I haven't used my magic in a long time," he said, taking a deep breath. "But I think I can fix this. Come here and I'll show you."

He reached out a hand and Ava stepped closer, setting her cup on a nearby table. His touch was surprisingly cool. Too cool. She almost pulled back—the temperature felt wrong, unnatural—but he was already guiding her over the fallen trunk.

"Careful where you walk." He helped her through the hole and out of the house, then pulled her toward where the trunk had split in two. The tree had withered, the leaves turning brown and sad. She had been lucky Rune wasn't seriously injured during the quake.

"Ready?" Thorben asked, his stare intense. Ava dipped her head, and he placed her hand on the rough bark of the trunk, covering it with his own. He breathed in slowly, his exhale a whisper against her cheek. His scent of mint drifted beneath her nose, reminding her of yesterday.

"Trees have a spirit," he said quietly. His voice dropped into a register that vibrated in her chest.

"*Revive your spirit,*
Let life renew,
Flow earth's blood,
Return to yourself true."

The tree moaned, and the leaves shivered as if a strong wind quickly blew through. The branches heaved themselves off the ground, its trunk moving to its original position. The part that had been sawed in half gradually melded back together. Brown wrinkled leaves filled with color as they plumped into shape. The base of the tree reached for its missing half, thankful to be whole once again. Finally, the tree sighed, its branches resting peacefully in place, the leaves rustling a quiet 'thank you'.

Thorben stepped back, his breath quick, and his eyes slightly misty as he studied his work.

"That was beautiful." Ava touched the restored trunk, marveling at the seamless repair. "You're a phytomancer. Why didn't you tell me?"

"I wanted to see your reaction." He dusted his hands, but his gaze never left her face. "You work with souls, seáh? In the liminal plane?"

"Seáh." She tilted her head. Where was he going with this?

"How deep can you go? Into the plane?" Those gray-blue eyes tracked her expression like he was memorizing it.

Ava shifted her weight. "It depends. Some souls are...more challenging than others." She thought back to yesterday. When she had reached out, his soul had been subdued, like it was immersed inside a thick liquid. She had never encountered a soul like that before. Her fingers twitched toward her phylactery—she wanted to reach for it again, understand what she'd felt. That underwater sensation, like his soul was trapped, muffled...

"Have you ever gotten lost?" The question came quick, almost hungry. "In the plane?"

Her stomach tightened at the memory—ten years old, drowning in thickness, Zoya's panicked voice pulling her back. "Once. When I was young."

"But you found your way out." He moved closer, and she caught herself leaning back. "How? What technique did you use?"

"I...I'm not sure. Mother Zoya helped me." The air between them felt compressed. "Why are you asking so many questions about my magic?"

Thorben's expression softened into something apologetic, vulnerable even. "Forgive me. I've been...alone for a long time. I've forgotten how to make normal conversation." A self-deprecating smile tugged at his mouth. "And your magic is fascinating. I've never met a druis before."

The tension in her shoulders eased. Of course. There weren't many of them. "It's fine." She managed a small smile. "I'm just...not used to people being interested in the technical details."

"Then I'll try to be less interrogative." But even as he said it, his gaze dropped to her phylactery, studying the way it rested against her arm.

Her fingers twitched toward it protectively.

"Let's see what we can do to the inside of the house." He carefully stepped back inside, offering a helping hand to Ava as she followed.

"Usually, magientists use some kind of energy source to help with their magic," Ava said. He had asked about her magic—she could ask about his. "But you didn't."

"Luckily, nature has its own energy," he explained. "Powerful life flows through the earth, the trees, the wind. It has its own spark of strength and is enough for most mages." He paused, his expression somber. "The earth has always been my friend, even when I was not much of one."

Ava heard the regret in his voice. "So, you can't use magic on the house, then?" she teased, attempting to lighten his mood. She grabbed a broom to clear away the fallen leaves.

"That would be so much easier," he sighed, giving her a lopsided grin. "But no. We will have to fix this the old-fashioned way."

He measured an overhead beam. Ava swept the debris into neat piles, trying to focus on the work instead of the questions still swirling through her mind.

"Your phylactery," Thorben said suddenly. "How does it work exactly?"

She paused mid-sweep. "It stores essentiae."

When he gave her a quizzical look, she explained. "Essentiae are objects that have a soul bonded to them. It protects them until I can guide them safely to Empyrean."

"Protects them from what?"

"From getting lost. Or destroyed." She frowned. "Why?"

"Curious." He jotted something on a piece of wood, marking measurements. "And the souls inside—can you communicate with them?"

"Of course," Ava nodded. "It's part of my magic. Why do you want to know? Are you looking for someone that was lost during the landslide?"

"Oh," Thorben shook his head. "Neyá. I'm just trying to understand how it all works." That apologetic expression again, softer this time. "Your magic is remarkable, Ava. Surely you can understand my fascination."

She could. But something about the way he cataloged her answers made her skin prickle.

"In any case, I think it might rain soon. Your aunt won't be happy if she gets wet while she sleeps."

"There, you are correct." Ava set the broom in a corner, imagining the verbal blistering her aunt would spout if that were to happen. "A soggy Rune is an unhappy Rune."

Thorben chuckled as they got to work. Together, they tore out the crumbled wall and roof. Thorben was able to keep most of the structural beams, setting them to their original positions.

After a morning of labor, Rune's roof was fixed, and the wall was smooth on the outside. There was still more work to do on the inside, but at least the rain and wind couldn't get in.

"Thank you for your help." Ava and Thorben stood side by side, viewing their progress.

"I've forgotten the satisfaction to be had by working with my hands," he murmured.

"Do you not build things anymore? Or grow your own garden?"

"I used to, when it was needed, but I haven't done it in a long time. I mostly helped with planting and the harvest." The last sentence he said with distaste, as if he had been forced to do something he hadn't wanted to.

What had happened to cause such dislike of his own magic? Most people embraced their gifts, learning and growing through the years, some becoming powerful mages.

"Why don't you use your magic anymore?" she asked, steering the conversation away from herself.

A shadow crossed his face. He went to collect his tools, and Ava thought she may have offended him, so she stooped to help.

"I was ashamed," he finally answered, dipping his chin to his chest. "Who wants to be able to grow plants?"

"But it's a part of who you are," Ava argued, handing him a ruler. "You can feed entire villages, regrow forests, create flowers of every kind, maybe even make new ones no one has ever seen. That's a really useful gift to have."

He considered her words before standing. "Could I reconnect severed souls?" The question cut through the air between them. "Could I access the liminal plane like you do?"

She blinked. "Neyá, but—"

"Exactly. Your magic is far more valuable." He held her gaze with uncomfortable intensity. "You can touch death itself. Guide souls to their afterlife. Enter planes most people can't even perceive." "I suppose sometimes we forget our possibilities until someone comes along to remind us."

Ava relaxed slightly. His questions were odd, but maybe his loneliness explained it. Still, something nagged at her. The way he asked felt less like curiosity and more like...cataloging. Like Toby examining a broken mechanism, taking it apart to understand how it worked.

Was Thorben taking her apart?

He accepted the ruler, brushing his fingertips against hers. The coolness of his skin made her pull back instinctively.

"But being with you..." he said quietly, "is reminding me of what my magic could be."

"Ava?" She jumped at Rune's voice coming from the kitchen. What did he mean by that? Before she could ask, he spoke.

"I'll finish packing." Tools clinked as he gathered the last items from the floor.

She needed space to breathe. The questions, the intensity—it was too much. Ava ran her hand over her face and turned away to see what her aunt needed.

"Help me hang these herbs, will you?" Rune had varying types of plants tied in bundles scattered on the kitchen table.

"I will, but first, you should come with me," Ava said, grasping her hand. She wanted her aunt to see what Thorben had repaired.

"Alright, alright, don't be so pushy," Rune groused. But when they reached the room, Thorben was gone. He'd left without even saying goodbye.

"Oh, *mé veláh.*" Rune put her hand to her heart. "You fixed so much this morning, thank you. How did you do all this?"

"Do you remember the man that helped pass out healing salves yesterday? He was here this morning and did most of the work."

Rune slid her gaze sideways and raised her eyebrows. "A man?"

Heat crept into Ava's cheeks, but not from attraction—from confusion. "He offered to help."

Rune studied her flushed face, then squeezed her shoulder. "How does this man's soul feel to you? Is his smile genuine?"

Ava hesitated. Yesterday in the liminal plane, his soul had been wrong—submerged, muffled, like something trapped underwater. She'd never felt anything like it. And today, all those questions about her magic, her phylactery, her abilities...

"He has an excellent smile," she said instead.

Rune's eyes narrowed. "That's not what I asked."

"His soul is...unusual." Ava chose her words carefully. "But he's been alone for years. That changes a person."

"Hmm." Rune didn't look convinced. She patted Ava on the shoulder and headed back to the kitchen.

Alone in the doorway, Ava stared at the repaired room. Thorben had asked so many questions. About her magic, her phylactery, the liminal plane, forbidden techniques. Each answer she'd given felt like handing him pieces of herself.

But he was lonely. Of course he was curious.

Still, that nagging feeling wouldn't leave.

She moved to the window, searching the garden for any sign of him. Nothing.

Her chest tightened. Why had he left so abruptly?

She was overthinking this. He was probably uncomfortable with prolonged social interaction. That made sense. Everything made sense if she just thought about it logically.

But as she touched the repaired wall, she couldn't stop the question churning in her mind.

What was he hiding?

Chapter Nine

The morning after Thorben vanished from Rune's room, Ava found her aunt in the kitchen talking to empty air.

"*Seáh*, I understand," Rune murmured, nodding at the space beside the herb cabinet. "But she's not ready yet."

Ava's stomach dropped. "Auntie? Who are you talking to?"

Rune blinked, focusing on Ava as if surfacing from deep water. "Was I speaking aloud? I thought..." She trailed off, confusion flickering across her weathered face.

"You were talking to someone." Ava moved closer, searching her aunt's eyes. "Who?"

"I don't...I'm not sure." Rune pressed fingers to her temple. "Sometimes I hear voices. Or think I do. Old age, *mé veláh*."

But Rune wasn't that old. Seventy, perhaps seventy-five. Not ancient.

Ava reached out instinctively, letting her spirit brush against her aunt's. What she felt made her breath catch.

Rune's spirit was fraying. Like fabric worn too thin, threads separating, gaps appearing where there should be wholeness. Underneath, something else stirred—older, deeper, tired beyond measure.

Ava pulled back, heart hammering. She'd never felt anything like it. A spirit shouldn't feel that way. Shouldn't be coming apart at the seams.

"Auntie," Ava whispered. "Your spirit—"

"Is fine." Rune's voice sharpened, snapping Ava back to the present. "Don't fuss. I'm simply tired." She turned away, busying herself with the morning tea. "You should go to the city. Didn't you have errands?"

Ava wanted to argue, to demand answers. But the set of Rune's shoulders, the tremble in her hands—her aunt was barely holding on.

Whatever was wrong with Rune's spirit, it was getting worse. And Ava had no idea why.

She swallowed around the lump forming in her throat. If she wanted answers—if she wanted a cure—she needed to act now.

"Before I go, will you make a remedy for me?" Ava asked. "I need something that will help with night terrors. And delusions."

"Are you having troubles?" Rune asked, her eyebrows drawing together.

"It's not for me," Ava began hanging the herb bundles, avoiding Rune's concerned stare. "It's for someone at the temple." Which, Ava reasoned, was technically true.

"It's not Zoya, is it?"

"Neyá, I promise. It's only for a friend who needs help."

"Hmm," Rune eyed her but said nothing else. "Alright, grab the jar of dried somnus."

Ava went to the wall of herbs. "And the quieting frigilia," Rune said over her shoulder, collecting a bowl and pestle.

Ava grabbed a jar filled with black flowers. "I don't see the frigilia." She scanned the shelves. The jar was missing from its usual place.

"It should be there, I haven't used it in a while," Rune said, crushing ingredients together.

Ava kept searching and finally her eyes caught on the jar at the far end of the shelf. She reached, bobbling it from its perch. "Got it."

"Take out two flowers each and grind them together," Rune instructed. Ava did as requested and passed the ground mixture to her aunt. "Liss and gardilian will rid the body of any current toxins and help the other herbs be more effective." Rune paused, staring at the empty space again. "*Seáh*, I'll tell her." She wiped her hands on her apron. "The frigilia will stifle the visions while the somnus will give rest."

Ava's chest tightened. Another hallucination. A conversation with someone who wasn't there.

Rune poured hot water into the herbs. She spoke an incantation and the kitchen filled with a bitter smell. Ava wrinkled her nose. The mixture of herbs and liquid fused together, creating a bright orange tonic.

Rune handed her the bottle. "Be careful who you trust. Sometimes, people are not what they seem."

Was Rune talking to her? Or still to the voice only she could hear?

Ava didn't know why Flip wanted this particular remedy and it occurred to her that maybe she should have asked. But Rune needed that cure.

She went to the front room and put the tonic safely into her travel bag. Hope loosened the lump in her throat slightly. If she could meet with Flip's knave soon, perhaps Rune would be healed in a matter of weeks.

Before the fraying got worse. Before her aunt disappeared entirely into those voices.

A knock on the front door broke her from her thoughts. She opened it to find a woman from the local messaging service dressed in a blue pinstripe shirt, blue corset, and matching pants.

"A tube came for you this morning," she said, handing over a rolled letter sealed with wax.

Ava immediately recognized the Realm of Souls insignia.

"Thank you," Ava said breathlessly. It finally came. Maybe she wouldn't need Flip's deal after all. She accepted the note, her chest tightening.

"No problem," the messenger replied. "I'm surprised it even came through. We had so many cracks from the quake, most messages are stuck in the chutes." She saluted Ava and went back to her steam cart to deliver the rest of the mail to surrounding villages.

Ava closed the door and leaned against it. Her request to travel through the purdah had finally arrived. She was afraid to open it.

Taking a deep breath, she broke the seal.

Greetings, Avalina Llahenór,

Thank you for your request to travel through the purdahs. Unfortunately, we cannot grant you permission at this time. We are sorry for any inconvenience.

Purdah Regulations Office

Realm of Souls, Commodore Alistair Van Alst VII, Presiding

Ava's head fell back against the door with a thunk. Now, her only option was to speak with Flip's knave. She hoped he would be willing to fulfill her request. Rune's spirit was disintegrating, and Ava had no idea how to stop it.

The airbus station was packed with people trying to get to the city. She pushed through the crowd, desperate souls brushing against her with every step. So many spirits, too much pain, and all of it seeping into her like water through cracked stone. Some were still dirty from the quake, others carried children and bags of whatever they had left. Ava wondered where they would all go.

The airbuses were one of two types of public transportation, the other being the steam train which was dirtier, slower, and didn't run as frequently.

Ava hefted her bag over her shoulder. She had stuffed Dáhlia's glad rags and Flip's tonic inside. She could return the clothes first before heading to the temple. She aimed for the airbus docked in the last landing station. This aircraft was less crowded and a bit smaller, and she hoped it would get her to the city faster.

"Avalína."

She spun. Thorben stood three feet away, his gaze lingering on her bag. His utility belt and work vest were gone, replaced by a simple dark coat. He carried nothing—no bags, no tools.

"Thorben." Her pulse kicked. "What are you doing here?"

Something flickered across his face. "I'm...looking for someone." His gaze quickly scanned the crowd, but then his eyes found hers again. "And you?"

"Going to the city." She shifted the weight of her bag, conscious of the tonic inside. "To see friends."

"How is your aunt this morning?" The question came quickly, his attention snapping back to her with uncomfortable focus. "Is she well?"

Ava hesitated. Rune's fraying spirit flashed through her mind—those gaps, that exhaustion, those voices. "She's...the same."

"The same?" He tilted his head, no longer scanning the crowd. "What does that mean exactly?"

"Just tired." Why did this feel like an interrogation again? "She's been through a lot with the landslide."

"Of course." His expression softened into something sympathetic. "And her illness? You mentioned she was unwell."

Had she mentioned that? Ava tried to remember their conversations. "She's managing."

"What are her symptoms?" He moved closer, lowering his voice as people jostled past. "Perhaps I know of something that could help. Plant remedies, herbs..."

"It's not that simple." Ava stepped back, needing space. "It's more...spiritual than physical."

Interest sharpened in his eyes. "Spiritual? Her soul is damaged?"

"Not damaged. Just..." She stopped. Why was she telling him this? "I need to go. My airbus is boarding."

"Of course." He didn't move. "Will I see you again? To finish the repairs?"

"I'll send word." She turned away, but his voice followed her.

"Avalína? Be careful in the city. Things are...unstable right now."

She looked back. He was already walking away, apparently having abandoned his search for whoever he'd been looking for.

Her chest felt tight. The station was enormous—multiple piers, dozens of airbuses, hundreds of people. What were the odds they'd cross paths?

Unless he'd been waiting.

She shook her head, climbing the airbus steps. She was being paranoid. The landslide had everyone displaced, traveling, searching for resources. Of course she'd run into people she knew.

But as she clanged up the steps and dropped a coin into the slot, she couldn't shake the feeling that Thorben's questions about Rune felt less like concern and more like...cataloging.

The scent of sweat and old grease hit her as she entered the wide double doors. Some airbuses were several decks tall, but this one had a single deck. The benches were dingy red velvet, the ironwork worn from travelers' hands over time. Ava slipped into a front seat, behind the captain's control room, a cloud of dust making the light hazy.

The airbus lurched into the sky, and immediately Ava felt it—the weight of every soul on board pressing against her awareness.

Fear. Loss. Grief so sharp it cut.

A woman three rows back sobbed into her hands. Two children clung to their father, eyes hollow with shock. An elderly man stared at nothing, his spirit fractured by whatever he'd witnessed during the landslide.

Ava tried to block it out, but she'd never been good at that. Her druidic magic made her permeable to suffering, and these souls were drowning in it.

She reached out instinctively, sending calming waves to the woman, the children, the old man. Tiny threads of comfort, barely enough to ease the sharpest edges of their pain.

But there were so many. And each one she touched pulled at her, draining something essential. Her head began to ache. Her phylactery grew warm against her arm, resonating with the distress surrounding her.

More sobs broke out. A child's wail. Someone retching in the back.

Ava pressed her forehead against the window, trying to find something solid to anchor to. But even the clouds outside seemed to reflect the grief—gray, heavy, threatening rain.

By the time the airbus finally docked, she was shaking. Exhausted in a way that had nothing to do with physical tiredness and everything to do with carrying too much pain that wasn't hers.

She stumbled off, gulping fresh air, forcing herself to straighten. She couldn't afford to break down. Not when Rune needed her.

But souls, she was so tired.

The airbus finally docked, and everyone somberly filed out. Ava breathed a relieved sigh to be in the open air at the top of the pier. The breeze whipped strands of her ebony hair out from her aviatrix cap, and she hastily shoved them back.

"This way, please, this way," a boisterous voice called. A massive ship was docked several piers away with the emblem of the commodore painted on the hull. Ava realized this was the ship Mergen had seen the other day.

The door to the main cabin swung open and a large, tall man with jet black hair tied back at the nape of his neck walked out. He wore a stiff suit boasting several buckles on the vest and Ava recognized him as the commodore. He stepped aside and allowed several people behind him to file out onto the deck.

They looked to be from different realms, except for Lleu Priam, who was a druid she was familiar with. He had come to the temple once or twice to talk to Zoya, but it always seemed to Ava that Zoya did not enjoy his visits.

"The landslide off the island was unfortunate," a tall man in light brown robes said as he walked next to Van Alst. Ava guessed with his tanned skin and short white, blond hair he must be a mage from the Realm of Winds.

"It truly is," Van Alst replied, his hands running over his large stomach. "But we are close to a breakthrough that will transform the way we do things, including helping to find souls that have been lost. Our world will become more prosperous and united as never before."

A chorus of "ahs" followed his statement, and Van Alst smiled smugly.

"How can we trust this idea of yours will work?" another mage asked. "Plans of the truest intentions always come with risk." She turned over-sized, tinted goggles toward him, her shimmering skin reflected the light. Ava caught a glimpse of large ears tucked beneath dark, silky hair. She must from the Star Fyre Realm. "I do not want my realm to be caught in the crossfyre of your experiments."

Van Alst's nostrils flared. "My plan will work. It has been formulated by the very best mages in the Realms and tested extensively." He paused for effect, making sure he had everyone's attention, then raised his voice. "We have been experimenting with an untapped source of energy. I believe this force to be so powerful it will remove boundaries, forging new and influential relationships throughout the Realms. It will be revolutionary."

The assembled party paused, their faces thoughtful at Van Alst's words. Ava herself couldn't believe what Van Alst was promising. What breakthrough could he possibly be offering?

A woman wearing a simple toga tied at one shoulder leaned against the railing. The strands of her long white hair blew in the breeze and Ava's breath caught when she saw the woman's eyes. Multicolored pupils scanned the skyes, catching hues of every shade, dancing and sparkling in the light.

"When will you be telling us of this breakthrough?" A woman with obsidian skin cocked her head. Light winked off different sized gems that were embedded in her face, arms, and neck every time she moved. People from the Black Sands Realm used precious stones to signify status in their culture. With the amount of gems she boasted, Ava thought she must be highly respected. "So far, the only thing I see is your island crumbling beneath you."

Spots of color burned in his fat cheeks. "My invention is in its final stages. Everything you know will change."

Ava lost the conversation as Van Alst herded them to a set of stairs. He paused at the top, his head suddenly lifting to search the busy walkway below. He zeroed in on Ava.

The moment their eyes locked, her druidic magic flared in alarm.

Wrong. Everything about him felt wrong.

But it wasn't just him. Through his gaze, she felt...others. As if many spirits were pressing forward, watching her, seeing her, hungry and desperate and furious all at once.

Van Alst's lips curved into something that might have been a smile and her own spirit recoiled in horror.

The hairs on her neck rose and her breath came short.

What *was* he?

Chapter Ten

Her legs moved before her mind caught up, feet clanging against iron as she spun away from Van Alst. Don't look back. The corridor stretched endlessly—why was it so long?—until finally she reached a corner and threw herself against the wall. Air rasped in her throat. Her fingers trembled against cold metal, and deep in her chest, something still burned from where his gaze had touched her spirit. Wrong. Everything about him was wrong.

She pushed hair away from her face, trying to steady her breathing. That magic—his magic—it didn't feel like anything she'd encountered before. Corrupted, maybe. Like something ancient had been twisted into shapes it was never meant to hold.

And why had he looked at her like that? As if he recognized something?

Ava tentatively reached out her spirit, touching the surface of the liminal layer. It opened for her like a long-lost friend, inviting her in. She kept to the shallows, knowing if she succumbed to its depths, she might not find her way out.

The distance between her and Van Alst had lengthened, his presence lost in the sea of souls surrounding her.

Pulling herself out of the layer, she sighed and shoved herself off the wall. She didn't have time to think about the Magisterium or Van Alst. She traveled the length of the corridor, eager to get to Toby and Dáhlia's shop.

When Ava opened the shop door, she was met with absolute chaos. Machinery parts had been tossed to the floor, shattered into pieces. Oil spilled through the grated floors, dripping to the levels below, and the entire space smelled of grease. Dáhlia came in, her glad rags and hands filthy, her curly, chestnut hair in a high, messy bun.

"What happened?" Ava asked as she stepped over a relief valve.

"Some jackhole decided to raid our shop, that's what." Dáhlia's eyes sparked as she wiped grease from her cheek.

Toby came in, wiping his forehead with a towel. "They got into my workroom."

"Our invention?" Dáhlia asked.

"It's fine, thank the Five," Toby replied. "But I can't for the soul of me figure out what they were after."

"What do you mean?"

"Well," Dáhlia said. "This room is in shambles, but it doesn't look as if anything has been taken. They threw all the machine parts on the floor and just...left."

The destruction pulled at her attention—something about the pattern felt wrong. Machines torn apart, but not methodically. Not like someone searching for valuables. This looked like a fight. Like something had raged through the space, destroying everything in reach, then suddenly...sto pped.

Parts worth hundreds of coins scattered across the floor, untouched. Tools left hanging on their pegs.

A shiver traced her spine. It was almost as if whoever did this had been trying to destroy something, then argued with themselves about it. Changed their mind mid-rampage.

That didn't make sense.

"Did they steal any aircraft?" She gestured toward the stairs leading up to the sky pier.

Toby and Dáhlia exchanged wide eyed looks and quickly clanged up the stairs onto the sky pier. Ava hurried after them.

Six docks stretched along the pier—two for the twins, four for customers. Relief flooded through her when she spotted her ship still tethered in its berth.

"They took my byke!" Toby's voice cracked in disbelief. "I can't believe those bastards took my skybyke."

The orange byke's dock stood empty, his helmet abandoned on the side bench like a discarded shell.

"Well, now you can't kill yourself on that thing," Dáhlia retorted and went back below to continue cleaning.

"I'm sorry." The words felt inadequate as she touched his arm. "For what it's worth, I thought the byke was fantastic."

Toby's fingers caught hers before she could pull away—not grabbing, just...lifting them. Holding them as if they were something delicate he was trying to understand.

Cinnamon and vanilla cut through the grease-smell of the shop, and suddenly the afternoon felt warmer than it had moments before. She looked up. Light caught in his dark hair, glinted off his glasses. A smear of grease marked his cheekbone—she almost reached up to wipe it away before catching herself.

His thumb traced the ridge of her knuckles. Once. Twice. The touch sent heat spiraling up her forearm, settling somewhere behind her ribs where she'd been trying not to feel anything for years.

This was why she'd stopped letting herself stand too close. Why she'd learned keep every conversation light and surface-level, never diving into the depths where old feelings might still be waiting.

He'd made his choice.

She eased her fingers free, trying to make it look casual. Natural. As if her pulse wasn't doing complicated things in her throat.

His gaze followed her hand down to her side, something unreadable crossing his face before he blinked it away.

"Is Rune alright?" he finally asked, returning his gaze to her face.

She shrugged a shoulder. "For now." Rune's fraying spirit flashed through her mind. "The Purdah Regulations Office denied my request to travel."

"They did? Ava, I'm sorry."

"I'll figure something out." The tonic was heavy in her bag. She wanted to tell Toby about striking a deal with a knave but couldn't. He probably wouldn't approve.

"What about the house?" Toby asked. "Can I come over later to fix it?"

"You don't need to." Heat crept up her neck. Mentioning Thorben shouldn't make her self-conscious, but somehow it did. "We had some help from a nearby villager who's an elemental mage. He healed the tree, and we started the repairs."

"Oh?" Something shifted in his posture—barely noticeable, but she'd known him long enough to catch it. "Who?"

"His name is Thorben. I'm surprised I've never met him before. Do you remember him from when you lived there?"

"No." Toby's gaze wandered out to the horizon. "I'm glad you had help. I was going to come out until this happened."

"It's fine. Thank you for the offer, though." Ava shoved her hands in her back pockets. "You have your own catastrophe to handle."

"Indeed," Toby sighed, waving a hand for her to lead the way back to the shop.

Inside, Dáhlia and Aamina were collecting items and putting parts that were not broken back onto their shelves.

"Why would someone come here and trash our place?" Dáhlia threw a broken flywheel into a bin with a crash. "I don't even think they took anything."

"Well, whoever it was stole Toby's byke. He would say they took something." Ava bent to grab a crankshaft. Toby vanished into his workroom, a mumble his only farewell.

Aamina worked nearby, dropping bearings and lugs into a bucket one at a time—clunk, clunk, clunk. Little Sister, the porcelain doll Toby had made her, dangled from her other hand.

The girl paused, studying something small in her palm. Then—quick as a skybyke—she bolted for her apartment, the door slamming behind her.

"Uh oh. I think she found a new accessory for her doll."

Aamina loved to adorn Little Sister with trinkets, fabric, or baubles she found. The doll currently had several sewn-on buttons, a little golden chain, three glass beads, and a patch of bright blue fabric from one of Ava's old shirts.

Dáhlia rolled her eyes. "She's always collecting random bits of junk. Maybe she will become a druis."

"What do you mean by that?" Ava gave her friend a playful shove.

"You carry all kinds of odds and ends," Dáhlia laughed. "Perhaps I should get Aamina a utility belt for her birthday."

"You totally should," Ava said, nodding. "Besides, she would make an excellent druis."

"She would." Dáhlia agreed. "As long as she is happy doing it." Her gaze lingered where her daughter's form had disappeared. "Something interesting happened in my kinship group yesterday. Rayna Callistus, the metallurgist mage from Black Sands, stopped by."

"Why would she visit your kinship?"

"She's an avid teacher." Dáhlia replied, returning to the clean-up. "She likes to visit all the learning groups while she travels."

"Is she the one with all the diamonds in her skin?" A box scraped along the counter as she set it in place. "I've seen a few people from there, but never with so many gems. She was on Van Alst's ship this morning."

"That was her. She said all the Magisterium were invited by Van Alst to celebrate the Day of the Five."

After the landslide, meeting Thorben and having him fix her house, and the denial from the Purdah Regulations Office, the Day of the Five had totally slipped Ava's mind.

"She said Van Alst had a big announcement that would affect every realm," Dáhlia continued.

"I overheard Van Alst and the Magisterium speaking on his ship. He said something about a breakthrough and how everyone would be more prosperous."

Dáhlia snorted. "How would that be possible? The Realms are so cut off from each other by the purdahs that the only ones who can pass through are government officials and people with enough money to bribe them."

"Did Mage Callistus say anything else?" Her finger tapped the counter-top, mind jumping from one possibility to the next—traveling to different realms, finding a cure, saving Rune.

"Not really," Dáhlia replied. "Whatever Van Alst is organizing, she didn't seem to have much faith in it."

She straightened so fast her hip bumped the counter. "What if Van Alst has a plan that would let us travel freely through the barriers?"

Hope—dangerous, desperate hope—bloomed in her chest. "Dáhlia, the Purdah Regulations Office denied my request. But if Van Alst can change how the purdahs work while keeping the Realms intact..." Her words tumbled faster. "We could go anywhere. Black Sands. Star Fyre. We could find a cure for my aunt."

Before Rune's spirit unraveled completely. And those voices became all her aunt could hear.

Maybe Van Alst's breakthrough—whatever it was, however wrong his soul felt—could save Rune.

She was running out of options. And time.

Chapter Eleven

"She's here."

Van Alst's office occupied the highest building in the city, windows stretching from wall to wall—a panoramic view of everything he governed. Airships drifted past, sunlight glinting in and out of those scheming eyes.

Lleu Priam sat opposite him, fingers steepled. "You're sure? My sources haven't heard anything about her."

Van Alst's fist slammed into the desk. "Well, maybe your sources need their eyes cut out so they can hear better."

The fury on his face vanished—just *gone*—replaced by something almost serene. Then the rage returned, laced with petulant irritation, like a child denied a toy.

Three emotions in as many seconds.

"How do you know it was her?" Priam rose from his seat, keeping his voice level. Watching the souls war for control of that bloated body never got easier. The man was a walking argument with himself, and Priam found himself appalled—not for the first time—that he shared blood with this shambling mess.

Still. Useful messes had their place.

"We don't even know if she survived all those years ago," Priam added.

"I felt it." Van Alst settled back into his chair, hands smoothing the front of his vest with sudden fastidiousness. "When I saw the soul in her eyes, I knew. It was... familiar." His lids lowered, savoring the memory. "And if she's here, you know Vivia will be here too. She'll protect her niece with her life."

Priam's finger tapped his chin—once, twice—considering. If the druis and inyanga had returned to the Real, something must have triggered it. Did they know what he was planning?

He decided it didn't matter. Their years of immaculate preparation would hold against anything that old healer and pathetic druis might attempt. Every angle accounted for, every contingency mapped. But, now wasn't the time to ignore a potential threat, however minor.

"What did she look like?" Priam poured Star Fyre spirits into two glasses, the liquid thick and glittering.

"Dark hair." Van Alst's eyes slid closed, remembering. "And her eyes... deep turquoise. Like the healing waters of the Realm of Winds."

"Hmm." The glass passed from Priam's hand to Van Alst's. The windows beckoned, and he crossed to them, the cool silky liquor coating his tongue as he savored both the drink and the view.

"We can't take chances on them ruining our plans." Three decades of work. Years of traveling the Realms and collecting pieces of an ever-growing puzzle. Failed attempts littered the path behind them, but now—finally—they had everything they needed. "The research and experiments all support our theory. We've worked too long and too hard for it to fall apart now. The Realms need to unite, to be together again, under one rule."

A grunt from behind him. "We need to be proactive next week. I won't have them taking my glory again on the Day of the Five."

So predictable. Priam's lips curved slightly. "What would you like to do?"

Van Alst swirled his glass, the motion oddly graceful for such thick fingers. "If they're here, the other three may have survived."

"Highly unlikely."

"You weren't there." The growl came from somewhere deeper than Van Alst's throat.

Priam paused, glass halfway to his lips. He needed to be careful. "I know. But you've told me many times what happened that night. Surely they're in the afterlife."

Van Alst sank back into his chair, brow furrowing. "Their bodies were dead, but I was unable to find where their souls had gone. Vivia destroyed the mages I sent. I should kill her just for that."

A fat finger jabbed toward Priam. "If Vivia has hidden that brat for this long, she could also be hiding the rest of them." The remainder of the liquor vanished down his throat. "Set a bounty. Anyone with information about Vivia and her—" the word dripped with contempt "—*family* will receive compensation."

"As you wish."

Van Alst heaved himself upright, his large frame bumping the desk's edge. That flushed face twisted again—anger, confusion, determination, fear—cycling through expressions like shuffling cards before landing on bitter resolve.

"They will not stop me." Barely a mumble, more to himself than Priam.

"Of course not." Priam raised his glass. "After the demonstration, you, our ancestors, and our progeny will be honored instead of the Five. It will be an event to remember."

Van Alst nodded, already turning toward the door, muttering under his breath—words too low to catch, but Priam could guess. Always the same arguments with himself, the same circular conversations.

Fascinating, really. And disgusting.

The door closed.

Priam returned to the window, swirling the last of his drink. Below, the city sprawled—oblivious, trusting, *weak*. Van Alst thought himself a visionary, a revolutionary about to reshape the Realms.

Let him think it.

When Van Alst was gone—and he would be gone, eventually consumed by the chaos in his own skull—Priam would show them all how the Realms should truly be commanded. Not through borrowed power and fractured minds, but through cold precision and unwavering will.

He smiled into his glass.

Patience was, after all, the virtue of those who planned to win.

Chapter Twelve

A t Toby's shop, the three of them had restored order to the chaos. Goodbyes said, Ava caught a stepping lift and descended into the swale. Shadows fell across her face as the platform moved, the smell of earth slowly engulfing her.

Reaching into her pack she pulled out her black leather wired glove and slipped it on her left hand, buckling it at the wrist. Rune had insisted she learn to defend herself years ago. The swale wasn't safe, especially during evening light.

The lift jangled to a halt. She hauled open the door.

"Ava."

Instinct took over. Ava sidestepped and punched out her hand, grabbing a fistful of fabric. Flip stumbled from the shadows, his shirt tight in her grip.

"What are you doing?" Ava growled. "I about sliced your lips off."

"But you didn't, thank the Five." Flip brushed off her hold, sullen. "Did you bring the tonic?"

"Seáh."

"Great. Let's go." Flip caught hold of the strap on her bag and hauled her into the darkness. She batted away his hand, the smell of his body odor too strong for her to be so near. He raised an eyebrow.

"I can manage without you pulling me along," Ava huffed.

"Fine. Stay close."

The main paths to the temple were familiar territory and usually safe enough. These dark, winding passages? Dangerous. Used by people avoiding capture. Flip led her through a complex maze—ducking under iron beams, dodging water dripping from above. Her boots sloshed through muck that made her gag. He moved quickly and keeping pace took effort.

After a dozen turns, he stopped. She nearly collided with his back.

"Shh..." Flip held his fingers to his mouth.

"The girls need to be ready to go by tomorrow morning," a loud, angry voice bellowed. "We don't want to keep those highflyers waiting."

A large shadow passed by, and Flip and Ava shrank into the darkness. After a few moments, Flip peeked his head out and motioned her forward. She crept out of the passageway and froze. A boarded archway stretched over weathered double doors, the gold paint fading and chipping. The name of the parlous house was written over the top in big, red letters—The Scarlett.

"We're going 'round back." Flip maneuvered toward another dirty aisleway, skipping over puddles. Ava followed—gingerly.

"Here." He raised a flap and slipped inside. Ava ducked in behind him and was instantly hit with the heavy smell of incense. Her eyes watered, the perfume catching in her throat. Covering her mouth with her elbow, she coughed. The smoke in the room made it difficult to see. As her eyes adjusted, several iron beams supporting a large gathering room came into focus. Sheets of fabric separated bed spaces and she could hear moaning several sections away.

"What are we doing here exactly?" Ava whispered, covering her nose and mouth. Flip didn't seem the least bit bothered by the smell. Apparently, he was used to it.

"Shh! Just keep up," he said over his shoulder. Ava rolled her eyes but followed.

He led them across the room to a door, hidden behind a panel. Flip pulled out a small vial, poured it along the shank, and mumbled a spell. To Ava's surprise, it popped open.

"Do you have magic other than being a druid?"

He shrugged. "I've discovered a few handy tricks here and there. Let's hurry. We don't have much time until he gets back." He cranked open the rusty door and stepped inside. Stale, putrid odor wafted out and Ava gagged.

On the floor lay a small girl, covered in filth.

Ava's breath caught. The girl couldn't have been more than four-teen—maybe younger under all that grime. Curled on her side like some-thing broken and discarded. This was what Flip had been hearing through the wall every night. This was why he'd risked coming back.

Flip dropped to his knees beside her, all the street-smart bravado draining from his face.

"Gabrie, it's me," he said, touching her shoulder. She moaned and rolled over. Flip frowned. "She's been poisoned with a spellcasted drug to forget everyone she knows. It's been giving her nightmares. I can hear her screaming at night on the other side of the wall." The last sentence he mumbled, and Ava almost reached out to comfort him.

He snuffled, wiped his nose, and held out his hand. "Give me the tonic."

Ava dug in her bag and handed it over.

"Here, Gabrie, drink this." Flip went to uncap the bottle. The girl sud-denly stood and slapped him across his face, the sound echoing around them. The tonic flew to the floor.

"You!" She screeched. Her eyes were hazy and wild, her mouth sneer-ing in hate. "What do you want from me, Shaitán?"

Flip stepped back, his mouth a grim line. Barely moving his lips, he whispered over his shoulder, "I'm going to grab her from behind, you make her swallow the tonic."

"Wait—what?"

Before Ava could comprehend Flip's orders, he dashed behind Gabrie and threaded his arms through hers. Locking her limbs with his, he forced her into a sitting position. His legs wrapped around her waist, pretzelling so she couldn't move.

Gabrie twisted and flung out an elbow, gouging him in the ribs. Flip grunted. "Hurry!"

Ava scrambled to grab the tonic off the floor. Gabrie snarled and hissed, trying to bite Ava as she came closer. Ava tried to pour it into her mouth, but the girl twisted away.

"Grab her hair and yank her head back." Flip ground out.

Ava hesitated. How could she be so rough with someone who didn't deserve it?

"Do it," Flip snarled.

Ava tightened her grip on the vial. She snagged the girl's hair in her fist, she pulled it tight, and grimaced when her fingers squished between the dirty strands. Wrenching Gabrie's head back, she poured in the remedy.

"She needs to drink all of it," Ava said over the girl's gurgling. She gagged, trying to spit it out, but Ava shoved her hand under Gabrie's chin, forcing her to swallow.

Flip kept a tight hold, waiting. "How long until it works?"

"It should be fairly quick."

Gabrie's body went slack. Flip paused and then relaxed his hold. He crawled to sit in front of her and stared into her dirty face.

"Gab?" he whispered, nudging greasy strands of hair away from her face. "Can you hear me?"

Gabrie bolted upright. Her panicked eyes went from Flip to Ava.

Then she let out a blood curling scream.

"Shh!" Flip put his hand on her mouth, trying to keep her quiet. "I thought you said it would work?"

"It should have!" Ava protested.

"Ow!" Flip snatched his fingers back. Blood dripped from them. "She bit me." Flip grabbed a dirty cloth from his pocket, wrapping it around his injured hand. Gabrie took a big breath and let out another loud wail. Quick, heavy footsteps trod through the outer room. Flip eyes widened. "We need to get out of here."

"What's going on?" A deep voice echoed in the chambers. Before Ava could move, Flip slipped out the door and into the shadows.

"Flip!" Ava whisper shouted. "Wait—"

The door banged open. A large, tall man stepped into the room, blocking out what light there had been. Gabrie screamed again, making it difficult for Ava to think. Her only exit was blocked, and the smallness of the space was closing in around her.

The man paused and a slick smile spread across his wide face. "Found your way into my house, did you?"

"No, I—" Ava stood, reaching for the tab on her glove, but he was quicker. He lashed out and seized her arm, dragging her against his chest. His other hand caught her wrist, wrenching it behind her back. Ava's chest was pressed against him, her face inches from his. His smile widened, showing straight white teeth.

"Hmm," he bent, running his rough stubble cheek against her. Ava shivered in disgust. "Why would a pretty lass like you want to come in here?"

Gabrie whimpered on her mat. He frowned, his head whipping to her and then back to Ava.

"Did you come for her?" He jutted his chin in Gabrie's direction, his bald head shadowed in the light. "That is a wasted effort, I'm afraid. She's already mine. But, I think I will keep you," he put his nose against Avas hair, inhaling deeply. "I could get a high price for a doxy like you."

"No—" Ava twisted, trying to reach the tab on her glove.

"Yes," he whispered against her cheek. She pulled away from him as his malicious pale eyes raked over her frame. He zeroed in on her phylactery. "You're a druis?"

Ava remained silent.

"Even a higher price for you then," he smirked. "You can stay here with her while I send a few tubes. I have several buyers who would love an exotic such as yourself."

He threw her on the floor next to Gabrie and Ava skidded into the dirt.

"No!" She lunged for the door. It slammed in her face. "You can't do this!"

"No one steals from me, druis," he said, chuckling. "And no one comes in and leaves without me knowing."

Ava heard him click a new lock into place, leaving them both in complete darkness.

Ava sat in the corner of the filthy room listening to Gabrie whimper. Sometimes she would speak, but it was mostly gibberish. Ava was surprised the tonic hadn't worked. Rune's potions were always effective. Was Rune's sickness impairing her abilities to create potent remedies?

She thought back to the ingredients, but they seemed correct. Her stomach sank. What if she had grabbed the wrong jar? The frigilia hadn't been in its usual place. Had she put in an incorrect ingredient?

Ava dropped her head into her hands. If she had, it was her fault the tonic hadn't worked. Now, Gabrie was still incoherent, and they were both imprisoned with no way out.

And where had Flip gone?

Trusting him enough to follow him to this swale pit had been a mistake. She knew better than to let desperation cloud her judgment. But here she was anyway, locked in a filthy room because she'd been so focused on helping Rune that she'd forgotten to protect herself.

She huddled in the corner, reserving her strength and listening to the sounds of the night. People came and went, some laughing, a few crying.

And during all that, she watched Gabrie. When the big man's voice boomed on the other side of the door, Gabrie would curl into a ball on her mat and cry. She was trapped inside a disrupted reality, and it broke Ava's heart. The echo of frantic voices searching but fading into the vast emptiness—she knew that feeling. Ava squeezed her eyes shut, bracing herself for the childhood memory as it crept into her thoughts.

She'd been ten.

The forest was dark, but she wasn't afraid. The souls had been beautiful. Glowing, gentle things that swirled around her like ribbons of light. When she'd closed her eyes and reached out her spirit, the liminal layer had opened like a door she didn't know existed. She'd tumbled through. They'd led her deeper—showing her a sparkling waterfall, settling her inside a small alcove of trees that shimmered with their presence. She'd laughed, delighted, thinking this was the best hiding spot ever.

Then she'd tried to come back.

The layer had felt different from the inside. Thicker. Like water, but not water. Like air, but heavy enough to drown in. When she pushed against it, tried to surface, she couldn't find which way was up. Couldn't tell where the liminal plane ended and the Real began.

Panic had set in then. The kind that tasted like copper and made her chest too tight to breathe.

She'd screamed for Rune. Cried until her throat was raw. Begged the souls to help her find the way out. They'd tried—gentle, concerned, swirling around her in patterns she didn't understand. But they couldn't make her solid again. Couldn't push her back through to the world she belonged in.

Hours had passed. Or maybe days. Time felt strange in the liminal layer, stretched and compressed all at once.

She'd heard Rune calling for her. Desperate, terrified calls that echoed through the forest. Her aunt had been right there—close enough to touch if only she could break through the thickness between them. But Rune didn't have druidic magic. No amount of yelling or screaming could make her aunt see the girl trapped deep between worlds.

The souls had stayed with her through it all. Humming soft songs that had no words. Keeping her company in that terrible, beautiful, drowning place where she couldn't tell if she was floating or falling.

It had been Zoya who finally found her. The priestess had walked into the forest at dawn, reached out her own spirit, and pulled. Like grabbing a rope and hauling with everything she had. It had hurt—that sudden snap back into her body, the weight of flesh and bone after floating for so long in that in-between place.

She'd collapsed into Rune's arms, sobbing. Couldn't stop shaking for hours afterward.

Rune had held her tight. Whispered fierce promises against her hair. *Never again. Zoya will teach you how to control it. You'll never be trapped like that again.*

But the fear had stayed. Twenty years later, and the thought of diving deep into the liminal layer still made her chest tight and her remember what it felt like to drown in something that wasn't water.

A door slammed in the parlous house. The man yelled something unintelligible. Gabrie flinched at the sound.

Ava pulled the tab on her wired glove in and out, the zip-zipping filling the cold silence. She couldn't wait to use it on the man that had imprisoned Gabrie. At least when Ava had been trapped, it was her own fault. Gabrie was innocent.

Ava let the wire retract, She scooted closer to Gabrie. The girl winced at Ava's touch.

"Shh," Ava whispered. "I'm not going to hurt you."

Gabrie pressed against the opposite wall, hissing and spitting. Her eyes were round and wild, the pupils dilated.

"Would you like me to sing?"

Gabrie stared at her.

Ava hummed. After a few moments, Gabrie relaxed. Putting words to her melody, she let the song overtake her, pouring her heart and soul into the lyrics. It lifted and dived, flowing through her. Gabrie slid to the floor, her eyes drifting closed. Ava kept singing until she heard Gabrie's deep, even breathing as she caught a few moments of peaceful sleep.

After what seemed like hours, the noises in the parlous house quieted. The rain from above plunked on the iron roof, creating a steady, entrancing rhythm. Ava let her head loll against the iron wall and Thorben slipped through her mind. He had been right about the rain.

Chapter Thirteen

"I told you, she's mine." The man's voice woke her.

"You said you had a young girl for me in your message," a feminine voice replied. "I came all this way and now you tell me I can't have her?"

"Last week my server ran off. I need one to replace her. But, I have something else that might interest you."

Ava's neck ached from leaning against the wall for hours. She cracked open her lids to see Gabrie already awake, wild eyes darting back and forth between her and the iron door.

Standing carefully, Ava crept forward. That filth wasn't going to sell Gabrie—or her.

Heavy silence. Then the door dragged open.

Ava didn't waste a second. She zipped out her wired glove out, the laser bright in the darkness.

"What the—?" The man's question was cut off as Ava wrapped the hot wire around his wrist. The stench of burning flesh filled the space. He screamed and dropped to his knees. Ava followed him down and put her lips inches from his ear.

"No one owns me," she whispered. "Or Gabrie. Let us both go and I won't slice your hand off."

He shouldered her in the stomach, knocking her to the floor. Her grip on the wire tab broke free. He twisted out of the burning loop, groaning as it separated from his flesh.

Ava scrambled upright, putting herself between the man and Gabrie. Behind him, she caught sight of three people, casually watching. Two men with frowns on their faces and one tall, elegantly dressed woman. Her long, auburn hair cascaded over her shoulders, and she wore the largest feathered hat Ava had ever seen. The woman gazed at Ava with a bemused smile.

"This one isn't quite under control yet, eh Rachit?" she snickered.

Rachit held his wrist against his shirt, blood dripping off his arm. His eyes spit hatred, but he carefully stayed out of reach.

"She's nothing, Marselle," Rachit dismissed. "Caught her in here last night trying to help the other one escape."

"She's obviously not *nothing*," the woman said, gesturing to Ava with a lace-gloved hand.

The door. Ava focused on getting her and Gabrie out. That's all that mattered. She didn't want to be imprisoned in the small room again, but she also couldn't leave without Flip's sister.

"Where's the one I came for?" Marselle said.

"She's in there." Rachit motioned slightly with both arms, careful not to let go of his injured wrist. "But, like I told you, I need her." Marselle peered into the darkness, and Ava heard Gabrie whimper.

"You're not taking her." Ava shifted, moving between them and Gabrie. She pulled out the tab on her glove, the white-hot wire glowing in her eyes. Marselle's gaze shifted to Ava.

"Oh, I believe I will be," she replied, her hand motioning behind her. "Falcon? Your assistance please."

One of the men behind her stepped forward and grinned, missing several teeth. Reaching behind him, he pulled out two broad swords from a holster on his back. Ava swallowed, her grip on her wire glove tightening.

Falcon flipped the blades.

"Don't damage the merchandise," Marselle chimed.

He lunged forward with a sword. Ava sidestepped, pivoting, the white-hot wire spinning with her. Marselle and Rachit gave them a wide berth, a small smile on her face as she watched.

Falcon's swords sliced in the air. One descended behind Ava, catching her hair—several ebony strands fluttered to the floor. She booted him in the chest, and he stumbled backwards.

Two more steps toward the exit.

Palms together, she let the whip retract and recharge. Falcon grinned and raised both swords above his head. In a graceful arc, he brought them down, a breath away from Ava's face. She dodged but the swords rotated toward her again, this time aimed at her chest. Regardless of which side she chose, part of her was getting sliced.

Pinwheeling right, Ava strung out the whip, encircling the sword closest to her. With a sharp tug, the wire sliced through the metal. It clattered to the floor. Falcon glared at her.

The glow from her wire flickered and she glanced down. The last blow had damaged the fibers.

A chuckle and a soft clap sounded behind her.

"Are you going to let her get away with that, Falcon?" Marselle teased.

Falcon's fury burned in his eyes. He slung his remaining sword back and forth between his hands. Wheeling the blade, he jumped and flipped. Ava raised her hands, the laser whip stretched between them. Falcon's sword hit hard. Ava's arms vibrated as they met with the wire, shredding it in half.

The laser retracted leaving Ava with the broken half in her other hand. Out of options, she fell to the ground and curled into a ball. Her arm burned from being sliced open.

Falcon sheathed his sword. He grabbed Ava's injured arm and hauled her to her feet. Pain rippled through her shoulder, but she gritted her teeth and let her body sag. Not expecting her weight, he stumbled.

Ava moved. She looped the partial piece of wire around his throat and twisted.

Falcon dropped to the floor, his face turning purple.

"I said," Ava whispered into his ear. "You're not taking her."

Falcon's legs scuffed against the dirt floor and his fingers scrabbled at the wire, desperate for breath.

Ava's body suddenly convulsed. Pain shot from a pressure point against her neck. Her fingers cramped into odd angles and her legs buckled, giving way beneath her. Ava toppled to the ground. She lay frozen, next to Falcon who was still trying to breathe.

Marselle dusted off her fingers. "Can't have you killing my mate, dearest. I don't like to use my magic on people unless I must. However, I do prefer Falcon alive."

Falcon hauled himself from the floor and wrapped Ava's wrists as she lay immobile. She trembled in the aftershock of her nervous system being jolted, and painful prickles skittered along her body as her nerves slowly regained sensation.

Marselle circled them, her maroon velvet skirt swishing on the dirty floor. She lifted a lock of Ava's dark hair and rubbed it between her fingers, her spicy perfume filling the air. She returned Ava's furious gaze with a curious one.

"I'll give you one thousand for both of them," she said, sliding her hand back into her glove.

"One thousand?" Rachit scoffed. "The woman is worth that alone. She's a druis."

"Druis or not, I don't think you want to risk keeping her." Marselle eyed his wrist. "You never know when she'll get around to taking the rest of that hand off."

"But..." Rachit argued, trying to decide if bargaining for more was worth it. "She's sneaky. That door was locked when I left yesterday. I came in last night and she had managed to melt it." Ava's eyes cut to his cruel face. Flip had melted the lock, not her.

"Hmm." The woman tapped her finger against her cheek, thinking. "Alright. I'm feeling generous today, especially since you are injured. I'll give you twelve hundred for the pair. That's more than a fair price for the girl, and you won't have to keep watching your back."

Rachit glanced at her indecisively. Ava silently threatened him with a look. "Twelve hundred. I'm not sure that one—" he pointed to Gabrie, "—would have made me any money anyway. And don't tell the others I gave you a deal, Marselle. It's bad for business."

Marselle nodded, smirking. "Of course, Rachit. We wouldn't want that." She motioned to the man behind her. "Falcon, take them to my airship please. Gehrue—the funds."

Ava frantically pulled at the bonds on her wrists. She couldn't be shipped off to some unknown place.

What about Rune? Who would take care of her? Who would make sure she ate, that she didn't wander off during one of her delusions?

And Thorben.

The thought sliced through her panic like ice. She'd never see him again. Never hear his voice or feel that cold presence that had somehow become...comforting.

They'd barely started. She didn't even know him yet—not really. All those questions she'd been too afraid to ask, all those moments she'd been too careful, too guarded.

Gone.

She'd be dragged to another realm, and he'd never know what happened to her. He'd think she'd just...left.

Her chest tightened. She couldn't allow that to happen.

"As always, pleasure doing business with you," Marselle sang over her shoulder.

Outside, Gabrie's wild eyes swiveled back and forth, twitching when a bright patch of light hit them. Gehrue watched her, sorrow in his features. His grip was gentle, but firm. As Ava studied him, his other hand flexed, glinting. Ava's eyes widened. He had a mechanical arm.

He raised his eyebrows at her, and Ava looked away. Spellcasted mechanized arms or legs weren't unheard of, but they were very, very expensive.

Gehrue's gaze shifted from her to Marselle as she emerged from *The Scarlett*.

"We have a problem," Gehrue said, stepping toward her, his voice deep.

Marselle raised her eyebrows.

"She's been inked."

"What?" Marselle moved to inspect Gabrie. Gehrue turned her, moving aside her tattered shirt. Leaning in, Ava strived to see what they were discussing. Gabrie's back was exposed. A swollen, intricate design was tattooed in her flesh. It was bloody, dirty and from the looks of it, infected.

Marselle pursed her lips in distaste. "That's problematic, but it looks fresh. Maybe it hasn't taken over completely. We'll find out soon enough. Let's go."

Marselle led the way through the swale. Falcon dragged Ava along, guiding them through routes foreign to her. She was completely lost. Would they take her to another realm to sell her? Or make her a slave on one of the knave ships? How would she ever get back to Rune?

"We're here." Marselle abruptly stopped. "You can come out. No one followed us."

Flip appeared from the shadows. His face was dirtier than before, his clothes torn, but his slick smile was firmly in place.

"You—" Ava lunged for him, but Falcon held her.

Marselle turned to her shipmates. "You can release them."

Falcon cut through Ava's bonds. Ava bolted smashed her fist into Flip's smug grin. He fell hard, his lip bleeding.

"That's for leaving us." Ava ground out.

"I got you out, didn't I?"

His words hit something inside her. She wasn't going to be sold or shipped off to another realm. She could go home—to Rune.

To Thorben.

Relief flooded through her, sharp and overwhelming. She'd get to see him again. Ask those questions. Stop being so damn careful all the time.

Almost losing everything had a way of clarifying what mattered.

"I was right about you, druis," Marselle said, her dark green eyes alight. "You are a force to know. I'm going to have to keep my eye on you."

"Will someone tell me what in the souls is going on?" Ava spat.

"I am Marselle, captain of *The Sky Dragon*." She swept a hand to her companions. "You already know Falcon. My other shipmate is Gehrue. Sorry for the unpleasantness."

Ava glanced from Marselle to Flip and then to Gehrue where he was gently speaking with Gabrie. Flip had managed to find his way to the terrified girl, his arm over her protectively.

"How did you get us out?" Ava asked.

"We owed Flip a debt." Marselle turned to him. "Our debt is now paid."

Flip nodded, his arm tightening around Gabrie. "It is. Thank you."

A debt. Flip had a debt with a knave captain. How? When? What had he done to earn that kind of leverage?

She'd thought she knew him—street rat, petty thief, knave running cons in the swale. But this? Connections to captains like Marselle? The resources to orchestrate a rescue like this?

Who was he, really? What other secrets was he hiding?

"Excellent. We must be heading back." Marselle moved to leave but paused. "Don't get caught again, druis. We won't be able to get you out a second time." She gave Ava a wink and turned to leave.

"Wait—are you the knaves Flip said would help me?"

Marselle's eyebrows lifted. "Not that I'm aware." She glanced at Flip. "Is there another knave ship docked here?"

"The *Fairlight*." Flip answered, mouth drawn.

"Ah."

"Wait. Can you help me?"

"Unfortunately, I have other matters I need to see to." Marselle frowned.

"Please," Ava said. "My aunt needs a cure and I'm all out of options here. I need someone that can navigate to the other realms."

"Why can't you do it yourself?"

Ava hung her head. "I've tried, but I have no way of getting through the purdahs or even off this realm. And I can't leave my aunt while she is sick."

Marselle pursed her lips and finally sighed. "I'm sorry I can't be of assistance. The captain of the *Fairlight* is a good man, but he will ask a high price. You better have something valuable to bargain with, druis."

Ava's shoulders sagged. If she had been able to get Marselle's help, at least she would have an inkling of the person she was dealing with.

"You give a good fight," said a gravelly voice. She turned to find Falcon, a look of admiration on his face. He placed a hand on his heart and extended the other to Ava. "I would be honored to fight by your side any time."

Ava hesitantly accepted his Ili greeting, not sure what to say. The crew disappeared into the dark tunnels of the swale, leaving Flip, Gabrie and Ava alone in the clearing.

"I didn't mean for you to get caught, you know," Flip said, his face apologetic.

"You didn't mean for me to get caught?" Ava's anger came back in full force, heat filling her face. "I could have been sold. I could have been taken away from my home and everything in it trying to save her."

"But." Flip pointed his finger at her. "You didn't. That's what matters."

Ava heaved a loud sigh. Who was this poor girl to Flip anyway? She was too young to be his companion…at least Ava hoped that wasn't the case. Gabrie whimpered and Flip turned his attention back to her.

"Gab, shh, it's alright," Flip mumbled. "I'm here."

Gabrie kept trying to pull away from Flip, her arms wildly flinging at him. "Gab—stop," Flip tried to grab her wrists, but she twisted out of them.

"I think she's trying to show you something," Ava motioned to her. "Gehrue wanted Marselle to look at her back."

Flip's eyes instantly became alarmed. Swiveling Gabrie, he pushed aside her tattered shirt.

"Neyá. No, no, no…" He stared at the ink. "That bastard branded her. Shit!"

"Branded her? What do you mean?"

"She needs to get away from here." Flip started, moving fast. "If Rachit finds out Marselle let her go, he will try and take her back. Rachit inks them using a locator spell mixed with his blood, branding them as his property. He can find his girls from miles away. We've got to get it off her. If we don't he will always own her."

"What are you going to do?" New concern for Gabrie rose in her chest.

"I was going to take her home, but we live too close. She needs to be somewhere farther away. I had hoped to get her out before she was inked." Flip rubbed his face in frustration. "I wasn't fast enough."

"Let's take her to the temple and get her cleaned up." Ava suggested. "Then, we can board an airbus and go to my house. My aunt is there. If anyone can help, it's her."

"Like she helped last time?" Flip turned to Ava, his eyes filling with angry tears.

"I'm sorry the tonic didn't work." Guilt tugged at Ava's gut. "Auntie's remedies are almost always effective."

Flip turned back to Gabrie, brushing the hair off her face. The girl's eyes were empty, staring at nothingness.

"Who is she anyway?"

Flip adjusted Gabrie's shirt, trying to cover her exposed skin. "She's my sister," he said faintly. "I had to get her out of there."

His sister.

The pieces clicked into place. The desperation in his eyes. The reason he'd risked everything—including her—to get Gabrie out.

She'd misjudged him. Completely. He wasn't just some swale rat looking out for himself. He was a brother trying to save his sister from a nightmare.

"You did what you needed to." Ava stepped closer, her voice soft. "My aunt can try something else. I'm sure once she sees her, she'll know what to do."

After a moment, Flip nodded. They guided Gabrie through the swale's hollow pathways, the heavy silence filled with worry for an innocent girl strung between them.

"Wait." Flip paused and reached into his back pocket. He shoved a piece of paper at her. "Here's the coordinates for the knave's ship. A deal is a deal. Go now. They should be there for another few hours."

Ava accepted the note, but cast a worried glance at Gabrie. "What about her?"

"I'll take Gab to the temple and meet you at the airbus station in two hours."

Ava nodded and gently withdrew herself from beneath Gabrie's arms. "See you then."

Flip could handle himself. He'd proven that much. And Gabrie needed someone who knew these tunnels, someone with connections and resources she was only beginning to understand.

As Ava ran, she unfolded the note. Level 78, pier 256, docking station B. Risking the closest stepping lift, her heart raced as she prayed to the Five she would make it to the top in one piece.

Chapter Fourteen

T he stepping lift clattered to a stop and the doors screeched opened. Ava squeezed through, her feet clanging on the loose iron grates as she ran.

Signs welded onto each pier showed their numbers. Ava hastily followed them...235, 248, 252...Finally, she reached pier 256. She grabbed the ladder and hoisted herself up.

When she reached the top, she paused to catch her breath. This pier had 5 docking stations, pier B being the second on the right. It was empty.

"Damn it!" Ava cursed, sucking in a breath. She pushed herself off the guardrail and kicked a discarded piece of metal, watching it bounce. It skittered to a stop near a pair of black, scuffed aviator boots.

"Taking your anger out on an inanimate object may come back to punch you in the face, *elehi*. Even everyday items can hold a grudge."

Ava's eyes traveled upward at the voice, taking in the man's cobalt blue duster jacket, dark hair, and roguishly handsome smile.

"Who are you?"

"I'm more wondrously curious who you are," he replied, moving toward the edge. His duster jacket flipped open in the wind as he rested his hands against the iron railing. "And what you are doing on this pier."

Ava huffed and waved her hand toward the empty dock. "I was looking for a ship."

"Which ship?" His gaze swiveled to her, his dangerous, dark eyes ringed in kohl. He waved a hand toward the clouds, the rings on his fingers sparkling in the light. "I happen to know quite a few captains in these skyes. I might know who you are trying to find."

"I was looking for the *Fairlight*," Ava explained. "I was told it was docked here."

"Are you seeking passage? I can assure you, that ship doesn't take passengers."

"So, you know it?" Ava asked, the pressure on her chest releasing. "Can you tell me where it is?"

"Why are you so interested?" His dark eyes glinted.

"A friend said someone on the ship could help me."

"Well, you know how knaves are..." He grinned, mischievously. "Filthy, dishonorable company. They aren't to be trusted, *elehi*."

Ava scrutinized his grin, suddenly understanding. "You're from the ship."

He raised an eyebrow. "What makes you think I belong to a knave airship?"

"Why else would you be in the exact location where the *Fairlight* is supposed to be docked? Also, you have avoided all my questions."

The man pressed his lips together, mouth quirking up. "Guilty as charged." He swept a theatrical bow. "Declan, illusionist mage and knave extraordinaire."

"Where is your ship, *knave extraordinaire*?" Ava tilted her head. "The docks are empty."

He swept a glance down the walkway and turned back to her, an amused grin showing his dimple. "*Seáh*, so they are. What is your name?" he asked. "If I didn't know better, I'd say you were a knave. Being in a place where a knave vessel is supposed to be docked, not answering me about who you are...?"

A huff of laughter escaped her at his implications. "I'm Ava."

He raised his eyebrows at her. "Just Ava?"

"Ava, druis to the Temple of the Five. Not extraordinary in any way."

"Ah," he said. "I highly doubt that. Now, Ava, druis to the Temple of the Five, why are you searching for the *Fairlight* and her crew?"

Ava took a deep breath. "Sir—"

"Just Declan, love," he interrupted, his grin and dimple flashing at her again.

"Declan," Ava tried again. "My aunt is extremely sick." The words came out rougher than intended, scraping against the exhaustion lodged in her throat. "She needs medicine. I was hoping a knave ship would be willing to help me find a cure."

"What kind of sickness does she have?"

"Delusions mostly, sometimes lasting for days. She believes she's talking to someone else, someone that doesn't exist except in her mind," Ava explained. "She's an inyanga, but I've researched and tried everything she has and none of her own medicines seem to work. I don't know what else to do. There must be something in another realm that can help her."

His dark eyes studied her face, roaming over her frame, examining her clothes. Heat crept up her neck under his scrutiny. She crossed her arms, then uncrossed them, unsure where to put her hands. "Interesting. And what are you offering as payment?"

The only thing of value she carried were souls and most people couldn't access them unless they had druidic magic.

"I...I don't know. What would you want?" Ava patted her belt, trying to think of what she could offer. "I don't really have much—"

"How about a trade?" Declan tapped his finger on his full lips in thought. "I've been commissioned by someone, like yourself," he waved a hand at her, "to find a missing soul. But the spirit they want me to find has been gone for some time. I could greatly use a talented druis's assistance."

"How long has it been missing?" Ava feared the soul may have already dissolved into the ether if it hadn't been collected.

A shadow crossed Declan's face and his eyes dropped to his jacket, his hands smoothing over the fabric. "A little over three months."

Sometimes, three months was long enough for a soul to be absorbed into the liminal plane. For his sake, Ava hoped the spirit he was searching for had the willpower to stick around until she could find it.

"If I find this missing soul you'll find a cure for my aunt?"

"Seáh."

"How do I know you will hold up your end of the bargain?"

"Knaves may be thieves, scoundrels, and low lives," Declan murmured. "But we hold to our word."

Ava wasn't completely convinced she could trust a knave but then again, what choice did she have? She had to find something, and she was out of options.

"I'll need something the soul owned then," Ava said. "An item they loved or highly valued would be best."

Declan's hand disappeared into the inside pocket of his jacket and withdrew a thick ring of solid silver. He gazed at it—really gazed, like a man looking at the only thing anchoring him to the world—before placing it in her palm. His fingers trembled as he let go.

"This was hers," he said quietly. "I believe it would be the thing she cherished most."

Ava accepted it, running her thumb along its smooth surface. She carefully nestled it in a pocket of her utility belt.

Declan watched it disappear, but returned his gaze to her face, his eyes bright once again. He clapped his hands together, startling Ava with his suddenly roguish smile. "Let's meet back here, say, in five days?" he offered. "I'll be able to spread the word to my fellow knaves and between us, we should be able to find something."

Ava dipped her head in agreement. "I'll be here."

Declan gave her a sideways grin. "I'll be looking forward to it, elehí." He winked, stepped off the platform into the open air, and disappeared.

A gasp tore from her throat. She ran to the edge of the dock. His body was nowhere. She sighed. Illusionist mages were so dramatic.

Ava made her way to the airbus station, her mind reeling. She clanged down a set of stairs and spotted Flip and Gabrie standing next to a gangplank that led to a community airbus. Gabrie had donned fresh clothes and a hat, her eyes wildly scanning the deck and the busy crowd.

"How is she?" Ava asked when she reached them.

"She's calm, for now." Flip held Gabrie's arm with unexpected gentleness. "Gab, do you remember Ava?"

"Seáh llaéh, Gabrie." Ava stepped forward. "It's an honor to meet you."

Gabrie didn't acknowledge her. In the light, her eyes were the same bright blue as her brother's.

"How did Gabrie end up at *The Scarlett*?"

"That bastard, Rachit, got hold of her a few weeks ago. I've been trying to get her out since."

A shadow of frustration flitted over Flip's face. Ava's dislike of him melted just a little and she moved to Gabrie's side. "How are you feeling, Gabrie? Do you think you can travel a bit?"

Gabrie looked back at Ava, her stare blank. But, she wasn't screaming, so Ava took it as acquiescence.

"Ok." Ava nodded. "Let's go."

The zeppelin's massive balloon swelled into the sky, its golden hull a multilevel deck of compartments. The platform was filled with people coming and going. Ava's heart hammered the entire time, terrified that someone would recognize them and report back to Rachit.

The vessel lifted into the air and was soon descending into the station closest to Ava's house. By the time they reached her station, Ava's legs felt like they'd been filled with sand. Each step required conscious effort. She helped Gabrie down and guided them along the dirt road, Flip supporting his sister on the other side.

When they walked into Ava's home, Rune could be heard in the kitchen, talking to someone.

"Auntie?"

"In here," Rune called. "Neo told me you were coming so I made an extra plate."

Neo? Another hallucination, then. Ava didn't want to spook her by bringing an unexpected visitor. Best to prepare her first.

"You can take Gabrie to my room." Ava pointed to the other end of the cottage. "Let me tell my aunt you're here."

Flip nodded and he and Gabrie hobbled off.

In the kitchen, smells of yeast and fresh bread made her stomach grumble. Rune was elbow deep in flour, several loaves already proofing.

"Auntie?"

"Hello, Rubi. Neo said you were coming home for dinner." She chuckled to herself. "You know him and those machines."

"Actually...I met someone who needs help."

"Oh no! What happened?" Rune asked, pausing mid knead.

"Um, she doesn't seem to know who she is or where she is." Her fingers found a bowl of dough, picking at it absently. "Would you mind taking a look at her?"

"Of course." Rune dusted off her hands and untied her apron. "Bring her here, *mé veláh*."

Ava went to her bedroom. Flip and Gabrie were sitting on her bed in silence, Flip's arm possessively over Gabrie's shoulders.

"My aunt can see her, but—" Ava paused, not sure how to explain to Flip that Rune was in the middle of a delusion. "Well, just do whatever she says, alright?"

Flip raised his eyebrows at her but said nothing, following Ava to the kitchen.

"Auntie, this is Gabrie and Flip. Gabrie needs your help."

"Child." Rune circled the table to stand in front of Gabrie. She frowned and gently touched Gabrie's cheek. "*Yah propía fintú a Shaitán circa yah.*"

"What did she say?" Flip whispered.

"She said Gabrie has the look of a *Shaitán*." Dread spread through Ava's stomach, heavy and cold.

"A *Shaitán*?" Flip's eyes widened. "*Shaitáns* have ice magic, don't they?"

Rune bent slightly so she could look into Gabrie's eyes. After a moment, she rubbed the girl's shoulders comfortingly. "Rubi, please grab a mortar and pestle from the shelf."

Flip gave Ava a curious look at being called Rubi, but she shrugged and did as asked.

Rune went to the shelves, choosing jars and reading labels. "Fiery poppy for burning out the hallucinatory tonic already in her system," she murmured. "Frigilia and somnus, of course."

She poured the ground flowers into a vial and spoke an ancient Ili incantation. The liquid sparkled with a blackish orange glow. Rune's competency eased Ava's worries, but also confirmed she'd probably ruined the first tonic.

Guilt twisted sharp beneath her ribs. She'd failed Gabrie the first time. She couldn't fail her again.

"There we are." Rune set the tonic near Ava.

"Auntie? There's something else," Ava said. "She's been inked."

"Inked?" Rune paused. Flip delicately turned Gabrie, sliding the thin fabric away from her back.

"Oh dear." Rune stepped closer, bending to inspect the tattoo. "This is terrible. Inking was banned years ago. It absolutely must be removed."

Rune looked into her eyes. "I can eliminate the tattoo, but there will always be a slight trace of his blood within you. It is difficult to separate one's blood from another's that has been bound by spellwork."

Gabrie didn't acknowledge her words. However, Rune appeared to find an acceptable response within the girl's eyes. She let go of Gabrie, grabbed a basket, and headed outdoors. Ava motioned for them to stay put and hurried after her aunt.

Rune made her way through the flowers and herbs, hands lovingly touching several. Stopping at a robust yellow blossom, she bent to cut it from its stem. "Oubliette for forgetting," she said and placed it in her basket.

She moved toward a patch of blood red blooms, then paused, frowning. "I need trilofloris to purify the blood, but they haven't flowered yet." Her fingers touched the closed buds. "I'll have to find something else, but it won't be as potent."

Feeling eyes on her, Ava glanced sideways. Thorben stood near the garden wall. When he noticed her, he smiled and waved.

She trotted over. Maybe he could help. "Thorben. What are you doing here?"

"I said I'd come check on the repairs, remember?"

"Oh, seáh." Ava ran a hand through her hair. In all the chaos, she'd forgotten. "Now isn't a good time for that, but could you do me a favor?"

"Of course."

"Could you make the trilofloris bloom? We need it to make a tonic."

Thorben's eyes found the closed bud. He walked along the fence and when he reached it, tilted his head, considering. Then his hand extended toward the plant—not quite touching, more like coaxing. The flower gave off a faint glow, then unfurled into a perfect crimson bloom. A rich, heady fragrance filled the air between them.

He looked tired from the effort, but something like pride flickered across his face.

"A yah ageremé," Ava breathed. Their gazes met. A new light shone there—softer, more open—and for a moment it felt as if part of him had melted away, giving her a glimpse of who he truly was beneath all that careful control.

"Oh!" Rune straightened, delight crossing her face. "There's one! How did I miss it?" She swept her thumb over the silky petals and carefully cut the blossom.

"Rune," Ava said. "I want you to meet..."

But Rune was already heading away, lost in her task. "And let's add a little decovetis to make sure it doesn't happen again." She snagged two leaves from a vine that cascaded over their garden wall.

Ava shrugged apologetically to Thorben. "She sometimes doesn't recognize reality. It's...something I'm trying to fix."

Thorben watched Rune enter the house. "I'm sorry."

"It's alright. Thank you, again," she squeezed his arm. "For the flower. And the repairs." Before she could leave, he snagged her fingers and dropped a kiss on the back of her hand.

"I'll come by later." He said, the corner of his mouth lifting slightly.

She left him in the garden and willed her heart to stop pounding so hard.

Back in the kitchen, Rune methodically plucked petals from the yellow flower and stamens from the red, setting them into a bowl with the leaves. She ground them into a fine powder.

"Please grab a jar of ointment off the shelf in the pantry."

Ava retrieved it and Rune mixed the herbs with the ointment. She closed her eyes and spoke, a beautiful Ili spell falling from her lips. The ointment glowed faintly, and the calming scent of a sunny meadow filled the kitchen.

Rune moved to Gabrie, tonic in one hand and healing ointment in the other. "I know you are there somewhere, child, locked deep inside yourself. Can you reach out, be brave, and swallow this medicine?"

Gabrie's eyes suddenly went wild. She lashed out, her arms swinging violently. Flip grabbed her from behind, pinning her arms in place.

Rune pursed her lips. "I was afraid of that."

"Of what?" Flip ground out between his teeth.

"The inking spell has a tendency to make its host defy any type of removal." Rune set down the cream. "Hold her very still. Let's get the tonic in first and then the cream will be easier to apply once she's lucid. Hold her head back."

Flip tightened his grip. Grimacing, Ava held Gabrie's head by her hair, saying a quick prayer to the Five.

"It will be over in a moment." Rune soothed. She quickly poured in the tonic and pressed Gabrie's mouth closed.

She swallowed it down and the wildness in her eyes gradually faded. She slumped against Flip, exhausted but lucid.

"Gab?" Flip whispered. "Gabrie?"

She moaned and slid to the floor.

"She'll be alright." Rune assured them. "Here." She handed the healing ointment to Flip. "Put this on her back. Quickly, before she comes around. Removing the ink won't be pleasant."

In Ava's bedroom, Flip applied the ointment. The tattoo sizzled and bubbled, blood oozing as Rachit's mark sloughed away. Gabrie whimpered but didn't fight. Ava reached out with her soul—cool, calming waters—and the girl relaxed.

"A *yah ageremé*," Flip whispered. "For helping her."

"A *mé ceanáh agereyáh*. You're welcome."

Ava left clean clothes on the bed and closed the door quietly. Flip wasn't the nicest person, but his love for Gabrie was genuine.

Through the kitchen window, Thorben wandered through the garden, his hand extended toward wilting stems. They straightened under his touch. A closed bud bloomed. Another. Another.

He paused, staring at his own hands like he didn't quite recognize them. Then that small smile returned—steadier now. More certain.

Maybe he was finally seeing what she saw. That his magic wasn't worthless.

That *he* wasn't worthless.

Chapter Fifteen

After washing and changing into loose, comfortable clothes, Ava found Rune in the kitchen talking to invisible Neo. She grabbed fruit from a bowl and headed outside, needing air and quiet after the chaos of the day.

The breeze blew against her face and she savored the coolness against her skin. She hadn't put shoes on and as she walked, the grass tickled the bottom of her feet with its long thin touch. Her loose shirt blew in the breeze, her nipples tingling in response to the freedom of not being confined in a corset vest.

Ava plucked her damaged glove from her back pocket. She sighed. Replacing the wire wasn't difficult, but the spellcasted cord it needed to work properly wasn't easy to find. Ava grabbed a few tools from the shed and headed to the gazebo, dropping her things on the small bench near the stone fyreplace. Blankets were still laid out from last night where she and Rune had slept. The fyreplace was cold, but there was a pile of wood stacked next to it and she piled several logs inside the fyre box.

Ava grabbed an herb bundle from a basket and ran it roughly along the side of the stone. The foliage ignited and a spicy sweet aroma filled the air as she nestled the kindling bundle between several logs. She breathed deeply, letting the worries of the day fade with the light.

Satisfied with her fyre, she turned to the damaged glove. The broken wire came away easily. She wound new cord onto the spool, attaching the other end to the thumb tab.

"Mind if I join you?"

Ava spun and pulled out the brand-new laser wire on her glove, already sparking white hot between her hands.

"It's you," she said. Tension drained from her shoulders. Thorben stood, fyrelight dancing on his skin, a small smile on his lips. "What are you doing here?"

"I came to see if I could finish your aunt's room." Thorben gestured to the house behind him. "But I saw you come outside so I thought I would say hello first."

Her gaze followed the movement of his arm as he hooked his thumb into the pocket of his pants.

His tight, black leather pants.

"Are you alright?" He pointed to her bandaged arm.

She glanced down. "Oh, yes. It's been a strange day. You would never believe what happened."

Thorben stepped closer, stopping when his body was inches from hers. She looked up through her lashes, meeting his gaze.

"Try me," he murmured, his gray-blue eyes whispering unknowns. He guided her to a small love seat in front of the fyre, her glove landing on a nearby table.

Thorben's closeness set her heart racing. His scent—forest mist and rain—enveloped her. When they'd settled on the loveseat, mere inches apart, she told him of helping Gabrie, where they had found her, how they had been caught in the parlous house and almost sold to knaves.

Thorben tensed, his body rigid. "Did they hurt you? Is that how you got the cut on your arm?"

"Well, sort of. But everything is fine now." she flipped her hand dismissively. "I've never been in a parlous house before. It was so sad. And terrifying."

Thorben stared into the flames, a muscle in his jaw twitching, the fyrelight flickering in his eyes.

"What are you thinking?" she asked.

"I was thinking I've just found you. In an instant, you could have been taken away. I never would have seen you again."

"We haven't known each other very long," Ava said quietly. "I'm sure you would have been fine."

Thorben shook his head, turning to fully face her. "I wouldn't have. You are special, Ava."

The words landed soft but heavy, settling somewhere deep in her chest. Special. When was the last time someone called her that? Or looked at her like she was more than capable hands and a competent soul?

Her throat tightened. "I don't feel very special."

"Then you're not looking closely enough."

"Thorben—" Heat crept into her cheeks. She turned the conversation. "How have I never known you before now?"

"I..." Thorben paused, his eyes seeking answers in the fyre. "I'll tell you what I can." He sighed, his face somber. "I was raised in Syldan. I...have family there."

"But why am I meeting you *now*? I've lived my entire life in this house and your village is merely across the lake. My aunt has treated people from there."

"I believe..." Thorben glanced at her through his thick lashes. "When you need a certain person in your life, they will arrive at that precise moment. They will give you strength to keep living, to have hope instead of despair, to be able to look forward to the next day. And when you meet that person, they will unravel you even as they make you whole."

"Have you met people like that before?" she whispered.

He grinned. "A few. But never someone who is unraveling me as much as you are, Avalína."

He said her name with breathless purpose. Chills raced down her spine. He glanced sideways, his eyes roaming over the garden. Ava followed his gaze.

"What is it?"

Thorben's eyes came back to rest on her face. "Nothing," he whispered, tucking an ebony lock behind her ear. His thumb traced the line of her jaw—and suddenly, Ava felt something shift.

The air thickened. Humid. Heavy. Like breathing through silk. The fyre-light took on a strange quality, casting everything in deep blue shadows that shouldn't exist.

Her heart kicked—she knew this feeling.

The liminal plane.

Alarm raced through her. She pulled away—or tried to. His hand tightened on her neck, gentle but firm.

"Don't." Not a command. A plea. "Please don't go." His gray eyes held hers, darkening to storm clouds. "Trust me, Avalína."

Trust him? His hands were firm, and his eyes begged her to believe him. She focused on his face, the feel of his hand against her neck. Solid and real.

And the strangeness, it felt...familiar to her. It wasn't quite the same as her childhood terror. The drowning sensation hovered at the edges, yes, but it didn't consume her. Something else pulsed beneath the fear—understanding. Like her soul had been waiting for this and knew what could be expected here.

She should pull away and escape whatever this was.

But the heaviness called to her. Terrifying and familiar all at once. This was the place she'd avoided for twenty years. The place that had nearly consumed her as a child.

And she was choosing to stay in it. For him.

"I believe you are unraveling me," he whispered, his breath skimming across her lips. Shivers ran through her at his barely-there touch and she found that, even in the unsettling surrealness, she didn't want to leave.

Every sensation felt amplified. His cool touch burned brighter and his scent stronger in her lungs.

Part of her whispered warnings. This isn't right. This isn't normal.

But another part—deeper, older—recognized this place as safe.

His gaze pulled her under—the eagerness behind those gray clouds. Her stomach fluttered. When was the last time someone had looked at her like this—not as a problem-solver or caretaker, but as a woman they desired?

Years. A decade of buried wants trembling at the surface, demanding to be felt. But she was so tired of being careful, of being the strong one, the responsible one, the one who sacrificed everything.

Just once, she wanted something for herself.

She bit her lip. His gaze flickered, then darkened.

Thorben cupped her cheek, hand rough against her sensitive skin. She leaned forward and pressed her lips to his. The velvet of his mouth tasted like fresh mint and evening rain.

He sampled her, once, twice. "*Mé talé.*" He whispered against her lips. "My treasure."

Ava melted.

Thorben's hunger crashed down. His fingers tangled in her hair, as if he were as starved for a person's touch as much as she. It made her want him more. Her fingers curled in the fabric of his shirt, pulling him closer.

Thorben lifted her onto his lap. A gasp escaped her as he settled her legs on either side of him. A primal need surged through her, and she instinctively rocked against him, earning a deep throated moan.

Ava crushed her mouth to his. He tilted his head and deepened the kiss, his thick tongue sweeping through her mouth, his fingers digging into her ribcage. He tasted her lips and her neck, leaving the tingling sensation of mint and magic on her skin.

Thorben's hands slid down her sides and gripped the hem of her shirt. His thumbs snuck under the loose white fabric, caressing the skin under her breast. She shuddered.

He was watching her, waiting to see if she would allow him more.

For a moment, she wondered what in the souls she was doing. But before the thought had time to completely form, she pushed it away. Taking a leap of faith also meant taking a measure of risk. She was tired of not taking risks.

Ava grabbed the underside of her shirt and lifted it over her head. Her breasts raised as her arms did, her pink rosebud nipples coming within inches of Thorben's mouth.

Her skin was bare to the breeze and the strange atmosphere wrapped tighter around them. Humid air caressed her like fingers. The dark blue light made everything dreamlike—as if they existed outside normal time and space.

She should be terrified. This felt too much like that day when she was ten, lost and drowning in something she couldn't escape.

But Thorben was here. His hands solid against her ribs. He wouldn't let her get lost. His storm-gray eyes watched her with an intensity that made her forget to be afraid.

She listened to their breaths mingling in the air. His fingertips danced along her spine, his cool touch delicately laced with magic. His hands trembled.

Was he nervous? Or perhaps it was something else. Restraint?

No. He knew something she didn't. She could feel it in the way he gazed her, like he was memorizing this moment. Like he couldn't quite believe she was here, in this strange space with him.

He slipped off his green shirt and tossed it to the side. Ava's eyes widened. His chest glimmered in the fyrelight. He pressed her palms to his bare skin, his thumbs lightly stroking the backside of her hands. His skin was cool to the touch. His sucked in a breath as he watched her face, searching for something. A shaky hand brushed against Ava's cheek.

"Thorben, are you alright?"

"Don't stop," he whispered, his voice dark agony. "Please."

His head fell back, breath shuddering. Every muscle taut, trembling—like her touch was both agony and salvation.

"Am I...hurting you?"

He leveled his gaze, those dark storm cloud eyes searing. "You could never hurt me, Avalina."

She nodded, unsure what to say. Instead of wondering what he meant, she focused on his skin—smooth and firm. As she traced the dip between his muscles, a finger circling around his nipple, he shuddered, his eyes squeezed closed as if her touch brought enormous amounts of pain—or pleasure.

She caressed the path of hair that ran over his stomach and disappeared beneath those black leather pants. His muscles twitched beneath her hands, and she brought them to his waist, hooking a finger on the waistband of his pants.

She paused. "Why—"

Before she could finish, he brought her head to his and crushed her lips beneath his own, fervently, desperately. Ava let go of his waistband and snuck her arms around his neck. His lips savored her, dipping, tasting, discovering hidden places. He maneuvered her head back, his mouth trailing cool kisses along her jaw and throat. Ava arched her back, her fingers digging into the muscles on his arms, shivering as the moist breeze blew across her wet skin.

"Are you cold?" he murmured, his lips a gentle tickle on her flesh. Ava shook her head. Her gaze wandered over his chest, his sculpted stomach.

Thorben brought her fingers to his mouth and kissed them one by one. "I've never..." he sighed and blew out a heavy breath. "Souls, Ava, you are unraveling me." His words were quiet, reflective.

"Is that a good thing?" Ava teased. Another shiver—this time from the absence of his touch.

"You *are* cold," he murmured. "Let me—"

"Why does your skin shimmer like that?" Ava blurted. She let her palm rest over his heart. "Are you from Star Fyre?"

His eyes immediately hooded, and his hands dropped to her thighs.

Her neck flushed hot. Why had she asked that? Why couldn't she just let herself feel without needing to understand everything?

His thumbs rubbed small circles on her thighs as she berated herself. The silence stretched. Would he answer at all?

"I...It's a long story," Thorben finally said, his eyes reflecting the flames of the fyre. "It's...not something I'm proud of."

The thick air around them shifted slightly, responding to his emotion. Or maybe she imagined it. Everything felt strange when she was with him.

"Does it have something to do with..." She gestured vaguely at the space around them. "With whatever this is?"

His jaw tightened. "In a way." He brushed her hair over her shoulder, clearly changing the subject. "It's my burden, not yours."

Something in his voice—regret? shame?—made her chest tighten. He was holding something back. She wanted to push, to demand answers, but the shadows in his eyes stopped her.

Whatever haunted him ran deep.

Thorben wrapped his arm around her waist. "Let's get you warm." He kept one hand on the skin beneath her breast while the other snagged his discarded shirt. He lay beside her on the blankets by the fyre.

They both stared into the flames in silence.

Ava reached out with her spirit, gently nudging him. His soul was still quiet, hiding in thick shadows. It bothered her that she couldn't feel it. What was wrong?

"What are you thinking?" Ava asked instead.

"I'm thinking I want so much more of you than this," he whispered, his touch pressing into her waist. "But I don't want you to hate me for it."

"What? Of course, I couldn't hate you..." Ava looked into his troubled eyes. Thorben searched her face and Ava thought she saw regret, but it quickly disappeared.

A quick kiss to her lips. "I'm sorry I said it." He tucked the blanket closer. "Can I hold you?"

Ava gave him one more curious glance before settling back into the crook of his arm. The warmth of the fyre and the soothing motion of Thorben's hands steadily stroking her side sent her into a relaxed trance.

Exhaustion pulled at her consciousness. The thick air thinned and the dark blue shadows faded into the forest. Sound returned—cricket song, wind chimes, the ordinary crackle of fyrelight.

The world snapped back into focus.

Ava's eyes flew open. Thorben was still there, laying beside her, but something had changed. The strange atmosphere was gone. Just normal night air and familiar darkness.

"What..." She started to ask, but he tucked the blanket closer.

"Shh. Rest, *mé talé*."

She wanted to ask why everything had felt so different. Was that part of his magic? What did he have to do with the liminal plane? But her eyes were already closing.

Tomorrow. She'd ask tomorrow.

As sleep claimed her, one thought lingered warm in her chest: whatever that strange place was, she'd go back without hesitation.

For him.

Chapter Sixteen

S he had touched him. Kissed him. Run her fingers over his skin, sending electric tingles shooting through him—the sensation almost painful.

Painful. What a pathetic understatement for the devastation of being touched after ten years of nothing.

Thorben had forgotten the intimacy of experiencing another's touch—until that moment. He'd almost not gone through with it, terrified of discovering he'd feel nothing at all.

But he had. Oh, how he had.

When Ava's lips brushed against his, she slipped into the liminal level with him—the first person in a decade capable of existing in that dark blue abyss—and he could barely breathe, barely think.

The cascade of her ebony hair fell around them like a curtain, blocking out the strange blue shadows of the liminal level. His hands had moved of their own accord, sliding over her skin, pulling her closer. Never close enough. When her palm flattened against his chest, he'd nearly broken apart.

And her lips. Utterly devastating. She'd tasted like honey and salvation, spicy and floral and wild. For those few minutes, there had been nothing but breath and heat and fingers tracing lines of fyre across his skin—it tore at the edges of his soul in a way he would never recover from.

And her warmth...it had been the worst of it. Alone in the cold space between worlds, and then fever-hot skin against his, burning away the chill that had settled into his bones.

Her presence in his world felt...right. As if she belonged amongst the blue shadows, born to exist alongside them.

Had she noticed?

He moved a tendril of hair away from her face. She sighed in her sleep.

And suddenly, the screaming came back to him.

Ten years—what felt like a lifetime ago—he'd run after druids and druises who came near the liminal level, trying desperately to get their attention. Shouting until his voice went raw. Reaching for them with hands that passed through their shoulders like smoke. Begging, pleading, cursing.

They had only seen the souls.

That's when the true horror had settled in. If the people with druidic magic couldn't see him—the ones who walked between worlds, who guided the dead, who understood the liminal level better than any-one—how would he ever escape?

The first year had been the worst. He'd clung to hope like a drowning man, convinced someone would notice. Someone would help. His sister would find a way. The curse would break on its own.

It hadn't.

By year three, he'd stopped screaming. The loneliness had scraped him raw from the inside out. He'd forgotten what being alive felt like. What it meant to exist as more than a ghost trapped between worlds.

By year five, he'd started wondering if he'd ever been real at all.

Then *she* spoke to him.

"Will you help me?"

Four words that had shattered a decade of silence.

He'd frozen, terrified that if he moved, if he breathed, the miracle would end. That she'd realize her mistake and he'd vanish.

But she'd kept looking at him. Expecting something.

And in that moment, nothing else had mattered. When you've spent a decade drowning, you don't question the hand that pulls you up. You just grab on and hold tight.

He hadn't expected that hand to be warm. Feminine. Or to feel like salvation and ruin all at once.

He should be figuring out how her ability to enter the liminal level could break his curse. Instead, he was watching her breathe and thinking about how her hair caught the evening light.

He'd been so careful, at first. Every conversation calculated, every question designed to probe the depths of her magic. He'd told himself he was gathering data. Building a strategy. Finding the key to breaking his curse.

But somewhere between her exhaustion and kindness, watching her save strangers and listening to her sing to lost souls, he'd stopped studying her and started just...*knowing* her.

The way she checked on Rune three times every night, her footsteps soft so she wouldn't wake anyone. How she preferred Star Fyre Spirits to hot tea and hummed while she worked, different melodies depending on her mood. And he knew the exact sound she made when she was trying not to cry—a small hitch in her breath she thought no one could hear.

These weren't research notes. These were love notes.

The realization sliced through him like a blade.

She'd become more than his hope of breaking the curse. She'd become his lifeline. And the terror of losing her had crashed through him with more force than any physical sensation.

The worst part? He couldn't stop it or control what was happening inside him. She was pulling apart every wall he'd built, every bitter justification, every calculated plan. Remaking him thread by thread. He hadn't anticipated caring more about keeping her than freeing himself.

Could he use her to gain his freedom? Would she set him free if she knew the reason he had been cursed? The woman who had sentenced him to this terrible existence had taught him that loving someone meant giving them the power to destroy you. But Ava was teaching him something else entirely—that being destroyed might be worth it.

If she pulled away and never touched him again, he'd have nothing.

He couldn't survive that. Not now that he knew what it felt like. What *she* felt like.

But lying there with her weight against him, her breath ghosting across his neck, the careful threads of his control were coming loose.

His plan wasn't working. Worse—he didn't want it to work anymore. He wanted Ava. He needed her to look at him the way she had tonight, like he was worth touching. Worth keeping.

And that possibility terrified him more than another decade in the liminal level ever could.

Chapter Seventeen

Ava stretched in the morning light, a soft smile on her lips. Sensing something was missing, she rolled over.

Thorben was gone.

She touched her lips, remembering his kisses and his words, replaying in her mind. How could she possibly hate him? He was holding something back, and she was determined to find out what.

Ava stretched and glanced toward the kitchen window. Rune was making breakfast, while Gabrie and Flip sat at the counter. She tiptoed to the house through the damp grass, shivering as the cool morning dew seeped between her bare toes.

The smell of lavender and lemon oatcakes wafted throughout the house, and her stomach grumbled when she entered. Talking and laughter drifted from the kitchen—Rune's bright voice, Flip's lower rumble, Gabrie's delighted squeal.

Ava paused in the doorway, throat suddenly tight. When was the last time their cottage had held this much sound? This much life?

She continued to her room where she grabbed clothes—turquoise shirt, leather corset, utility belt—then paused at the jingle from her phylactery. Inside, her fingers found the cold circle of Declan's ring. Worn smooth at the edges.

She had to find this lost soul—for him and for Rune's cure. She remembered the pain in his eyes when he'd handed it over, the way his fingers had trembled.

Finding a length of black string from the bottom drawer, she threaded the ring onto it and tied it around her neck. The cold silver lay against her collarbone.

Satisfied, she checked her pockets for forgotten items, then pulled on her boots.

"Another! Sing another!" Rune laughed as Ava entered the kitchen. "Avalína, mé veláh, esprí aluta, joyous morning to you. Would you like breakfast?"

Gabrie was eating with gusto as Rune placed cake after cake onto her plate. Thank the Five, the tonic had worked. Flip watched his sister eat, barely taking bites himself. Gabrie finished her oatcake, and he slid one of his onto her plate.

"I'd love breakfast." Ava went over to kiss Rune on the cheek. "How are you today? Feeling alright?"

"Fit as a flywheel, as always," Rune answered, overturning another oatcake.

Ava turned to Gabrie and Flip. "How are you?"

Flip gave a curt nod. "Good, thanks."

"Flip is a terrible singer." Rune pointed her spatula at him like this was crucial information. "Sing us a temple song."

Flip's cheeks reddened, but he sang anyway—a truly off-pitch rendition of a sacred temple song. Ava pressed her hands to her ears. Gabrie grinned around a mouthful of oatcakes.

"That really is terrible," Ava admitted, accepting a plate from Rune.

"I have a tonic for that," Rune offered. "You'd sing like a sky syren within minutes."

"No, thank you." Flip shook his head. "I take pride in being terrible. Means they don't make me perform at temple."

Rune set a cup of tea in front of Ava. She snagged her aunt's arm. "Rune," she said quietly, "Do you remember anything from last night? Did you have visitors?"

Rune paused, thinking. "Other than you and these two lovelies? I don't believe so. Why do you ask?"

"Do you know anyone named Rubi or Neo?" Ava watched her aunt's face carefully. Her smile slid.

"Rubi? Neo? Why would you ask about them?" Rune whispered, her shoulders stiff.

"You were speaking to me as if I were Rubi last night. You don't remember?"

"*Neyá*." Rune's mouth set into a firm line. She quickly turned back to the stove to flip more oatcakes.

Ava frowned. Sometimes Rune couldn't recall who she was talking with during her delusions. But this time, Rune clearly remembered Rubi and Neo. Ava wondered why those particular names bothered Rune so much.

Ava headed to the airship station. It was safer for Flip and Gabrie to stay at the cottage for now. Rune was happy to have a little girl she could spoil, and Flip wasn't leaving his sister.

A prickle skittered across her skin halfway there. She paused, scanning the crowd—villagers heading to the city for work, errands, family visits. Nothing unusual.

"Thorben!" Ava put a hand to her thumping heart. "Mother of the temple, you scared me."

"Sorry." Thorben's grin came too quickly, nervous at the edges. He reached out, hesitated, then tucked a strand of hair behind her ear. His fingers lingered a beat too long, trembling slightly against her skin. Last night crashed through her—his mouth, his hands, the desperate way he'd held her. Heat pooled low in her belly.

"Where did you go this morning?" The question came softer than she intended.

His gaze skimmed the trees, the crowd, anywhere but her face. "I need-ed to—" He stopped. Started again. "I'm not used to..." His jaw worked. "It's been a long time since I woke up next to someone."

The admission hung between them, raw and uncertain. Something in Ava's chest loosened. He wasn't pulling away—he was overwhelmed. "It's been a long time for me too."

His eyes finally found hers, relief flickering there. "Are you going to Seráya City today?"

"I need to work on my airship and get it flying." Even though Ava had been denied access through the purdahs, she still needed a functional zeppelin.

Thorben's brows lifted. "You didn't tell me you had an airship. Why are you always taking the airbus?"

"It's in pieces at the moment. Would you like to come with me? I can introduce you to Toby and Dáhlia. I'm sure they would love to meet you."

He caught her hand, fingers threading through hers. The gesture seemed to surprise him as much as her—like his body moved before his brain caught up. Her breath caught.

"I should—there's work. Homes from the landslide." The words tumbled out too fast. "I'll see you when you get back?"

It sounded like a question. Like he wasn't sure she'd want him to.

"Alright." She held her breath, waiting.

Thorben leaned in—then stopped halfway, uncertain. His gaze dropped to her mouth. Fresh rain and something darker, earthier. He kissed her finally, but it was nothing like last night's desperation. This was careful. Tender. Asking permission for something he'd already been given.

When he pulled back, his thumb brushed her jaw. She watched him leave, the way his shoulders held too much tension, skin sparkling in the early morning light. He glanced back twice like he was checking she was still there.

Her stomach flipped.

He wasn't smooth or confident. He was a disaster.

And somehow that made her want him more.

Shaking her head, she boarded the airship and chose a place near the back. The pilot flared the burners which filled the balloon with hot air. The whir of the propellor settled around her, the noise giving her space to think. How had she come to be in a relationship with a handsome man she barely knew?

She envisioned them building a house in Dasírli Forest, planting a garden, making love in the grass. Perhaps they would have children, a little boy, with Thorben's beautiful dark hair and her blue-green eyes.

The clank of the ship docking startled Ava from her thoughts. She gathered herself and headed to Toby's shop. When she entered, she saw that the parts room had been reorganized and the door to Toby's invention room was sporting several new locks.

"I'm glad you're back," Dáhlia said from behind the counter, then stopped mid-thought. Her eyes narrowed. "Wait. What's that smile about?"

From the doorway to the workshop, Toby glanced up from the brass fitting in his hands. His gaze caught on Ava's face—and something shifted in his expression. Too quick to name. Gone before she could read it.

"What smile?" Ava tried to school her features.

Toby looked back down at his work. "Morning, Ava." His voice came out carefully neutral.

"Morning, Toby." Ava replied, trying to hide her smile but failing miserably as it overtook her face. "Um, what smile exactly?"

"That one." Dáhlia pointed at her accusingly. "The one you are trying to not make right now." She moved closer, putting her hands on Ava's shoulders. "You...have been with someone." Dáhlia's eyebrows rose in surprise.

Ava shook her head, but Dáhlia wasn't fooled.

"Oh, my skyes, you have. Who is it?"

She handed Dáhlia's clothes back. "I met someone after the landslide. He helped me fix our house when a tree smashed through the roof. And he kind of saved my life when I went over the edge."

Dáhlia sucked in a breath. "What in the world were you doing at the edge?"

"A few souls were lost. I couldn't leave them."

"Hmm." Dáhlia raised her eyebrows. "What else?"

"Nothing else." The lie heated her cheeks.

Dáhlia gave her a hard finger jab on the shoulder. "Nothing else my ass—"

"Astrophysics!" Ava said loudly shooting Dáhlia a look as Aamina strolled into the shop, clutching Little Sister.

"*Seáh*, astrophysics is definitely interesting." Ava shoved Dáhlia back to the counter. Dáhlia rolled her eyes and made a 'you & I will talk later' motion. Ava waved her off and turned to Aamina. She hand-signed, 'Hello.'

"*Esprí aluta*. Joyous morning, beautiful." Ava crouched so she was face to face with her. "Tell me about the accessories Little Sister is wearing today."

Aamina held the doll out for Ava to examine. Pointing to each trinket, she explained in hand language where she had acquired them. A button from Dáhlia's coat, a small cog wheel and glass lens from Toby's shop, a patch of fabric from a shirt Ava had given her ages ago, and a large silver buckle.

"Whenever we are missing something small, we always know where to look." Dáhlia smiled adoringly at her little girl. She gave Aamina a squeeze and a kiss on the cheek. "Will you help Mommy today? I have some homework from kinship, and I really need an assistant."

Aamina instantly narrowed her eyes.

"What? I promise, it won't be that bad." Dáhlia argued.

Aamina frowned and pointed to the kitchen area in their apartments. Dáhlia hung her head and then threw out her hands. "I only melted the one pot. I got it after the fifth try. Give me some credit."

Dáhlia took Aamina's hand, trying to convince her everything would be fine as she was dragged off to help with that day's homework. Ava laughed at the 'help me' expression on the little girl's face.

"Oh, Ava." Dáhlia turned back. "Before you distracted me with your secret smile, I was going to tell you we are taking our invention to our client today. I promised Aami she could see the ship, but I could use some help watching her while we install it. Would you be able to come with us?"

"*Seáh*. When?"

"This evening. It should give you plenty of time to work on your zep."

Ava agreed to go and then went to change. She was itching to work on her ship, he was so close to being finished. The engine was repaired and there were a few final touches still needed on the deck and control panel.

If she wanted to find Declan's lost soul and bargain for a cure for Rune, she needed to get her airship flying. The soul he wanted could be anywhere on the main island or the surrounding smaller ones. Using her own method of transportation to search would be easier and faster than relying on public transport.

Ava headed down the walkway taking in the new line of customer projects. There were several airships docked and a huge gold and black skycoach rested in the nearest bay.

She found Toby under the belly of the machine, only his legs visible.

"Hey." She crouched down. "Thanks for finishing the suspension lines yesterday. You didn't have to do that."

He rolled out on the dolly, goggles pushed up on his forehead, a smear of grease across his cheekbone. "It wasn't much. Thirty minutes, maybe."

It had been at least two hours of work. She'd done suspension lines before.

"I partially inflated the balloon to make sure they were the right length," he said. "Now, you can finish your engine and install chairs and any details you want inside the cabin."

"Well. I appreciate it." She touched his shoulder briefly—just a friend thing, the kind of casual contact they'd shared for years.

But Toby went very still under her hand.

When she pulled back, he was already rolling back under the coach. "Let me know if you need help with the engine," he called, voice muffled by machinery. "Shout loud. I'll be here under this coach's pretty skirts."

Ava frowned at his retreating form, then shook it off. Toby was always very focused when he was deep in a project.

Ava left Toby to his skycoach and went to bury herself in her own engine. As she neared, her heart skipped a beat. The beautiful cream fabric of the balloon pressed against black ropes that reached up and over like a lover's arms. The balloon hovered above the dark mahogany ship, beckoning people to walk on board. His wings were delicately folded in, tensed with strength and ready for flight. *The Spirited Gent* was elegant, simple, and completely hers.

She checked the tension on the rigging, making sure it hadn't come loose from the quake before she jumped on board. The burner was still lit but set low. The heat brushed her cheeks as she gazed into the mouth of the balloon. He was almost ready.

She grabbed the accelerometer from the floor where it had fallen and put it into place. After threading the cable on the side, she moved to the control panel to calibrate the equipment.

She and Toby had co-designed *The Spirited Gent*'s engine. She'd wanted something beautiful and fast; he'd wanted to pursue a vision. Together, they had created an engine using not only steam, but a separate housing configured for a black powder capsule. By inserting the capsule and pressing the hammer, the black powder would release into the fyrebox, creating a massive amount of pressure. The pressure supercharged the engine, giving a burst of speed while also being able to maintain flying for longer without loading more wood. The intense heat from the powder pushed energy into the pistons which spun the propeller on the back of the ship. Dáhlia had spellcasted the seams on the engine and the boat to ensure her ship would be sturdy and stable while using the propulsion system.

She couldn't wait for the test flight.

Leaning over the control panel, she craned her neck to read the compasses. Both seemed to be reading accurately.

The blast hit without warning.

Pressure slammed into her ears. The zeppelin shrieked against the cantilever beams, metal screaming, the whole ship rocking sideways. The dock disappeared as the airship tipped away—

She was falling.

The ropes. Grab the ropes—

Her hands closed on empty air.

Chapter Eighteen

T oby heard an explosion and a second later the screeching of metal against metal. A tremor traveled along the pier, rattling through his bones. He shoved himself out from beneath the skycoach's engine and stepped onto the walkway, glancing out over the city. Movement caught his eye. He turned just in time to see Ava's ship slipping off the pier.

"Ava!" Toby ran.

The last time he'd felt this terror, they were sixteen and she'd fallen from the roof of the temple. She'd been trying to collect a wayward soul. He'd caught her—barely. Skinned his palms raw breaking her fall, and she'd laughed in his arms like it was nothing. Like he'd always catch her.

Maybe she hadn't been on her ship. Maybe she'd disembarked.

He slid to a stop as the gondola slid off with a screech, bobbing into the open air. His gaze raked the deck, desperately trying to confirm Ava wasn't on board.

He found her holding tightly to the wheel with one hand, the other struggling to open the ailerons. Her mouth was set in a grim line, determination to save her ship plain on her face.

"Shit!" Toby's heart pounded in his ears, sweat breaking out on his skin. He had to get to her. *Now.*

Toby hunted for anything he could throw to catch the ship and haul it back. Even though her balloon was inflated, her ship still sank, quickly dropping to the lower levels. If the balloon hit any of the outreaching steel beams and was punctured, it would explode, killing Ava and whoever happened to be close.

A swinging rope caught Toby's eye. The leftover length from the suspension lines he'd installed was swaying, teasing him to try and catch one. He swallowed and jumped down to the edge of the blasted dock, her ship twenty feet out. The ledge creaked under his weight but held. Pressing his lips together, he widened his stance, chest tightening.

And he jumped.

A scream tried to escape his throat but was shoved back by the force of the wind. The air whipped through his hair, his glasses coming askew. The rope slapped him in the face, mocking him for his choice.

Toby wrapped his hands around it and held on. It reached the end of the line. His shoulder popped as the rope jerked. He screamed, the pain exploding through his arm as his body swung beneath the hull.

Part of him wondered why he had just jumped. But, it was Ava. Of course he would go after her. She had been his first kiss behind the temple, and later, they fumbled through awkward intimacies in his workshop. She was his experience at heartbreak when they grew up and realized friendship fit better than forever.

He'd made peace with that years ago. She was safe in the category of: people I love and protect.

Except his sister was in that category too, and he wouldn't be dangling from a rope with a dislocated shoulder for Dáhlia.

The thought skittered through his pain-fogged brain and lodged there, uncomfortable. Gritting his teeth, he focused on putting one hand above the other as he climbed toward the deck. His shoulder screamed in protest. He kept climbing anyway, the rope swinging madly.

The boat suddenly dipped, and his body swung toward an outreaching steel beam. He tucked himself into a ball, squinting his eyes shut.

"Holy hell!" The metal beam gouged a line into his back. Tears blurred his vision. Unable to move, he focused on breathing, in through his nose, out through his mouth, until the first wave of pain washed over him.

He had to keep moving. He looked upward, gauging the distance. Only a few more feet. His split skin pulled in agony with every move, and he prayed he wouldn't pass out before he reached the top.

Finally, he hauled himself over the side. His bad shoulder hit the floor and he groaned, needles of pain raking along his insides.

Ava was still at the helm, her black hair whipping in the air as she struggled to miss beams and platforms. She reached up blasted hot air into the balloon, trying to level it out. Toby trudged toward her, holding his arm across his chest. Her eyes widened when she caught sight of him.

"Toby! How did you get on here?" She glanced to where he was holding his arm. "Are you hurt?"

He motioned to the control panel with his good arm. If he stopped to think about his injuries, he might pass out. "What's the situation?"

She pulled the ropes again, setting the fyre high, attention back on the controls. "I'm trying to slow him down by putting more hot air into the balloon," Ava said, adjusting a lever. "The fyrebox isn't prepped, and the accelerometer isn't working. The ailerons need extended, but I'm afraid they will be ripped apart by the beams."

"Keep doing what you are doing." Toby hobbled over to the fyrebox. "Hold steady and straight and keep the burners lit."

"What are you doing?" Ava hollered over her shoulder.

"We need power to get out before we crash." Toby snagged a kindling bundle from the pile. He struck it on the side of the housing, threw it into the fyrebox, and slammed the door shut behind it.

"We haven't tested the engine yet!" Ava's voice pitched high. "We don't know what it will do."

"It's damn well time we tried it, don't you think?" His intuition told him it would work, but his mind frantically tried to solve the how before he had to hit that hammer. Heart pounding in his ears, he threw open the barrel housing and shoved a black powder capsule inside. The engine would work. It had to.

"Prep the hammer." He took the first mate's place in front of the control panel and cranked closed the exhaust valve to ensure the engine would get maximum thrust once they tapped into the black powder.

Ava pulled out a valve to the left of the wheel. The city's levels rolled by, putting the people and the ship in more danger with each passing floor. Onlooker's faces were pressed against windows, with their mouths in an "o" shape while others stood at railings and landings, watching the airship fall.

"Toby—Is this going to work?" Ava turned her wide turquoise eyes toward him, and his words momentarily caught in his throat.

He leaned in, close enough to smell the spicy soap in her hair. "Do you trust me?"

Her mouth firmed, jaw set with that familiar determination. She nodded.

He straightened, letting his injured arm go. Pain laced from his shoulder to his fingertips, but he could still move his fingers. He lifted his hand slightly, ready to give the signal.

"Now?" Ava asked, her hand wavering above the hammer.

"Not yet." Iron beams protruded haphazardly in all directions. A platform forty floors below was getting closer every second. If they lit the box now, they might ram into a beam. If they waited too long, they would land on the lower level and explode into a fiery blaze. Two more levels and they would have enough room to angle the zeppelin enough to miss both.

He hoped.

"Get ready. Right ten degrees rudder," Toby said.

Ava hurriedly turned the wheel. "Right ten degrees rudder."

"Ready?" He held his hand a little higher, watching the ship turn, the bow pointing into the clearest path through the outreaching steel.

"Now!" He threw his hand out.

Ava jammed the piston into the panel. A loud boom thundered behind them, and a burst of black smoke exploded out of the back of the engine.

The boat lurched forward, throwing them both off balance. Toby grabbed a handrail, steadying himself. Thankfully, Ava's feet were planted firmly, and she had a white-knuckle grip on the helm, her face stern as she concentrated on steering the ship.

The hull scraped against a steel beam, kicking its trajectory sideways. Wood cracked and split beneath them.

"Toby!" Ava screamed in panic.

"Stay steady." He pulled a lever, adjusting the right aileron. The ship swung wide, the other side crashing into an opposite level. Crunching of wood against metal filled the air. People ran from the balconies and platforms, trying to avoid the debris.

"Hold on! Don't let go! Ailerons extending." Toby threw a lever.

Ava held the wheel steady, her face squinted in concentration. He snagged the levers for the side wings, pulling them open. Locking the ailerons in place, he pressed the handles for both elevators to gain as much lift as possible.

The ship shuddered as powder exploded in the fyrebox, puffing black smoke. Toby clutched the elevator levers, pulling hard, using every ounce of strength to keep them steady. His shoulder burned with the effort, the pain flashing lights in his eyes.

The ship rocketed past the levels of the city and burst into the clouds. The zeppelin zipped through the airstreams, ruffling the air traffic in its joyous haste to get its first taste of the sky. Airships and turbo props blew their horns at them in indignation, but Toby didn't care.

They had made it out and were airborne. Their engine had worked. The speed and power the black powder configuration had saved them. He couldn't help the grin spreading over his face as he turned to Ava in triumph.

"We did it!" She shouted.

His breath caught. Watching Ava fly was like seeing a soul for the first time. Her grip strong and steady, ebony hair streaming behind her, soot-covered face aglow with the same brilliant smile she'd worn walking into the shop this morning.

That smile.

The one that hadn't been for him.

She'd been glowing then too—flushed and bright and more alive than he'd seen her in years. Happy. Someone was making her happy.

And he'd thought: *Good. She deserves that.*

But now, watching her laugh in triumph, wind whipping her hair, looking at him like he'd built the piers—

Something sliced through his chest. Sharp and present. Like tearing open an old wound that he'd thought was healed.

They'd been kids together. He'd loved her the way you love someone when you're young and stupid and think love is enough. Then they grew up and grew apart—physically and emotionally. She needed things he couldn't give her—magic, power, and someone extraordinary. He was just Toby. Good with machines, useless with spells.

So he'd let her go. It had been logical. Except he'd just jumped off a dock for her. He'd climbed a rope with a dislocated shoulder, back split open, barely able to breathe—and the only thought in his head had been: *Keep her alive. Nothing else matters.*

It took him by surprise. Ava had always been someone he could trust, a loyal and caring friend. But, experiencing her, in this moment, made him question his cataloging of where she belonged in his life.

Perhaps he had been inaccurate.

They brought the ship down on an upper platform. Ava's hands shook on the controls, but she managed the landing with a little encouragement from him.

Dáhlia was waiting at the dock, Aamina clutching her neck. His sister's face had gone pale.

"What happened?"

Toby ran a hand through his hair, wincing as pain laced through his shoulder and back. "Someone set explosives to Ava's pier."

"Why would someone do that?"

Toby shook his head. "I don't know, D."

"And you jumped." Her voice came out flat. Shocked. "I saw you. Right off the dock."

"I'm fine." Toby climbed over the railing, his shoulder screaming.

"You're bleeding through your shirt." She shifted Aamina to her other hip, the little girl signing something frantic. "Your arm is—Toby, you could have died."

"But I didn't."

Dáhlia's gaze cut to Ava, who was checking the balloon. When Dáhlia looked back at him, something in her expression shifted. Her mouth softened into something sad. "Oh, Toby."

It wasn't a question, but recognition. Dáhlia had always said he loved Ava more than he cared to admit. He had just done something incredible—or something stupid.

"Don't." His throat tightened.

"I'm not going to say anything." She touched his arm with her free hand, careful. "But you can't keep pretending you don't love her."

She wouldn't tell him to confess. Wouldn't push him to act. Dáhlia knew him too well. He'd only move when his brain finally caught up with his heart.

"Come on." She tugged his good arm gently. "Let's get you some of Rune's ointment and call a healer before that shoulder sets wrong."

Toby followed his sister, glancing back once.

Ava stood at the railing, hand smoothing over the wood. Talking to her ship like it could hear her.

He'd jumped off a dock for her.

And she didn't even know why.

Chapter Nineteen

Since her normal dock had been destroyed in the explosion, they'd landed at a lower public pier.Since Ava's normal dock had been destroyed, they cautiously landed her airship in a lower, public deck. The pier's mooring constable charged demanded an outrageous fee for a non-scheduled dock. Ava went to protest, but Toby waved it away and handed over the coins. The constable's lip curled smugly until Toby quietly stepped into his space, initiating a short, intense conversation that left the shorter man bobbing his head in acquiescence. Satisfied, Toby walked away with Ava, a protective hand on her lower back and as they returned to his shop.

Dáhlia called in an inyanga to examine Toby's hands and shoulder. The healer hummed as she examined his back, commenting on the effectiveness of the ointment they'd already applied. The healer hummed and mumbled as she looked over his back, commenting on the effectiveness of the ointment they had already used Rune insisted they always keep a tin on hand, and it was the first thing they'd grabbed when they returned to the shop..

"I think your pier was blown to bits by a phlogos mage,." Dáhlia said after the healer finally left. "Only a mage with fyre magic could do that sort of damage to the beams of a pier. The strength of the chemicals needed plus the complexity of a spell to explode at a certain time would take a lot of skill. No one was here last night or even the night before except us. Right?"

Toby nodded.

"That means whoever did it was targeting you specifically, Ava." She gave her a pointed look and a shiver traveled over Ava's spine. "Know any fyre mages you've torqued off recently?"

"Um, no?" The run- in with Rachit flitted through her mind. He wouldn't have the resources to sabotage her vessel would he? How would he even know it was hers?

The clock chimed the hour, and Dáhlia glanced over, sighing. "We can talk about this later. We need to deliver the locating device. Ava, are you feeling up to going with us to keep an eye on Aami?"

"Sure," Ava said, pulling Aamina into a fierce hug. "We can pretend to be knaves on an adventure."

Aamina grinned, showing her small, perfect teeth.

"Don't get into trouble," Dáhlia muttered, putting a hand on her hip. "I do not want to call the inyanga again. She isn't nearly as good as Rune, and she charges a fortune."

Toby and Dáhlia loaded their invention while Ava put Aamina in a dress Dáhlia had already laid out for the occasion. Ava ducked into Dáhlia's bathroom and scrubbed the soot from her face, wincing as the cloth passed over the tender spot on her forehead. The inyanga's salve had worked—barely a bump remained—but it still ached.

She stared at herself in the mirror. Exhausted and filthy, but alive.

She'd almost died. Again.

The thought should terrify her, but all she felt was...nothing. Numb. The adrenaline had burned through her, leaving only ash.

She needed to see Thorben.

"Ready to go?" Dáhlia asked, walking in. She took one look at Ava and softened, a small smile pulling at the corners of her mouth. "You need clothes. Again."

"It's not funny," Ava grumbled.

"It is a little," Dáhlia said, pulling some clothes from her closet. "You get filthier than Aami does and that's saying something. Here, wear these. You'll feel better when you're clean." Dáhlia had already changed into a beautiful corset of camel brown leather with gold metal details she had spellcasted herself, a full dark mocha skirt with slits on both sides, and knee-high leather boots. Her ears were adorned with golden hoop earrings, and her hair was elegantly swept into a small knot on top of her head.

"I can't keep wearing your clothes."

"Then maybe you should leave some of yours here," Dáhlia suggested. "Let me fix your hair." Dáhlia swept Ava's long, dark tresses into a top knot, allowing several curls to fall elegantly around her face and over her back. Satisfied, she left, giving Ava some privacy.

Ava dressed quickly. Dáhlia had chosen a black vested corset with delicate silver snaps, a low cut, flowing turquoise shirt and black aviatrix pants. Donning her utility belt, the ring necklace and her phylactery, Ava returned to the common room.

"Everything is loaded and ready," Toby announced, coming through the door. He grabbed a drink from the counter, then paused when he saw Ava.

"How is your head?"

She touched the tender spot absently. "Fine. Barely a bump. How's your arm?"

He rotated his shoulder, wincing. "Sore. The inyanga said it'll take time."

Ava nodded. A beat of silence.

"We should go," Dáhlia called from the workshop. "Don't want to be late."

Ava grabbed her things, grateful for the interruption. She needed to get through this delivery, then she could go home. See Thorben. Tell him about the flight, the fall, how Toby had jumped after her like a complete lunatic.

She smiled at the thought. Thorben would be horrified. Protective. He'd probably lecture her about being reckless.

She couldn't wait.

Toby and Dáhlia's ship, *The Twilight*, was docked in the first bay of their personally owned pier. Their zeppelin was an amalgamation of old ship bones with new, cutting-edge designs. Dáhlia had spellcasted the ropes, creating extremely fine metal wires woven throughout. They shone like silver, wrapping over the cobalt blue balloon. The hull of the ship sported a delicate filigree pattern. They hadn't installed their new engine system in it yet, but now that they knew it worked, Toby was excited to add it.

Ava guided Aamina to the passenger seats, making sure Little Sister had a seat too. Toby strode past, sending a wave of cinnamon and vanilla over her nose. He now wore a brown and cream pantsuit, with a form fitting corset vest. His white shirt billowed out at the arms, and his hands now sported leather gloves. A pocket watch was attached to his lapel and the chain swung methodically when he moved.

"Safety straps please!" Dáhlia's mothering orders brought Ava back to the moment. She settled herself into the black leather seat next to Aamina and fastened her buckle. Aamina tapped Ava on the shoulder and gestured to her doll.

"Of course, I can buckle Little Sister." Ava leaned over and attached the clasp, pulling it snug. "There."

Aamina smiled at her in thanks. Dáhlia took the first mate's position. Toby and Dáhlia worked like the team they were, moving levers and adjusting dials without needing words. The airship lifted smoothly away from the dock.

Ava watched them, something wistful tugging at her chest. Twin magic—not literal spellwork, but the kind that came from years of knowing someone completely. Reading each other's minds, moving in perfect sync.

Would she and Thorben ever have that?

They were so new. He'd been alone for ten years, she'd been buried in exhaustion. They were still learning each other—the way he tensed when he was hiding something, the way she hummed when she was nervous. Small things. Beginning things.

But maybe one day they'd have this too. The thought warmed her.

The commodore's personal piers were located in the middle of the city, several levels higher than the rest of the residents. It was rumored that every edge of the enormous island was visible on a cloudless day from his window.

The flight took minutes and soon they were ringing into the dock, communicating with the mooring master they were coming in.

They disembarked and were met by an official from Van Alst's party. He escorted them to a conference room, the wide arcing windows drawing them speechlessly inside. The clouds were sparse, the sun glowing in muted crimson and apricot, signaling evening's approach.

"You can see everything from here," Dáhlia said dreamily, her nose inches from the glass. Toby gently took Aamina's hand and went to stand beside his sister. Ava watched the three of them, her heart aching just a little. She had Rune, but it wasn't quite the same.

The doors suddenly opened, and Lleu Priam strode through, his long brown robe billowing behind him.

"Druid Priam." Ava offered her hand, the other resting on her heart in a traditional Ili greeting. Priam's gaze went from her outstretched hand to her face. Ava paused, waiting.

"I'm Avalína Llahenór." When Priam still didn't move, she raised her hand a little higher. "I'm...a druis at the temple." He stared at her intensely, a curious and irritated look in his dark, observant eyes. She dropped her arm. "I've seen you visit with Mother Zoya. She is a wonderful keeper."

She exhaled slowly. Heat crept up her neck. His reaction to her was bewildering, and it set her on edge. He took two quick steps toward her.

"You have eyes the color of luminescent flowers on Star Fyre," he said quietly, his voice smooth and dangerous. He studied her hair, locking on the small silver chain Dáhlia had clipped on her ear. "And hair like a Black Sands night."

Ava stepped back, putting space between them. "Ah, thank you. I'm told I take after my mother."

Priam's eyes narrowed further, studying her clothing, finally landing on her phylactery. "Your mother? Who is she?"

"Ah, I don't know, actually." Ava slid a glance to Dáhlia and Toby, hoping they would save her from this awkward conversation.

"Do you have other family? An aunt perhaps?" Priam's eyebrows quirked upward, his gaze never leaving her face. Cold slithered down her spine. What was Rune to this man?

"Druid Priam, I see you've met our friend, Avalína." Toby walked over, Aamina still holding his hand.

Priam peered at her one more time before turning his attention to Toby. Sliding a smile into place, he addressed the twins. "Master Wynstann and Mage Wynstann, *Seáh llaéh*."

Toby nodded. "I have your order."

"Wonderful." Priam clapped his hands together. "Shall we get it installed onto the master ship?"

"Will you take Aamina?" Toby asked Ava, passing the little girl over.

"Of course." Ava took Aamina's small hand in her own. Priam gave Ava one last look before leading them away.

What a strange man. Even Flip hadn't set her on edge like this. She wanted to peek at his soul in the liminal level, to see what it would tell her. But Aamina was pulling on her hand, anxious to go exploring.

"Should we get started on our adventure?" Ava asked and Aamina nodded eagerly.

The commodore's ship was the grandest Ava had ever seen. It had to be ten times the length of Toby and Dáhlia's zeppelin with windows and decks from each of the seven levels.

"Look, Aamina." She pointed. "You can see the flags at the top of the main mast. I wonder what the helm looks like. I bet the control panel is complex. Let's go see."

She kept a tight hold of Aamina's hand as they followed Dáhlia, Toby and the crew on board. As they ascended the gangplank, Ava's awe grew with each step toward the impressive airship.

When they reached the top, she paused, the view of the city sprawling as far as she could see. Piers of every height blocked the sun while airships bathed in the light. Mountains glimmered in the northern part of the island, their colors crisp against the hues of the sun.

She dropped into a crouch to whisper into Aamina's ear. "Have you ever seen anything so beautiful?" Aamina shook her head, clutching her doll tighter. "I bet Little Sister is excited to see what else is on this ship, right?"

Aamina nodded, and Ava lifted them both, carrying her as they toured the ship, leaving Dáhlia and Toby to their work.

The deck itself was massive, taking up much of the front of the ship with a wide-open space at the bow. Currently, people were decorating tables and setting out glasses. She set Aamina down and took her hand.

"What's all this?" Ava mumbled.

"We're decorating for the Day of the Five." A petite woman approached, her arms full of paper lanterns. "Van Alst has a party planned."

She set her load on a nearby table. "It's going to be enchanting. The party is set for sundown when the souls come in. I can't wait to see it from this high in the air. It will be my first year serving during the holy day." She grinned, her excitement shining in her large brown eyes.

"I'm sure it will be beautiful," Ava smiled. "I'm Ava." She held out her hand and the woman accepted.

"Kit," she replied. "Will you be attending the party?"

"Neyá. I'll be with the temple. I'm a druis."

Kit's eyes got big and round. "Wow. I bet having all those souls come at you at once is overwhelming."

She shrugged. "I couldn't do it without the other druids and druises. We are stronger when we are together."

A light flickering in the distance caught Ava's eye. A ruby red soul was lazily winding along the deck. Could that be the soul Declan was looking for? Reaching out, Ava introduced herself. It ventured closer, curiously examining Ava. Finally, it wrapped around Ava's wrist, and she welcomed it, sending a message of comfort and peace.

Kit was commenting on Little Sister's dress and baubles, and Aamina was telling her about each and every one using her hand signs. When they were finished, Aamina tugged on Ava's hand and pointed at the back of the deck.

"Oh, right." Ava turned to Kit, keeping her spirit's attention on the soul on her wrist. "Can you tell us about the ship? We've never been here before."

"Sure." She motioned for someone to take the lanterns. "Let's see. This level is for entertainment, as you can tell. There will be tables, chairs, and a dancing space. The back part of the ship," Kit said, pointing toward the stern, "has a small theater, and several areas for dining. And of course, through there is the helm and control room. The captain's cabin is directly behind it. The levels below us are private rooms, offices, kitchen, engine and storage rooms."

"You know a lot," Ava said. "How long have you worked here?"

Kit nodded, blonde hair blowing in the breeze. "I've been serving for almost five years, but this is my first time working on deck during a party."

Dáhlia emerged from the control room, waving them over. Perhaps Ava could get a few minutes to bind the soul while they installed the machine.

"We need to go. It was good to meet you, Kit. Thanks for the information." Ava smiled, pulling Aamina along behind her.

"Here you are." Dáhlia took Aamina from Ava. "Come in and see."

She paused and pulled the ring from beneath her shirt, offering it to the red soul. It continued to circle around her wrist, not interested. Ava's shoulders sagged. This wasn't the soul Declan was looking for then. She fished out several essentia from her utility belt, humming a tune. The soul quickly picked a red silk bow that perfectly matched her color. Ava tucked it into her phylactery and quickly joined the others in the control room.

Toby was crouched, securing the soul locator to the floor. Priam stood off to the side, and his eyes narrowed when he noticed her. Ava's heart kicked. What was it about her that bothered him so much?

Her gaze drifted to the control panel. She browsed through dials, levers and switches, her mind spinning with the thought of captaining such a grand vessel.

"There is our famous duo!"

Ava whirled as a voice boomed through the room. Van Alst VII barged in, his footsteps heavy on the floorboards. He was even larger in person, his tall frame dwarfing everyone in the room.

Van Alst strode over to the machine and bent to inspect it. "It works, doesn't it?" he asked Toby and Dáhlia.

"Seáh, sir," Toby replied. "I can show you now, if you would like."

"Yes, yes. Let's see it." Van Alst's eyes fixed on the machine as Toby turned the crank. The device whirred to life, the dial spinning wildly before snapping into place.

Van Alst turned, following the gauge's direction.

It pointed directly at Ava.

Chapter Twenty

Ava took a step back, her pulse kicking hard against her ribs.

She'd seen anger before—grief-stricken families lashing out, desperate souls raging against their fate. But this was different. Van Alst's fury wasn't hot and wild. It was cold. Calculated. Like he was deciding whether to kill her now or later.

"What—What is she doing here?" Van Alst sneered. Spittle formed at the edges of his mouth and his eyes blazed.

Priam placed a calming hand on the commodore's arm. Looking down his nose at Ava, he answered, "This is a guest of Master and Mage Wynstann, sir. I don't believe you know her."

"I—I don't?" Van Alst gritted his teeth, visibly trying to rein in his emotions. He puffed out a breath, then absently ran his hands over his belly and the silver buckles on his vest.

Ava followed the gesture, her gaze snagging on the empty space where the last buckle should be.

An oily smile plastered itself onto Van Alst's face. "I'm sorry, my dear. Sometimes my emotions can be...unexpected." He laughed it off. "What is your name?"

Her soul quivered. The sensation rippled through her chest, an instinctive recoil she couldn't explain. Something about this man agitated her spirit—made it twist and pull like it wanted to flee her body entirely.

She didn't want to be rude, but every fiber of her being roared for caution.

"It's...Avalína."

"Why is the locator pointing to her?" Van Alst asked Toby, his gaze never leaving Ava's face.

Those bright blue eyes felt like knives. Dissecting and hungry.

"I suspect it's because she is a druis and very good at what she does." Toby moved closer to Ava, his shoulder nearly brushing hers. "She often has several essentiae within her phylactery. The machine is sensitive to any soul not within a body. If they are bonded with an object, souls can be detected since, technically, they are ready to move on."

Van Alst's eyes narrowed, still locked on her face.

The liminal layer vibrated.

Ava's breath caught. The plane thrummed with unease, a discordant hum that set her teeth on edge. She tilted her head, listening. Something was wrong. Very wrong.

Cautiously, she stretched out her awareness and dipped her spirit into the liminal plane.

Van Alst's soul was near. She could feel it—close, present, hovering just beneath the surface of reality.

But something about it felt... off. Twisted. Like staring at a reflection in warped glass.

She reached further, trying to understand—

A lash of heat scorched through her soul.

Ava gasped, the pain blinding and immediate. It tore through her chest, her head, her very essence—white-hot and vicious.

She retreated as fast as she could, yanking herself back from the liminal plane. But the damage was done. Her head pounded, the pain loud and throbbing behind her eyes, and her knees buckled.

She sank to the floor, both hands clutching her temples.

"Ava!" Dáhlia ran to her side, dropping down beside her. "Ava, are you alright? What's wrong?"

Breathe in...

The pain clawed behind her eyes, bright and relentless. Her spirit felt raw, scraped clean, like Van Alst had reached inside her and burned everything he touched.

Breathe out...

She'd guided souls for twenty years. She'd experienced grief, rage, despair—every emotion a dying soul could carry. But she'd never been attacked by another person's soul.

Breathe in...

The headache pulsed with her heartbeat, each throb a searing reminder: In the liminal plane, he could hurt her. But...how?

Breathe out...

The pain dulled to a manageable ache. Ava blinked hard, forcing her vision to clear.

Van Alst stood over her, hands resting on his large belly, that smug smile curling his lips as if he'd just won something. Like her pain delighted him.

Priam glanced back and forth between them, a frown creasing his face.

"Sir, we have several other matters needing attending to before the celebrations," Priam reminded, his tone carefully neutral.

Van Alst strode confidently past Ava toward the door, his steps heavy and deliberate. Before he could exit, he swiveled on one foot—as if a thought had suddenly occurred to him, redirecting his path entirely. He knelt next to her, close enough that she could smell the boat burned bourbon on his breath.

He tried to reach out a hand but didn't seem to have the strength to touch her. His face contorted, muscles twitching beneath his skin like they were at war with each other. Then his hateful eyes abruptly filled with a bright kindness, his expression softening into something extraordinarily genuine.

"I'm so glad you are here." He gave a wink.

In an instant, the kindness was wiped off his face. The fury returned, cold and absolute. He straightened, pulled at the hem of his coat, and stomped out of the cabin, angrily muttering to himself.

Ava stared at the closed door, her heart still racing.

Dáhlia leaned over and said into Ava's ear, "That guy is a freaking gearbox. How is he the leader of the realm?"

Ava let out a shuddering sigh. "I don't know."

She pushed to her feet, Dáhlia steadying her with a hand on her elbow. The room tilted slightly, then settled. The headache still throbbed—a dull, persistent reminder behind her eyes.

Toby frowned at the door Van Alst had just exited. "Something's wrong with him."

"Wrong doesn't cover it." Ava pressed her fingers to her temples, trying to ease the pressure.

The way Van Alst had looked at her—like he'd seen a ghost—but wanted her dead and alive at the same time.

"Did you see his face when the locator pointed at me?" she asked quietly.

"Like he wanted to murder you on the spot," Dáhlia said flatly.

Ava's stomach turned, remembering the wink. What had that been about?

Toby's jaw tightened. "We should leave. Now."

Ava nodded, but as they headed toward the door, one thought circled through her mind, cold and insistent: Why did it always feel as if more than one pair of eyes was looking at her from behind Van Alst's piercing gaze?

Ava's throat tightened. There was only one way that could happen. And it wasn't by accident.

Chapter Twenty-One

V an Alst slammed open the door, lifted the nearest vase, and hurled it across the room. It shattered against the wall, water and flowers falling to the floor. Priam quietly closed the door behind them.

"I thought you took care of her!" Van Alst roared into Priam's face, his spittle flying as he searched for something else to throw.

Priam's lip curled and he brought a sleeve to his cheek, wiping it clean. "I had a fyre mage set charges on the cantilever beams at the dock," he said calmly. Van Alst's tantrums were irritating, but they usually gave Priam a read on how Van Alst was managing his situation. "The balloon hasn't been inflated the entire time it's been there. It was odd luck it had been filled."

"Luck or not, she will ruin this for me." Van Alst growled, rounding on him. He stopped inches from Priam's face, his blue eyes livid. Van Alst towered over him, and Priam had to tilt his head upward or be left staring at the commodore's double chins.

"Did you know she can enter the liminal layer?" Van Alst ground out.

Priam's eyebrows rose. He had been trying to breach the liminal plane for years with Van Alst's help and had never succeeded. Taking a step backward, Priam buried his envy. It would serve him no purpose here.

"Yes," Van Alst sneered. "I know *you* can't do it, but she did. She reached her soul out and tried to touch mine."

"That is...surprising. She didn't see the real you, did she?"

"Of course not," Van Alst snorted. "I singed her soul before she got too close."

"Are you sure it was her? You are the only druid I know that can travel through the liminal plane and that is because you have studied it for a thousand years."

Van Alst absently gazed at the airstreams, a delighted glint in his eye. "She hesitated when she entered. She is afraid."

"Fear is a powerful motivator," Priam said receiving an agreeing grunt from Van Alst.

"Even though she has the ability, I doubt she knows why," Priam offered. "She seems genuinely clueless. Wherever Vivia is, she has kept the truth from her."

"Vivia...The only person who knew me as I once was..." Van Alst's eyes went glassy. This was what happened when the forbidden wasn't heeded. A person would go mad, their memories of past lives clouding the present.

"Sir," Priam prodded, quietly at first. When Van Alst didn't move, Priam said it a little more loudly.

Van Alst's eyelids fluttered. "Oh. You needed something?"

"Yes, as I was saying," Priam cleared his throat. "I don't believe Avalína knows the extent of her past. At least, not yet."

"We need to find Vivia." Van Alst shook his head, trying to dispel the fog. "She always did have a protective streak."

"I have several who believe they have a lead." Priam grimaced as he watched Van Alst put himself back in working order. "So far, they've only tracked her within the city."

Van Alst pointed his finger at Priam, some of his initial frustration back in his eyes. "You have two days, Priam. I want to see that girl's body soulless."

Priam nodded. He would gladly fulfill that order.

"Before you leave, Priam, bring the mage you assigned the task of removing our dear Avalína to my retribution room." Van Alst said, shrugging out of his jacket. "Afterward, I'd like some entertainment." Van Alst went to a metal shelf behind his desk and poured himself a glass of boat burned bourbon.

"And when you do find Vivia," he called to Priam as he was leaving. "I'd like a visit with her personally."

Priam walked out of the office, insulted Van Alst ordered him about like an assistant. He had much more potential than being an errand mage. It was only a matter of time, he told himself. Van Alst and the ancestors would not last long, especially if Vivia and her druis niece were here.

He dreamed of a future as he would have it. Van Alst gone and he, the Master Druid of the Realm of Souls, the only person left fit to lead. The other realms and their representatives would be...persuaded...that they would need him to know their loved ones made it to the afterlife. It would ensure their dependency—and cooperation.

And now, they had the locator. He could duplicate it, adapt it, and use it to his specifications. Priam would be the owner of a powerful collection of essentiae, ready to serve.

That was something the ancestors didn't understand. Souls weren't worthless bits that needed to bond or simply move on. They could be powerful—a strong, moldable force—more important than anything the other realms could create. Souls would become the new currency—and he would have them all.

Priam took the stairs to the levels below, stopping before a metal door. He motioned the guard to open it. The smell of burnt flesh wafted out. Priam covered his nose and stepped inside.

A mage was chained to the floor, his hands and wrists blistered and raw from where he had desperately tried to burn his way through the metal cuffs.

Priam tut-tutted. "Did you believe I would be stupid enough to give you cuffs you could melt? Why is everyone insulting me today?"

The mage stared hard at him with hatred in his golden eyes. "Why am I here? I did my job."

Priam shrugged. "You did, but you failed. The ship slid off the pier and blasted into the sky. Van Alst was not happy when he saw her this morning."

The mage paled.

"Oh, yes." Priam went on. "He saw her. And now, he would like to see you."

The mage's face paled even more, and he trembled. "No. I did as I was asked. It's not my fault she lived."

"Van Alst doesn't see it that way," Priam replied, turning to the guard. "Take him to the Retribution Room and make him comfortable."

"No!" The mage struggled as the guard dragged him out the door. Priam could hear his screaming protests and shook his head in disappointment. That phlogos mage was a particularly talented one and Priam hated to see good talent go to waste.

Chapter Twenty-Two

R une set the dish aside and wiped her hands on her apron—or was it Rubina's apron? Neyá, Rubina had been gone for...how long now? Rune blinked, steadying herself against the counter. The present day settled back into focus. She had been worried about Ava all day and could sense something was amiss.

Ava worked hard at the temple, and collecting souls was like breathing to her. She would go to any lengths to save one, no matter what it meant to her own safety.

And that often got her into trouble.

Through the window, Rune caught movement in the garden. Ava stood beside the herb beds, and though Rune couldn't see who she spoke to, she knew. The ghost. Or soul. Whatever he was. The one only Ava could see. Her niece's face was soft, almost luminous, in a way Rune hadn't seen in years. Perhaps ever.

Love. Ava had finally found it.

And Rune was about to destroy it.

The truth would steal this from her—this brief, shining moment of happiness. Ava would learn she wasn't meant for simple joys like love and garden conversations. She was meant for sacrifice. And for saving a world that had already taken everything from her once before.

Rune's throat tightened. If only she could give Ava more time. If only Rey hadn't forced her hand.

But there were no more days to give.

Rune set herself in the common room with some hot tea, waiting for Ava to enter. She had already given Flip and Gabrie dinner and some calming tonic for the child's nerves and she was asleep. Flip never left Gabrie's side, his eyes tracking every shadow that crossed their small cottage. He hadn't given Rune any information on what had happened to them exactly, but she was glad they were there.

Gabrie had the sweetest disposition. Just this morning, the child had touched Flip's scraped cheek—three deep gashes from whatever they'd fled—and within moments, the skin had knit itself closed. The girl hadn't even realized what she'd done, just smiled and gone back to her breakfast. Anatomic magic, without question, even if Gabrie herself didn't know it yet.

Rune lifted her cup, letting the bright floral notes of the hot beverage settle over her tongue.

The front door swung open, and Ava trudged in. Her hair was a tangled mess, grime smudged across her cheek, and the weariness in her movements made Rune's chest ache. Thirty years old and already carrying the weight of decades.

"Mé veláh," Rune said, setting her cup aside. "My dearest, are you alright?"

"I'm fine," Ava said tiredly, dropping her bag near the door. "It's been a long day."

"Come sit and relax." Rune patted the overstuffed chair next to her. Ava plopped down, leaned her head back and closed her eyes. Rune remembered a young Ava, how she would climb into Rune's lap without asking, her small hands pulling at Rune's sleeves to hear another story. Sometimes, she would tell Ava of things that had happened to her in a previous life. How Ava had loved those adventures.

Now, Rune ached for her niece, seeing the weariness in her bones. And Rune was going to make it so much worse, taking away what little peace—and love—Ava had managed to find.

"What have you been doing?" Rune asked, smoothing the blanket over her lap, putting off the inevitable.

Ava paused, as if to tell her aunt something about her invisible soul. But, she shook her head and finally said, "Toby and Dáhlia delivered an invention to Van Alst today, and I went with them to keep an eye on Aamina."

"You saw—" Rune caught herself. "Van Alst?" Her heart beat a little faster. After as many years as she had endured, she knew coincidences did not exist.

"Seáh," Ava replied. "He was so strange, Auntie. It was like...like he couldn't make up his mind how to act toward me. He was angry, but then he smiled, and it was so...hopeful. I'm sure I've never met him before. And my soul, it didn't like him at all."

Rune closed her eyes, sinking deeper into the cushions. Van Alst had no doubt known exactly who she was.

It was time to tell Ava the truth.

Revealing the ancient truths about their lives would be difficult, but part of her was relieved. After all these years, Rune could begin the end of her own journey, and it started with this story.

However, the other part of Rune was sad, because out of all the lives she had lived, this had been the best one, the most joyous one, the one she had been able to cherish with her niece.

"Mé veláh, I believe it is time for me to tell you something," Rune said quietly.

"Can it wait until tomorrow?" Ava murmured, almost asleep in the chair.

"There may not be a tomorrow," Rune said, looking at her weathered hands. If Rey had recognized Ava, it wouldn't be long before he found them both. Ava peeked an eye open, and Rune held her turquoise gaze. "You must hear this."

"Alright." Ava sighed, her ebony hair falling into her face as she straightened in the chair.

Rune began, her voice steady despite the tremor in her hands. "Once, as you know, our world was whole and complete. It was beautiful, full of light and life. But the inside was not healthy, and as time went on, we, the mages, druids, inyangas, and others of magical talents, sensed the internal upset."

Ava visibly relaxed as Rune spoke, the narrative familiar, and a lump formed in Rune's throat. That day had transformed her entire life and the lives of her family. Or was it families? How many times had she lived this? The memories bled together—ten lifetimes of waiting and preparing for this moment.

"Our world cracked, oceans dribbling away and mountains collapsing. The Magisterium came together to find a solution. They talked for weeks, trying one thing and another, but nothing worked. After much discussion, they decided they needed talents beyond their own. They found them in the form of an inventor, two mages, and a young druis, all within the same family..."

Rune's words faltered, thinking about the day when the Magisterium had come knocking on their door. "There were six mages on the council at the time. Mage Veerva, Mage Bell, Mage Falk, Mage Shea, Druid Baraz, and Druid Rey," as she said the last name, her lip curled slightly.

"The family accepted the Magisterium's request. Not everyone agreed on how things were to be done, but in the end, they set aside their differences and created a way to keep our world from total destruction."

Over time, the details had faded from common knowledge, and Rune had let them fade. Better that way. She didn't want the details of what had happened spoken about in whispers for however long she was still needed in the physical realm. Her family were simply people, trying to be the very best versions of themselves to save everyone they knew and loved.

Realizing she had drifted off into memory, she blinked. Ava was watching her intently, concern creasing her brow. Rune cleared her throat and forced herself to continue, though each word felt like pulling up stones from a deep well. "Rubina, the mother of the family, was an astral mage and the best at what she did. She knew all the stars and could plot their coordinates and where they would travel. She could manipulate gravity to have a certain pull or push where she wanted it. Powerful indeed." Rune gave a small smile, warmth blooming in her chest at the memory of Rubina. "She was also a good friend."

Ava leaned forward, her elbows propped on her knees. "What do you mean 'a good friend'?"

Rune lifted her hands for patience. "Wait and listen. I will tell you more than you want to know before I'm through. Dorienne, Rubina's beloved daughter, was a manipulation mage and very talented, but still learning her skills. She was headstrong and anxious to prove herself."

Rune paused, the cup trembling slightly in her hands as she drank. It was difficult to talk of this after so many years of keeping it to herself. The memories were bittersweet, and it hurt her to have to lay this burden on Ava. She wished she could wait, if only to give Ava more time to enjoy life.

"Neo was an inventor." Rune's voice softened, and for a moment she could see him clearly—covered in grease, grinning as he showed her yet another contraption that would probably explode. "He and Sebastion worked together to create the formula for which the temple now uses to bond souls. This method is what bonded the Magisterium to the sections of the world that were slowly moving apart. Neo was a true engineer, always tinkering with anything he could get his hands on," she chuckled. "I remember caring for him multiple times as a boy, he was always getting himself hurt creating one contraption or another."

Ava stared at her, eyes wide with dawning realization, and Rune's tone softened. "The young druis, she was a jewel. Only a toddler when it all happened, but she was powerful even then. Souls would find her and curl up beside her while she slept, drawn to her light like moths to flame. Or sometimes—" Rune's lips twitched with the memory, "—she would play with them at night when she should have been sleeping." Rune gave her a pointed look. "Her mother and father loved her dearly and they did everything they could to protect her. She helped save the world, you see, even then. She kept the Magisterium's souls close by her side so they would stay to do what they had promised."

"Who was she?" Ava whispered.

Chapter Twenty-Three

T he air left Avalína's lungs. Rune's bright blue eyes held hers, steady and certain. "It's you, of course, *mé veláh.*"

"I don't understand—that's impossible." The words came out strangled. Ava's hands gripped the armrests. "This happened a thousand years ago. There's no way I was there."

But Rune's eyes were bright with clarity.

"Have you ever wondered why you can feel a soul's emotions so clearly? Why you can see and know things about the liminal plane that other druids and druises cannot? Why you crossed over accidentally as a child?"

Ava's stomach dropped. She had wandered too far into the forest, trying to collect a group of wayward souls. They had led her to a stream with a cave, and she had been so intent on being with them her spirit had crossed through the curtain separating the planes. She had been greedily swallowed by the liminal level, the pressure of being inside its existence pressing against her chest. Her ears had popped, and her body grew heavy, the unexpected weight making her sluggish and slow.

But the spirits...they were more vibrant than ever. Ava recalled their utter brightness—joy and tenderness radiating from them like heat from the sun. When they'd sensed her anxiety, they had cocooned her, soothing and keeping her safe.

Rune and the others had searched frantically for days. Ava had screamed until she was hoarse, but no one could hear her. She was trapped in the liminal plane, unable to free herself.

Until Zoya had come.

A spirit from Ava's little group had guided Zoya to the void where Ava was trapped. Zoya's voice had cut through the pressure, steady and calm, talking Ava through the curtain separating the liminal plane from the physical realm. Step by step. Breath by breath. Until Ava had stumbled back into the Real, gasping and shaking.

It had been the scariest moment of Ava's life.

Ava put her head into her hands and leaned forward in the chair, trying to brush off the memory. "There is no possible way, Auntie, no way at all." Her voice cracked.

But even as she said it, pieces were clicking into place. The liminal plane. The way spirits always found her.

"Who am I?" The words came out as a whisper. "If this is true, who am I? Am I Ava? Or am I...someone else?"

Her hands were shaking. The only way she could have been there was to have her spirit moved from cadaver to cadaver through the years. But that wasn't her life. Was it? Had there been other lives she couldn't remember?

Rune nodded, plucking at the blanket over her lap. "It was you, and I will tell you how. But you must listen with your spirit and not your head, for it won't make sense unless you do."

Ava straightened. If she had been there a thousand years ago, what did that mean for her now? Where had her soul been through those years?

She lifted her gaze to her beloved aunt's weathered face. "Alright. I'm listening."

"After we accepted the Magisterium's request, we worked day and night trying to find answers. You, even young as you were, had a magnetism spirits couldn't resist. There was one in particular you would tell us about that stayed by your side night and day. You described him as silver fyre and said he was your best friend." She smiled, looking at Ava. "You told us his name was Palo."

Ava's breath caught. The silvery being in Empyrean—the one who'd known her name, who'd said he missed her.

Palo.

He'd been there, all this time.

Her vision blurred with tears.

"We delivered our solution to the Magisterium," Rune continued. "After much discussion, they accepted it. We created the purdahs, binding a spirit to each realm in its own protective covering. But the earth needed balance, and so it forged the liminal level to compensate."

"Wait—we saved the Realms?" Ava jumped to her feet. The room tilted. She grabbed the chair back to steady herself, then started pacing. This was too much. Her family. Her aunt. *Herself.* All of them—legends.

"How is this possible?" The laugh that escaped sounded broken even to her own ears. Ava stopped pacing. "But how am I here? Right now? How did I survive all this time?"

"Do you remember the ending of the story?"

Ava thought back. "Some say they celebrated together. And others say..." The words stuck in her throat. Rune nodded, encouraging her to finish.

"And others say Willihad Rey destroyed them all," Ava whispered.

The words hung in the air between them. Destroyed. Murdered. *Her family.*

"That's right." Rune's voice was heavy. "After the earth stabilized, we celebrated. But, later that night, I overheard Rey speaking with a fellow mage. He was very jealous and threatened, I think, that an entire family could do such a wondrous thing. He planned to murder all of you, to secure his rule over the Magisterium. After hearing it, I ran and told your father. The plan was for all of you to enter Empyrean together, so at least in the afterlife, you could still be a family. And your father had hoped he would devise a way for all of you to return.

"He brought all of us into the garden," Rune's chin trembled, but she went on. "You took one glance into the pond, and the portal opened. Your father asked Palo to take you first, even though he couldn't see him, he knew Palo was there. I'll never forget how your small body went limp when your spirit left."

Ava knelt in front of her aunt, tears from Rune's eyes dripping onto her hands. "Oh Auntie..."

Everything made sense now. The liminal plane. Why it had always felt like hers, even when it terrified her. Because she'd been there first—a toddler sent to Empyrean, touching that plane before she even understood what it was.

The weight of it pressed against her chest.

"Then, the death mages arrived." Rune swiped a hand at her wet cheeks. "I was younger at the time, of course, and strong. Being an inyanga doesn't mean I am only a healer. I ran to my room, grabbed some poisons I had been working on and ran back. But I was too late."

Ava's stomach turned to ice.

"Our family had been slain." Tears dripped over Rune's wrinkled face, her voice cracking. "I threw the poison over the murderers and cast a lethal spell. I have never wanted to kill anyone as much as I did that night."

Rune's fingers were twisted in the blanket, knuckles white, anger burning in her eyes. Ava gently stroked her pale hands. "I'm sorry you had to do that."

Raising her wet lashes, Rune took a shaky breath. "It wasn't your fault, mé veláh."

"What about everyone else?" Ava whispered.

"Well, the portal was gone, and without you to guide everyone, there wasn't much I could do," she explained. "I hoped everyone would stay long enough for me to bond them. I searched for something to use as essentiae and found three coins in your father's pocket. But I couldn't see their spirits."

"Because you don't have druidic magic," Ava whispered.

"Yes," Rune answered. "But I knew someone who did."

"Who?"

"Sebastian."

"*The* Sebastian? The one you talk about sometimes?"

"Have I spoken of him?" Rune's eyebrows rose. "Interesting. I didn't realize I had."

"It usually happens during your hallucinations." Ava's throat tightened. "You called Toby Sebastian once."

Toby. Who looked like the man her aunt had loved a thousand years ago.

"Oh my," Rune sighed. "I bet he thinks I'm crazy."

"You are not crazy," Ava assured her, squeezing her hands.

"I was crazy for Sebastian, though," Rune grinned, and Ava saw sweet memories float through her blue eyes. "He was with us often and had even helped Neo a bit with creating part of the process of bonding. He was the light that kept me going after losing all of you. He helped to find Rubi, Neo and Dorienne's spirits. They had stayed close by in the garden, watching and waiting. Sebastian bonded them to the coins I gave him."

"Auntie..." Ava's voice broke. Her parents. Her sister. Here. After a thousand years. Rune's answer to the question burning in her heart might give her something she had always wanted but thought she would never have. "Where are the coins now?"

"I have kept them safe for a thousand years." Rune ran a hand lovingly over Ava's hair, and the tension in Ava's shoulders eased. "It has been my responsibility, my honor, to do so."

"But how have I not felt them if they're here?" Ava was always sensing spirits wandering into their forest or occasionally finding an essentia that had been lost to time. She couldn't fathom how she hadn't detected her family when they were so close.

"Sebastian took them to a mage to seal them," Rune explained. "He had the same concern. He said if any druid or druis could sense them, they wouldn't be safe."

Ava nodded. It made sense. Another thought suddenly struck her. "Wait—are you truly my aunt?"

"I am," Rune smiled. "I am your father's sister."

"But how are you here after all these years?"

"I have been able to continue my task by taking on new cadavers. My soul has gotten used to moving from one body to the next, even though I seem to lose a little bit of myself here and there..." she gave Ava a bemused smile.

"That explains the hallucinations." The word came out hollow.

Not ill. Worse. Rune's spirit was simply wearing out, losing pieces of itself with every transfer. No medicine could fix that. No magic could heal it.

Ava's hand went to the ring beneath her shirt, fingers pressing against the thick metal through the fabric. The cure she'd been so desperate to find. Useless now. If Rune had been physically ill, Ava would have had a fighting chance. But degradation of a spirit? There was no cure for that.

She was losing Rune. Truly losing her. And there was nothing she could do.

"I suppose it does," Rune laughed lightly. "Well, I'm sure you have seen people at the temple who were ready to move on even though their physical forms were still in good condition."

Ava nodded. From time to time, people that desired the afterlife left their physical body behind, exchanging it for the sweet, care-free existence of Empyrean. Sometimes they were young, sometimes old, and other times they were simply done trying to survive in their current situations.

"The temple has kept my secret for a long time." Rune's smile faded. "By helping me live and protect you and the coins, they serve the Five. We have been keeping you safe until the time you were needed again."

"Needed again? What do you mean?"

Rune leaned forward and met Ava's eyes. "I believe Rey is here, now, like I am."

The room spun. "What?"

The man who'd murdered her family. Who'd killed them in cold blood after they'd saved the world. He was here. Alive. Walking around.

"How? Where?"

Rune's eyes glazed over, and she leaned back in her chair, a dreamy smile on her face.

"Auntie," Ava said, shaking her hand. "Auntie don't hallucinate now. Where is he?"

Rune gazed at her niece, her bright blue eyes like a cloudless, carefree sky. "Who dear?"

Chapter Twenty-Four

V an Alst—or Rey, as he'd been called a thousand years ago—had many voices in his head offering suggestions on what to do with the phlogos mage. The souls he'd bound over the centuries each had opinions, desires, and magic they wanted him to use.

Today, some voices wanted mercy—most notably the soul whose body he had usurped. But he'd learned a long time ago that voice was never worth listening to.

'*Throw him off a pier and be done with it,*' a metallurgist's voice suggested.

'*Sacrificial lambs are always worth their weight...*' another snickered—an anatomic mage who'd forgotten his calling.

However, as usual, the loudest, most obnoxious voice won out. Rey's own voice—the one that counted. And Rey wanted the mage to suffer slowly, joyously, until his soul wandered into the ether.

Rey walked quickly to the Retribution Room, the excitement of torture setting his endorphins on fyre.

The iron door creaked. The mage wearily looked up at him from his place on the floor. He had been chained to the iron grates, the flesh on his wrists bloody and burnt from where he had tried to escape.

There was a metal trough in the middle of the room, separating Rey from his prisoner. It was an unwilling barrier between the two men, holding disturbing possibilities for the evening and wood for a fyre. Chains and manacles dangled from the ceiling directly above the trough on a track, the backward and forward motion giving them a measure of confined freedom.

There were no windows, and Rey lit several candles on ledges along the perimeter. The flames jumped, eager to bend to the will of the phlogos mage's magic.

"There's no need for that," Rey said quietly, walking around the trough. He knelt, brushing his fingertips along the prisoner's dirty collarbone. Beneath his sensitive touch, the heartbeat pounded, blood rushed through veins, the body quivering in exhaustion.

Rey reached inside himself, past the chattering voices, until he found the magic he was looking for. The anatomic mage inside him had resisted at first—decades ago— but now his magic rose willingly, twisted by centuries under Rey's control.

Rey pressed his fingertips harder against the mage's flesh. Through his ancestor's power, Rey located each and every hair follicle beneath the skin. He forced them to grow, accelerating months of growth into seconds, pushing the hairs through flesh that wasn't meant to accommodate such speed.

The mage screamed as his body rejected the sudden rush of growth. Rey reveled in his pain, drinking it in. The mage's skin wept blood, the capillaries bursting, crawling with an intense itch he couldn't scratch.

Rey let go, his breath labored as he stepped back. Thick, scarlet blood trickled down the mage's arms, scalp, and face. His hair had grown an inch, maybe more.

"I did my job," the mage sobbed, scrambling away. "I planted the charges. I set them to go off when she crossed the barrier. It wasn't my fault."

"I know you set the charges," Rey replied through Van Alst's lips. He wiped his fingers off with a handkerchief from his vest. "It was bad luck for you she survived. However, I cannot let failure go unpunished. What kind of leader would I be if I allowed everyone to simply 'try' and then accept low caliber results?"

Rey opened a large leather box that had been placed on a table. Metal tinged against metal, the bright sounds contrasting to the dark acts they were capable of doing. Rey ceremoniously laid the forging tools on a small side table: hammers of varying weights, chisels and punches in graduated sizes, and a box of iron nails. Behind him, the mage whimpered.

"Since you are a phlogos mage, you will appreciate this craft," Rey said, conversationally. The tools had served him for over five hundred years, encouraging him time after time to use them again, insisting they would still perform admirably. "I've honed my abilities, being tutored by a very reliable source. He taught me the intricacies, the desires, and the...pleasures of the flame. As I'm sure you are familiar."

Rey lifted a large set of polished tongs. He turned them until the mage's bloody, sniveling reflection stared back from the polished metal. Smiling, he set the tongs beside his other tools. "Now, let's get started. Light the fyre in the trough."

The mage simply glared, dirty hair hanging over a swollen gray eye. Defiance burned in his gaze, and Rey's spirit grinned in glee.

"This will go much easier for you if you follow instructions," Rey turned, his lips curling at the corners. "If not, I will light it and your torture will be much worse. Now, will you light the fyre, or will I?"

Rey secretly hoped the mage would continue to oppose him. The anticipation of following through with a threat made his blood rush. But he waited. Patience always made the outcome more euphoric.

The mage slowly rose from his seated position, and Rey raised his eyebrows in surprise. He limped toward the trough, his gaze throwing hatred.

'He doesn't deserve this, and you know it,' a small voice mumbled. 'Why do you delight in being so cruel?'

"Stop talking, coward," Rey growled through Van Alst's mouth. The soul who owned this body had no magic, no power, nothing but his conscience and his pathetic cadaver. Rey shoved the voice down deep where it couldn't interfere.

The mage surveyed the room at his grumble but continued his walk. Pausing at the bin, he blinked slowly—and then spat onto the logs. "I will not."

"Very well." Rey called the guards in. "Put our prisoner in the manacles."

The mage fought, which Rey thoroughly enjoyed watching. Their prisoner punched one guard in the face, breaking his nose. Reaching toward the flames on the candles, he drew them to himself. They settled in his palm, and he began to spell cast.

Rey felt one of his bonded souls stir with interest inside him. The phlogos mage. He recognized his own kind, his own magic. For a moment, Rey almost let him surface—let him show this lesser fyre mage what true mastery looked like.

But it was too risky. He couldn't afford to lose focus.

Before his prisoner could finish the incantation, the other guard slammed his elbow into the mage's face. The flame spluttered out, and the mage's head lolled backward. Quickly, both guards lifted him, slamming the eager, cold cuffs around his wrists.

"I like to do things in an orderly fashion." Rey couldn't help the eager grin that slid onto his face. "Since you are being punished for services not rendered, I will return the favor. My services of leaving you alive after contracted work no longer apply."

The mage moaned, his chin coming to rest against his chest, his now long brown hair sticking out in all directions.

"I told you." The mage tried again, his words slurred. "I did what I was paid to do. I watched her. I tracked her. I planted the charges, and her ship fell off the pier as planned."

Rey slid the contraption with the cuffs to the back of the room so he could light the fyre. The mage cried out as his body swung haphazardly, jerking to a stop when the track reached its end.

Rey muttered a spell—the phlogos mage's incantation, secured along with his soul centuries ago. The kindle caught immediately, flames leaping higher than natural fyre should. He fed it more wood, the borrowed magic making it burn hotter, hungrier.

"Your job was to terminate her." Rey pointed out, ignoring the mage's sounds of pain. "And she lives. That is a failure on your part." Turning to his instruments, he lovingly laid each one in the trough to heat and the mage's eyes rounded.

"What else do you want? I could tell you about the mechanic. Or where they live."

"I've seen the shop, and I know all about the mechanic," Rey replied, bored. "That's easy information. You would need to provide me with more than what I already know."

His eyes wildly scanned the room as if an answer might be written on a wall.

"Ask me anything. I followed her for days."

Rey paused. He was anxious to continue, but he was also curious what else the mage had seen. "I'm listening. Enlighten me."

"Her name is Avalína Llahenór. She takes the airbus back and forth to the city. She visits the temple regularly, I believe she is a druis or someone who works there," he rambled.

"I know she is a druis!" Rey bellowed, rage flooding through him. He grabbed the hot tongs. The metallurgist's magic let him grip the heated metal without flinching. Another soul's anatomic knowledge whispered exactly where to press for maximum pain—the nerve cluster on the inner calf, where the tissue was thin and sensitive.

Rey clamped the tongs onto the mage's leg and squeezed hard.

The mage howled, the tongs devouring the thin fabric on his legs. His hands curled into fists as his body spasmed. He kicked desperately, trying to loosen the hold on him, but Rey was too strong.

The acrid smell of burning flesh filled the air. It penetrated Rey's senses like a soothing smoke. He closed his eyes, savoring the moment.

Inside, other voices stirred—an artist who wanted to burn patterns into his skin, an illusionist who wanted to make the mage see his own death before it came, a wind mage who whispered about suffocation. So many souls. So much power. All his to command.

Rey finally yanked the tongs off, leaving a charred circle of burnt skin. The mage hung his head, sobbing.

"I know who she is," Rey said again, his voice dangerously quiet. He needed to find the druis and Vivia and eliminate them both—again. He moaned in frustration. Why couldn't they move on already? He shoved the tongs back under the coals, and turned away.

But something his prisoner had said came back to him. "You said you trailed her to the airbus. Where did she take it?"

The mage didn't move, and Rey realized he had passed out. How disappointing. Snagging the chisel from the trough, he pressed into the mage's chest. Instantly, the mage woke, screaming.

"Where did she take the airbus, mage?" Rey seethed. He dropped the chisel to the floor, and grabbed the mage by his bloody shirt.

"Das...Dasírli Forest," the mage whispered before blacking out again.

Rey shoved him away. He hung limply in the chains, unconscious. Rey sighed. No sport in torturing an unconscious man. Besides, he had what he needed—Dasírli Forest. That's where the old healer was hiding the druis.

The voices inside chattered with suggestions: the artist wanted to carve the location into the mage's skin as a reminder, the wind mage wanted to suffocate him, while the coward's voice begged for mercy.

Rey ignored them all. He had his own plans for Avalína—plans that required her alive. For now.

Chapter Twenty-Five

"Ava!" Flip hissed, shoving at her shoulder. "Ava, wake up!"

"What?" Ava rolled over, eyes gritty, blinking at Flip. His blue eyes were wide with panic. He shoved himself into her space, stale breath making her jerk back.

"They're here!"

"Who?"

"Rachit's men. They've come for us."

Ava sat in bed, her loose shirt dropping over her bare shoulder, the ring still around her neck. "Are you sure?" Ava and Rune's conversation replayed itself in her mind from last night. It could be Rachit's men...or someone much worse.

"I don't think it's Rachit," Ava mumbled, her eyes sliding to the window.

"What?"

"Long story." Ava threw the covers off and dropped her feet quietly onto the floor. "But they are probably more dangerous than anyone Rachit has working for him."

Flip nodded, oddly accepting Ava's explanation. He peeked out the window and ducked, meeting her eyes. "Whoever they are, we need to get out of here."

Flip melted into the shadows. He was surprisingly good at that.

Ava pulled on black pants and boots, grabbed her phylactery and utility belt, and strapped on her laser glove as she hurried to her aunt's room. Her heart hammered against her ribs.

Rune was already sitting in bed, scanning the windows. Lightning flashed. A shadow crossed the bed covers.

A chill shot down Ava's spine. Souls, they needed to move.

"Auntie," Ava whispered. "Are you here? Are you with me?"

"We are out of time." Rune turned to her, her azure eyes lucid, but filled with worry. "They are here for you. You must go."

"I'm not leaving you." Ava yanked open a drawer, pulling out pants and an oversized long sleeve shirt. Rune scooted to the edge of her bed and slid to the floor. "He's found us."

"Rey?" Ava spun, handing her aunt the clothes. "You said Rey was here, like you and me. Has he been using cadavers like you? Who is he?"

Glass exploded into the room. Ava threw herself over Rune. Shards bit into her back. When she straightened, a metal canister spun on the floor, hissing.

The smell of chemicals choked the air. Gas wafted out in thick waves. Ava coughed, the mist coating the back of her throat. Her mouth burned, heat melting her from the inside out. Rune dropped to the floor, gagging, and Ava knelt next to her, trying to swallow the pain.

"There's no time for a nap!" Flip raced in, grabbing them both by the arms. Ava and Rune stumbled behind Flip as he dragged them away from the smoke.

"There must be a..." Ava coughed into her elbow, blood spattering her shirt. "...nebulis mage outside." Her throat became raw as the acid burned the sensitive flesh at the back of her throat. They stumbled through to the kitchen where Gabrie was waiting, her eyes large and frightened.

"Hurry." Rune croaked, ushering them toward the door. "You all need to go."

"Not without you," Ava said, gripping her elbow. "I'm not leaving you by yourself."

Flip glanced between them and gave Gabrie a slight nod. "We'll go out the front. Head to the tube station and hide."

"They're probably waiting out front, and the tube station is too far on foot," Ava coughed. "Let's go out back. The garden fence will give us cover. We can run to the forest."

"Alright. We'll do it your way. What happens if we get separated?"

"Head to the village across the lake," Ava replied, herding Rune to the back door. "Look for the circle of cabins. Thorben should be there. He can help."

Gabrie dropped her bag and ran to Rune, giving her a tight hug. "Thank you for letting us stay. I've never eaten such wonderful food in my entire life." Rune kissed the top of her head, whispering something in her ear. Gabrie grinned and went back to Flip.

They huddled at the back door and listened. Rain pattered on the roof, making the grass glisten. Voices filled the air to the left side of the house where Rune's room was currently releasing smoke through the broken window. They needed to move while their attackers were on the other side of the house.

"Ready?" Ava whispered. "Go!"

Ava flung open the door and veered right, Rune close behind. Flip and Gabrie sprang from the house, fleeing into the garden shadows.

"Watch out!" Flip's yell echoed over the garden.

Flames erupted in a circle around the house, rain doing nothing to dampen them. Ava stopped short. The fyre roared in her face, heat searing. Rune slammed into her from behind, arms wrapping protectively around Ava.

They'd scaled the fence.

"Quick! This way!" Ava grabbed Rune's hand and ran through a gap in the flames. Heat scorched her legs as they stamped through. Ava aimed for the flowerbed, hoping their attackers hadn't spread fyre powder through the flowers.

Ava caught a glimpse of Gabrie and Flip jumping from shadow to shadow. They ran along the perimeter on the opposite side of the garden, heading for the gate into the forest.

Rune coughed but ran steadily, white hair flowing behind her, damp and loose from its braid. Ava's chest tightened with love and fear for her.

"Almost there," Ava huffed, squeezing Rune's hand. "Just another few—"

The earth lurched beneath her feet. Ava pitched forward, knees slamming into wet dirt. The ground rumbled. A dark figure emerged from the shadows. He crouched low, his hands digging into the soft dirt of their garden soil. Words tumbled from his lips, and the earth groaned and rolled in response.

Ava drew out the thumb tab on her glove. The wire zinged with electric charge, rain drops sizzling at its touch. She took three slow steps toward the mage. His eyes lifted, his mouth pausing midspell. On the fourth step, Ava spun. Her arms stretched into a graceful arc that, at any other time, would be absolute beauty in motion. Now, the pirouette was deadly grace, slicing through the mage's neck. A scarlet curtain of blood flowed, covering his flesh. His eyes were an empty stage as his head tipped into the grass.

The body tilted, fingers lifting limply from the dirt. It landed with a dull thud. A brown and black soul slithered out slowly. Ava stood, letting the wire retract with a sharp zing. "Your soul won't be heading to Empyrean, swale rat. Into the ether you go."

The soul twisted on itself, seeking a way to return to its body. Ava turned her back on him. He would be captured by the prince of Tartarean's wooden flute melody, tortured, and left to rot in a hell of blood and ice.

"Auntie, are you okay? We need to move."

Rune nodded, and Ava grabbed her elbow, slick from the rain, and steered her toward the gate.

In her peripheral vision, Ava caught a glimpse of another mage emerging from the other side of the house. They were halfway through the garden, the forest dark and welcoming beyond the fence.

She hadn't seen Flip and Gabrie since they had sprinted out the door, and she didn't want the mage to find them. Her gaze raked the garden shadows, but they had disappeared. Pressing her lips together, Ava turned toward the forest. If she couldn't see them, then the mage probably couldn't either.

The sound of footsteps made her spin. Her hand went to the thumb tab, but she froze when she saw who it was.

"Thorben! Souls, you scared me." Ava pressed a hand to her chest. "Take Auntie. I'll be right behind you."

He frowned, not moving.

"What's wrong?" Ava asked. "We need to go!"

A fyreball lit the garden, illuminating Thorben's face. Rune ducked, covering her head—blind to the ghost standing right beside them. He looked from Rune to Ava, eyes desperately helpless.

"Thorben!" Ava screamed.

His lips firmed. He gripped Ava's hand—the only person he could touch.

"Hold onto your aunt," he ordered.

Ava clasped Rune, linking them together, and they ran. Bursting past the garden gate, they tumbled into the shadows of the canopy. Thorben dropped Ava's hand and dove to his knees, palms pushing against the dirt, his eyes closed in concentration. The trees at the edge of the forest began to grow, speaking and groaning as they twined together, their branches reaching for one another, creating a thick web of tangled limbs.

Soon, neither the house nor the garden could be seen from behind the growth.

The forest was quiet. The canopy kept the rain away, and Ava wiped at the wetness dripping off her cheeks and nose. The fyre mage had tried to follow them, but Thorben had grown a massive, long bramble making it impossible to pass through.

Thorben looked at the blood spattered on her shirt. "Are you hurt?"

"My throat feels like it's on fyre, but it will wear off." Rune coughed lightly beside her. "Auntie, are you alright?"

"Fine, fine." Rune waved her off, standing a bit straighter.

"Good. I'm going to head them off and make sure they don't come around," Thorben said. "My magic isn't very strong. If they follow the thicket far enough, they could get through."

"Thank you," Ava whispered.

Thorben nodded and jogged into the forest. She had no idea what he'd been doing out there, but he'd been here when she needed him. That was what mattered.

"Why are you thanking me? I didn't do anything, silly girl." Rune turned back to the wall of limbs, still rustling from their sudden growth. "But I do wonder what got into those branches."

"Auntie, Thorben helped us." Ava gestured toward where he'd disappeared.

"Who?"

"The soul who—never mind." Ava brushed off her pants. "Let's get to Syldan and meet with Flip. Hopefully they got away."

The forest enveloped them in warm darkness, but Ava's anxiety didn't ease. She jumped at every sound, hand hovering over her wire glove. After several minutes of quiet, she relaxed slightly, hoping the fyre mage had left.

These assassins were trained, skilled, deadly. Not the kind who'd work for a swale snake like Rachit.

Which meant...

"Auntie, you said Rey was here." Ava spun to face her aunt. "Was he one of the mages who attacked us?"

Rune bent to pick up a fallen branch, using it as a makeshift staff before answering. "Neyá. I have reason to believe he is inside Van Alst."

"What?"

The words didn't make sense. Ava stepped back, arm folding around her stomach. "Are you certain?" Was that why her soul had reacted the way it did when she saw him? Could her spirit have recognized him after all this time?

"Seáh." Rune's voice trembled, but her eyes were fierce. "Van Alst is not Van Alst at all. He harbors Willihad Rey's soul. Rey is a skillful druid who's had a thousand years to hone his craft. I've been watching him. It's why I knew the time to bring you back was now."

"But why? What can I possibly do against someone who has been keeping himself alive for a thousand years?" Ava's heart was loud in her ears.

"Other than Rey, you are the most powerful druis the world has ever known. You've spent time in Empyrean and returned—no one else has done that. Rey has trifled with the forbidden, and only someone with tremendous druidic power can break him from his host." Rune paused, placing her hand on Ava's shoulder. "Zoya and I have taught you everything we know. Your ability to traverse the liminal plane, to understand souls the way you do, is unique. If you use your skills, call on the liminal plane, and trust your instincts, you can pull him from the body he clings to. You are the only one who can break Rey's bond on Van Alst."

Ava bit her lip. Rune's hand slid off, leaving a heavy burden in its place.

Her time in Empyrean had strengthened her druidic magic? That would explain why only she could see through the portal. And the liminal plane? Ava shook her head. She couldn't think about that right now.

"Now he's found me, and he's found you." Rune's hands shook. Frowning, she crossed her arms and walked ahead. "And he wants us both dead."

"What?" Ava took three quick steps to catch up. "Why?"

"Rey always wanted to be idolized." Rune stabbed the earth with her stick as she walked. "He believes *he* is the true hero of our history, not the Five Pillars and certainly not our family. As the honoring of the Five has grown, so has his bitterness. He wants to be seen as the valiant one, the one who sacrificed. Having us here reminds him he can't take what he wants without a fight."

"What is he going to do?" Ava wondered aloud.

"I don't know. But it's my guess that whatever he is planning he will do it on the Day of the Five. There's no better way to rewrite history than doing it on a day that's already holy." Rune fixed her eyes on Ava. "And by getting rid of the only people who can stop him."

Chapter Twenty-Six

"**W**here did they go?" Gabrie's whisper was barely audible over the crackling flames behind them.

"I don't know, but we'll find them." Flip huffed, shoving through the bushes, branches clawing at his arms. His life had been defined by survival in the darkest parts of the swale. The tenebrous gloom had always been a friend, a constant veil of protection. And now was no different.

Ava and Rune had run across the garden and had practically been incinerated. He wasn't stupid enough to do that.

The undergrowth gave way, revealing an old fence barely holding back the forest. Flip kicked at a rotted board. It clattered to the ground, leaving a gap wide enough to slip through.

"Let's go." He grabbed Gabrie by the wrist.

"What about Rune?" Gabrie's voice pitched higher. "We can't leave her."

"We'll meet them in the village." When Gabrie didn't move, Flip turned to her. "Ava isn't going to let anything happen to Rune, you saw her with that laser whip thing."

Gabrie nodded slowly, and with one more look back to the garden, she and Flip slipped through the fence.

Thirty minutes later they entered the village. Morning sun peeked over the island's edge, roofs glistening from rain. Their feet crunched on brittle leaves. Woodsmoke wafted from the chimneys while wind nudged the hanging laundry. Stacks of logs waited against the houses. The central fyre pit was cold.

Oyamnís Lake stretched in the distance, its muddy bottom exposed. Flip remembered the day it had drained over the edge of the island and into the biosphere. There would be no portal for the souls to travel through on the Day of the Five. He wondered what Mother Zoya and the druids were going to do when the souls came in and there was nowhere for them to go.

"What do you think?" Gabrie whispered, pointing to a worn cabin set apart from the others. No smoke rose from its chimney—probably empty. "Let's sit outside and watch for a bit."

Gabrie snuggled next to him, leaning against a tree, rough bark digging into their backs.

As they settled in to wait, Flip's mind drifted to the night before.

He'd been asleep, Gabrie snoring softly beside him, when voices woke him. He'd tiptoed out to find Rune and Ava deep in discussion in the common room. He'd meant to give them privacy.

Then he heard it: "There may not be a tomorrow."

His feet stopped moving.

So Flip stayed in the hallway, pressed against the wall, listening to a conversation that would change everything. After Ava and Rune finished speaking and sat in heavy silence, Flip returned to bed. His head spun with questions and his lungs wouldn't fill properly.

How could Ava have been there a thousand years ago?

What did Rune mean, hopping cadavers?

Most importantly—where would he and Gabrie go when this place became a target?

Flip had seen what happens when a world falls apart. His parents—no money, only habits. When their addictions became too much, they'd sold Gabrie to Rachit at *The Scarlett*. Then they'd died of an overdose.

He didn't miss them. Didn't have to worry about saving them from their own messes anymore. Now it was just him and Gabrie. He could take care of her better than their parents ever had.

But their sanctuary with Ava and Rune was about to become dangerous too. Now he'd have to watch for Rachit's men and whoever wanted to harm Ava and Rune. Someone at the temple knew they were here. What other secrets was the temple keeping?

It didn't matter. What mattered was keeping Gabrie safe. If the temple was tangled in some ancient scheme, he wanted no part of it.

Tomorrow. After a good night's sleep and some breakfast, he and Gabrie would leave Ava's place and find somewhere else that was safe.

But morning brought fyre instead of breakfast.

Now here he was, hiding in a village he didn't know, waiting for the two people he'd planned to abandon.

A half hour later, Rune and Ava appeared at the edge of the woods. They reached the group of houses and stopped, surveying the village.

Something was wrong.

Gabrie started to signal them, but Flip grabbed her arm. "Wait. They don't feel right." He reached out with his spirit, trying to sense their souls. He wasn't as good as Ava, but he could occasionally sense a bonded soul. These beings were void. Empty. Ava's soul had a brilliance to it, a beacon for spirits in the liminal plane. He could pick her out anywhere.

"It's not them," Flip whispered, his stomach clenching. He shrank farther into the shadows, pulling Gabrie with him. His hand shook as it gripped her arm.

Whatever the hell they were, they weren't human.

The imposters nodded to each other, then split off—one taking the right side of the cabins, the other the left. The Ava look-alike came dangerously close to their hiding spot.

"We need to move," Flip whispered. They slunk behind the empty house, into the welcoming darkness of the woods. Flip boosted Gabrie into a tree with low-hanging branches, then followed. From here they could watch without being seen.

The village was waking. People stepped from their homes, sleepy and bright, readying themselves for the day. Someone started the fyre in the main pit.

The imposters ignored the townsfolk, walking stiffly toward each other like they were learning to use their bodies. Their faces remained blank even when they spoke.

Goose bumps crawled up Flip's arms. What in souls' names were they?

Then the real Ava and Rune emerged from the forest on the opposite side of the drained lake. Rune leaned heavily on Ava, their steps slow and measured. Exhausted, but human.

"Shit," Flip whispered. "Ava and Rune are coming."

He slipped past Gabrie and landed softly on the ground with bouncy feet.

"What are you going to do?" Gabrie asked, shifting her weight on the branch.

"I'm not sure, but stay there, okay?"

Gabrie's blue eyes stayed glued to Rune, her adoration and fear shining through.

"Don't let her get caught, Flip," Gabrie said quietly. "She can't be caught."

Flip nodded. In the short time they had been at Rune's house, he had encountered it too—that sense of belonging, of knowing someone cared about them. Even possibly loving them. He didn't want to see either of them get hurt. Which was why, without any idea what he was going to do, he tiptoed away from Gabrie and toward the two people who had extended the comforts of a home he and Gabrie had never had.

Chapter Twenty-Seven

When Ava reached the village, she forced herself to smile despite the trembling in her hands. She'd just cut off a man's head. Watched his soul slither into the liminal level, condemned to Tartarean.

Her first kill.

She'd guided thousands of souls to their afterlives. But this was different. This was her hand holding the blade and her decision to end a life.

The earth mage's eyes flashed through her mind—that moment when he'd realized what was coming. Had he deserved it? He'd been trying to kill her, trying to kill Rune. It had been self-defense.

But her hands still shook. Ava wiped her palms on her pants and instead focused on the village ahead. The homes were small, peaceful. Children's laughter drifted on the morning air. People going about their chores, unaware of the danger stalking toward them.

Her chest tightened. Ava hoped desperately she wasn't bringing death to their doorstep.

Movement caught her eye. Flip, sneaking along the edge of a cabin, keeping to the shadows. Relief flooded through her—he and Gabrie had made it.

Ava started to wave, but Flip's frantic gestures stopped her. He pointed behind her, his face pinched.

Two figures approached. One tall, dark-haired. One shorter, white-haired. They moved stiffly, wrong. As they drew closer, Ava's stomach dropped.

Her own face stared back at her. And Rune's. But their eyes—burning red spheres where eyes should be.

"Vjáme." The curse hissed through Ava's teeth.

"Avalína Rose! That is no way to talk," Rune chided, then followed Ava's gaze.

A menacing growl cut through the morning air. Rune's mouth opened. Closed. The color drained from her face as she stared at her own double stalking toward them.

"Vjáme," Rune whispered.

"Exactly." Ava grabbed her aunt's arm and dragged her behind a house.

The Rune look-alike reached behind its back. Metal scraped against metal. A long scythe emerged, curved blade catching the light. The edge looked sharp enough to split souls. Ava dropped her aunt's arm and took a defensive stance, pulling out the wire tab on her glove. "Auntie, go!"

Rune stumbled backward. Flip appeared from nowhere, ducked under Rune's arm, and half-carried her toward the forest. Gabrie's terrified face appeared in the trees, reaching for Rune.

The scythe whistled through the air.

Ava threw herself sideways. The blade missed her throat by inches and struck the ground with a loud ping, sparks flying.

The Rune-clone bared its teeth—too many teeth—and growled. Ava's stomach lurched. That was Rune's face. But twisted into something vile and wrong.

"You're going to regret impersonating my aunt." Ava retracted the wire and pulled it out again, preparing herself. The wire zinged out, white hot, vibrating with excitement.

The Rune-clone swung again, her silvery-white hair flowing and red eyes ablaze with joyful hatred. Ava looped the arc of the laser whip over her head, dodging away from the clone's reach.

"I will send you into the depths of Tartarean," it said in a gravelly voice that scraped like rusted metal. It held the scythe with one hand, the other pointed at Ava. "You will not be a part of our new world."

"Your new world?" Ava brought her hands to her chest, the wire zipping back. "Not if you're running it."

The replica grinned widely, its teeth sharp and pointed. It lunged toward her, the scythe held high above its head. Ava pulled the tab, the wire whirring out. She spun, her head missing the fall of the scythe by inches. At the last minute she twisted, her wire grazing the side of her assailant's ribs. A small slice of fabric and flesh sheared off, leaving a deep gash.

It roared, angry. Swinging the blade, the creature swooped low, trying to cut Ava's legs from beneath her. Ava jumped, her wire connecting with the monster's shoulder. She yanked the laser whip forward, and a large slice of flesh slid off, landing with a heavy squish on the ground. Dark blue liquid flowed down its arm.

"Who will be in charge of this new world?" Ava panted, circling. The clone tried to lift its injured arm, but it hung limp.

"A world without barriers. A better world," it hissed. "A place where a true magientist will rule."

Magientist. The ancient word for those who combined magic and science. Rey's obsession.

Something slammed into Ava from behind.

The Ava look-alike wrapped an arm around her throat, cutting off air. Ava's fingers scrabbled at the arm—solid ice, impossible to grip. She dropped the tab. The wire retracted wildly, slicing through air.

Ava hunched forward, using momentum to flip the body over her head. It crashed into the ground with a hard thud.

She tried to scramble away, but icy fingers grabbed her shirt. Ava pitched forward and her face smashed into dirt. The taste of blood and earth filled her mouth.

Weight crushed down on her back as the imposter straddled her. Ava struggled to lift her head, spitting mud. The weight on her back was impossibly heavy and cold. Like a glacier pinning her down.

Foul breath ghosted across her cheek—rotting meat and frost. She turned her face away, gagging.

Spells tumbled from its mouth. Ancient, cold, dark words.

Ice exploded through Ava's chest.

She gasped, but no air came. The frigidness spread like poison through her veins. Not the cold of winter—but of death. True death, where souls don't go on to Empyrean, but dissolve into the ether.

No. She needed to be here. With Rune. With Thorben. With—

Frantic, Ava kicked and twisted away, anything to dislodge the weight.

The bitter cold spread deeper. Shards of ice pierced through her heart and lungs, freezing her from the inside out.

Ava screamed.

The sound echoed wrong—hollow, distant, already half in the other world.

Ice crystallized on her lashes and they froze open, unable to blink. Her lips went numb. Her ears burned with cold so intense her head felt like it would split.

She could feel her soul separating. Peeling away from her body. Being dragged down, down, down into frozen darkness.

The Rune-clone laughed—a sound like breaking glass. It took the scythe's edge and dragged the tip slowly along Ava's cheek.

The blade pierced her skin. Blood welled up, but instantly froze into ruby gems that clung to her cheek. The cut burned with frostbite, ice crystals forming in the wound.

Ava gritted her teeth. She couldn't even scream anymore.

"Goodbye, Druis," it whispered, raising the scythe.

Ava stared. She wanted to see it coming—and know who she needed to destroy once her spirit was free.

A blade erupted through the clone's throat from behind.

Blue ooze sprayed. The creature's burning eyes flickered, dimmed, went black. Its hands released the scythe and it toppled sideways with a heavy thud.

Flip stood behind it, chest heaving, dagger dripping blue. His blond hair fell over determined blue eyes.

He didn't hesitate. He grabbed the fallen scythe, stepped over the Rune-clone's body, and swung at the Ava imposter still pinning Ava down.

The blade sang through air. And then through flesh.

The Ava-clone's head tumbled off its shoulders.

Blue fluid burst from its severed body like a geyser. It splashed over the ground, across Ava's face and hair, soaking her. The smell hit her—metallic ice, chemical cold, wrongness.

The corpse's grip released. It slid off her back and crumpled to the ground, lifeless.

Ava couldn't move.

The Tartarean magic had taken root. Ice crystals spread through her veins like poison. Her heart beat slowly, sluggishly, each beat weaker than the last. Her lungs struggled to pull in air—freezing from the inside.

She tried to speak, but nothing came out except a feeble moan. Her teeth chattered uncontrollably behind blue lips. Darkness crept in at the edges of her vision.

"Ava!" Rune's voice. Ava heard running footsteps and then her aunt was there, dropping to her knees beside her.

"Ava, breathe. Mé veláh, breathe." Rune's hands hovered over her, shaking. "We need help. I don't—I can't—this is dark magic, I can't fix this—"

Her voice cracked. Tears streamed down her wrinkled face. Ava wanted to wipe them away, but her arms wouldn't move.

"Flip!" Rune looked up, desperate. "Find someone. Anyone. An anatomic mage, a healer, I don't care—anyone!"

Flip nodded, already running. "I'll be right back."

"Oh, mé veláh," Rune sobbed. Her hands stroked Ava's arms, trying to warm them. Impossible. Ava's skin was ice. Literal ice. Frost formed where Rune touched. "This isn't how its supposed to end. I saved you for something greater than this, I promise—" Her voice broke completely. She pressed her forehead to Ava's. "Don't leave me. Please don't leave me. Not after everything."

Ava tried to squeeze her eyes shut, but they wouldn't move. Everything was numb. Everything was cold.

Her mind slipped into wintry darkness. The edges of the world faded—village sounds, Rune's voice, even the pain.

A melody drifted through her thoughts. The prince's flute, haunting and beautiful, calling her to Tartarean.

Ava's body relaxed and the fight drained out of her. The melody wrapped around her like a promise of rest.

Maybe the dark afterlife wouldn't be so bad...

Maybe it was time to stop fighting...

Chapter Twenty-Eight

Thorben had made sure the mages would never walk in the Real again before following Ava and her aunt. When he had arrived, two wraiths were lying on the ground, sliced to pieces, and Flip and Rune were leaning over—

Ava. Frozen and turning bluer by the second. Thorben had to help, even if it meant breaking a boundary he had sworn never to cross. Watching Ava fight for breath ignited something fierce in his chest—not the desperate calculation he'd felt for ten years, but something more raw. No one deserved this, especially someone as giving and innocent as Ava.

He ran into the forest, snagging a particular flower from its perch beneath a tall tree, before he entered her house. Inside, their morning routine was already underway. His sister, Natalia, and her husband were in the kitchen, working side by side to make breakfast. Two girls skipped into the room, holding hands and wearing matching dresses. His throat closed. The oldest girl—blond curls, round cheeks—moved exactly like their mother had. He pressed his palm harder against his face.

A decade ago he would've wanted this—Natalia's kitchen, the girls' laughter, the ordinary warmth. Now he wanted Ava breathing. The rest could wait.

He rushed to the hearth and placed the flower into an empty vase sitting on the mantle. Thorben spellcasted, drawing his magic through the bud. It took a moment, but soon the flower blossomed. He encouraged it to bloom more, the flowers rapidly multiplying in the vase before they started shooting over the lip and curling themselves over the fyreplace.

"Mama, look!" the youngest daughter pointed.

Thorben pushed the magic harder. Bursts of pinks and blues spread over the wall.

"What's happening?" the oldest asked quietly.

Natalia dropped the cup she had been holding, and it crashed to the floor. "Those are...friendship flowers, my love. My brother and I picked them when we were children." She whispered.

Thorben coaxed another bloom open—the same way they'd practiced as children, before everything broke between them. Natalia's breath hitched. Her husband, Dellyn, pressed his lips together.

"Thorben?" Natalia whispered. He couldn't answer—she wouldn't hear him. And he was running out of time. Ava was dying, and he needed his sister to move.

"What is he doing here?" Dellyn's voice had an edge Thorben hadn't forgotten. "I thought he was gone."

Thorben made the flowers spread quickly, over the ceiling, out the door, and into a path leading directly to Ava. Looking back, he prayed his sister would follow.

"Apparently not," Natalia breathed. "Let's see what he wants."

Natalia and the girls raced outside, Dellyn trailing behind. Thorben continued the pathway of flowers until they had reached the huddle of Rune and Ava. Natalia froze.

Rune grabbed the scythe sitting next to her and spun, ready to fight. Natalia held up a hand, scooting the girls behind her with the other.

"It's okay," she said. "I'm here to help. What's happened?"

Rune eyed Natalia, her wide-eyed girls and companion behind her. Rune's shoulders slumped and she dropped the scythe. "My niece, she's..."

Natalia gasped when Rune stepped aside. Ava's body had become almost solid blue, her eyes darting back and forth in panic. Natalia placed a hand on Ava's arm, closing her eyes. She grimaced, her face contorting the longer she held on.

Flip returned, his face red from running. "Rune, I checked in the village and no one—who the hell are you?"

Rune grabbed Flip's wrist. "She's here to help. Now hush."

"This is dark ice magic," Natalia murmured, ignoring Flip. "I am familiar with it, unfortunately."

Thorben sucked in a breath. He had suspected, but Natalia confirming it made his insides squeeze.

Thorben's powers had never been much, but Natalia had always had an exorbitant amount. When they were young, Thorben remembered her being overwhelmed and terrified of her magic. He had always pushed her to do more, be more, know more. Until it had hurt her. He needed her now and hoped she would be brave enough to help Ava.

"This magic is strong." Natalia pressed her lips together. "Dellyn, take the girls inside. I have to help, and I don't want them to see this."

He frowned, but did as she requested. "I'll be here if you need me." He put gentle hands on the girls' backs, ushering them inside the house. He spoke quickly and quietly to them, closed the door, and stood guard. Thorben was thankful Dellyn took care of his daughters with such affection, even if he and Dellyn hadn't gotten along.

"Everyone step away." Natalia moved her hands outward. She swallowed hard and Thorben's heart swelled. He had always loved his sister, even when he wasn't sure how to express it. He was grateful she was willing to try. "Thorben, can you get my chapbook? You know where it is."

Thorben did. He remembered the day Natalia had made him bury it and hide it from her. It was the same day she had killed their rabbit and burnt her hands from the power of the ice. That day she had vowed to never use her magic again.

He raced through the forest, coming to a large rock they had played beside every day as children. Underneath was a small niche where he had placed the chapbook and several other items in a box. After all these years, he was honestly surprised it was still there.

He rushed back and placed it next to Natalia. The minute his hand released the box, it appeared next to her. Rune gasped.

"Thank you, Brother," Natalia said. Thorben would have answered, but he knew she couldn't see him or hear him. So, instead, he stood by and watched, his chest tight and his stomach in knots. If Ava died, his hope of freedom died with her.

Natalia unlocked the latch and removed a small leather-bound book. Thorben's throat thickened as she flipped through the pages, the memories of her carefully writing down the spells she might need one day flashing through his mind. She pressed the book open at a page near the end.

"Who are you?" Rune whispered, leaning back a bit from Natalia.

"Someone with a very dark gift, I'm afraid," she replied with a sad smile. Placing her hands on Ava, Natalia closed her eyes and spellcast. When she opened them, they were no longer gray blue, like Thorben's, but a bright white.

"*Dark ice magic, of deathly cold,*
Melt now away, release your hold.
Disappear and liberate this soul,
Leave no trace, make her whole."

Thorben, Rune, and Flip watched as Natalia chanted. Her wrinkled and scarred hands bore down on Ava's chest, and Ava's eyes rolled back into her head.

Natalia's lips pressed together in concentration. Her nose dripped blood, but she didn't let go.

"Nothing's happening!" Rune reached for her, but Flip held her back.

"Don't," Flip said. "Give her a chance."

Natalia's fingers trembled. Her face turned into a grimace, her arms quaking as she tried to draw the magic out.

Suddenly, Natalia was thrown back as bursts of ice exploded from Ava's body. Flip threw himself over Rune, the shards burying themselves in his jacket. Natalia scrambled up, her white eyes burning, her hands and fingers stretching out, straining toward the cold.

Natalia closed her fists, her voice roaring out from her throat—and the ice fragments halted. She whispered a command and every piece of ice gravitated towards her. She gathered the pieces into her arms and absorbed them. Each shard melted into her body, leaving whisps of moisture in the air.

Her eyes were a swirling white snowstorm as she stood, silent and still. Thorben wanted to reach out, to make sure she was alright, but he couldn't. His little sister had taken a chance and had faced her greatest fear for him—and for Ava.

Natalia leaned over and coughed, her breath coming out in a white puff of cold, misty air. Then, she fainted.

Thorben ran and knelt beside her. He wanted to hold her, touch her, but he didn't dare. Dellyn ran over and crouched next to his wife.

"No, no, no." Dellyn moved her head to the side, wiping the blood from her nose with his shirt. "You can't leave me. You don't belong there. You belong here!"

Natalia's eyes flickered open just enough for her gaze to meet Dellyn's. Thorben let out a choked sigh.

Natalia turned her head, eyes widening. "Thor? You really are here." Smiling, she lifted her hand, trying to touch him. Before she could, her eyes fluttered closed, and she fell unconscious again.

"Damn him." Dellyn's jaw worked as he lifted Natalia. "Thorben! You've taken enough. Stay away from her."

He lifted Natalia's body and stalked to the house. Thorben watched in desperation, his heart hollowing out with each step Dellyn took. Dellyn had blamed him for the rabbit, the burned hands, the years Natalia spent afraid of her own power. But Thorben had seen what she could become—if she'd just stopped running from it. Dellyn had wanted her safe. Thorben had wanted her to own her magic and become someone great.

Ava coughed—small, weak. Thorben spun toward her as Rune pulled her upright. She pressed Ava's hair back from her face, placing a kiss on her slightly less blue forehead. Thorben dropped beside her, and air finally filled his lungs. She was alive. His hope was breathing.

"Auntie, I'm so cold," Ava mumbled, curling onto her side.

"I know. We'll get you warm." Rune wrapped her arms around her, searching for somewhere to go. "Everything is going to be alright."

Thorben leaned close—near enough to catch the scent of her skin, to feel the ghost of warmth from her hair. "I'm here, *mé talé*," he whispered, his voice fracturing. "I won't leave you."

Ava's eyes flickered open. "You're back," she mumbled. Something in Thorben's chest cracked—relief and guilt and terror braided together. Ava's soul pulled at his like gravity—senseless, inevitable. Even trapped in the liminal plane and cursed, his spirit bent toward hers.

"I'm back," he whispered, reaching out to touch her, but stopping. He didn't want Rune to panic any more than she already was.

Rune eyes welled. "I never left you, Avalína."

Flip returned, touching Rune's shoulder gently. "That cabin's empty," Flip said, jerking his thumb toward it. "We can rest there."

Thorben looked where Flip indicated. The cabin. His cabin. Abandoned since the day he'd destroyed everything inside—since the witch had stolen his life and left him raging in the liminal plane.

Rune and Flip carried Ava to the house. Villagers slowed, staring at the commotion. Thorben tracked their curious faces, their whispers. He wanted to lift her himself, shield her from their stares, carry her somewhere safe. But his touch would drag her into the liminal plane—make her vanish in front of everyone. He followed them inside. They laid her on his sofa—the one he'd nearly ripped apart the day everything ended.

Flip and Gabrie coaxed a fyre to life in the hearth. The cabin was a wreck—Thorben's rage and a decade of emptiness layered together. He'd thrown everything—chairs, books, the frame his sister had carved—when he'd realized that witch had cursed him.

Soon they'd hear what happened here. How he'd trusted someone and she'd stolen everything, including his soul. And now he was back, watching the woman who'd become his living treasure fight to breathe on a ruined sofa.

Chapter Twenty-Nine

The fyre rippled eddies of warmth against her face, waking her. The smell of woodsmoke and pine filled the cabin, and she inhaled deeply, the scent flowing through her tired muscles. She tried to blink away the blurriness and found Thorben crouched beside the sofa, watching her.

"Welcome back," he smiled. "How are you feeling?"

"Sleepy." Ava yawned and scooted herself into a seated position. The blanket slid off, exposing her bare shoulders.

"Where are my clothes?" Ava blurted, hurriedly trying to cover herself.

Thorben's gaze flicked away from her bare shoulders, deliberately focusing on the fyre. Ava's cheeks burned as she clutched the blanket tighter, her nipples puckering against the rough fabric.

When Thorben's gaze returned, it had darkened. Ava's pulse kicked up, heat flooding through her despite the lingering ice magic.

"You, ah...were covered in blue muck," Thorben cleared his throat. "Your aunt washed you off and burned your clothes."

Ava stared at him. Had he watched Rune undress her?

"Don't worry," Thorben assured her. "I waited outside. Are you hungry? Thirsty?"

Ava shook her head. Her brain felt like it was loose, rattling inside a skull that was too big for it. She scrunched up her face. "Ow, my head hurts."

"It's the ice magic. But I think Natalia got it all out of you."

"Natalia? Ice magic?"

"Seáh. Tartarean magic is powerful."

Thorben blurred—two of him wavering. Ava squinted, trying to focus despite the pain. She leaned back and gathered the blanket to her, rubbing her head. "Where is Auntie? And Flip and Gabrie?"

"They went outside to talk so they wouldn't disturb you," Thorben answered. "I'm sorry I woke you myself. I didn't mean to."

Ava's hand crept to her neck, searching for Declan's ring. It was there, settled in the hollow between her breasts. Thorben tracked the movement, his jaw tightening.

"Whose ring is that?" he asked.

"It belongs to a knave." Ava scooted the blanket more firmly around her shoulders. "He wants me to find a soul for him."

Her spirit quieted, drawing inward. She'd thought she needed Declan's missing soul to trade for a cure—but now she simply wanted to find it because his heart had seemed so lonely without her.

Grimacing, Ava put a hand on her stomach. "Oh, I might be sick."

Thorben quickly poured her a cup of tea from a kettle hanging over the fyre. "Here. Your aunt made it for when you woke."

Ava inhaled—ginger, cardamom, cinnamon. The tea Rune always made when she was ill. The scent sank into her muscles, loosening the ice-locked tension. No matter how old Ava was, she would always need the comforting presence of the woman who had raised her.

"Do you want me to leave?" Thorben whispered. His fingers hovered near her face—almost touching a damp curl—before he pulled back.

"Neyá. Will you stay?"

Thorben nodded, settling onto the floor near her—close enough that his forest scent mixed with the tea's warmth.

Ava stared into the dark amber beverage. "How did you draw out the ice magic?"

Thorben's exhale was slow, measured. "I didn't. I asked my sister."

"Your sister? Is she the family you have here?"

"Seáh," Thorben answered carefully. "Natalia is my younger sister, and a Tartarean mage."

"I've heard of Tartarean mages," Ava said thoughtfully. "But I've never met one. They are very rare." The Tartarean mages Ava had heard about could rarely break away from the evil that ran through their blood. Ice magic has its own hold on mages, and it often caused destruction and chaos as the magic overcame them. Her gut tingled, realizing how close she had come to drowning in it.

"Natalia is very special." He gazed into the fyre, memories flitting through the storm in his eyes. "She always has been."

If Natalia had magic that was linked to Tartarean, could she see souls like Ava? Did she guide them to the dark afterlife?

"How does her magic work?" Ava asked.

Thorben shifted closer—not quite touching. Why was he being so distant? Had the attack made him rethink their relationship?

"I don't really know. Natalia's magic is powerful, overwhelmingly so I think, and she hasn't used it since we were children."

"Why?"

"She's afraid of it," Thorben said, his hand resting near hers on the blanket—so close their fingers almost brushed. "I think she believes if she practices dark ice magic it will create an evil inside of her she won't be able to control. The last time she tried to wield it, she killed our rabbit, almost killed me, and in trying to save me her hands got burned so badly she still wears the scars."

Ava was exceptionally skilled, but she had never hurt anyone with her gift. Living with something sinister and unpredictable would be difficult for the best of people.

"She put aside her fear of her magic because you asked her to." Ava mused. "She must love you very much."

Thorben was silent. Ava's eyelids were heavy, and they drifted closed, her body relaxing into the warmth until Thorben murmured, "In saving your life she almost lost hers. She is the bravest soul I know. I have always believed in her."

"Where is she? I'd like to thank her."

"Her husband took her home and told me to stay away."

"Why?"

"Dellyn has never cared for me." Thorben's sigh held regret. "But, he is good to her, even if he doesn't want her to use her magic."

Ava reached toward him—fingertips grazing his jaw before he caught her wrist gently, holding her back. His sudden distance made her stomach tight. What was wrong?

"Everyone's fear has its own price," Ava replied, setting her hand in her lap. "I'm thankful she values you more than her fear."

"I am too," Thorben whispered, his gray-blue eyes darkening as he studied her face. He leaned closer—close enough she could feel his breath against her lips, mint and promise. But he didn't close the distance. His gaze flicked toward the front window—checking they were still alone—before returning to her.

"I want to kiss you all night," Thorben whispered, his gaze dropping to her mouth. "But you need to heal first."

Ava leaned toward him, the space between them crackling. She could almost taste the coolness of his breath—mint after hot tea. Her mouth parted slightly, eyes half-closing.

"Let me tell you what I want to do to you," he murmured, his voice dropping lower. "When you're healed. When I can finally..."

"Finally what?" Ava said, in little more than a whisper, her eyes locked on his.

"When I can finally make you moan for other reasons."

Ava's cheeks burned, but she needed to ask. "What would you do to make me moan?" Her voice came out quieter than she intended.

Thorben's grin turned wicked, his eyelids lowering. "First," he began, his voice like velvet dragging across her skin, "I would kiss every knuckle, one by one, until you're trembling. I would turn your hand over," he continued, his gaze tracking the motion as if he could see it, "kiss your palm, your wrist, feel the pulse beating there. I would kiss you until you beg for breath. I would dip my tongue into your mouth and learn every taste of you. I want to nibble your neck and press my nose against the skin behind your ear...inhaling the perfume of your hair."

Thorben paused, leaning so close she felt the ghost of his breath along her jaw. Her eyelids dropped closed, her entire body attuned to his words, to his nearness.

"Then what?" she whispered.

Thorben's smile was predatory. "Then I would kiss your jaw, that spot behind your ear, the crest of your breast...until you gasp for more."

Ava sucked in a quick breath.

"This blanket would end up across the room. I would map every inch of your skin—your back, your hips, your ass filling my hands. I would lick the hollow of your belly button, lick my way down between your thighs. I would take my time with you, Ava. Hours, if you'd let me. My lips crave the taste of you."

Ava's heart pounded against her ribs, his words skimming along her skin and leaving a trail of hot desire.

"I want to worship your breasts," he continued, his voice rough. "Suck your nipples until you're writhing. Roll them with my tongue, bite them gently, then harder when you beg for it. I want them red and swollen from my mouth."

Ava's core clenched, and her nipples torturously dragged across the rough fabric of the blanket. Wetness escaped her center, her inner thighs slippery with her arousal. She wanted it, wanted him.

"I need you screaming my name when you come. I want to feel you clench around my fingers, watch your face as you fall apart for me."

Ava moaned, her hand fisting the blanket, her head falling back.

Thorben's breathing had roughened. "Souls, Ava," he muttered, "you have no idea what you do to me. I want to see all of you," he said, his voice raw. "I want you spread open for me so I can slide my fingers through your wetness, find that perfect spot inside you, feel you squeeze around them. I want to taste you while my fingers fuck you slowly. And I want you begging—begging for my cock, for more, for anything I'll give you."

Ava whimpered, her core clenching at his words. She ached, empty and wanting. Every word made it worse—or better—she wasn't sure.

"I need you beneath me," Thorben said, his voice nearly breaking. "Trembling, gasping my name while I'm buried inside you. I want to feel you come around my cock, squeeze me until I can't think."

Their heavy breathing filled the cabin, the crackling fyre giving them permission for more.

"I..." Ava's voice caught. "I want you to touch me. I want your fingers inside me. I want—" She met his eyes, her cheeks burning. "I want you inside me. All of you."

Thorben's eyes went black, pupils blown wide. "Ava..." His voice was shredded.

"I'm not finished." She lifted her hand toward his mouth, and he caught her wrist—held it there, his lips a breath away from her fingertips. "Don't," he said roughly. "If I taste you, I won't stop."

"I want your mouth on me," Ava whispered.

"Where?" His voice was gravel.

Her blush deepened. "My..."

"Say it." He leaned closer, his breath hot against her cheek. "Tell me where you want my mouth."

Ava couldn't. She couldn't speak anymore. Her core was tight, her nipples hard, her skin practically on fyre while flames of need melted her from the inside out.

"I know where," Thorben said, his gaze dropping between her legs. "I want to taste you there. Spread you open with my tongue, make you come on my face. I want to devour you until you can't remember your own name."

Ava surged forward, desperate—but Thorben caught her shoulders and held her back. "Not yet," he breathed. "If I kiss you now, I won't stop. And you need to heal."

Voices drifted from outside—Rune and Flip returning.

Thorben stood quickly, putting distance between them. But he paused at the back door and turned. "Ava."

She looked up, still flushed, still aching.

He crossed back to her in three strides, cupped her face—and kissed her. Deep, claiming, devastating. His tongue swept into her mouth, tasting her thoroughly, and she melted into it with a sound that was half-moan, half-sob.

Then he pulled back, breathing hard. "Soon," he promised, his thumb grazing her swollen lower lip. "I'll see you soon."

He was gone before she could respond, the back door clicking shut.

Chapter Thirty

"Oh, *mé veláh*, you're awake." Rune entered through the front door, shattering the moment like glass.

Ava startled, the blanket slipping from her trembling hands. She scrambled to pull it back up, her skin still feverish, her lips still swollen from his kiss.

Rune's hand landed on her forehead. "You look flushed. How do you feel?"

"Um—" Ava's voice came out rough, wrecked. She cleared her throat, huddling deeper into the blanket, trying desperately to push away the ache still throbbing between her thighs. Damn Thorben and his filthy promises, putting visions in her head—his mouth between her legs, his fingers inside her, his cock—and then just walking away.

"You seem better," Rune commented, limping to the teapot. "I see you've had some tea."

Ava groaned. Her body was strung taught, and not only because of the mages and the assassins. She forced herself to breathe in through her nose, out her mouth. Her shoulders relaxed, her thighs stopped quivering.

She glanced up at her aunt, who was looking into the teapot. Rune could have been killed. Her spirit gone forever. Righteous anger surged through Ava. How. Dare. They. She would *not* let that happen. Ruining cadavers was one thing, but destroying the one spirit that had held goodness and hope for the Realms for the last thousand years? Unacceptable.

"You're hurt." Ava frowned.

Rune waved away her concern. "*Neyá*, I'm quite alright. I've had worse, I assure you."

"Auntie—"

"Stop. This is not your fault," Rune said, as if she knew where Ava's head was going. "If it is anyone's fault it's mine for not telling you sooner who you were and why we are here. I could have prepared the both of us better."

Rune picked up bits of things here and there, her hands needing something to do. Ava surveyed the cabin for the first time. There was a small kitchen area with a wooden table, several chairs in another corner with a rug, and a doorway in the back led to a bedroom. There were broken dishes and vases strewn about, as if someone had thrown them against the walls.

A knock sounded from the front door. Natalia pushed it open slowly, peeking her head inside. "Can I come in?"

"Of course." Rune moved a chair near the fyre and poured her a cup of tea. "You need some of this too, I'm betting."

Natalia took it gracefully and sat in a wooden chair, setting a small bundle she had brought on a side table. She took a sip and sighed. "That is delicious. Thank you."

"Drink it all. It will do you good." Rune poured herself a cup and sat next to Ava. Natalia put the mug in her lap, memories flashing through her eyes, as she looked around the cabin. They were the same gray blue as Thorben's, but her hair wasn't dark like his. It was blond and short, surrounding a heart shaped face with a pert nose smattered in freckles. Eventually, her gaze landed on Ava. She smiled.

"I brought these for you." Natalia held out the bundle. "They might be a little small, but better than nothing."

Ava opened it to find a cream-colored dress with a blue sash. "A *yah ageremé*. Thank you," Ava said, warmed by the gesture. At least now she could get out of the itchy blanket.

"A *mé ceanáh agereyáh*." Natalia acknowledged Ava's thanks and took another sip of tea. "I'm sure you are wondering what happened."

"Thorben explained it a little," Ava said quietly.

Natalia straightened. "You've seen him?"

"I met him the day of the landslide. He helped us repair our house."

Natalia turned to Rune. "Can you see him? Hear him?"

"Not yet, but he seems to be a wonderful young man."

Natalia scoffed and shook her head. "Thorben is only wonderful when he thinks there is something to be gained. I love my brother, but even I can admit he is not selfless."

Ava straightened from her slouch on the couch. "Are we talking about the same man? Because he has been nothing but kind and helpful to me."

"I'm glad to hear it." Natalia said, frowning.

"Are you saying he is a bad person?" Ava's muscles tensed.

Natalia sighed, her thumb rubbing the rim of the cup thoughtfully. "The Thorben I remember thought he was better than everyone else. He loved me, and we had a special bond, but he didn't care for anyone else unless he thought they had something he could use. He treated others with disrespect and contempt. My mother and father never knew what to do with him, other than give him a wide berth."

Ava processed Natalia's words. That didn't sound like Thorben at all.

"One of the girls in the village doted on Thorben," Natalia continued. "She wasn't beautiful or special in any way, she simply loved him from the moment she saw him. He was her world." Natalia paused. "She dreamt of being with him when they got older, but he wasn't interested. She tried, once, to get him to go with her to the city. He was so offended she had asked. As an answer, he insulted her and her family, telling her he would never be seen with someone as homely, untalented, and unconnected as she was."

Ava's mouth dropped.

"He believed he was perfect, above the rules, and destined for something great—to be someone great—in the Realms. And he didn't think it would happen in this small village. So, that night, hurt and angry, the girl left. No one saw her or heard from her again for years." Natalia looked into her tea. "One day, a beautiful woman arrived. She had long, wavy locks of blond hair, the bluest eyes I've ever seen, and the fairest, most shimmering skin. We thought she had come from the Star Fyre Realm. Thorben instantly wanted her. He believed she was the one to bring him to his ultimate destiny."

Natalia paused, staring into the fyre. "They were coupled in a week. He was so in love with her, he would do anything for her. People couldn't believe their eyes, he was so changed. After about three months, Thorben came home one evening and she wasn't there. Instead, a short woman with plain brown hair and brown eyes sat where his companion normally did. He demanded to know what she had done with his partner. She told him she was his companion—had been all along."

Ava and Rune looked at each other and back at Natalia.

A wave of dizziness crashed over Ava. Thorben had never mentioned a companion. He'd had his tongue in her minutes ago. Her stomach dropped.

"Who was she?" Rune asked.

"Remember the girl Thorben had insulted? When she ran away, she ended up in the company of a *Shaitán*, a very powerful mage who offered to teach her everything she knew. After learning the magic of Tartarean, she returned. She wanted to show Thorben he was a normal person whose destiny was not some remarkable thing.

"He was coupled with the very person he had sworn never to be with, someone he thought beneath him. She took away her illusion, explaining to him they had had three very happy months together, and regardless of her appearance, he could have that happiness, if only he would see it."

Ava asked quietly, "What did he do?"

"Well, he didn't respond well at all," Natalia said. "He flung her out of his house, screaming she was an ice demon and a traitor. We could all hear the pottery breaking as he threw it against the walls. For his selfishness and shortsightedness, she cursed him."

"When did this happen?" Rune asked and Ava froze, afraid to hear the answer.

She locked gazes with Ava. "About ten years ago."

Ava leaned forward, her mind a jumble of thoughts. Ten years ago. Had Thorben been cursed and alone for ten years?

"Ava, I need you to listen." Natalia spoke low. "I can see from your face you have feelings for him. Be careful. Thorben usually doesn't do anything without a reason."

Ava's heart thumped heavily, her gut churning. Had he befriended her—been *intimate* with her—to get something? "What could he possibly want with me?" she murmured.

"I don't know." Natalia shook her head. "But my guess would be he thinks you can break his curse."

"Thorben has said nothing about it." Ava's eyes were hard on Natalia. Had he planned on wooing her just to exploit her druidic magic? Ava's soul screamed no, but her mind spun with unanswered questions and flawed logic. Her body still throbbed with wanting him—which made the betrayal cut deeper.

Ava lifted her chin. "What if you're wrong?"

Natalia sat back in her chair. "I sincerely hope I am. For him and for you, I truly hope he has changed."

"What happened after he was cursed?" Rune asked, pouring Natalia more tea.

"After that night, we never saw him again. Dellyn and I assumed he was gone, that his soul moved on. When he came into my house this morning and made flowers grow everywhere I knew it had to be him."

"So, you haven't seen him in ten years?" Ava clarified.

"Not until today. Not until I...drew the Tartarean magic out of you." Natalia tapped a finger on her chin. "You are a druis, *seáh*? I used to be able to see souls, when I was younger."

"You did? Do you have druidic magic?" Ava asked, eyebrows raised.

"Not exactly," Natalia said. "The only souls I could see were the evil ones. The ones destined for Tartarean."

Ava had heard rumors that someone owning dark ice magic could access the liminal layer but had yet to meet anyone with that ability. It made her wonder what Natalia was capable of with her magic.

"It was frightening," Natalia continued. "To be an innocent girl that drew wicked, dishonest spirits like a beacon of light in the darkness they dwelled in. I tried, one time, to get them to leave me alone." Natalia glanced at her hands, sighing. "The only thing I accomplished was scarring my hands and knowing I didn't ever want to use my magic again."

"Thorben said you had always been very gifted," Ava murmured.

"Well, I didn't want it. I ignored them and my magic until eventually it faded to a point where it didn't consume me. The souls stopped finding me, and I couldn't see into the liminal plane anymore. It was a life of quiet. A life I could live in."

"Thank you for facing your fear for my Avalína." Rune leaned over, grasping Natalia's wrinkled hands with her own, two pairs permanently and perfectly flawed for two very different reasons. "It was a true act of bravery."

Ava thought about her own fears of the liminal level. Since she had accidentally crossed over and not been able to return, she was terrified it would happen again. Natalia feared her magic too. It made Ava feel a little less alone.

Natalia squeezed Rune's hands in return. "I'm glad I was able to do it."

Just then, an apple appeared on the table next to Natalia. Thorben held a basket of fruit, a tray of dried meat and several small pies.

Natalia's eyes went wide. "What...?"

Thorben set the food on a nearby table. Natalia's mouth dropped open as brother and sister looked at each other.

"Thor?"

"It's me, Nat." Thorben took Natalia into his arms and leaned his head against her short blond waves. Natalia cried into his shirt as he wiped tears from his own eyes. "I'm here, Nat. I'm here. I've been here every day. I'm so sorry I couldn't have done more for you. I've enjoyed watching you thrive and seeing the girls grow. Mom and Dad would have been so proud of you."

"I don't understand," Natalia hiccupped and gave a giddy laugh. "How are you here after all this time?"

"Where did she go?" Rune stood, dropping her teacup onto the floor. "Natalia?"

Thorben and Natalia exchanged a glance. Natalia slowly untangled herself from Thorben's embrace.

Rune's hand flew to her chest. "Souls, girl, what happened?" Rune scanned the cabin as if whatever made Natalia disappear might get her next.

"What do you mean?" Natalia raised an eyebrow.

"You." Rune pointed at her. "What are you doing disappearing and reappearing? It's unnerving."

Natalia turned to Thorben. "What you touch disappears, doesn't it?"

Thorben nodded. "It took me awhile to figure that out. Everything seems real to me."

Ava's eyes went wide, her breath stopping.

Every time Thorben touched her, she disappeared.

The garden. His hands on her skin. His mouth on hers. That strange floating sensation, like the world had gone distant. She'd thought it was desire, thought it was the liminal plane calling to her. But it was HIM. His curse. Pulling her into wherever he existed.

She'd vanished from the Real—and hadn't even known.

Rune took a step forward and kicked a piece of clay. It skittered to Ava's feet. She lifted it, turning the shard over in her hand. A broken cup. Part of the set he'd destroyed when he'd raged at the woman who'd cursed him.

In this house. On that couch where she'd just been lying, nearly naked, listening to him describe all the ways he wanted to claim her.

The same house where he'd loved someone else and then destroyed everything when that love turned to ash.

"I..." Natalia glanced at Thorben, her hands in the air trying to find the right words.

"You said Thorben had been angry," Ava murmured, raising her gaze to Natalia. Her suspicions raced through her mind, and she refused to look at Thorben. "He had thrown things. Yelled at her to get out of his house."

"You told her." It wasn't a question.

Natalia nodded. "I wasn't...I didn't...Oh, Thor, I'm sorry."

The moment they'd just shared in front of the fyre—minutes ago—inside the very house where he'd lived with his companion. Heat pushed its way up through Ava's body, her head pounding with it. Why had he not told her? What other things was he keeping from her? Maybe Natalia had been right, and she couldn't trust him to be honest.

Thorben took a step toward her but paused when Ava glared at him. "Mé talé, please."

"No." Ava held up a hand. "You don't get to talk to me right now. You kept the truth from me. You had an ellú, a companion. We spoke of—" Ava stopped her words, remembering Rune was still in the room. "We had—a moment—in this house."

"Living here with that woman isn't a fond memory," Thorben said, taking another step toward her. "She deceived and lied to me."

"Don't come near me." Ava's heart pounded in her ears.

"Ava, I would have told you." Thorben made his way to stand in front of her. "You were the first person who had spoken to me, seen me—even touched me—in over ten years. I didn't know what to think other than I wanted to be with you all the time. I needed it—needed you. And the more I was with you the more I knew that meeting you was no accident."

Ava's voice shook. "What does that mean? No accident? Were you looking for me? Did you seek me out because you thought I could break your curse?"

"No, I—" Thorben ran a hand through his hair. "I'd given up. I stopped looking for a way out years ago. And then you appeared. You could see me. Touch me. I thought maybe...maybe I was being given a second chance."

"How does it work? Exactly?" Ava thought back to Natalia's warning. "How are you planning on breaking it?" Ava held her breath. Please don't admit Natalia's words are true, her mind begged. It would break her spirit—the one that was trusting him more every day.

Thorben looked at his feet. "She told me the curse could only be broken by an act of complete selflessness." His jaw worked. "Something I've apparently never been capable of."

The room filled with a heavy silence. Ava heavy breathing filled her ears.

"Ava. Who are you talking to?" Rune asked. "Did the ice magic give you hallucinations?"

"Neyá, Auntie. I have been a fool, that's all." Ava dropped the broken cup, the shard clattering against the floor. She grabbed the dress Natalia had given her, clutching the blanket tight around her shoulders—suddenly desperate to cover herself, to stop feeling so exposed.

Thorben's explanation didn't make her feel better. It made her feel used. "I'm going to change."

Ava slammed the door to the bedroom and froze.

The bed. His bed. Where he'd slept with his companion for three months. Where he'd—

She gagged, pressing a hand to her mouth. She'd almost let him touch her in this house. Almost let him fulfill every filthy promise he'd whispered while she melted for him.

And all along, he'd been keeping this from her.

Chapter Thirty-One

Alistair Van Alst VII studied himself in the mirror. For once, the voices inside his mind were quiet—giving him a rare moment to see what they'd made of his body.

And he hated it.

His once chiseled, handsome face had gone pudgy with all the extra food they made him eat, and his stomach hung low over his waistband. The hair on his head was thick, wavy and black. He liked having it frame his face, but they always made him pull it back into a low ponytail. His piercing blue eyes were kind and gentle now, but when *he* took over they became cruel and hateful.

Sensing his thoughts, Rey rose within him. The concern in Alistair's eyes shifted to a mocking stare. He tried to fight it—pushed back with everything he had—but as always, Rey easily overtook him.

"Quit pouting," his lips said without his permission. Rey's voice, using his mouth. "I make you a better man than you could ever have been on your own. Besides, we have company."

Rey grinned in anticipation and ran a hand over his buttoned shirt, tucking it into his pants. Appearances always mattered. Giving a curt nod, he left the bathroom, entering his bed chambers where two women from a local parlous house were waiting. He had directed them to be dressed in temple garb, complete with phylacteries strapped to their arms.

"Ladies," he opened his arms. "Welcome."

Both were young, expressions bright. They could have been intoxicated, but Rey didn't care. They were here under orders to perform a service.

'Ugh, this again. Can't you be more original?' A voice muttered in his head.

Another chimed in, 'At least these girls seem to want to be here. The last one cried.'

'Could we not do this today? We have so many other pressing matters,' said a stuffy voice.

'Why are men all the same? I swear, if we spent as much time planning as we did fucking, we would be in charge of all the Realms by now,' from another.

Rey clapped his hands to his ears, pressing his lips together. Could they shut up for once? "Be quiet," he hissed. "I am in charge here."

The smile on the brunette faltered, her eyes looking back and forth. The redhead's grin got wider as she sauntered over to him, and she laid her hands on his broad shoulders.

"I'm Shayreen and you are absolutely in charge," she purred, guiding him to the bed. Rey let his hands drop to his sides, trying to shake off the voices. Shayreen's fingers danced along his buttons, undoing them slowly as she pushed him into a sitting position on the bed. Rey sighed, allowing himself to fall into the fantasy he had paid for. He refused to let the others ruin his good time.

"Laurette, come over here and entertain him while I massage his shoulders," Shayreen instructed.

Laurette's confidence returned. She stood in front of him, combing his hair away from his face. His thick fingers glided along the sides of her ribs, the silken corset tight on her trim waist. Reaching the top of her vest, he tugged on her shirt, her dark-skinned breasts popping out. His cock swelled in response. Her nipples were large, soft, brown—he rolled them in his fingertips, making her shudder. Heat shot through him, and tingles skittered through his stomach.

'Souls, those are gorgeous,' a voice commented.

'They are for feeding children, not for ogling, you moron,' another huffed.

Rey paused. He was ready to tell them to keep their opinions to themselves, but they quieted so he continued. Taking the sizable bud into his mouth, he ran his tongue over it, and she moaned lightly. Her reaction made him throb, and he grabbed both breasts, massaging them in his large hands.

Laurette threw her head back, allowing him more access. She slid onto his lap, holding his head in her hands. Having her rub against his erection sent a shudder through him, and it gave him a sudden confidence boost—he could do anything to her, and she would enjoy it.

He pressed his thumbs against her pulse and dipped into another soul's magic, using it like it was his own. His vision changed, allowing him to see inside Laurette's body—blood flowing through veins, heart pumping steadily, lungs expanding with each breath. He focused the magic on her heartbeat, causing it to pulse faster. Laurette gasped in response, her dark eyes suddenly alarmed.

A smile crept onto his face. Focusing on her blood flow, he increased it, making it pulse where she would feel it the most. Her eyes widened, her mouth forming an 'o' at the sudden sensation. He pushed the magic harder and forced her pelvic muscles to contract rhythmically.

"Souls—" she gasped. Deep, loud moans escaped her throat, and she squirmed as tingles of electricity zipped along her spine, hitting her exactly where he wanted it to. Her body became wet and tight, perfectly ready for him.

Shayreen rubbed his back and slipped his shirt over his broad shoulders and thick arms. She removed her own shirt, rubbing her nipples over his back, lightly nipping at his skin with her mouth.

Rey's fingers curled under Laurette's thighs, squeezing until a small squeal escaped her. He rotated his hands until they cupped her core. He was pleasantly surprised when his fingers found her pants open at the crotch. His fat fingers pressed against her, slipping inside her folds, once again taking her nipple inside his mouth.

'Well, that's handy,' a voice murmured.

'I would have never worn something so demoralizing,' another said, seeming to roll its eyes.

'Of course not, you weren't in her line of work,' said another.

Rey growled a warning to the voices.

Laurette screamed and jumped back, falling to the floor. Blood dripped from her nipple.

Alistair was horrified. He wanted to apologize, but he couldn't get his mouth to work. Rey had a firm hold. The arousal pumping through his body sickened him and he thought he might throw up. He reached for her, but Laurette's eyes were wide and she took a step back. Her arms were wrapped around her torso, holding her breasts, blood staining her clean, white shirt.

An apology rose to his lips. I didn't mean—his own words, his own horror at what Rey—what he had done. Before Alistair could speak, try to make it right, Rey clamped down on his will, shoving him back to the dark corner where he kept him trapped.

"Enough!" Rey yelled, standing. He yanked off his pants, letting his erection spring forward. The women exchanged looks—one scared and the other intrigued. A smile curved over Shayreen's lips. Rey knew this part of his body still looked good and worked even better.

Shayreen waved Laurette off. She didn't wait. Holding her shirt in place, she scooted out the door.

"We don't need her anyway," Shayreen purred, guiding him to the bed, her eyes raking his frame. Her appraisal soothed his nerves, the feeling of power flowing through him again. The tip of his cock twitched, the cool air skimming across it, urging him to touch it.

Rey reclined on the bed, positioning himself to watch. Shayreen's curly auburn hair fell over her fair breasts as she leaned over him. Her skin was dotted with freckles, her nipples a soft pink. Her breasts weren't large like the other girl's, but he massaged them anyway, pinching her nipples hard. She let out a small cry but allowed him to keep going.

Her pants were crotchless too, so he moved her on top of him, sliding her slickness against his cock. The intensity of her wetness shot adrenaline through his body, and he jerked. His stomach wobbled with the effort of moving her, and he groaned.

He entangled his fingers in her red locks and guided her mouth to him. She opened readily and sucked hard. He was long, thick, and had yet to find a woman who could fit his entire dick into her mouth. This girl was no exception.

Her tongue ran along his length, casting wave after wave of sensation through his body. Breathing heavily, he pushed her head faster and faster. He wasn't close to coming, but her mouth slickly sliding over him sent him into euphoric bliss.

'Why do men always need to be in control?' someone whined.

'Because women like it that way,' came a haughty answer.

'That is such a chauvinistic thing to say,' said a third.

'I'm tired of screwing chicks,' piped one. 'Can we get a guy next?'

The voices crashed over each other, a dozen conversations at once. Rey's control wavered. Even he couldn't silence them all. He paused his pumping, his grip tightening in the woman's hair. She peered up at him, saliva dripping from her lips as she massaged his shaft. "Would you like me to sit on you, Commodore?"

Rey would like nothing better than for her to continue, but the fucking voices in his head would not stay silent. Nodding, he lay back and allowed her to position herself. She stroked the head, his precum sliding through her fingers. His eyelids slid closed. With a knee on one side of him and her foot on the other side, she slowly slid onto him, settling herself.

Her tight wetness made him groan, and he relaxed, letting her do the work.

"Oh," she sighed, her eyes rolling back in her head. "That feels so good."

'She's just saying that. It never feels that good,' a voice scoffed.

'Then you apparently had terrible lovers,' came an answer.

'I had plenty of good lovers,' huffed the voice.

Someone else volunteered, 'My wife liked it from behind.'

Rey hurled himself off the bed, and Shayreen tumbled to the floor. "Stop talking! All of you!"

Shayreen peered around the room. "There isn't anyone here but us, Commodore."

Rey's eyes swiveled to her, his blood rising. The damn voices would not stop, and he couldn't concentrate. Pointing to the door, he sneered. "Get. Out."

With one last curious look around the room, she gathered her clothes and disappeared.

Alone, Rey finally released his grip. Alistair collapsed back into control of his own body—exhausted, violated, disgusted. He stared at his reflection in the mirror across from the bed.

This was his body, face, hands.

But nothing he'd just done had been his choice.

He covered his face with his palms and wondered, not for the first time, if anyone would ever free him from this nightmare.

Chapter Thirty-Two

Ava watched Rune and Natalia speak quietly, not really hearing their words. Instead, she gazed around the dusty cabin—broken pottery, shattered dreams, the bed where he'd loved someone else.

Or maybe—maybe Natalia was wrong. The Thorben who'd whispered filthy promises against her skin wasn't the same cruel boy—

Ava caught herself mid-thought and pressed her palms against her eyes.

Stop making excuses for him.

This was what women did, wasn't it? Found reasons to believe the best in men who hadn't earned it. Convinced themselves that this time would be different, that he was different.

Were all his acts of kindness calculated? Testing her to see what she could do for him? Ava didn't have time to fall apart over a liar. And she refused to be the kind of woman who ignored every red flag because a man made her body sing.

Ava pressed her hands to her head, fingernails scraping her scalp. She needed to focus. People were trying to kill them. Their house was destroyed—again. And the Day of the Five was—

"Oh no," Ava said, raising her head. "We need to get back."

"Get back where?" Natalia asked.

"To the temple," Ava replied. "The Day of the Five is tomorrow. I need to check in with Zoya. The lost souls will be coming, and the lake is nonexistent. There will be no portal for them to enter."

Rune nodded. "They will need every druid and druis they have to gather the oncoming souls. Without a portal to enter Empyrean, there will be thousands of souls needing guidance."

Dread pooled in her belly. Rune had brought her back from Empyrean because she believed Ava could break the bond Rey had with Van Alst. To try and draw out a powerful druid, on her own, was insanity wrapped in hope.

They said their goodbyes to Natalia. Flip and Gabrie waited outside, but Thorben was gone.

The walk home was quiet. When they got closer, smoke rose from Rune's destroyed cottage, filling her nose with acrid reminders. Inside, black burn marks bloomed up the walls and glass shards covered the floor.

"Another round of remodeling," Ava sighed. "Grab what you need and we can go to Toby and Dáhlia's. I'm going to get my things."

Rune headed for the kitchen. Ava went to her room, refusing to let the tears fall. Her mind wandered back to Thorben. What was he doing? Would he dare come back?

Outside, Flip was convincing Gabrie she couldn't stay there by herself. The mages might return and the house was in ruins.

"I can't go back to the city!" Gabrie cried. "Rachit might find me."

"He ain't gonna find you," Flip insisted.

Gabrie hiccupped. "How do you know that, Flip?"

"The location spell is gone," Rune assured her. "Rachit can't find you."

"Would you like to stay with my friend Dáhlia?" Ava asked. "She has a little girl. You'll be safe there."

Gabrie sniffled. "Really?" She glanced between the three and finally nodded. "Alright." They made their way to the airbus station, the weight of numerous worries on each of their shoulders.

When Ava disembarked in Seráya City, Thorben was waiting.

Ava's breath caught—half anger, half something she refused to name. His skin shimmered in the light, more translucent than she'd realized. Because now she knew. He was cursed, caught between existence and the liminal plane. A ghost who could touch her just enough to make her disappear.

He stepped forward, mouth opening. "Ava, please—"

"No." She held up a hand, her voice firm. "Not now. Not here."

"I need to explain—"

"You needed to explain *before*." Her eyes burned, but she refused to let the tears fall. "Before you touched me and made me feel—" She cut herself off, jaw clenching. "I have work to do. Souls to save. That's all that matters right now."

"Ava—"

She turned her back on him and walked away, Rune and the others following. He trailed behind, silent, and she felt his presence like a brand between her shoulder blades.

At the temple, a frazzled Zoya rushed between rooms. She'd been coordinating with the other temples in the Realms about how to collect the spirits that would be arriving without the portal to guide them. She promised to update Ava once they had a plan.

Since Ava's next concern was the twins' invention, they went to Toby's. If the machine was central to Van Alst's plans, she needed to warn him.

When Dáhlia opened the door, her eyebrows rose, but she graciously let them into the apartment. Aamina peeked around her mother's legs.

Gabrie's eyes skittered around the room. Aamina slowly emerged from behind her mother. She walked up to Gabrie, waved 'hello', and offered her Little Sister.

Gabrie managed a small smile despite her tear-stained face. "Is that your doll?"

Aamina nodded shyly.

"She's beautiful," Gabrie whispered, touching one of the trinkets gently. "I used to have a doll like this."

Aamina's face lit up. She took Gabrie's hand and tugged her toward the common room, already chattering in her wordless way.

Ava's chest tightened. Two girls who'd been through too much, finding comfort in each other. She prayed to the Five that when all this was over, she will have made their world brighter.

Flip and Gabrie seated themselves in the common room, Rune hugged Dáhlia, and Thorben stood off to the side, curiously surveying the group.

"What's going on?" Dáhlia whispered to Ava after Rune let her go.

"I'll tell you in a minute. Where's Toby? He needs to hear this."

Toby walked in fresh from the shower—nothing but low-slung pants, toweling his hair. His stomach muscles flexed. Vanilla and cinnamon filled the room.

Four pairs of female eyes swiveled his way. He froze.

Ava tracked his arms, his shoulders, that easy confidence. It was his casual pause that reminded her they were all friends here.

From the corner of her eye, she saw Thorben stiffen, his eyes glinting.

"Um, Dáhlia I didn't know we were expecting company." Toby slowly lowered the towel, the muscles on his arm contracting. Flip grinned, gazing appreciatively at his tall frame.

Thorben's expression went carefully blank, but his hands curled into fists at his sides.

Ava forced herself to look at Toby's face—only his face—suddenly desperate to prove she wasn't affected by Toby's bare chest. Or by Thorben's presence burning behind her. By any of it.

"We have a problem," Ava said.

"What do you mean?"

"I think something terrible is going to happen." Ava scrubbed her hand down her face. "Could you put on a shirt?"

Toby's lips pressed together. He disappeared and returned moments later fully dressed.

Ava exhaled—relief or disappointment, she wasn't sure. She glanced at Thorben. He'd moved to the window, watching the air traffic with rigid shoulders and a tight jaw.

She couldn't explain his presence to the others. Couldn't tell them about the cursed mage who'd made her body ache and her heart break.

So she let him stand in silence, brooding in his corner like the liar he was.

"Right." Ava wiped her palms on her pants and went to sit next to Rune. "Toby," Ava started. She wanted to have all the information before she told them her theory. "Can you tell us exactly how you came to create the locator? From the beginning."

"Sure," he replied, taking an empty seat. "Dáhlia and I met a druid at the High Flyers Sky Bar. He hired us to develop a method of locating a soul based on its substance, or its genetic makeup so to speak. It began with an idea, a dream really, of pushing our combined scientific and magic capabilities. I wasn't sure it could be done until he came to me with an exact formula for what a soul is once it's released from the body." Toby shook his head in wonderment. "It's amazing really. That a spirit could be thought of as tangible, in a way."

Ava's mind whirled. A druid who wanted a device to locate souls.

"Go on, Tobias," Rune encouraged.

Toby rubbed the back of his neck and continued. "Dáhlia and I tinkered with methods to locate a soul, and we were able to stabilize the chemical properties to within about a mile range. Ava, you've seen it work."

She nodded. A soul having an explicit configuration and a druid who knew how to do it. Her stomach hurt as she processed the possibilities. "Do you know what he wanted to do with those souls, Toby?" she asked quietly.

"He said he wanted a way to find every soul, so that no spirit would be lost."

"Neyá." Rune sliced her hand through the air. "There is more to it than that. Finding a formula for the makeup of a soul would have taken hundreds of years' worth of study and experimentation. A single person would not be able to do this alone. He had to have had help."

Ava and Rune exchanged glances. If someone needed a long time to study souls and create a formula, there was only one person who could have done it—Rey. And the druid who asked it to be commissioned had to have been Priam. They delivered soul locator directly to them both. Ava's hands began to shake.

"He seemed extremely knowledgeable," Dáhlia said, quirking her mouth to the side.

Rune's eyes misted over. She pressed a hand to her face, releasing a soft sigh.

Aamina slid from Dáhlia's lap and crossed to Rune, offering her small hand. Rune smiled, the expression transforming her tired face, and lifted the little girl into her lap. Her arms wrapped around Aamina like she was the most precious thing in the world. Rune and Aamina whispered together, both looking at the doll and her trinkets.

"Is that a silver buckle?" Rune asked.

Ava's head snapped up. "A silver buckle? Let me see."

She knelt in front of Aamina. The buckle seemed familiar. Ava's pulse quickened. "Where did you find this, Aami?"

Aamina pointed toward the shop.

Ava stood slowly, dread settling in her stomach. "Toby, I think I know who destroyed your shop."

"What? How?"

She held out her hand to Aamina. "May I borrow Little Sister for a moment?"

Aamina handed over the doll. Ava carried it to Toby, pointing at the silver buckle. "This is from Van Alst's vest. He was missing one when we delivered your device. If Aamina found it in your shop—"

"He was here," Toby finished, his face paling.

"Why would Van Alst break into our place?" Dáhlia asked.

Ava handed the doll back to Aamina. What had the commodore said? He had a breakthrough that would transform their world. Ava began to pace. "When I was in the city, I overheard Van Alst say to the Magisterium he had been experimenting with something, a new energy, a powerful, revolutionary thing."

"What type of energy?" Toby asked.

Ava's mind spun through the implications. Souls carried energy—pure life force. Gathered in massive numbers, what could they do? Fuel weapons? Machines? If that was what he was planning then thousands of souls arriving tomorrow would find obliteration, not peace.

Icy fingers of desperate fear crawled along her skin. She couldn't let that happen.

"If Van Alst gathers those souls before we do, they won't survive." She looked around the room, meeting each person's eyes." Souls are precious and not to be experimented on. Life is not for the taking under any circumstances, unless it is given willingly."

Her hands moved as she spoke, druis passion burning through her exhaustion and heartbreak. "If Van Alst thinks he can destroy them, he's wrong. I'll fight him with everything I have."

From the window, Thorben's voice came quiet. "You won't fight him alone."

Their eyes met across the room. Despite everything between them—the lies, the hurt, the broken trust—his gaze held nothing but fierce determination.

Ava's throat tightened.

"Rey doesn't value souls like you do, Ava," Rune said, her voice distant. "He's always experimented with them. Even when we were young."

Silence fell over the room.

"Who's Rey?" Dáhlia asked carefully.

Rune's hands trembled slightly. "Rey is a druid. A very old and very powerful druid. I have reason to believe he's bonded himself with Van Alst."

"That ain't possible." Flip stood abruptly. "Only one soul per body. It's forbidden—everyone knows that."

"Rey doesn't care about forbidden," Rune said quietly.

Toby leaned forward, frowning. "When you say 'old'...how old are we talking?"

Rune looked at Ava, then back to the group. "Nearly a thousand years."

The room erupted.

"A thousand—" Dáhlia's hands braced the counter.

"That's impossible," Toby said, shaking his head. "No soul survives that long outside Empyrean or Tartarean."

"He wasn't outside them," Ava said quietly, pieces clicking together. "He's been hiding. Moving between bodies and collecting souls along the way. That's how he survived."

"Like a parasite," Flip muttered, his face pale.

Gabrie moved back to Flip's side where he hugged her close. "Can he...can he take anyone?"

"Anyone that allows him to," Rune said, her voice heavy. "He is a druid by trade, but now has other spirits bonded to him, which gives him access to their powers."

Dáhlia's eyes widened. "Wait. You said 'when we were young.' You knew him? A thousand years ago?"

The silence stretched.

Rune's smile was sad, ancient. "I did."

"How?" Toby's voice came out strangled. "How could you possibly—"

"Because I'm the same age he is." Rune looked down at Aamina in her lap, stroking the little girl's curls. "I've been in many bodies over the years. Many lives. Waiting for Rey to reveal himself."

"You're..." Dáhlia pressed her hand to her mouth. "You're a thousand years old?"

"My soul is, yes."

Flip sank back into his chair. "Souls above."

Ava watched her aunt—the woman who'd raised her, who'd made her tea and bandaged her scrapes and sung her to sleep. The woman who'd lived ten lifetimes waiting for this moment.

"You've been hunting him," Ava whispered. "All this time."

Rune met her eyes. "Someone had to. He destroyed too many lives the first time. Our family's included." Her voice cracked. "I won't let him do it again."

The weight of that—a thousand years of hunting, of waiting, of living and dying and living again—pressed down on the room.

Toby broke the silence. "And now he's here. Inside Van Alst. With a soul locator that can gather thousands of spirits."

"On the Day of the Five," Dáhlia added, her voice hollow.

Ava glanced at Thorben, still standing at the window. His shoulders were rigid, his hands clenched. He'd been cursed for ten years and thought it unbearable. What must it feel like to be trapped inside Van Alst's body with Rey? A thousand years of captivity?

Ava walked to Thorben. They gazed out the window, side by side. Each with their own thoughts.

Below them, crowds bustled and a group wearing gray work suits caught Ava's eye. They paused to consult some paperwork and then began to repair a steel beam on the pier.

"Oh my souls," Ava whispered.

She turned back to Toby and Dáhlia. "The people wearing those suits—who are they?"

"The commodore's special maintenance units," Dáhlia said. "They verify structural integrity of the levels and work on his airships. Why?"

The woman who'd fallen through the beams had worn a gray suit like that. She must have been working on one of Van Alst's ships.

And Van Alst had trashed Toby's shop. Destroyed it. But stolen nothing. Why destroy the place unless he was looking for something? Unless he was trying to destroy something?

The soul locator.

Ava's breath caught. Van Alst's demeanor when they'd delivered the device—savage one moment, then suddenly kind. Like two people fighting for control.

What if one soul inside Van Alst was trying to *destroy* the locator while the other wanted to *use* it?

Her blood went cold.

If Van Alst's soul was still fighting, there might be a way to reach him. To separate him from Rey. But she'd need help from someone who knew Van Alst and worked on his maintenance crew.

"I know someone who can help." Ava turned from the window, her voice cutting through the silence. "Tomorrow is the Day of the Five and Rey will be waiting with that locator. We need to stop him."

Ava looked around the room—at Rune who'd waited a millennium, at Toby and Dáhlia who'd unknowingly armed a monster, at Flip and Gabrie who'd survived too much, at little Aamina who deserved better.

"How?" Dáhlia whispered.

"By reaching Van Alst." Ava's jaw set. "His soul is still in there, trapped and fighting for freedom. I need to break the hold Rey has over him. Maybe then Van Alst will be able to destroy the device himself."

"That's a hell of a maybe," Flip muttered.

"It's what we have." Ava met his eyes. "It has to be enough."

From the window, Thorben spoke quietly. "I'm coming with you."

Only Ava heard him. But she didn't turn around.

"Toby," Ava said, her jaw setting. "I wish your orange byke hadn't been stolen—we could get there so much faster."

Toby glanced at her, a clever glint behind his glasses. "Well, actually... I've been tinkering with a replacement. A prototype."

"Another byke?"

"*Seáh.* And this one is different. Black powder propulsion will get you there in half the time."

"Great." Ava checked her phylactery, her utility belt. "We leave now."

"Ava." Thorben's voice held an edge of desperation.

She turned toward the door.

Rune stood, gently setting Aamina aside. She crossed to Ava and took her hands. "A thousand years I've waited for this moment." Her ancient eyes held Ava's. "Come back to me. We end this together."

Ava's throat tightened. "Together," she promised.

She pulled away and headed for the door. Behind her, she heard Thorben move—felt his presence following.

At the threshold, she paused. Spoke without looking back, her voice low enough only he could hear.

"Don't."

One word. Final.

She stepped out into the evening air, Toby at her side. The landing pier stretched before them, city lights glittering like scattered stars.

Behind her, in the apartment, Thorben stood invisible among people who couldn't see him.

Alone in a crowded room.

Just like she'd felt when she'd learned the truth.

Chapter Thirty-Three

T oby steered her toward his latest creation—a sleek skybyke, smaller than his old one, with a single wheel in front and two in back. Black powder residue still dusted the fyre box.

Ava swung onto the seat behind him, fingers finding the harness straps. At the city limits, Toby yelled over his shoulder. "Hold on! Here we go!"

Ava barely managed to grab his waist before he pressed a button. Black powder ignited in the fyre box with a hollow boom, and the byke lurched forward. Her scream caught in her throat. They soared upward, diving and rising between clouds, a trail of black smoke ribboning behind them.

Her fingers tingled, grip slick on the harness. Wind tore through her hair, whipping tears from her eyes, and she couldn't stop the grin splitting her face. When Toby banked hard around a clock tower, she screamed—pure, startled delight.

Minutes later, they touched down outside her house, the byke bouncing gently on its tires. Toby cut the pistons and twisted to check on her.

"Are you alright?"

Her lips wouldn't form words. She managed a breathless laugh, fingers still locked around his waist.

Toby grinned and pried them off one by one, his calloused palms warm against her knuckles. "I'll take that as a yes." He released her hands. "You said fast, right?"

Ava took a deep breath, waiting for her heart to slow. The world felt too bright and sharp after the rush of flight.

"I...ah..." She shook her head, trying to focus. "Give me a second."

Toby swung off the byke and turned to unbuckle her, fingers quick on the straps. When he finished, his hand paused near her shoulder—just for a moment.

"Ready?" His voice was quieter than usual.

Ava nodded, not quite meeting his eyes. Something about the way he looked at her made her chest tight. Not uncomfortable. Just...aware.

"Let's get you off." He offered his hand.

Ava tried to swing her leg over, but her muscles had locked from tension. She toppled sideways, landing face-first against his chest. Toby caught her arms, steadying her as she stumbled, legs prickling with returning blood.

"Ow," she muttered into his shirt.

"Sorry about that," Toby said. "Should have warned you—if you tense up, the blood drains from your legs."

"That would have been nice to know, Tobias." She glared, but there was no heat in it.

He chuckled, steadying her until her legs stopped shaking. His hands were warm, solid, patient. Toby had always been patient with her.

Safe. The word sat wrong in her chest. She didn't want safe right now. She wanted answers.

Thorben's face surfaced—his eyes, the way he'd looked at her in that cabin. The words he'd spoken. She shoved the thought down. He'd had his chance to explain.

But his curse nagged at her. Stuck somewhere he shouldn't be. If he found a way to be truly selfless, he could get his soul back.

Would that change anything?

Ava stepped back, putting distance between them. "We need to hurry."

Her voice came out rougher than intended. Toby's expression flickered—something she couldn't read—but he only nodded.

"Lead on." He gestured, and they both walked into the house.

The hair on Ava's neck prickled. She paused in the doorway, scanning the grassy yard behind them. Nothing. No stormy eyes watching her, no shadow that didn't belong.

She shook it off. Toby's byke had been impossibly fast—there was no way Thorben could have followed. He was probably still standing in Toby's apartment, staring at the door she'd walked out of.

Good, she thought, and hated how much she didn't mean it.

Toby and Ava entered the cottage.

He paused in the middle of the common room. "What happened here?"

"Long story." Ava left a confused Toby and hurried to her room. She lifted out the small metal rod from a jar. It vibrated in her palm, bringing back the moment when Ava found her broken body from the fall through the maze of beams. She was relieved she could finally give this spirit a second chance at life.

"Let's get you bonded with a new form and see what you have to say." Ava tucked the rod into her belt and headed outside.

The skybyke waited in the dying light, Toby already mounting. She climbed behind him, this time without hesitation.

The excitement of the Day of the Five buzzed through the city. People hung emblems outside their doors representing each of the Magisterium's souls that had been bonded to the Realms: a multi-pointed star for Star Fyre, a sun on behalf of Lyte Realm, wind swirls for the Realm of Winds, mountains for the Black Sands, and a circle with a dot in the middle symbolizing the Realm of Souls.

Children ran past with painted faces, laughing. A woman hung a wind-swirl emblem above her door, humming. None of them knew what was coming tomorrow.

Ava's stomach tightened.

As they descended into the swale, the festival sounds faded behind them. Darkness swallowed the path, cool and quiet as a held breath. The temple door had been decorated, and it opened when they arrived. Instantly, they were ushered into the Passing Room to Zoya.

"Avalína." Zoya rose gracefully from the body she was washing, dropping her cloth into a bowl of clove water. Her gaze flicked to Toby, assessing. "Is everything alright? The other temples are working on a solution—I haven't sent for you."

"They may not need to." Ava plucked the rod from her phylactery. "Do you have a cadaver available for this soul? We might be able to get some answers from her."

Zoya's sleek black eyebrows raised. "Actually, I do have a vessel," she said, gesturing to the body she had been washing.

A woman, mid-forties. Rich auburn hair laced with gray, woven into several braids. A thin blanket covered her freckled skin.

"This woman left us a few hours ago. I can send a message to the family to see if it would be acceptable to use her as a cadaver."

"Yes, please," Ava said. "We need to be quick."

Zoya motioned for a servant and murmured instructions. The woman bobbed her head—to Zoya, then to Ava—and hustled out. "She will return soon. Why don't we sit in an alcove, and you can tell me what's happening."

Ava and Toby followed Zoya through a corridor lined with large arched doorways. The bricks crumbled in places, but the space held its grandeur. The hall held at least a dozen alcoves, all of which had plush seating, a rug, table, and a small fyreplace. Choosing one, Zoya entered and pulled a string that would ring a bell in the kitchen.

Once they were all seated, Zoya lifted an eyebrow at Toby, causing a small blush to creep to his face.

Ava cleared her throat. "Ah, this is Tobias, Zoya. He's a friend."

Toby smiled and nodded. "It's an honor to be in the temple, Mother."

Zoya's stoic expression turned soft. "Thank you, Tobias. It's a pleasure to have you." Zoya turned her gaze to Ava, her smile dropping. "Now, please tell me why you needed a cadaver so quickly."

Ava recounted the events and her and Rune's suspicions of Rey being bonded with Van Alst, but she omitted her own role from the histories. She was still processing that part of her life and wasn't ready for Toby or Zoya to know. Zoya listened intently, the grim line of her mouth her only sign of worry.

"I believe the soul in the essentia I have might know something that can help us," Ava explained. A servant entered, setting a tray of tea on the table. Zoya and Ava thanked her, and she quietly exited the room.

Zoya took a moment to pour herself a cup. Ava could tell she was pondering what Ava had said as she sipped. "As soon as we hear back from the family you may conduct a re-entry."

"Thank you, Mother," Ava said. Ava and Toby stood, ready to leave, but Zoya spoke.

"And as for Van Alst." Zoya set her cup aside and rose, dark eyes holding Ava's. "I have every confidence in you, my Avalína."

She wrapped Ava in her arms—warm, fierce, unyielding. "I loved you the moment I met you. You are a force. An ever-flourishing druis." Her voice dropped. "Be careful. Come back to me."

"Of course." Ava held on longer than she meant to, letting herself breathe in the familiar scent of clove and temple incense. When Zoya finally released her, she wiped a tear from the corner of her eye. Her smile trembled at the edges.

"Excuse me," a servant said, entering the alcove. "An urgent message, Mother."

Zoya accepted the scroll and glanced at Ava. She quickly unrolled the parchment and read it. "The family is honored we asked and has given you permission."

Ava nodded. "Let's get to it then."

The three went back to the Passing Room, and Toby stopped just inside the doorway. "I'll stay here," he whispered. "I'd like to observe, but not be in your way, if that's alright."

"Of course." Ava moved to the cadaver and plucked the metal rod from her phylactery.

She cradled the rod in her palm, humming low. The hum deepened, found melody, became words:

"*Prepare your soul, you are no longer alone,*

Leave behind your past to a future unknown,

Have hope, even if it is fragile and new,

Begin your journey, this form now belongs to you."

The soul materialized—a beautiful swirl of lavender and silver that filled the room with the scent of hydrangeas and rain. It wound through Ava's hair, making her smile despite everything, then followed her outstretched arm toward the cadaver. The wisp settled gently on the skin and soon disappeared.

"Look," Ava whispered excitedly. The body was breathing, and her eyes swiveled behind closed lids. Suddenly, they snapped open and scanned her surroundings, her gaze landing on Ava.

"Hello," Ava murmured. "Can you hear me? Can you see me?"

"Yes," she breathed. Bringing her fingers to her face, she moved them, watching them in wonder. "Where am I? What happened?"

"You're in the temple. We bonded you with a new body," Ava explained.

The woman straightened, the blanket falling to her lap. She gazed at her hanging breasts and long, shapely legs. "Am I...old?"

Ava smiled comfortingly. "You are not as young as you were, but this body has plenty of good years ahead. She is very beautiful."

Zoya brought over a mirror. The woman studied her reflection, taking in her almond shaped eyes. She touched her straight nose and full lips.

"I suppose this will do," she said quietly, though her fingers kept touching her new face, testing its reality.

"It will take some time to get used to," Zoya said comfortingly. "We will be here for whatever you need. Can you tell us your name?"

Her bright green eyes turned to Zoya.

"Estalyn," she said. "I work on the commodore's ship."

"What did you do there?" Ava asked.

"I'm a metallurgist mage. I've worked for the realm and the commodore for five years."

"Do you remember how you fell?" Ava asked.

"I...didn't fall," Estalyn said. "I was pushed." Her new hands curled into fists, knuckles whitening. Something dark moved behind her eyes—the memory surfacing.

"Why don't you start from the beginning?" Zoya asked gently.

Estalyn took a breath and nodded, rubbing a hand over her face. She absently gazed at her palm, and Ava suspected the sensations in a new body were very different.

"An announcement was made several months ago that they were seeking talented magientists to work on a special project for the commodore. I applied for the job as head metallurgist. There were seven of us in all. We were put on one of the commodore's working ships, and we sailed out to the edge, past Dasírli Forest. We were told not to speak to one another because we were working on separate projects.

"At first, the tasks were simple. Mundane. Metal alloys, basic spellcasting. Then they grew more complex—stranger. They gave me metals I'd never worked with and wanted impossible shapes. Eventually, I was told to design interconnected wires that would explode when activated." She swallowed. "I knew something was wrong then."

Ava's eyes widened. "Wires?"

Estalyn nodded. "Their requests seemed strange, so I started asking questions. I wanted to know how my creations were going to be used. No one would tell me anything."

"There were cords connected to each blast point on the underside of the island," Ava said slowly. "After the explosion."

"So, it worked?" Estalyn asked. "The charges went off?"

"Seáh, they worked. Part of the island exploded, and a huge chunk fell off into the biosphere. It drained Oyamnís Lake. You didn't know they were planning that?"

"Neyá." Estalyn shook her head. "But I peeked through the door." She shuddered. "Van Alst stood before a mirror, arguing with himself. Different voices came from his mouth— a woman's rasp, an old man's growl, something deeper that didn't sound human at all, and another trying to reason with all of them. As he spoke, his face shifted." She looked at Ava. "I've never seen anything like it. Can you explain how that is possible?"

Ava's mind raced. Multiple souls, each with their own voice, fighting for control of one body. Ancient, dangerous...and possibly very powerful.

"What were they arguing about?" Zoya asked.

"When to set the charges off," Estalyn continued. "Van Alst wanted the lake gone."

"He emptied it to ensure the portal to Empyrean would be destroyed. The souls won't have anywhere to go," Ava whispered, her spirit writhing inside her, burning with anger.

"Then what happened?" Zoya asked.

"He began ranting about the purdahs," Estalyn continued. "How the family that saved the Realms long ago had robbed him of his legacy."

Ava's blood went cold. *Her family.*

"He was practicing some spell when he caught me watching," Estalyn said. "So, I ran. He chased me through the corridor, caught me by the hair." Her voice flattened. "He said, 'It's a good thing you've completed all I hired you to do.' Then he dragged me to the rail and threw me over."

The silence that followed was absolute.

"Estalyn. I'm so sorry." Ava squeezed Estalyn's shoulder.

She nodded once, slowly, then rubbed her hands over her arms.

"Let's get you some clothes, and you can rest." Zoya rose and helped Estalyn to her feet.

"Wait—" Ava said. "Can I ask you one more question? Do you know why Van Alst wants the souls to stay and not move on?"

"I overheard a druid discussing a secret project with one of the other mages," Estalyn replied. "Tall with cold, calculating eyes. Spoke like everyone else was beneath him. They were talking about a machine that gathers souls and creates energy."

Priam. Ava's jaw tightened and she turned to Toby. "Does your machine do that?"

"Neyá." Toby adjusted his glasses, thinking. "It would take something extremely complex to transform a soul into a usable energy source."

"But maybe he has something that does." Dread filtered through Ava's bones. If Van Alst had a machine that could locate souls and then transform them into power, what exactly were they up against?

"How can we keep Van Alst from stealing all those souls?" Zoya asked, still holding onto Estalyn's arm.

"More curious," Toby said, "is why does he need such a large amount? What is he planning?"

Ava stared at the metal rod in her hand—empty now, Estalyn's soul settled into new flesh.

Tomorrow, thousands of souls would arrive for the Day of the Five. And Rey would be waiting.

She had less than a day to stop him.

Chapter Thirty-Four

"**H**e wants to destroy the purdahs." The words left her mouth before she fully understood them. Destroy the very bonds holding the Realms together. Who would—

But she knew who. Rey.

"How could he possibly do that?" Zoya's voice was quiet with concern. "The Realms will collapse. It would destroy everything."

Estalyn shook her head. "He didn't seem to think so. The voices said using the souls' power would be sufficient." Her gaze lingered on Ava, curious.

"We need to tell Rune," Ava said. "Thank you, Estalyn."

"Please give my regards to your aunt. I will pray to the Five. For you. For all of us," Zoya said. "And for you, Tobias."

Toby blushed but nodded his head in thanks.

Ava and Toby boarded the stepping lift in silence. Estalyn's words confirmed her worst suspicions about the device—but destroying the purdahs? The very bonds holding the Realms together?

A prickle of icy dread skittered through her. Thousands of souls would arrive tomorrow for the holy day. Thousands.

"I need to talk to Rune," Ava said, half to herself. If Rey wasn't the only one inside Van Alst, who else was there? Breaking one soul's bond was going to be difficult enough—but severing them all?

"I need to talk to Dáhlia." Toby's voice was hollow.

Souls. Ava glanced at him—really looked. His jaw was tight, shoulders rigid. She'd been so focused on Rey's plan that she hadn't considered what this meant for Toby. He and Dáhlia had been used. Their creation twisted into a weapon without their knowledge.

"It's not your fault," Ava said quietly, touching his arm.

Toby didn't look at her. When the lift opened, he stepped aside to let her exit first, then followed, shoulders slumped. "Dáhlia and I created it. Without us, we wouldn't have this problem."

"That's not true," Ava said. "Rey is the one planning this. You were a piece of his puzzle. That's all."

Toby said nothing. His silence was answer enough.

When they arrived back at the apartments, Gabrie and Flip were playing a game with Aamina while Dáhlia and Rune made dinner in the kitchen.

Thorben stood at the window. When Ava entered, his shoulders dropped—relief he couldn't hide.

So he hadn't followed. He'd actually stayed behind.

She wasn't sure if that made her feel better or worse.

"Mé veláh," Rune said. "I'm so glad you're back. Were you able to speak with the soul?"

"Seáh," Ava said. "We have news. You aren't going to like it."

Ava quickly recounted the information Estalyn had given them.

Thorben stood close—not touching, but near enough that she felt the chill of him. She hated that it still felt like comfort.

Toby watched the air traffic. Dáhlia worried at her lip.

"He's going to destroy the purdahs?" Rune asked, her eyes wide. "How?"

"By using the captured souls as the power source," Ava said. "And that's not all. Van Alst is harboring more than Rey. According to Estalyn he has more souls bonded to him."

"More?" Rune asked. "I suspected Rey had survived, but I never thought he would have collected others."

"No wonder he is a freaking gearbox," Flip muttered.

Rune dropped her head in her hands and smoothed back her hair, the fine wisps of silver sliding through her fingers. When she sat up, her lips were pressed into a firm line. "Rey was always fascinated with souls and what he could do with them." She paused as if sorting through old memories. "If he has figured out a way to collect souls over the years, he is more powerful than we first thought. I'd bet my crispy garden he can access the magic from each of them—explains how he's had such control in the Realms for so long."

"What are we going to do?" Dáhlia asked, rubbing her hands over her face as she paced.

"Ava will break the bonds the souls have on Van Alst." Rune's gaze found hers, heavy with meaning. "As she was always meant to do. Dáhlia, you and Tobias must find the device and shut it down before it captures any arriving spirits."

Toby ran his hands through his hair, thinking. "Dáhlia and I are on Van Alst's guest list for the party. We can go tomorrow night, find it, and disable it."

"Why wait?" Flip said, and four pairs of eyes zeroed in on him. "There are people going in and out of that ship right now getting it ready. We could snag a few boxes, get in line, and be on that ship in a breeze."

"That's not a bad idea," Toby said.

"I'll take you," Flip offered. "We'll blend in so well, you'll forget you're not actually there to set out party favors."

"Go." Ava turned to Toby. "Both of you hurry, before they stop deliveries for the evening. We'll be here when you get back."

"I better get some extra cots ready for everyone," Dáhlia murmured, going to her bedroom as Flip and Toby headed toward the door.

"Will you walk with me, Ava?"

Thorben's voice came from behind her. She didn't turn immediately—let the silence stretch, let him feel it.

When she finally looked, his expression was uncertain. Vulnerable in a way she'd rarely seen.

"Rune." Ava kept her voice flat. "I'm stepping out for a minute."

Rune opened her mouth to speak but changed her mind and instead simply said "Be careful, *mé veláh*."

Ava exited the apartment, Thorben following. Most metal doors along the corridor had already been decorated for the Day of the Five. A circle surrounding a dot was painted in a plethora of colors representing the Realm of Souls. Others had hanging paper cutouts, beads, or lanterns with the symbols of the other realms, to honor the Five.

She walked without destination, letting her feet choose the path. The air between them hung thick with everything unsaid.

"Ava—"

She spun on him. "Why didn't you tell me?" Her voice came out sharper than intended, brittle at the edges. "Did you think I wouldn't believe you? That I wouldn't have wanted to be with you?"

"No, I..." Thorben sighed, dragging a hand through his hair. "When I first met you, I was shocked you could even see me. You were the first person who'd spoken to me in ten years."

Ten years. The number landed differently now—not as excuse, but as context. Ava pressed her lips together, fighting the sympathy rising in her chest.

"That doesn't explain why you *kept* lying," she said. "Even after."

"How can I trust you?" She held her palms open—nothing hidden, everything exposed. "All I will ever ask of you is honesty."

Thorben's jaw tightened. "You deserve it."

"Then give it to me now." Her voice hardened. "All of it. Tell me what happened." She turned and continued down the corridor. "Not Natalia's version. Yours."

Thorben walked beside her, and this time he held nothing back. The loneliness that had hollowed him out. The desperation that made him willing to use anyone, anything. The souls in the liminal plane—his only companions for a decade.

"When you fell over that cliff, I didn't think," he said. "I just reached for you. Expected you to slide through me like everyone else." He stopped walking, forcing her to face him. "But you didn't."

Ava remembered the moment—his hands catching her, solid and cold. She'd been too terrified to question it then.

"I hadn't touched anyone in ten years," he said quietly. "I'd forgotten what it felt like to be real."

He looked down at his hands, laughed softly—a sound caught between wonder and grief. When he met her eyes again, something had shifted in his expression.

"Everything I thought I knew, you changed in a single moment," he said. "I didn't know what to think, how to feel. Only that I couldn't let you out of my sight. I had to be with you."

Ava raised her eyebrow at him.

"At first..." He swallowed. "At first I thought I could use you. Convince you to like me, and maybe you'd be able to break the curse." The words came out rough, like they cost him something. "I studied you. Asked questions I had no right to ask. Treated you like a puzzle to solve."

Ava's chest tightened. She'd suspected—but hearing him say it still stung.

"But the more I knew you, the more I realized I wasn't studying anymore. I just...wanted to be near you." His voice dropped. "You make me feel whole, Avalína. Even though I'm still cursed."

Ava's throat tightened. She looked down at her hands, not trusting herself to speak.

"I want to be with you." He reached for her hands, fingers sliding between hers before she could pull away. "But I know it's not fair to ask. You deserve someone whole. Someone who's at least visible to other people."

Ava tried to laugh, but it came out cracked. A tear slipped down her cheek—she hadn't given it permission.

Damn him. She was supposed to be angry. She *was* angry. Her tongue flicked out, tasting the salt of her tears.

"Ava—"

A white soul drifted through the corridor behind Thorben, weaving between paper lanterns and decorations. Whatever Thorben said next, Ava didn't hear it. Her spirit reached out instinctively—a gentle introduction. The soul turned over on itself, regarding her with something like curiosity, then continued down the corridor.

"Thorben." Ava's voice dropped to a whisper. "That soul—I need to collect it."

He turned, brow furrowing. "But—my question—"

"Later." She was already moving, following the soul's trail. If this was the spirit Declan had been searching for—

Thorben followed as Ava chased it down the stairs, footfalls clanking on the iron grating. A sign above them read "Level 50, Conservatory and Business District."

The conservatory sprawled across Level 50, a pocket of green surrounded by iron and industry. Trees, flowers, a small stream fed by pumps from outside the city—a garden suspended fifty levels above the ground.

People wandered the pathways, hanging decorations, murmuring prayers for lost loved ones. Tomorrow, those souls might return.

A sweeping iron staircase descended into the lush gardens below. Trees bowed over pathways, creating hidden canopies. Glass beads—spellcast to glow faintly—hung from railings and branches, catching the dying light. The smell of earth rose to meet them.

"I don't see it," Thorben said.

The white soul's wispy tail disappeared into a grove of trees, and Ava pulled the ring from beneath her shirt, the wide silver band mutely reflecting the light.

"It went this way." The cool metal handrail slid thickly through her palm as she went down the grand staircase. Her feet sank into the carpet of dirt.

"There." Ava pointed. The white soul swirled through branches, shimmering faintly in the evening light.

They wandered deeper into the conservatory, passing couples with bent heads and clasped hands, oblivious to everything but each other.

They stopped several trees away. Ava clasped the silver ring, letting a song rise from her chest—soft, coaxing. She reached out with her spirit, offering connection.

The soul observed her cautiously, sliding between branches and grasses, occasionally peeking out like a shy animal.

"Come, friend. Let's find you rest." The soul drifted closer, trailing a scent of flowers, sunshine, warm afternoons. She curved toward the ring, vibrating with recognition.

"Does this belong to you?" The soul flicked eagerly over the ring, looping around the silver band—

Then froze.

Before Ava could react, she jetted away, streaking back through the trees.

"Wait!" Ava reached out a hand, but it was too late. The soul had disappeared.

"What happened?" Thorben asked.

"I don't know," Ava said. "This ring belongs to her, I'm sure of it. Something spooked her."

On the way back, Ava collected two more souls—a soft orange one that smelled of crisp leaves, and a golden wisp that hummed contentedly as it settled into her phylactery. But she kept scanning the sky for the white one.

"I'm sure you'll find her again," Thorben said.

"What if I don't?" Ava slipped the ring back around her neck, the silver cold against her chest.

They climbed the stairs in silence, his presence beside her like a cold shadow. She kept her hands to herself. Safer that way.

At the top, the crowd thickened—shoppers in silk corsets and layered skirts, hats crowned with clockwork flowers that chirped at passersby. The upper-tier crowd, laughing, celebrating, hanging decorations for the festival. Oblivious to what was coming.

In less than a day, thousands of souls would arrive. Rey would be waiting. Everything might end.

"You never answered me," Thorben said quietly.

Ava's step faltered. "What?"

"Before the white soul appeared." He moved closer, not quite touching. "I told you I wanted to be with you. You never answered."

The festival noise swelled around them—laughter, music, the chirp of clockwork birds. Everyone celebrating a future they didn't know might never come.

Ava didn't have words. She'd spent so long being careful, patient, dutiful. And she was exhausted. Soul-deep weary of fighting herself.

A woman in a feathered hat strode toward them, heading directly for Thorben—through him, Ava realized. She'd walk right through him and never know.

Without thinking, Ava grabbed his hand.

The world shifted.

The air thickened instantly—humid, heavy, like breathing through silk. Colors deepened, sounds muffled, and the crowd around them seemed to move through water. The liminal plane. She knew it now, recognized its weight pressing against her skin.

But this time, she didn't fight it.

Because Thorben—

She stared at him. In the Real, he was handsome but faded, like a painting left too long in sunlight. Here, touching him, standing with him in the between-place...he was vivid. His dark hair gleamed. His skin held warmth it never showed before. His gray-blue eyes burned with an intensity that stole her breath.

This was who he really was. Who he'd been before the curse stole him from the Realms.

"Ava?" His voice was richer here too, deeper. "Are you alright?"

The feathered woman passed through the space where they stood, oblivious. Gone. They were invisible now—two ghosts in a crowd of the living.

To hell with it.

She pulled him into the shadow of a shop awning, her back finding the wall before she'd consciously decided to move.

"Ava—" His voice caught.

"I don't want to think anymore." She gripped his shirt, pulled him closer. "About Rey, or the souls, or any of it."

His hands found her waist, steadying her. Steadying himself. "What do you want?"

"You." The word came out raw. "I want you."

Something shifted in his expression—hunger breaking through the restraint he'd been holding. His mouth found hers, demanding, taking instead of asking. They were in public—or the ghost of public, the shadow of it. She was still angry. Wasn't she?

But his hands traced her corset, thumbs pressing where her nipples hardened beneath the fabric, and every sensation felt amplified in this place. His cool touch burned brighter. His scent filled her lungs. She stopped thinking at all.

"Thorben..." she hissed against his mouth.

"*Seáh, mé talé?*" Nibbling kisses against her throat, each word a vibration on her skin.

"People will see."

"No one can see you here." His grin was wicked, those vivid eyes lit with fyre. "You're in my world now."

She licked her lips. His gaze followed the movement, hungry. Every rational thought told her to push him away, but this--*this* was who he really was. Who he'd been before the curse stole everything. And she was the only one who could see him.

The thought cracked something open in her chest.

"I meant what I said in the cabin," he murmured against her ear. "I want to hear you scream my name when you come. Right here. Right now."

If the world ended tomorrow, she didn't want regrets. She wanted to be wrapped in the liminal plane—with him.

"Make me," she breathed.

Chapter Thirty-Five

Before she could speak, his mouth claimed hers. His tongue swept inside—not cool like before, but *warm*. Here in the liminal plane, he burned. She melted against the wall, letting him hold her weight as he slanted his head, deepening the kiss. Her fingers wound through his hair, and the soft moan that escaped her seemed to echo strangely in the thick air.

"Are you going to be loud?" he whispered against her lips. "I can make you scream."

Her breath came ragged as his fingers worked the laces of her corset. He tugged her shirt down over one shoulder, lips following the path of exposed skin. When he freed her breast, the liminal air kissed her flesh—thicker than normal air, heavier, making every nerve ending spark. Her nipple hardened before he even touched it.

He dipped his head, drawing her nipple into his mouth—warm, firm, *real* in a way he never was in the outside world. She arched into him with a gasp, fingers fisting in his hair. His arm banded around her back, pulling her close, and when he slid his thigh between her legs, she ground down against him without shame.

A moan tore from her throat before she could stop it.

Her eyes flew open, panic cutting through the haze. Over his shoulder, the world moved like a dream—shoppers strolling past in slow motion, their voices muffled, their colors muted. None of them looked her way.

A man in a tall cocoa-colored hat glanced their direction, frowning.

Her heart slammed against her ribs. Her skin went hot, then cold. *Could he see them?*

The man shouted—and a small boy raced past, earning a firm pat on the rump as his father sent him toward his mother.

Ava's breath rushed out. Not them. Not seen.

"What are you looking at?" He raised his head, pressing a kiss to the inside of her breast.

"That man." Her voice came out breathless. "I thought he saw us."

"Did that excite you?" One eyebrow arched, amused.

Heat flooded her cheeks. She couldn't answer.

"Interesting." He leaned back, dark hair falling into his eyes, studying her like she'd just revealed a secret.

He opened her corset wider, exposing her other breast to the heavy liminal air. When his fingers brushed both nipples, her whole body jolted—the sensation sharper here, amplified, electricity crackling from her chest to her curling toes.

"I've become used to people ignoring me." His palm pressed between her legs, firm and deliberate. "But watching you experience it..."

She bit down hard on her lip, trapping the cry in her throat. Her hips jerked against his hand.

He braced his arm on the wall above her head, caging her in, lips brushing her ear. "I can feel your heat," he murmured. "On my thigh. In my hand." His voice dropped lower. "I want to kiss you there. Taste you on my tongue."

The image hit her—his dark head bowed between her thighs, worshiping her on his knees. Her legs nearly buckled.

Seáh. She wanted it. Wanted *him.*

She leaned into him, lips finding his ear. Her cheeks burned, her voice shook—but she said it anyway.

"Do it. Put your tongue inside me."

His grip tightened instantly, fingers digging into her hips. The growl that rumbled through his chest sent a bolt of heat straight to her core.

He unbuckled her utility belt with deliberate care, setting it aside. Then her pants—slowly, one leg at a time, his knuckles dragging down her thighs, leaving shivers, as he stripped her bare. He tossed them beside the belt.

The liminal air pressed against her bare thighs—not cold, but *present*, like the atmosphere itself was touching her.

He dropped to his knees—and the sight of him there, this beautiful, vivid man kneeling at her feet, stole her breath.

Before she could speak, he hooked her legs over his shoulders and *lifted*. She squeaked in surprise as her back hit the wall, pinned, spread open, completely at his mercy. His storm-dark eyes burned up at her.

He held her gaze as he leaned in—and dragged his tongue along her slit. Slow. Devastating.

Her head fell back against the wall, a gasp torn from her throat.

"Look at me." A command, rough with want.

She forced her head forward to meet his eyes. He spread her open with his thumbs—and dove in. His mouth sealed over her, tongue and lips and heat, and the world dissolved.

His head moved between her thighs, relentless, and here in the liminal plane his mouth burned hot against her most sensitive flesh. She writhed, but he held her pinned, the iron ridges biting into her back—pain and pleasure blurring together.

Her arms flailed, desperate for purchase. Her fingers found the steel beams overhead and she gripped them hard. The leverage let her lift herself. She ground against his mouth.

He growled into her flesh, and the vibration shot through her like lightning. Her hips bucked against his face, beyond her control.

He fucked her with his tongue, nose pressed against her, then shifted higher and found the swollen bundle of nerves. He sucked it into his mouth. Flicked. Circled. Devoured.

She twisted in his grip, a puppet on strings of pleasure he controlled completely.

The climax built like a wave—pressure coiling tighter, tighter—then crashed through her in a surge of white-hot sensation. Her teeth sank into her lip, fighting to stay quiet, failing.

"Go on," he murmured against her flesh. "Scream for me. No one can hear you but me."

Permission granted, she shattered.

"Thor!" His name ripped from her throat as her body arched, hips bucking against his mouth, fingers white-knuckled on the steel above. She came apart completely, and he drank her in.

In the dark blueness of the plane, her heavy breathing was loud, sensual. It filled her ears as Thorben's tongue gentled, licking slowly and savoring the last trembles of her body. He moaned, low, and it vibrated against her oversensitive flesh. Aftershocks rippled through her—she felt powerful, desired, *seen.*

She wound her fingers through his hair and pulled his head back. His lips glistened, wet with her. When his eyes met hers, they burned—a gray storm shot through with heat.

He inhaled slowly, then blew a stream of breath across her swollen, trembling flesh. The contrast—her heat, his breath—made her legs go weak.

He kissed the inside of her thighs as he carefully lowered her, hands steadying her hips until her feet found the floor. Her legs shook.

"You," he murmured, bending to collect her pants, "are reminding me I can feel something other than loneliness."

Her head fell back against the wall. She had been his first touch in ten years. Her throat tightened. She reached for him, fingers tracing his jaw. "Then I'll keep reminding you."

He kissed her softly, then brushed his lips against her ear as if sharing a secret. "I also need to tell you...your pants are gone."

"What?" She threw herself off the wall. "Are you sure?"

He pressed a hand over his mouth. Following his pointed finger, she spotted the culprit—a small boy sprinting down the corridor, her black pants waving triumphantly above his head.

She lunged after him, yanking free of Thorben's grip.

"Ava, wait—!" He grabbed for her and missed.

"What are you doing running around like that, you parlous doxy!" An elderly woman laden with shopping bags jabbed a finger at her. "I'm calling security!"

Ava froze.

The air had thinned. The sounds sharpened. She was back in the Real—and Thorben wasn't touching her.

She looked down. Corset gaping. Breasts exposed. Bottom half completely bare.

"Vjáme!" The word came out strangled, horror flooding her veins. Before she could move, Thorben's arm banded around her waist from behind, yanking her back against him.

The world thickened. Muffled. The liminal plane swallowed them again.

"Where did she go?" The woman turned in a circle. "You can't hide, doxy. I'll find you. Security!"

Hot tears spilled before she could stop them. *Stupid. So stupid.* If Rune found out—if anyone found out—

She buried her face against his chest, shoulders shaking. Humiliation burned through her, scalding and complete.

"I'm sorry, *mé talé*," he murmured into her hair. "There's a shop a few doors down. We'll get you something."

His hand slid beneath her hair to rest against her bare back—steadying, apologetic.

At least the little thief hadn't spotted her utility belt—it lay where Thorben had set it. She laced her corset with trembling fingers, pulled her shirt down to cover her rear, and cinched the belt around it like a makeshift skirt.

Thorben kept hold of her hand as they walked toward the shop, cloaking her presence, ensuring her safety.

It was late when she returned to the apartment. She'd spent hours searching the upper levels for Declan's lost soul, until Thorben gently reminded her she'd be useless to anyone without sleep.

He kissed her softly at the door, promising to continue the search while she slept. She let him go reluctantly and crept inside.

Dáhlia, Toby, Flip and Rune stood at the kitchen counter, each with a glass of dark, sparkling liquid in their hands. They raised their heads when she entered, and her stomach dropped at the expressions on their faces. Had someone told them?

"What?" Heat crept up her neck.

Toby drained his glass and poured another from a black crystal decanter. "We couldn't find it."

The heat in her face vanished, replaced by cold dread. "What do you mean?"

"It wasn't there." He gestured toward the window with his glass, liquid sloshing. "We got on carrying boxes, snuck back to where Dáhlia and I installed the device, and it was gone. Only the bolts in the floor were left."

Her chest tightened. "What are we going to do?"

She moved to the counter, desperate for something to lean against.

"We need to find out where Van Alst put it," Dáhlia said, her mouth a grim line. "And the only way to do that is by asking him."

"Which isn't going to happen, of course," Toby said, staring into his drink. "Even if he was willing to speak with me or Dáhlia. Van Alst accepted an invitation from the ambassador of the Lyte Realm, and he will be on their ship all day."

"Then you'll need to intercept him at his exhibition," Rune said.

"We *are* on the guest list," Dáhlia pointed out.

"Do you really think Van Alst will let you prance aboard and ruin his exhibition?" Flip asked.

"Do you have a better idea?" Ava retorted.

"Souls, no." Flip crossed his arms and grinned. "I'm just saying you might need a little...distraction. Toby and I had no problem getting on the ship tonight, so it should be easy enough for me to return. I'll be your extra set of eyes and ears, don't you worry."

Toby set aside his glass and nodded. "We can get Ava's ship ready to go so we have a fast getaway should we need it. Ava? Can you draw the souls away from the device while we disable it?"

"Of course," Ava said. "But Priam and Van Alst—Rey—they know me. What if they figure out what we're doing?"

"You won't be doing anything that you aren't naturally called to do," Toby pointed out. "And I doubt they suspect that Dáhlia and I know anything. We will be at the party, as expected, just...with a purpose."

She nodded. He was right. It didn't stop her stomach from churning.

"Let's all try to sleep," Dáhlia suggested, stifling a yawn. "We'll fly fast first thing."

They set their glasses down in somber silence. Ava couldn't speak for the others, but the weight of what they faced pressed against her chest like a physical thing. If they failed—if Rey succeeded—

She couldn't finish the thought.

Dusky light filtered through the window as she lay on her cot, shadows stretching across the ceiling. Around her, the others settled into sleep—Rune's soft breathing, Flip's occasional snore, Dáhlia murmuring something behind the closed door to her side of the apartment.

Her people. Her family, cobbled together from crisis and choice.

If she couldn't break Rey's hold on Van Alst, none of them would survive what was coming.

Chapter Thirty-Six

R une had to try.

She had lain in Dáhlia's bed all night, turning the possibilities over in her mind. She needed to speak with Rey, convince him to stop this madness—or at least buy Ava more time.

Rune had left the apartments early. Her departure had roused Dáhlia, but Rune promised her she would be back.

At least, she hoped she would.

She pressed a quick kiss to Ava's hair before leaving. Rune would give up an eternity in Empyrean to make sure her niece was safe— she had been protecting her across ten lifetimes, so what was a few more days? Her niece was the most valuable person in her life, and she was more powerful than she knew. Rune wanted to take away this burden, if she could, for Ava's sake.

She reached a common space where several corridors veered off in varying directions, signs hanging to indicate the wings of the city. Rey's men would find her soon enough—it was only a matter of time. He had always been cunning and smart, but Rune suspected his mind was deteriorating fast. Her own thoughts were often jumbled, and if she had hallucinations as often as Ava said she did, she was running out of time.

Choosing the corridor closest to her, she walked toward the center of the city. She weaved through halls and passed by homes and shops. The commodore's apartments were on the highest level of the city, located at the midpoint of the crescent shaped multiplex. She turned left and walked a few paces before a sudden shadow blocked out the light. Her heart jumped.

It was about time. Perhaps Rey wasn't as perceptive as she thought.

"He couldn't be bothered to come himself?" Rune called out.

The man moved forward, the dim light revealing his handsome features. His fingers twitched as magic swirled within them. "Van Alst is a busy man."

"So I've heard," Rune grumbled. "Well, I'm an old lady, you know." She waved at the mage's magic swirling in his hands. "There is no need for theatrics."

"Wouldn't be the first time I've been beaten by someone I thought was harmless," he said, and Rune heard a faint smile in his words. "I can't take any chances."

"Very well." Rune held out her hands. The man ran his rough fingers over hers, turning them over. His thumbs slid along the inside of her wrists until he found her heartbeat. He placed a slight pressure against her pulse, and Rune's heart rate plummeted, her vision going black and her legs giving out. She had the vague awareness of being slung over his shoulder before she faded into unconsciousness.

Rune woke in a large room filled with books. They were piled on tables, in bookcases and baskets. Vast, sprawling windows overlooked the city, and from the amount of air traffic, she must be on a very high level. She shifted her hands, feeling the tight bonds grind against her wrists. A tea service had been placed before her along with a decanter of Star Fyre Spirits.

"They said you couldn't do anything to me, but I insisted your hands be kept tied," Van Alst's lips moved, but the voice that emerged belonged to a dead man—one she'd last heard a thousand years ago, standing over her family's bodies. "I know you better than anyone after all."

Her heart hammered against her ribs, but she pressed her lips together and kept her breathing even. She had to focus and see what he was truly capable of.

He reached for the spirits and poured himself a glass, the dark liquid sparkling. He offered nothing to Rune.

"I said the same thing," Rune replied, shrugging her shoulders as if they were truly having afternoon tea. "Why does no one listen to their elders?"

"Indeed." Van Alst's voice was friendly but his eyes wary and hateful.

"How have you survived this long, Vivia?" Van Alst asked. Rune's heart skipped a beat. *Vivia.* No one had called her that in centuries. The sound of it cracked something open in her chest—a door she'd kept sealed for lifetimes.

"The same way you have, Rey," Rune replied, staring at his blue eyes, trying to see through to his soul.

He chuckled. "So, you know who I am. Are you surprised?"

"Not really. You always do what is best for yourself, so naturally I assumed you would remain, regardless of what it cost you." Rune said. "Apparently losing your mind isn't a very high price."

"My mind is clear enough," Rey said. "Why are you surfacing now? If you wanted to stop me hundreds of years ago, you could have."

Rune sighed. The painful rope tying her wrists was distracting her, but she knew he wouldn't remove it. He was right to be wary. She had little strength left in her old body, but she still had a few tricks left to show.

"My strengths lie elsewhere, as you know. I wasn't sure you really had survived until I saw you ascend to office," Rune said. "Something about your face gave you away. I can see the souls fighting inside you, clawing for control."

"And you think that pathetic excuse of a druis can draw me out, is that right?" Rey huffed. "Not likely."

Rune wanted to smile but didn't. Rey thought himself to be beyond Ava's capabilities, and Rune was happy to not correct him.

"I haven't claimed these souls for myself, Vivia," Rey said. "I have done this for the Realms. My ancestors have given me use of their magics, and those powers have helped me rule."

"You mean you stole their magic," Rune retorted.

"I needed it." Van Alst held up a finger. "The purdahs your asinine family erected destroyed our livelihoods and kept us segregated for too long. The realms are cut off from each other, smothering our possibilities."

"What my family did saved everyone." Blood pounded in her ears. He had murdered her family because the council had agreed with their plan and not his. "Without our solution none of us would be here. Including you."

"We had time," Rey growled, leaning forward. "We could have found another way. But the rest of the Magisterium were too anxious about losing everything to gamble on a better alternative. And we've been stuck in your family's 'salvation plan' for the last thousand years." Van Alst's face reddened steadily as Rey's anger grew. "No free travel, limited resources in every realm, and cutting everyone, including me, off from their families. No one remembers it now, but I do. You think that's living?"

"Cutting off people from their families?" Rune hissed. "I *remember*, Rey. I *remember* how you murdered my family. I *remember* a thousand years of carrying the image of them—Rubina's hand still reaching for Dorienne, Neo's eyes open to the sky. Because of *you*." Tears burned at the back of her eyes, the thousand-year-old image gouging through her heart all over again. How dare he disparage the lives of her family.

"Then you will also remember that we used to be *free*. We were able to make our own futures instead of having them squashed by the barrier's limitations." He stood, setting his glass on the side table. "I plan on having that freedom again."

"How?" She scoffed in unbelief. Rey had taken more lives than she could count. Was he really going to gamble the Realms and all their inhabitants to fulfill a lost dream?

"After today, there will be no more purdahs," Rey said, a smug smile creeping onto Van Alst's face.

Even though she knew it was coming, her stomach dropped. "You can't get rid of the purdahs. The Realms will float away if they are not anchored."

"I can and I will."

"There is nothing in this world strong enough to destroy the barriers," Rune argued. She struggled for a way to change his mind, to make him see reason. If he did this, they would all float away into nothingness.

"Even after all these years, how little you know," Rey said. "Souls are the essence of life. They have incredible power."

"But you can't destroy them—they are the very thing your magic is inherently designed to serve and protect." Magic was woven deeply throughout a person, and Rune had experienced firsthand the pain of going against her magic. How could he do such a thing and not tear himself apart from the inside out?

"It's not destroying," Rey insisted. "It's a sacrifice that must be made for us to achieve true freedom."

"How many souls will you need to sacrifice to gain that freedom?" Rune asked. If he used the souls coming in for the holiday, the hearts of many people would be weeping for loved ones they would never see again. The thought made bile rise in her throat.

"Enough," Rey said, gazing out the window. "I've taken measures to ensure we have a plentiful amount."

"A 'plentiful amount'?" Rune choked.

"Let's just say the island is a bit lighter than it was." Rey said, raising his glass and slinging the rest of the liquid back.

"Oh, my souls," Rune breathed, realization dawning. "You were responsible for the landslide that drained Oyamnís Lake. You created hundreds—maybe thousands—of souls by destroying your own realm. And they won't be able to access the portal to Empyrean without the lake. You have cut off their gateway to paradise."

"I knew you would never understand." Rey shook his head, his mouth a grim line. "I am securing the future. You must see that. After today, the people of all the Realms will celebrate my accomplishment. They will call me a visionary, a hero. It will be a time of plenty, of forging new alliances..." He straightened and pointedly looked at her. "A time of new leadership."

"You will destroy everyone you are trying to rule!" Rune tried to stand, but pain shot through her bound wrists. The Rey she had known as a young woman had been cruel, evil, and ambitious. But the years had made him even more voracious for power, consuming everything he was, his entire soul dark and selfish. Looking at him now—Van Alst's handsome face twisted by Rey's ancient hunger—she saw how completely madness had consumed him.

"We will see," Rey smirked, turning toward the door.

Ava could stop him, Rune knew it deep inside. She prayed to the five souls bound to the Realms that they would reach out and protect her niece. Tears spilled over Rune's wrinkled cheeks, and she sagged back into the chair. Ten lifetimes of fighting, waiting, protecting—and it all came down to a young woman who didn't yet know the full weight of her own power.

Ava, mé veláh. Rune closed her eyes. *You were saved for this moment. Now show him what a thousand years of waiting was for.*

Chapter Thirty-Seven

Ava awoke to giggling as Aamina and Gabrie played in the common room. Stretching, she suddenly straightened, shoving hair out of her eyes. Today was the Day of the Five, and they had a long list of things to do.

"You'll need this," Dáhlia said, handing her a cup containing a dark brew. "Drink up and get your ship ready."

Ava nodded her thanks and took a sip. The bitter taste covered her tongue, making her gag. "What is this?"

"My black and tan morning brew," Dáhlia said, grinning. "It will get your blood flowing."

"Hm." Ava eyed the remainder of the dregs. Closing her eyes, she held her breath, and downed the rest. "That was terrible," she muttered, putting the cup on the counter and heading to Dáhlia's rooms to get dressed.

"You'll thank me later," Dáhlia called after her.

Ava opened the door and paused.

"Dáhlia, where's Rune?"

"I'm not sure," Dáhlia dropped a cup into the sink. "She had something to do this morning, so she left early. She said she'd be back."

Ava didn't remember Rune saying she needed to run an errand. Rune usually kept to their cottage and sent Ava to get what she needed from the city.

"Will you let me know when she gets back?" Ava asked.

"Seáh," Dáhlia replied.

"Oh, and can I borrow some glad rags?"

"Of course," Dáhlia said, raising an eyebrow at her. "You really should leave half your wardrobe here."

"I know." Ava turned, immediately slamming into someone.

"Whoa." Toby caught hold of her, the warmth of his hands seeping through her sleeves.

"Sorry," Ava said. "I need to, ah..."

"Oh." Toby released his hold and stepped aside so Ava could go into Dáhlia's rooms. She hustled by him, shut the door and let out a quick breath.

Toby had been her friend since they were children. Why did his nearness always make her pulse skip? She pushed the sensation aside—probably just the weight of the day pressing down on her.

Shaking her head, she tried to put it out of her mind. She had more pressing matters to think about. If she couldn't get her ship ready and stop Rey, the Realms would be gone and none of it would matter.

After a quick change, Ava and Toby climbed the iron steps to the pier. It was still early, the sun's rays glinting off the morning traffic in the airstreams. The breeze was cool and crisp, and Ava inhaled a cleansing breath.

"I'll grab a few tools and meet you at the ship," Toby said, turning to a small storehouse. Ava continued walking, slowing as her ship came into view. The morning light caught the waxed mahogany hull, and something in her chest loosened.

"If I didn't know any better, I'd say you prefer this ship to me." Thorben walked toward her from the other end of the pier.

"Well, you are both very handsome," Ava said, smiling. "Any luck finding the white soul?"

"Unfortunately, not." Thorben sighed and ran a hand through his hair. Memories of yesterday burst into her head and heat snuck into her cheeks. Ava swallowed, her gaze dropping to linger on his mouth.

Thorben stepped forward, and Ava fell into his stormy gaze. He didn't touch her, but studied her face, her lips, her eyes. His skin glittered in the light, and Ava's heart pumped faster.

She tipped herself on her toes and pressed her lips against his. He instantly opened for her, and she ran her tongue over his velvet mouth.

"Ava," he whispered, his fingers reaching for her. Ava wrapped her arms around his neck, slanting her head to the side. One hand found its way to her hair, and he entangled his fingers in her dark waves, gripping them and turning her head more. He trailed cool, wet kisses over her neck, and she arched backward, giving him more access.

A sudden jangle of tools made her jump. "Ava?" Toby climbed aboard the ship, a box of tools in his hands, working goggles shoved on his head. He scanned the deck and headed to the back of the ship, calling Ava's name.

"You need to let me go," Ava breathed against Thorben's mouth. Wrapping his fingers around her ribcage, he pulled her close, stealing several more kisses as her toes dragged on the ground. When he released her, Ava had to put a hand on the railing to not topple over. She took a deep breath and hustled aboard.

"Oh, there you are." Toby returned from the rear of the ship. "I didn't see you. I thought you were in the back. Ready to get started?"

"Ah...Seáh."

Toby bent to open the toolbox. Behind him, Thorben's mouth curved with mischief. "Behave yourself," Ava whispered to him. "We have a lot to do."

"Absolutely," Thorben murmured, that smile stretching into something wicked. Ava huffed but didn't say anything more. She hoped she could be productive among the distractions.

Surprisingly, Thorben was extremely helpful. Ava and Toby worked on her ship collaborating steadily. Thorben stayed close, fetching Ava tools when she asked for them.

Toby was equally stunned and curious despite himself each time things magically appeared beside her.

"Is your friend really a ghost?" Toby asked as a wrench appeared, clanging to the floor.

"Neyá," Ava said. "He sort of...lives in the liminal plane." It was the best way she could describe it without going into too many details. She didn't want Toby analyzing it like she knew he would—she just wanted to enjoy what she had without his persistent curiosity invading her privacy.

Finally, the balloon was stable, and the accelerometer reinstalled. Toby and Ava had devised a system for the smoke to funnel through a pipe out the back of the ship, so they weren't covered in soot every time it was ignited, making it safer to use. With only a few hours until the exhibition, Ava's aircraft was finally ready.

"She looks gorgeous," Dáhlia said as she walked aboard, carrying a tray filled with sandwiches.

"It's a *he*," Ava pointed out, snagging a sandwich. "*He* looks gorgeous. And you're right. We've worked hard getting him in shape."

The zeppelin's cream-colored balloon reminded Ava of a man's dress shirt, the black cables stretching over it like sexy suspenders. His deep mahogany hull had been waxed, making every inch of the wood smooth and shiny. *The Spirited Gent* had been painted on the side by Gabrie and Flip in beautiful thick lettering earlier that day. Ava's aircraft was sturdy, sensual, and made her feel like the sauciest aviatrix in the air streams. He was perfect for her.

Dáhlia tapped her chin, her brown eyes mischievous. "I think you're missing something." She held up a bottle of white whiskey. "If he is going to be our vessel of salvation, then he needs a toast."

Ava grinned and accepted a glass. She could almost feel *The Spirited Gent* quiver beneath her feet in anticipation.

After toasting *The Spirited Gent*, everyone hurried inside to get ready. Everyone except for Ava. Dread coiled tight in her chest, the finality of the day pressing down on her.

"Ava." Thorben snagged her hand before she could go. He tucked a dark curl behind her ear. "What's wrong?"

"What if I fail?" The words escaped before she could stop them, small and cracked. "What if all this comes to nothing?"

Thorben tilted her chin, until she was looking directly at him. "You are one of the few people I know that puts everyone before themselves. After that stunt at the edge of the island, your over-caring nature worries me." Thorben smiled as Ava huffed a small laugh. "But, you have also shown me how much joy there is to experience from embracing who you truly are."

Thorben tucked Ava's head against his shoulder, wrapping his arms around her. She sagged into him. "You will know what to do when the time comes."

Ava hoped he was right. Thorben kissed her gently before releasing her. Footsteps heavy with worry, Ava clanged down the metal steps, Thorben a few paces behind her and entered the apartment.

Dáhlia swished in from the bedroom, already dressed.

"You need to get ready," she said, her fingers picking at an unruly thread of silver embroidery that gently swirled back and forth on her corset of cobalt blue. Her hand, now covered in silver filigree lace, motioned to Ava's clothes. "You can't go in that."

Ava studied the glad rags, covered in soot and grease stains. "What? This isn't acceptable attire for a party?"

"Haha," Dáhlia retorted, striding toward Ava, her skirt of sparkling blue fabric billowing into a cloud as she walked. The fabric glimmered in the light, and Dáhlia tucked a loose strand into her mahogany hair, the rest falling elegantly down her back. Ava thought she resembled a goddess.

"You need a proper dress," Goddess Dáhlia said. "Come with me." She deposited Ava in her bedroom and waved to a gown of creamy ivory.

"Hurry, please," Dáhlia said, using her mothering voice.

"I'm not a toddler," Ava retorted, accepting the dress.

"Then quit arguing with me about what to wear," Dáhlia threw over her shoulder before closing the door behind her.

Ava sighed and shucked off her dirty work suit and scrubbed herself clean in Dáhlia's bathroom. Pulling her hair into a quick bun, she went to get dressed.

Ava lifted Dáhlia's dress, the luxurious fabric sliding over her fingers like water. For a moment, she just held it—this beautiful thing meant for celebrations, for joy. Not for stopping a madman from destroying everything. Tonight, the world would change if she didn't stop Rey. If she couldn't break the hold Rey had on Van Alst.

And Rune was still missing.

A tear slipped down her cheek. She swiped it away, hard. She *could* do this. Rune had kept her secret for a thousand years, bringing Ava here for a specific purpose. She wouldn't let her down.

Squaring her shoulders, she stepped into the dress and pulled it over her hips, the cool silkiness of the cloth making a small shiver travel over her skin. She buckled the silver clasps at her shoulder, leaving the other shoulder bare. Her arm slipped inside a sleeve, the fabric laced together in concentric circles. The full skirt swished as she moved, making her grin, just a little. She had never worn anything so divine and luxurious.

She grabbed her phylactery and utility belt but paused. Where would she put them? In past years, she had stood with other druids and druises surrounding Oyamnís Lake, in traditional temple garb, inviting lost souls to enter Empyrean through its waters when the portal opened. This year she wouldn't be with the temple and there would be no portal.

Sighing, she eventually decided to buckle the phylactery to her thigh and tuck Declan's silver ring on her finger. She shoved her wired glove beneath the corset, feeling better once she had found a place for her usual things.

Dáhlia burst into the room. "How long does it take to get dressed?" She huffed and then stared, horrified. "Your hair looks dreadful."

Ava patted it and frowned. "It does not."

"Sit." Dáhlia pointed to a chair. Ava did, the dress fluffing out in an ivory cloud of creamy air. Dáhlia brushed Ava's hair fiercely, making her wince. She then applied pins, shoving them in all directions.

"Will I have a scalp when you're done?" Ava groaned.

"You complain more than Aami does, hold still."

Dáhlia shoved in several more pins and stepped back. "There. Much better."

Ava went to the mirror. Dáhlia had swept her ebony hair into a large, loose braid that fell over one shoulder, the pins making the braid look full and billowy. Tendrils snuck out in exactly the right places, drawing attention to her pale face. The subdued ivory of the dress made her eyes look even more turquoise than usual. Dáhlia quickly dusted Ava's cheeks and shoulders with a shimmery powder and tutted her off to the common room where Flip, Aamina, and Gabrie were playing a game of cards. Thorben stood at the window, his lips pressed together, gaze fixed on something in the distance.

Flip gave a low whistle, and everyone turned their heads, including Thorben.

Ava's face burned, the pink in her cheeks complimenting her ebony hair and ivory dress. Thorben walked to her in awe and reached out to touch her face, stopping at the last second.

"You take my breath away," he murmured. "But," he said, holding up a finger. "I think something is missing." He walked over to the kitchen where Dáhlia had several large white flowers in a vase, their petals star-shaped with streaks of violet. He raised one to her hair.

"Hold very still," he whispered.

Murmuring a spell, Thorben's fingers danced with his magic. Starbursts of white and lavender nestled themselves within Ava's braid and over her shoulders. He grew them along her bodice and skirt, the blooms bursting into a fan of floral beauty. A sweet and heady fragrance filled the room.

"What in the skyes...?" Dáhlia murmured.

Ava touched a petal, its silky smoothness sliding along her skin.

"So that boyfriend ghost is real, huh?" Flip asked.

Ava sighed, her gaze lingering on Thorben's face. His smile was apologetic, and his hand twitched at his side—the gesture of a man who wanted to reach for her but couldn't, not without pulling her into the liminal plane in front of everyone. "He's real."

"There's that smile again." Dáhlia pointed. "I knew it! What's his name? Where is he from? How did you meet him?"

"Ah, his name is Thorben. I met him—"

"Did he make the flowers?" Gabrie interrupted. Both girls had come to inspect Ava's dress. Aamina had buried her nose in one, inhaling its sweet fragrance.

"Seáh. He's a phytomancer," Ava explained. "Someone who can grow plants."

"Why can't we see him?" Gabrie touched a flower. "Can he make me some flowers too?"

Ava laughed and glanced at Thorben, her eyebrow raised in question. He snagged another flower, his magic creating two wreaths of white, purple, and bright pink blooms. He plopped one on each of the girls' heads. Gabrie squealed in delight, and Aamina rushed to show her mother.

"Beautiful." Dáhlia kissed Aamina's cheek.

Toby came into the common room wearing a form-fitting midnight blue corset vest, the swirling silver embroidery matching Dáhlia's dress. His silver shirt billowed out at the shoulders, pleating in sharply at the cuffs, his pants tailored to fit snug. He carried a top hat of matching blue velvet.

Toby froze when he spotted Ava.

His mouth opened. Closed. Opened again.

"Avalína," he managed, his voice strange and tight. "You look—" He took several slow steps toward her, his dark brown eyes sweeping over the flowers cascading down her dress. "You're. The dress is—"

He bent closer to study the flowers, and Ava caught the familiar scent of his cinnamon vanilla soap, something slightly smoky underneath. His fingers hovered over a petal, not quite touching. "The structural integrity of these blooms is remarkable. They're not wilting despite having no root system, which means the cellular structure must be—" He stopped abruptly, color flooding his cheeks. His hand dropped to his side like he'd been caught stealing.

"What I'm trying to say is—" His throat worked. He looked up at her, and something flickered in his dark eyes—something Ava couldn't quite read. "You've always been—I've always thought—"

"Oh, for the love of the Five." Dáhlia rolled her eyes. "He's trying to say you look beautiful, Ava. Forgive my brother—he's forgotten how to use words that aren't technical specifications."

Toby shot his sister a look that could have melted steel.

"Thank you, Toby," Ava said, biting back a smile. He'd always been like this—brilliant with machines, hopeless with words. She moved toward the door, sending a small wink in Thorben's direction.

He didn't return it. His stormy gaze had fixed on Toby, and something flickered there that Ava couldn't quite name. Irritation? No—that didn't make sense. Toby was just being his technical, awkward self, like always.

Dáhlia cleared her throat. Toby turned and swept a bow to his sister. "And you, my dear, look ravishing as well."

"For what this dress cost me, I better look like the Queen of Star Fyre herself," Dáhlia harumphed. "*Elehí Ècie* has raised her prices."

Toby set his hat on the counter, and Dáhlia grabbed his arm. "Wait—what are those strapped to your back?"

"These—" He pulled out two revolvers, rotating them in his hands with ease. "Are my latest prototypes. I've adjusted the powder on the inside to give a high burst of momentum when the hammer is pushed—very similar to Ava's engine, but on a much smaller, more precise scale."

"Are you planning on shooting someone tonight then?" Dáhlia asked, eyebrows raised.

"Well, you never know," Toby shrugged. "We are walking into the Tartarean den so to speak. We may need some fyre power. I've been dying to try them out."

"Has anyone seen Rune?" Ava asked the room. Heads shook slowly in reply.

"Your aunt is very resourceful." Dáhlia touched Ava's arm. "I'm sure she's fine."

Ava nodded, wanting to believe her. If Rune were to have a hallucination without anyone there to help, who knows where they might find her. Ava smoothed her dress, her heart kicking hard. It was almost time.

"Flip, you are coming, *seáh*?" Dáhlia asked. "Toby has a few things you could wear. Although..." Dáhlia's gaze flitted between Flip and her brother. "They might be a little big."

"Don't worry about me." He waved them off. "I'll get dressed and meet you there."

"How?" Ava asked. "The security will be tough to get through."

"I have my ways," Flip winked at them. "Trust me."

Ava believed him. Flip had methods of doing things she didn't even want to know about.

Toby offered his arms to Dáhlia and Ava. "May I lead you to the aircraft, lovelies?"

Ava took his offered elbow. From the corner of her eye, she caught Thorben's expression darken—jaw tight, gaze fixed on where her hand rested on Toby's arm. A pang of guilt flickered through her, though she wasn't sure why. Toby was just being polite. She would have preferred to walk with Thorben, of course. She threw an apologetic smile his way as they climbed the stairs and headed to the pier to board *The Spirited Gent*.

At the docking station, Ava saw a head of tawny brown curls moving on the deck of the ship. Toby froze, his arms flinging backwards to keep Ava and Dáhlia from moving closer.

"Who in the souls—" Toby reached for his revolvers.

"It's fine," Ava said pushing his arm away. "I figured we would need some help piloting our ship tonight, and I had the perfect person for the job."

Ava veered around him and boarded the aircraft, making sure her dress didn't snag on the railings.

"I don't know how you thought of this crazy design," Mergen said, unwinding a rope from a dock cleat, grinning from ear to ear. "But I can't wait to try it the hell out!"

Chapter Thirty-Eight

After the others left, Flip headed to Dáhlia's room instead of Toby's.

"What are you going to do?" Gabrie shout-whispered, following closely. "You can't reveal yourself. If Rachit finds out, he will have a target on you so fast you won't stand a chance."

Flip placed a hand on her shoulder. "Ava helped us when she didn't need to, saving you from that awful place and getting caught in the process. I can't let her go to Van Alst's ship without an extra body that might make the difference between life and death—for all of us."

"I know." Gabrie's voice went small, her gaze dropping to her feet. "I just...I don't want to lose you. You're all I have left."

"You won't." Flip tipped her chin up with one finger, holding her gaze. "I'm not going anywhere. Not tonight. Not ever. Understand?"

Gabrie nodded her head even though Flip could tell she was uneasy about it. Hell, he was uneasy about it too. Being *herself*, even for a night, would be a challenge. She'd spent so long burying that person, she wasn't sure she remembered how to find her. Let alone wearing her own skin in a room full of strangers.

"Shall we pretend we are getting ready for the ball, then?" Flip's grin felt shaky on her face, but Gabrie's eyes lit up, and that was enough.

Together, they went to peruse Dáhlia's wardrobe.

Chapter Thirty-Nine

Mergen piloted *The Spirited Gent* like a dream, sailing smoothly through the burnt orange sky. Ava gazed out over the complex, surreal city. The amber light gilded every spire, bridge, and floating pier—fragile, all of it at stake. If they failed, nothing would remain.

Ships from every corner of the Realms dotted the horizon, their hulls winking at each other in the light, all to witness the Gathering of Souls. Some had rented high priced barters captained by the Realm of Souls' finest to float and hover in the best locations for soul watching. Others piloted their own vessels from visiting realms.

Sleek, sand-colored aircraft from the Realm of Winds grazed the skyline, their large sails and ailerons fueled by wind mages. Star Fyre ships flew lower, their long sapphire bodies sparkling with decorative silver scrollwork, pure white sails drifting silent through the air.

Black Sands representatives arrived in cylindrical shaped airships, the bottoms of the hulls scorched black from flying over volcanic heat. The brightest ships were from Lyte Realm, their tall angular masts reaching into the clouds while ribbons of color swirled magically across their frames.

The sounds of parties and raucous laughter floated through the air, extravagant decorations fluttering from ships in the breeze.

"This night amazes me," Thorben murmured next to her.

"Why?" Ava, of course, had always loved the Day of the Five. Her heart lived to find these souls. It was her reason for existing, the very essence of who she was.

He gazed out over the clouds. "When I was...younger...I used to think this was a way for living people to have closure, seeking those they had lost. But, after watching it for the last ten years, alone, I understand the souls and the peace they seek."

Ava lightly touched his cheek, her fingers lingering against the cool of his skin.

"I had given up hope. And then you saw me and started giving me orders." He quickly pressed a kiss to her open palm, and warmth bloomed through her at the feel of his lips on her skin.

"You needed something to do, and I needed the help," Ava sniffed, lowering her hand to the railing.

"Like I've said before, *mé talé*," he said, his smile warm. "You are unraveling me, one moment at a time, whether I like it or not."

Their airship breezed into Van Alst's main pier and docked. Mergen assured them she would fly a short distance behind should they need her.

Ava's hand was tucked into Toby's elbow as they walked to the gang-plank. The sleeve of his shirt pulled taut as he retrieved their invitations. Ava fixed her gaze on a flower at her bodice, refusing to notice the solid warmth of his arm beneath her fingers. The guard motioned them forward, and they ascended into the fray.

Ava's attention was instantly diverted the moment they climbed to the main deck, all of them silent with awe. A large hoop hung high above the guests with long white banners billowing out, attached to the railings below. Orbs of spellcasted light drifted through the air, casting everything in a warm, festive glow. String players occupied a platform beside the dance floor, their lively notes threading through the wind. Beside the musicians, an ice sculpture rose tall, the symbols of the Five carved into its gleaming surface.

Women wore lavishly layered gowns of satin and lace, some with leather corsets and top hats covered with feathers and mechanical animals that moved. A few donned small masks matching their gowns. The men were dressed beautifully as well, sporting trim pants and coats with leather gloves and hats. In honor of the occasion, many wore phylacteries on their upper arms to show their support of the temple.

"Van Alst isn't here yet," Toby said quietly as he guided the ladies into the party. Thorben followed, a silent, but supportive, guard.

Ava accepted a glass of champagne from Toby. He offered another glass to Dáhlia.

"I'm going to mingle. See what I can find out." Toby's form disappeared into the throng of people.

Suddenly, the crowd broke into cheers and applause. Members of the Magisterium trickled in, nodding and smiling as guests rushed to meet them. Dáhlia offered a traditional Ili greeting to a tall, tan gentleman. From his attire, Ava guessed it was the mage from the Realm of Winds, Demetrio Metharom.

Another member broke away from the group, gracefully moving to the champagne table, and Ava couldn't stop staring.

"That's Mariyana Clare," Toby said, coming to stand next to Ava. Mage Clare's shimmering black dress hugged her pale luminescent skin, the train gliding along the floor behind her.

"From Star Fyre Realm?" Ava asked, watching as her braided hair swung across her back in several long strands. Other braids were piled high on her head into a crown.

"See how the designs on her skin shimmer?" he gestured. "They use spellcasting to bond stardust to their skin creating a chemical reaction. Over time their bodies produce bioluminescence on their own."

Ava cocked her head to stare at him. "How do you know so much about it?"

Toby's cheeks colored a bit, but he shrugged his shoulders. "I asked her."

"You did? That's very...adventurous of you."

The flush crept toward his ears, and Ava wondered if there was more to speaking with Mage Clare than he was letting on.

Ava and Toby watched the crowd in companionable silence when a thought occurred to her. "Do you think she might know where Van Alst put the device? Or any of the other members of the Magisterium?"

Toby adjusted his glasses as he thought. "It's a possibility."

"Let's ask them," Ava suggested. "What do we have to lose?"

"Valid point." Toby grinned at her, his deep brown eyes twinkling. "It will give me another chance to speak with Mage Clare."

Ava rolled her eyes, fighting a smile. He was adorable when he was excited. Toby took a few steps, but quickly turned back. "Is—" Toby swept the space with his eyes. "Is *he* here?"

"You can tell Toby I am most certainly here, and I can see every time his eyes slide down to your—"

"He's here," Ava cut him off. "He'll help if there is any danger."

Toby nodded, his posture stiffening.

"Hey." Ava reached out to touch his arm. "Everything is going to be alright. I can feel it."

Toby squeezed her fingers, giving her a soft smile. "I hope you're right." He brought her hand to his lips, laid a quick kiss on her fingers, and strode away to find Dáhlia.

Beside her, Thorben went very still.

Ava glanced at him. "What?"

"Nothing." But his voice had an edge.

The liquid in her glass suddenly trembled as the ship shuddered beneath her feet. Large ailerons began extending beyond the railing, the massive wingspans preparing for ascension.

"This is it," Ava whispered to herself. The ship heaved forward, and Ava's chest tightened in anticipation. The hull rose into the sky, ascending rapidly into the approaching evening light. Anticipation skittered through her veins, ready to see the souls in the sky. But also trepidation. If they couldn't find the device in time, the souls might not survive the night.

"Priam said he saw you in the crowd." Van Alst approached Ava, his massive hand coming to rest on the railing. His eyes cut over her form, lingering on the slight swell of cleavage the ivory dress revealed.

Ava swallowed and tried to smile. "Tobias and Dáhlia invited me as their plus one." She surveyed the deck, trying to avoid his gaze.

A turbo prop unexpectedly zoomed by the plane, the wind from its wings pushing against Ava, making her hair flutter. Wing walkers glided along both wings, their sparkling attire flashing in the evening sunlight. Streamers of fabric billowed behind them, and Ava was lost in their otherworldliness for a moment.

"I'm glad you are here instead of with the temple," Van Alst said. "It's fitting for you to witness the realm's greatest moment in history."

"Wasn't the greatest moment when my family and the Magisterium saved the Realms?" The words came out sharper than she intended, but she didn't soften them. Her fingers trembled against her glass, but she kept her voice steady.

His large form towered over her, but she refused to shrink away. "You and your family burdened the Realms with their idea of saving." Van Alst's eyes crinkled at the edges as he smiled maliciously. "She is wrong about you."

"Who?" The question scraped out of her, thin and uncertain.

"Your aunt," he huffed, throwing back his drink. "How deluded she is."

Her lungs seized. "My aunt? When did you speak with her?"

Van Alst's face split into a cruel smile but suddenly contorted. He squinted, fighting with himself. Ava took a step back. His evil eyes transformed, and when he blinked, they were open and kind.

"She's safe," he gasped, straining for control. "I'll do my best to keep her safe."

"Wait—Who are you?" Ava tried speaking to the soul that had surfaced, but Van Alst growled, his hands bunching into fists.

"Shut up!" he raged. His eyes blinked rapidly, trying to focus. Waves of anger, resentment, heartache, and desperate hope poured off them. Her spirit ached to answer.

Thorben shifted side to side, and Ava shook her head. If he touched her or Van Alst, they would both disappear, and that could raise an alarm.

His features twisted again, and Ava's spirit leapt toward the souls inside him before she could stop it. They called to her, writhing in Van Alst's body. She reached out, dipping into the liminal level, striving to see them. A song formed in her soul, swelling and lifting.

But before it could pass her lips, Van Alst grabbed her by the wrist, wrenching her close. Ava twisted against his grip, her free hand pressing flat against his chest. She could feel them—the souls trapped inside him, writhing, reaching for her.

"You will not take another moment of glory from me," he sneered. "This will be *my* victory, and they will honor *me* at the temple. And you will help me."

Ava opened her mouth to demand what he meant, but a petite woman appeared beside him. "I heard there was an attractive man I needed to dance with." Her drawl was honey-sweet. "And here you are."

The handsome blonde patted Van Alst's arm, and he quickly dropped Ava's wrist. "Who are you?" Van Alst growled.

"Sugar, I am your personal entertainment for the evening." She planted a hand on her trim waist, her pink corset glimmering in the evening light. Looping her other arm through Van Alst's elbow, she began to lead him away.

"Wait—" Ava needed to ask him about Rune...and the device. The woman paused and turned back to wink. Ava gasped, astonished to realize she knew this woman.

"Fli—"

"Felicity is my name, sugar, and don't you forget it," she smiled wide and Ava's mouth dropped open. She couldn't believe what she was seeing. Apparently Thorben couldn't either because he was dead silent.

"Fe-Felicity," Ava murmured. Looking at Felicity was like looking at Flip's twin sister. Her hair was the same short cut, but instead of being dirty, it was clean and shiny, hanging slightly over one bright blue eye.

"You run along now, while I handle our commodore." She dismissed Ava with a wave of her hand. Grabbing a fistful of her bright pink skirt, she guided Van Alst onto the dance floor.

"Can you believe—?" Ava mumbled to Thorben.

"Nope," he shook his head.

"How did I not notice Flip was...a girl?"

"To be fair, he—er—*she* was very convincing." Thorben shook his head.

"What are you looking at?" Dáhlia said, swishing over to her.

"Um...Nothing." Ava took a long sip from her glass. She wasn't sure if Flip wanted his—her—secret known. She decided to change the subject. "Van Alst was here."

"What?" Dáhlia rounded on her. "What did he say?"

"He knows where Rune is."

"That swale rat," Dáhlia hissed.

"I need to find her." Ava's voice cracked. "What if she's hurt?"

Dáhlia rubbed Ava's shoulder. "We'll find her. Your aunt is tough. She won't let anything happen without a fight."

Rune knew Rey better than anyone. But would he kill her as revenge? Finish what he started? Her pulse roared in her ears, each breath coming shorter than the last. She didn't want to live this life without her aunt. She couldn't.

"Listen, Rune brought you here for a reason, remember? To stop Van Alst. She would want you to focus on that," Dáhlia's gaze was intent. "Did you ask him about the machine?"

"I didn't get a chance." Ava's fingers tightened on her glass.

"That's ok," Dáhlia straightened her shoulders, staring hard at Van Alst across the room. "I will be damned if he is going to get away with this."

"Maybe Toby was able to talk to Mage Clare," Ava said.

"Mage Clare knows nothing." Toby strode over, a frown on his face. "I think Van Alst hasn't told anyone what he is planning."

"Maybe he'll tell one person." Thorben pointed. Flip was leaning heavily on Van Alst's arm, giggling and drinking champagne like she had done it her entire life. Ava watched, aghast. At the same time, Toby caught sight of Flip.

"That girl," Toby said. "She looks familiar."

"She's from a parlous house, obviously. Have you been visiting those without me noticing?" Dáhlia snorted.

Toby shook his head. "Of course not."

"But her dress," Dáhlia's finger tapped on her glass, thinking. "I have one just like it."

Ava bit her lip to keep from grinning. Watching them puzzle it out was too entertaining to spoil.

Van Alst meandered over to a small platform, Felicity still on his arm, and turned to the crowd. "My delightful friends and guests. Thank you for being part of this year's Day of the Five. It is our one thousandth anniversary."

The crowd cheered in excitement, smiling and chattering.

"When I—" Van Alst chuckled and took another drink. "When the Five of the Magisterium bonded our realms, we couldn't have guessed how it would impact our abilities to grow business, be with our families, or limit our communication. We are grateful that each year, every lost soul from every realm comes here to find peace and sanctuary. We, the Realm of Souls, welcome all lost souls on this day."

A round of applause filled the boat. Van Alst raised his glass in acknowledgement.

Ava's heart tugged, and she gazed out at the horizon. A cloud of shimmering color bloomed in the distance, growing closer, brighter, larger by the second. Hundreds of them. Thousands.

The souls were arriving.

Chapter Forty

A va's hand absently pressed through the ivory fabric of her skirt, making sure her phylactery was still there. The surge of spirits was a small blush of color against the rose skyline. As they got closer, their essences tugged insistently at her innermost being. She moved to the edge of the deck, the souls naturally drawing her.

The spirits flowed forward, a wave of every color in the spectrum—blues, greens, pinks, yellows, golds, lavenders, and silvers undulating in the light. They sparkled and tumbled over one another, heading directly toward the ship—directly toward Ava.

"Oh no," she whispered. They were leaping and diving, tumbling over each other in their haste to find comfort and peace. Too late, Ava realized she was the magnet, drawing them straight to Van Alst and his location device, wherever it was. She suddenly understood what the commodore had meant when he said she would help him.

"Don't come this way! Go!" Ava tried to connect with them, but they sensed her power, and knew she was the person they needed to reach to arrive in Empyrean and their eternal peace.

"What's wrong?" Toby asked.

"The souls," Ava said. "They are drawn to me, and Van Alst will have what he wants. I need to get them away from here—away from him!"

Ava's innermost being whispered to her, insisting she dive into the liminal plane. Her whole body went rigid. What if she got stuck again? What if she couldn't get out?

Her arms raised of their own will, instinctively inviting the souls to come to her. She wanted to hold them, to comfort them, to weave her love through them and let them know they were safe with her. They arrived slowly at first, sliding through her fingers and swirling around her body.

More arrived, faster and faster. Their emotions flooded through her—panic and peace, anxiety and comfort, the bliss of finally finding someone who felt like home.

Her vision blurred with tears, her own spirit rising to meet them. The souls connected with her, coalescing into a blurring cyclone of color. Her hair swirled in the wind, the souls weaving through her ebony tendrils. Scents of briny waters, gardens, forests, spices, and rain bombarded her. Ava was lost in the sensation of them, the feel of coming home so thick it made the tears drip down her face.

Ava's heart ached for them and the time they had been lost in a world that was not where they belonged. A song rushed through her mind. It was a tune Rune had sung to her when she was young. Closing her eyes, Ava lifted her voice.

Her aria surrounded her, knitting itself throughout the souls. Ava's spirit felt complete as she connected with them, one by one.

Suddenly, a small painful tug pulled at her gut. Then another and another, like a flower's petals being plucked one at a time.

"What's happening?" Ava pressed a hand to her chest, her eyes flying open.

Flip bounded over, pointing and yelling. Toby's mouth clamped shut into a firm line and he turned, motioning to Dáhlia. On the horizon, the shadow of a small ship sailed, its position even with Van Alst's zeppelin.

Another piercing blow pulled at her, and Ava staggered. She watched as a soul zipped away from her, toward the small vessel.

"No!" Ava yelled and pointed. "Toby, the ship!" But Toby was already gone. Ava's knees buckled and she gripped the railing for support as more souls were ripped away. Soon, a continuous stream of color was pulled from Ava, the souls unwinding like a multicolored thread from a bobbin into the evening sky.

Ava desperately held on, as gut-wrenching pain racked her body. Dáhlia ran to Ava, supporting her even as Ava bent over.

"Hang on!" Dáhlia cried, flinging her arms around Ava.

Flip stood next to them, trying to catch random souls as they flew out of the mix. She saved several but most were torn away. She paused and took a step back, protecting Ava.

Van Alst walked toward them, his face flinching with each stiff step, as if he didn't want to go. When he was near enough, his countenance changed completely, his fierce blue eyes pleading. The only thing Ava could make out were the words "Help me." His face contorted, and he roared in livid fury.

Ava pressed her lips together, searching for the souls inside him. He was engulfed in a tangle of emotions—anger, pleading, hoping. She narrowed her focus to a single soul. Grappling with it, her spirit pulled hard, wrenching it out.

A soul of deep scarlet erupted from Van Alst's chest. It hovered around his head for a moment and then joined the swirling mass.

Van Alst's eyes went wild with rage. He howled in frustration, flinging himself away from her. He fought against an unseen power, his steps stiff and rigid, as if part of him wanted to stay.

As he tottered, Ava caught a glimpse of the white soul through the maelstrom—the same one that had fled from her in the conservatory.

"You came back," Ava whispered, and the sadness in Declan's eyes flashed in her memory. The white soul slipped in and out of the vortex, Ava losing sight of it several times in the melee. Ava was sure the soul Declan had lost was someone he loved. Maybe even his companion. If Thorben had been taken away, her heart would feel just as empty. She needed to gather her, for Declan's sake.

She thrust her hand out, offering the soul the ring. The white soul spun several more times before leaping from the whirling mass and tucking itself around Ava's finger. The ring became heavier as the soul bonded with it, and Ava breathed a small sigh of relief.

But saving Declan's lost soul had cost her. While she had been focused, other souls had been torn from her, the cyclone significantly thinning.

She was losing them.

"No!" Ava screamed. She had to do something. Shutting her eyes, she cautiously stretched her spirit toward the liminal level. Her soul barely touched the curtain that separated it from reality. The thick surface grasped at her like syrup, and she struggled to maintain a distance. Another soul was plucked away from her, and she fell to her knees.

"No..." she ground out. "I can't...go. I can't..." The old terror clawed up her spine—the memory of being ten years old, drowning in this thickness, unable to find her way back. Another soul was ripped from her, and she groaned.

Thorben bent, his voice a whisper against her ear. "You are strong enough, Avalína. I have faith in you."

A scream tore its way out from Ava's throat. She plummeted into the liminal level, her spirit drowning in the thickness of it. It sucked at her, and the plane was eager to have her, filling her lungs with a wet stickiness. Coughing and gasping for breath, she tried to get her bearings.

Inside the plane, the souls swirled in a magnificent rainbow of color, beautifully serene, and more brilliant than she had ever seen them. They embraced her presence, lovingly caressing her, welcoming her to their reality. Her hair floated around her face as if caught in an invisible tide, the ivory fabric of her dress drifting weightless against her skin.

On the ship, her friends were muted, their images wavering as if seen through a wall of water. Their shouts of panic at her disappearance reached her as distant echoes.

"You're here." Pride and relief wove through his voice.

Ava turned to see Thorben. She forgot how vivid he was in the plane, warm and solid in a way he could never be in the Real—and for one aching moment, she wished she could stay, just to be with him. But the souls churned around them, urgent and afraid, and there was no time for wanting.

A sudden prick of pain grabbed her attention—another soul, ripped away by Rey's machine. The remaining souls vibrated with agitation, pressing closer to her. "I need to help them. We can't let Rey use them to power his device."

Thorben pressed his lips together, thinking. "The only way out for a soul is to be guided by a druis or the prince's song."

As if summoned by the words, a familiar, lilting melody drifted along the current. Another soul disappeared, but this time Ava sensed it wasn't sucked in by the machine, but drawn away by something else.

"He calls the wicked to him," Thorben said, his mouth a grim line, looking out through the thickness. "It doesn't bother me, but I hear it."

"This is bad." Ava turned, taking stock of how many she had left. Perhaps a dozen continued to circle them, maybe less. "What am I going to do?"

"You could harbor them," Thorben suggested. Ava's mouth dropped open.

"I will not." She could go mad, like Rey, if the souls fought for control. Or she could lose her own soul entirely if one of them decided to take over. The risks were too high.

"Why? It would be a way to keep them safe until you could send them on."

"It would be...I couldn't...It's *forbidden*."

"Sometimes," Thorben said, stepping closer to take her hand. "Forbidden acts offer us an opportunity to take a chance on ourselves."

Ava stared into his fervent, whirlwind eyes, getting lost in them. "Take a chance, Avalína. Believe you are worth more than the rules of this world."

Thorben caressed her cheek and Ava closed her eyes, his touch firmer than she remembered. She had feared being consumed by the liminal level for twenty years. Now that she was here, she had two choices—stay or fight her way back.

Ava took a deep breath and lifted her lashes, the dark blue of the liminal level filling her vision.

"I'll be right here," Thorben reassured her.

Ava sighed. She closed her eyes and gave herself over to the plane, feeling the sway of its atmosphere and the depth of its existence. Her song lifted inside her, but it was different here, deeper and richer. She called to the souls, asking them, pleading with them, to take a chance on her.

At first, nothing happened. They seemed content to simply swirl to her song. Suddenly, a rosy, pink soul settled against her heart, melting into her chest. The soul rose within her, a bubbly, cheery voice that filled Ava's mind. She shifted on her feet, already feeling uncomfortable.

"We need to make room," she mumbled. "Can you calm yourself please?"

Immediately, the soul quieted. "Thank you."

Breathing deeply, she pulled the others to her. Streamers of all colors swirled to her, burying themselves against her stomach, legs, and back, sinking into her skin. Ava's spirit panicked as it was pressed in on every side. Soon, all of them were inside her, churning in a quiet, almost peaceful rhythm.

"You did it." Thorben's voice was hushed, reverent.

Ava winced, all the voices giving her an instant headache. "Seáh, but now how do I get back?" The souls crowded against her chest, her throat, making her feel off balance. Sweat broke out on her face and her hands trembled.

"Easy," Thorben gently touched her elbow. "Reach out your spirit, find the surface, and dive back over."

"You make it sound so easy." Ava blinked open a single eye, the pressure inside blurring her vision.

Thorben huffed a small laugh. "It's not, trust me. But you can do it."

Ava jammed her eyes shut, trying to find quiet amongst the cacophony of souls inside her. Centering herself, she stretched herself, hunting for the surface. *There.*

As she traveled back to the Real, a tug stopped her. She looked down—Thorben's hand, still wrapped around hers. He smiled at her, but something sad flickered beneath it. Then he let go.

His brilliance dimmed, the liminal plane fell away, and she was standing on the deck of Van Alst's ship once more.

Chapter Forty-One

T oby's pulse spiked as he searched the deck frantically. People were talking and drinking, unaware of the souls and what was happening. Several druids and druises were guests and concern crossed their faces, one stepping forward when he saw Ava disappear.

"Where in the skyes did she go?" Dáhlia stood, her arms that once held Ava now completely empty.

"I don't know," Toby mumbled, a lump catching in his throat. Ava had to be somewhere, she wouldn't leave.

"The device is on that ship!" The blond who had been with Van Alst grabbed Toby's arm.

"What?" Toby frowned, following the line of where her finger pointed. In the distance, a small ship was hovering on the horizon. "How do you know?"

"I'm a druis, you idiot." The blond woman's voice was sharp, familiar somehow, though Toby couldn't place it.

Toby pressed his lips together. "I'll go. Dáhlia, keep searching for Ava."

His sister nodded, already turning to scan the crowd. The blond woman gave him a quick grin and a thumbs up before she disappeared back into the crowd. He swore she looked familiar, but he didn't have time to think about it.

At the railing, he pressed two fingers to his lips and whistled—loud, clear, sharp.

"Come on, where are you?" Toby searched the sky, waiting. Lifting his fingers to whistle again, he suddenly saw *The Spirited Gent* swoop out from behind the commodore's ship and hover below the keel.

Toby leaned over the railing, trying to gauge the distance. It was a long drop and even further if he missed the ship's deck.

With a swift tug, he spun his hat to the deck. He retrieved a pair of fingerless gloves from his back pocket, slipping them on with practiced ease. A nearby cleat held a length of unwound rope, and he carefully wrapped it around his hands. He'd faced his share of close calls while working on ships and skybykes, but this deliberate leap off the ship's edge topped the list of his most foolish decisions.

His heart squeezed. He prayed to the Five Ava was alright.

He took a steadying breath and leaped over the side, aiming for the deck of *The Spirited Gent*. The wind whipped through his hair, and he gritted his teeth. As the railing came closer, Toby lifted his feet and barely scraped over, landing hard. The impact jarred him to his bones, and he groaned as he rolled. Pressing his hands into the decking, he stood and staggered to the front of the ship. When he appeared, Mergen jumped.

"Tobias, you damn gearbox, you almost made me tank the zep."

"Sorry," Toby muttered, pointing to the black dot in the distance. "We need to get to that ship."

"The one where all the souls are jetting off to? I was wondering what was going on." Mergen frowned and turned to him. "I'm assuming you'll want to get there fast?"

"Is the fyrebox lit?" he asked, hobbling over.

"Yep, ready to go," Mergen replied. Toby opened the barrel housing, dropping in a black powder capsule and then secured the latch. He pulled out the valve, prepping the hammer.

"Ready?"

"Hell, yes." Mergen said, tightening her grip on the wheel. Toby smashed the piston into the panel. A split second later, *The Spirited Gent* burst into the upper airstreams, heading straight for the small zeppelin on the horizon, black smoke trailing behind them.

Tobias couldn't help the grin spreading over his face as they sped through the clouds. Generally, he was a very careful, calculating person when it came to risks, but his love for speed often overrode his sensible side. Flying through the air did something to his insides he couldn't get enough of. Mergen had a wide smile on her face too as she let out an enthusiastic shout.

The aircraft neared the smaller ship, and Toby opened the exhaust valves, releasing the steam. Mergen held onto the wheel to keep the ship steady while Toby pulled hard on the flaps. They quickly glided to a stop above the ship, and Toby nodded with satisfaction. They had built the engine and the airship well.

Below, two people were walking along the deck of the small ship. He waited until they went to the other side before grabbing a rope.

"Stay close," he told Mergen.

"Absolutely," she nodded. "I'll fly him underneath to catch you if you fall." She gave him a wicked grin.

"Gee, thanks." Toby grabbed another rope and stepped to the railing. "Why in the realms am I always jumping off ships?" He muttered to himself.

"Probably 'cuz you care about her," Mergen said, easy as commenting on the weather.

Something twisted in his chest. All those years of convincing himself he'd hidden it well, that no one could see what he'd buried so deep—and Mergen tossed it out like common knowledge.

He didn't answer. He launched himself over the railing before Mergen could say anything else, letting the wind swallow whatever his face might have shown. His shirt billowed out as he swung, once again, onto the deck of a ship. Landing better than last time, he took a moment to steady himself. Two mages stood waiting, glaring at him.

"Evening gents." Toby brushed off his vest, keeping his hands steady through sheer will. Two mages. Two guns. One ship above, one below. Device not on deck—probably secured below.

"Have either of you seen a locator device? I believe it may have been misplaced."

The mages shared a look.

"It seems you are the one misplaced," a mage with rich ebony skin said, his Black Sands accent rolling off his tongue, his esses hissing like zees. The diamonds embedded in his face sparkled in the dusky light. A crisp click drew Toby's eyes to the flint striker in the mage's palm. Sparks danced in his hands and he spellcasted, the embers growing until a fyreball churned in his grip.

"You have heard fyre is the natural enemy of aircraft?" Toby casually moved his hands over his head, reaching for his pistols still strapped to his back.

The fyre mage grinned. "Like we say in our realm, 'Fyre is your friend...until it decides otherwise.'"

Reaching his arm back, he hurled the ball. Toby spun and grabbed his pistols in the same breath. The scorching flames grazed his cheek, the heat searing his skin. Clicking the hammers on his pistols, Toby set his mind's eye on the exact position of the mages. He rotated and fyred.

The first shot hit the fyre mage in the arm, blasting a hole through his flesh. He roared in pain. Opening his hand, the mage muttered a quick spell. He closed his fist and the flames died out leaving a charred dent in his arm. The smell of burning skin polluted the crisp, clean breeze of the evening.

The second shot whizzed by the other mage, his prism eyes wide with astonishment. The heat of the bullet singed his long white, blond hair, close to his ear.

"What magic is this?" he asked.

"It's not magic," said Toby, his grin purely for the joy of inventing. "It's science."

Toby's thumb rotated the barrels, an empty capsule dropping to the deck with a small clink. The mages were wary now, and both took a step back, eyeing his pistols.

He cocked the hammers again, this time taking careful aim. Both mages' eyes widened and they turned, but not fast enough. Two shots, two hits—both mages crumpled, legs buckling beneath them. Howling in pain and fury, they fell to the deck.

Toby spun the barrels, dumping two more empty capsules. He flipped his pistols into their holders and sprinted to the back of the aircraft toward the captain's cabin. He threw open the door and raced inside.

The locator device was there, but it was...different. Someone had modified his original creation. The urn burned bright, drawing souls in and then bonding it with others. A gauge was now attached, and it steadily crept upward.

Toby was positive he didn't want that lever to reach the top.

Backtracking several paces, he withdrew a single pistol and cocked the hammer, aiming directly for the glass canister. He hoped blasting it wouldn't kill him.

The two mages staggered into the captain's cabin, one wielding an arrow made of fyre and the other producing streaks of electricity bouncing between his fingers.

"For skyes sake," Toby muttered, grabbing the other pistol. "Why do I have to keep shooting you?" He spun and aimed.

The fyre mage released his arrow, and Toby ducked, rolling over his shoulder. The arrow whizzed by, slicing a hot streak into his flesh. The pain laced through his arm, and he almost dropped his pistol.

Gritting his teeth, he landed on his knees, shooting. The first bullet hit the fyre mage in his other arm. The second bullet went wide.

Sparky fury lit the electric mage's eyes, and he flung a current. It collided with Toby's torso, making his heart skip a few beats and his body instantly freeze. He tipped over onto his side, gasping for breath. The electric shock rode through his body, his hair painfully tingling as it stood stiffened.

Toby had fallen on top of his right arm, which still held his pistol. The current began to subside, and Toby's muscles slowly relaxed. He painfully curled his fingers around a trigger.

The electric mage approached, and Toby waited, his breathing loud in his ears. A tan hand, filled with small electric sparks moved into Toby's range of vision. When he was within inches of Toby's face, he rolled, aiming upward. His arm was still slightly numb, but he pulled the trigger. The shot hit the mage's neck, and he fell with a thump onto the floor.

Toby got his wobbly legs under him and stood, facing the mage who now had a fyre flail in his large hands. The hot ball dangled off the end of the baton by a chain of flames. Toby cocked his guns.

"There's no need to go overboard, now," Toby raised his hands in mock surrender. "You throw that at me and neither one of us are getting off this ship until it crashes beneath us."

The mage ignored him, holding the baton tighter. He grinned as two more orbs of fyre burst from the tip. Then, with a huge roar, the mage swung the fyre flail, the globes heading directly for Toby's chest. Toby dove for the opposite side of the cabin, and the flail embedded itself in the wood, making the entire ship shudder and groan, the flames hungrily eating the wooden walls.

A burst of fyre brought Toby's attention to the doorway. The blaze from their earlier altercation had spread, and now, he was trapped between two walls of flame and a mage. The electric mage was unconscious, or probably dead, on the floor. The container holding the souls was brighter now, filling the cabin with white light. He had to shut it down.

Suddenly, a blast rocked the ship and Toby hit the floor. Wood smoke filled the space and his eyes stung, his glasses fogging. Wiping his fingers against the lenses, he tried to clear his vision. Putting one hand in front of the other, he crawled toward the locator. Neither mage came into his line of sight as he moved. If he could deactivate the device, he would consider his job finished.

A large, booted foot stomped in front of his face. "Going somewhere, scientist?"

Toby peeked over the rim of his glasses. The fyre mage was grinning, the surrounding flames roaring in delight. He shoved Toby onto his back, pinning him in place. His pistols skittered across the deck.

Blazing white-hot heat flowed through the mage's hands, scorching Toby's shirt and turning it to ashes. The mage's fiery grip pressed on his bare skin, searing his flesh. The heat rocketed through his body.

Toby screamed. Pain like he'd never known scorched him from the inside out. His back arched, chest burning, lungs seizing. He curled onto his side, writhing, fingernails scraping against the floor in desperation. The flesh on his chest sizzled, the smell of burning skin filling his nose. His stomach heaved, trying to vomit out the sensation.

And then the touch of the fyre mage was gone.

Toby cautiously squinted open an eye. The mage towered over him, his eyes wide in shock. A long thin rod of what looked to be ice protruded from his heart.

A large man leaned over him, blocking out the heat of the fyre with his body. The sharp tang of grease and engine oil cut through the smoke.

"Aya, boyo, let's get you outta here." He lifted Toby, his touch like a cooling balm against his hot, scorched skin. Toby's eyelids were heavy, and he tried to force them open. There was something he needed to do—the device, the souls, Ava—but the thought scattered like sparks before he could catch it.

Chapter Forty-Two

Ava slammed back into reality. Her hand shot out, catching the railing before her legs could buckle. Thorben was instantly by her side—but here, in the Real, he was diminished again. Less solid. Less vibrant. The liminal plane had shown her the truth of him, and now she couldn't unsee what this world took away.

"Are you alright?" he asked.

Ava nodded, gazing out over the deck. The party continued—music, laughter, the clink of glasses—all of it pressing against her skull like a vice. Several druids and druises mingled in the crowd, collecting random souls seeking solitude, but those without druidic magic were oblivious to what had been occurring.

Ava looked out at the horizon toward the small aircraft Toby was supposed to be on. A burst of flames leapt from the ship, erupting into the sky. The crowd turned toward the explosion, murmurs floating among them, guessing about the sudden fyre at the edge of the horizon.

"Oh no." Ava leaned toward the railing. "No, no, no..."

"Is Toby on that ship?" Thorben asked.

"He is supposed to be finding the locator..."

"I'll look for him. I'll be back as soon as I can." Thorben dissolved into shimmer and light, gone between one heartbeat and the next.

Wait— How was he going to reach a ship miles away? How had he just vanished like that? In all their time together, she'd never seen him—

The souls inside her writhed and her questions scattered.

Several spirits tried taking control of her body, but she forced them back. This was her vessel. She would not allow it.

Dáhlia and Flip appeared at her side, each reaching out a supportive arm. Her legs had almost given out, and she was thankful they were there. They helplessly watched as the ship on the horizon burned brighter with every passing moment.

Suddenly, the flaming ship tilted, and a deafening boom thundered through the evening sky.

"No!" Dáhlia screamed. "Toby!"

The commodore's vessel rocked hard as an invisible wave of force sent the guests sprawling. Crystal shattered. Someone screamed. Ava's knees hit the deck, pain shooting up her thighs, and she grabbed for Dáhlia's arm as the world tilted. Around them, guests clutched each other, champagne pooling between the boards, the sharp scent of alcohol mixing with smoke carried on the wind.

"Toby..." Ava whispered. If he'd been on that ship when it blew—if Thorben hadn't reached him in time—

Tears blurred her vision. *Toby.* His presence in her life had been a constant, steady thing since childhood—and now that steadiness was gone. The souls inside her stirred, offering comfort.

A dangerous quiet filled the air, sharp and loud. People cautiously stood. Everyone held their breath as gazes flickered across the deck, searching for answers no one had.

The members of the Magisterium rose and searched the crowd for Van Alst.

Without warning, another wave swept through them—not physical this time, but something deeper. It started in Ava's bones, a hum that built until her teeth ached and her vision blurred at the edges. The vibration crawled through her blood, her muscles, the soft tissue of her lungs. She couldn't breathe. Couldn't think. The souls inside her buzzed like angry bees trapped in a jar, battering against her ribs, her skull, desperate to escape the sensation.

Then it passed, leaving her gasping.

Ava breathed deep, struggling to keep control. She kept her eyes glued to the horizon, on the small ship that was still aflame.

"Toby isn't on the ship." Dáhlia's voice was barely a whisper, tears slipping down her cheeks. "I would feel it. He's alive. He has to be."

Ava gripped her friend's hands hard, praying to the Five she was right.

Van Alst stood at the railing, one of the few who hadn't fallen. His smile was a blade, triumphant and sharp.

"My dearest friends," Van Alst said, his arms going wide. "Magisterium—you have all witnessed a phenomenon." He couldn't contain the look of glee in his eyes. "I have dissolved the purdahs. The islands still stand, and we are now able to move throughout the Realms without restrictions. Our world is free!"

A single clap came from the back of the deck. Ava turned to see Priam, a smug smile on his face. The clapping gradually became louder until the entire deck was on its feet, applauding and cheering.

"What happened?" Dáhlia whispered next to Ava.

"He used the souls to destroy the barriers," Ava choked, tears flowing down her face. They had failed—*she* had failed. "The purdahs are gone."

Ava, Dáhlia, and Flip sat motionless as the party revived around them. Music swelled. Glasses clinked. The Magisterium members buzzed with excitement—total accessibility, families reunited, free trade, unlimited travel—as if they hadn't just watched thousands of souls burn to make it possible.

Ava's stomach turned. The islands seemed stable now, but for how long? And at what cost?

She studied the horizon, desperate to see *The Spirited Gent's* appearance, to see Toby safely on board.

"Look." Dáhlia pointed. Ava's airship was a dot on the horizon, but heading toward them, wings at full capacity.

The floor behind her thrummed with heavy footsteps, and Van Alst approached, his face exultant.

"You, druis, will no longer be needed," he said. "And if you would like to keep your aunt alive, I suggest you come with me quietly."

Cold washed through her. The souls inside stirred, restless, pressing against her control—eager for a fight she couldn't give them yet. She squinted, trying to hold them back, to keep them calm until she could safely send them on.

"What have you done with Rune?" Dáhlia stood, tugging Ava closer. Her golden-brown eyes blazed as she stepped toward the commodore.

"I haven't killed her yet, if that's what you want to know," Van Alst said, curling his lip. He peered into his drink, and mumbled to himself, "I will, though. If I can get them to stop talking long enough."

"You kill her, and I will make sure your life is a living hell," Flip ground out next to Ava.

Van Alst's eyebrows arched upward. "What is it to you?"

"She—"

"She is my aunt," Ava interrupted. The spirits rose inside her, flooding her limbs with borrowed strength. "The only family I have left. And you will do as *we* say."

Giving Dáhlia and Flip's hands one last squeeze, she released her friends and called on the spirits inside her. One rose to the surface, and Ava accepted its offer. She grabbed Van Alst by the wrist and squeezed.

Van Alst dropped his drink. It crashed to the floor, shards of glass skittering across the deck. Ava's vision shifted. Van Alst's body became transparent—lungs expanding, heart pounding in syncopated rhythm with her own, blood rushing through veins she could almost taste. The anatomic mage's magic hummed through her, electric and intoxicating.

Pushing the magic into him, she took over his muscles, making his legs move forward, his steps jerky and unsteady.

"You will go with us, commodore." The voice that came out wasn't quite hers—lighter, sharper. "Or I will make your body do things you won't enjoy."

Beside her, Dáhlia and Flip exchanged glances, but followed.

"What are you doing?" Van Alst ground out. "I am destined to lead our new world."

Ava tipped her head, fascinated as the commodore's body fought her, his heart pumping hard in anger and fear.

"Where are you taking me?" he asked.

"Somewhere with fewer eyes." She smiled, and it didn't feel like her own. "I am not going to allow you to mislead these people anymore. Your time is over, Rey." Anger flooded her—hers and theirs tangled together, impossible to separate. The souls churned with righteous fury, and she let it carry her, forcing his body to walk faster, reveling in the borrowed power.

Ava yanked opened a heavy door, shoving him into the captain's cabin. He crashed to the floor with a disdainful grunt. Dáhlia closed the door behind them.

The anatomic magic subsided, and the spirit quietly drifted to a corner of Ava's mind. Slowly, her vision came back to normal—colors sharpening, edges solidifying.

The captain's cabin was oppressively lavish. Velvet drapes the color of dried blood. A mahogany desk cluttered with maps and decanters. The lingering smell of pipe smoke and something sweeter beneath it—incense, maybe, or decay. Every surface gleamed with gold leaf, as if Van Alst needed constant reminders of his own importance.

Ava's gaze wandered back to him as he struggled to stand, his legs still wobbly from her control.

"I have worked too long to allow a nothing druis like you take away my future," Rey's voice sneered, inhaling deeply. When his eyes opened, they had shifted—dark cobalt, ancient and cold. His smile tilted at the corner, wrong on Van Alst's face. He lifted a small bag of powder from his pocket, pouring some into his open palm.

"Run, Druis." The voice that slipped through Van Alst's lips wasn't Rey's—silky, amused, savoring the word like a cat batting at a mouse. "Run." His hand ignited in flames.

Ava frantically called to another soul inside her, but she wasn't fast enough.

Rey threw the fyre ball, and all three women ducked. It blew past Ava, smashing into a table. The flames gnawed at the wood, starving and excited at their bountiful feast.

Ava searched the souls inside her. She didn't have an elemental mage with the gift of water that she could sense. The souls tumbled over one another, anxiously offering their help.

"You will never forget how it feels to have all those souls inside of you." He laughed, raspy and low.

Another flame rolled toward them, low and hungry. It caught the hem of Dáhlia's dress and raced upward, devouring the edge of the delicate fabric in seconds. The smell of burning silk filled the cabin.

Dáhlia screamed—a raw, animal sound that Ava had never heard from her.

"Dáhlia!" Ava lunged forward, but she was too far. Dáhlia was already batting at the flames, her hands slapping uselessly, her face twisted in panic. The fyre climbed toward her bodice, her hair—

Water crashed over her. Flip stood beside her, chest heaving, an empty jar clutched in white-knuckled hands. The mage flames still burned, unperturbed by mere water.

Finally, Ava found a spirit inside her that could help. She pulled at it with all her strength, releasing a spray of liquid. The fyre consuming Dáhlia's dress dissolved instantly.

Ava turned back to Rey, jaw set. He had set flames on her best friend, taken her aunt, and ruined the lives of countless souls throughout history, including her family's.

It needed to end.

Rey mumbled a spell, fyre once again growing in his hands. Reaching deep inside herself, Ava chose a soul that was offering his magic. She breathed deeply, absorbing the power. The magic drifted through her bones, and the air instantly became visible, tangible, and changeable in her eyes.

She mumbled the spell the soul fed her, letting the unfamiliar words shape her mouth.

The temperature plummeted. Frost crept across the windows in delicate fractals. The fyre on the table sputtered, choked, died. Van Alst's flames shrank to nothing, leaving only a small char mark in the center of his palm. Ava's breath came out in white clouds, and she could feel the cold settling into her joints, her fingertips going numb—but the soul inside her thrummed with satisfaction, and she let herself feel it too.

Ava smiled—or the spirit did. She couldn't tell anymore.

"Clever girl," Van Alst murmured. "I see your power. The enjoyment of having others' magic at your disposal is intoxicating, isn't it? Tell me, are you going to keep them when we are finished here?"

His words made Ava pause, because he was right. Feeling the power of those inside her *was* intoxicating. And it had been easy, so easy, to assume their magic and make it her own.

Van Alst grabbed Flip by the arm. She thrashed and twisted, cursing at Van Alst, her skirt tangling in her legs as she was dragged away.

"No." A puff of white escaped Ava's lips, the heat of her breath hitting the coldness of the room.

"Yes," Van Alst sneered, his face changing yet again. "Felicity, correct? Felicity, I can feel your heart, it's beating way too quickly. I'm going to slow it down for you."

Flip unexpectedly pivoted, clocking Van Alst in the face with a hard right hook. Van Alst's lip burst open, and he shook Flip, growling. Suddenly, Flip's eyes rolled skyward, and she went limp, Van Alst's grip on her tight.

"Stop!" Ava stepped forward, the fabric of her dress stiff and crackling in the cold. She frantically searched inside her for something else—anything else. But, one wrong move, and he would stop Flip's heart for good.

Van Alst suddenly flew backward. Flip sank to the floor, her dress pooling around her like bruised petals.

Van Alst crashed into an ornate table on the other side of the room. He brushed off an unseen force from his jacket, the fabric ripped.

"I couldn't find Toby," Thorben said to her, appearing by her side. "I'm sorry."

Ava nodded once. She couldn't think about Toby. Not yet. Not if she wanted to keep standing.

Van Alst frowned at his now ruined coat. "You are all so short sighted! Why can't you see what I've done is for the Realms? For you? For us?" He hefted himself up, smoothing his hair away from his face. "Ava, we are a pair of unique individuals, the only ones who can harbor spirits in this way. Can't you see that *we* hold the power here? Your druidic magic is even stronger than mine. I have never seen a person able to do what I can do."

He took a step toward her, offering his hand, his words churning in her mind. "We can do this together. We can build our new world—make it beautiful, flourishing, available to every person in every realm to enjoy."

Ava studied his eyes—bright, blue, intelligent. Scheming and hopeful in equal measure. He lifted his hand a little higher.

"Together, we can make this world the way it should have been from the beginning."

The souls inside her buzzed, restless with warning. She could feel their distrust like a pressure behind her eyes, a chorus of no, no, no thrumming through her blood. But beneath that—beneath their fear—she felt her own exhaustion. Her own desperate need for this to be over.

What he said made sense. In the way poison made sense when you were dying of thirst.

She took his hand.

"No!" Dáhlia leapt forward, but Van Alst was already dissolving into shimmer and shadow, pulling Ava with him.

Chapter Forty-Three

D ropping into the liminal level was easier this time—but something was wrong. The familiar thickness pressed against her, yet the space itself was different. Darker. Emptier. No souls drifted past. No faint glow from the world above. Rey hadn't just pulled her into the plane; he'd dragged her somewhere deep, somewhere she'd never been.

She breathed deep, forcing her pulse to steady. Her body remembered this place, its imprint from the last journey still on her skin. But Thorben wasn't here. She couldn't see anyone except Rey.

Beside her, he chuckled. "See? Powerful. It took me years to master that."

His fingers tightened around hers. She glanced down—still holding his hand—and her stomach turned.

"What you fail to understand, Rey," Ava said, squeezing his hand in return. "Is that I only want to be in this level to understand it, to make me a better druis, rather than to rule it."

The smile on his face tipped, and before he could retract his hand, Ava drew on the souls' magic inside her. His body became translucent—lungs, veins, the steady pump of his heart, all of it laid bare. All of it hers to control.

She focused on the liquid, cooling it, freezing it, the cold melding her hand to his. Van Alst screamed.

"You've always had a cold soul," she murmured. "A druid who would murder a family simply because he was afraid of them." Ava murmured more spells the souls told her. "A true coward, only able to take what he wanted by imprisoning others to do his bidding."

Van Alst dropped to the floor of the plane, his body flailing to be free of her grip.

"The souls inside you deserve their afterlife," Ava said, "wherever it may be."

A haunting melody drifted along the thick waves surrounding them, and Ava considered the murky blueness. She tipped her head, listening.

"Do you hear that?" Ava's grin felt wrong on her face—too wide, too sharp. The giddy madness was partly hers and partly theirs, tangled together, and she let herself sink into it. Just for a moment. Just to feel the power. "That is the prince's song. And he only calls to those souls who are corrupt. Will you answer it, Rey?"

"No!" Van Alst's hand and arm were completely blue, the fingers ice white. His face contorted with emotions of rage, pain, and terror. "I won't go! This body is..."

Ava let her druidic power rise. Her voice swelled from somewhere deep inside her—powerful, clear, echoing through the thick air like a bell struck underwater.

"No—make it stop—" His voice cracked, desperate. "I can't go there. I don't belong. I'm a druid."

A soul of deep russet brown surged from inside him, his body jerking in refusal. It zipped away, following the prince's melody.

Another followed—glittery blue and white. Then two more: one burning orange and red, the other a deep violet. All of them vanishing into the fog, answering the call.

"How many more?" Ava ground out. Sweat slicked her palms despite the cold.

"No more..." Van Alst murmured. Attempting to stand, he used his good arm to lift his body, his other arm frostbitten and immobile. Ava reached her spirit out, searching him.

"Liar!" Ava screamed. She pulled on the other souls inside Van Alst, her voice surrounding them in a thick cloak of sound. Van Alst writhed on the ground, and two more erupted from him.

Van Alst sprang forward, grasping her wrist with his good arm.

The plane *shifted.*

Ava's ears popped. Pressure slammed against her chest, her lungs—like being dragged underwater without warning. She was falling, dropping through layers of thick, syrupy fog, the darkness swallowing everything until she landed in a space so cold and empty it felt like the bottom of a well.

He laughed—a mad, delirious sound that echoed from everywhere and nowhere.

"You forget, *druis*," Van Alst spat. "I have been doing this far longer than you." He opened his mouth and began to sing, his voice deep and rich, full of longing and trust.

Ava staggered back, trying to escape the overpowering weight of his song. The floor sucked at her feet with every step, thick and clinging, and she tripped, landing hard.

Thorben—

She searched the haze frantically, straining for any glimpse of him. But this wasn't the plane she knew. Rey had dragged her somewhere deeper, somewhere Thorben wouldn't find them. She was alone.

Something yanked at her core—a hook buried deep, *pulling*. Ava doubled over, bile rising in her throat, as a faint white-pink soul tore free from her chest and drifted into the ether.

He was stealing them. Her souls.

"The liminal level has many layers to it," Van Alst said, suddenly beside her, very close to her ear. "You would know had you studied it as long as I have."

Ava squinted her eyes, his voice echoing through her mind. "You have sacrificed the souls of others for your personal gain," she gritted out. "What you have done goes against the very thing druidic magic represents."

"Sacrifice is necessary for change," Van Alst said. "But sacrifice without gaining change—that is the worst possible outcome."

More souls ripped free—three, four, she lost count. Each one left a hollow ache behind, a coldness where warmth had been. Her arms wrapped over her waist as if she could hold herself together. The crowded fullness she'd carried since the harboring was gone, replaced by a terrible, echoing emptiness.

She struggled to stay conscious.

"Now you know what it is like to have something ripped away from you," he sneered. "I will make sure you don't return."

Ava's heart thrummed wildly in her chest. Her vision swam. Her head pounded. Her legs refused to work. She was a heap of ivory skirts on the cold ground, hollowed out and helpless.

"I believe we have them all, save one." Van Alst smiled. "Yours."

Van Alst whispered a song, a bold, sweet melody that pierced Ava's spirit. She screamed, her body feeling as if it were ripping in two from the inside out. Her ears rang with pain, her fingers and toes numbing.

The fluted melody drifted into her consciousness, sweet and terrifying. The music spoke to her, offering comfort and something else—words she somehow understood.

Ava stopped screaming long enough to listen. Her lips moved, her voice barely a whisper, shaping the song the prince gave her.

"*You sold your soul for a price, commodore,*

Long ago, in fear.

Now, you must answer to the prince,

For your lifelong debt is near."

Van Alst's eyes became wild when he heard the prince's melody. Ava's voice mingled with it, dancing and harmonizing. Her eyes closed in weariness, but she sang on, reaching, pulling, striving to free him from the body he had claimed to be his own.

"Get out!" Van Alst screamed, his true voice emerging. His face had changed, contorted in righteous anger. "You cannot control me anymore!"

A black and red ribbon burst from inside him. Van Alst slumped onto the ground, his eyes rolling into the back of his head. The black and red soul zipped through the air, frantically searching for somewhere to go.

"He's all yours, prince," Ava whispered. The flute melody surrounded them, and the soul whirred anxiously, trying desperately to escape the sound. Ava released one last note, claiming the final chord of their melody, sealing Rey's soul into the darkness, into the depths of Tartarean.

Ava slumped forward. The quiet that followed was absolute—a ringing emptiness where the battle had been. Tears leaked from the corners of her eyes and she focused on simply breathing.

Van Alst lay near her, unconscious. Ava reached out, wanting confirmation. There was a single soul left in him and it felt...peaceful. Sighing, Ava pressed herself into a sitting position and surveyed the plane.

She couldn't see anything in any direction, dark blue mist surrounding her on all sides. The silence was absolute.

"Thorben?" Ava's voice cracked, and it echoed back to her in the thickness. "How am I going to get us out of here?" she mumbled. Another moan made her glance toward Van Alst. She scooted over to him and pressed a hand to his forehead. His skin was dry and cool.

"Where am I?" He whispered, his eyes fluttering open.

"In the liminal level."

He sat up, wincing. His arm was still frozen, and he touched it delicately with his other hand. "I..." he whispered, his voice velvet soft. "I can feel," he tried moving his other arm, but grimaced with pain. "Sort of."

"Do you know your name?"

Van Alst lifted his bright blue eyes, stunned revelation inside them. "They're gone."

"Who?" Ava tipped her head.

"The ancestors." A content, relieved grin filled his face. "I've been controlled by them since I was a youth."

"What is your name?" she asked again.

"I'm Alistair," he replied. "Alistair Van Alst VII."

"Well, Alistair Van Alst VII," Ava forced herself to stand, her beautiful ivory dress now torn and wrinkled. The flowers had written their farewells in long streaks of dark purple pollen in smudges and smears on her gown. She sighed. "I'm afraid we are in a place I don't know how to leave." Smiling at him, she offered him her hand. "At least I'm not alone this time."

"We're stuck?" Alistair's gaze flitted back and forth.

"For now," Ava said, choosing a direction to walk. "Let's see what this place is made of."

Ava and Alistair explored, him cradling his frozen arm and Ava wandering in confusion. No matter which way they walked, it seemed they were getting nowhere, every place looking the exact same. Dark blue fog surrounded them, thick and sticky.

Ava turned to Alistair. "Did you hear that?"

He paused to listen. "I don't hear anything."

Ava was certain she heard someone calling her name. "It's Thorben!" Ava raced toward his voice, but encountered only more empty space, his voice never reaching nearer.

"How...? I don't understand," Ava stopped to catch her breath. "He has to be here somewhere."

"It's more likely an echo," Alistair said.

Ava raised an eyebrow.

"The ancestors bonded with my body when I was very young," Alistair said. "They were always making me do things that got me into trouble. One day, as punishment, I was put in an old helium cave." He shifted his arm and Ava could tell he was in pain, even though he said nothing about it. "The cave echoed, and everything seemed like it was coming from everywhere all at once. Echoes are fascinating things. Have you ever studied them?"

Ava shook her head, wishing he would get to the point.

"Sound reverberates off particles in the air. If a sound is made at a high pitch, or frequency, it will cut through the space, without an echo."

"How do you know all this?"

"After the cave incident, I decided to try and prepare myself in case I got stuck in a situation like that again. I spent a lot of Rey's sleeping hours awake, studying and reading, trying desperately to find a way to get rid of him and the ancestors. I have no magic of my own, and he and the others took over almost every part of me. But, I still had my intelligence, so I researched, hoping and praying that someday I would learn something that would set me free."

Ava remembered what it had been like having multiple souls inside her. How easy it would have been for them to overtake her, losing her own voice in the process. Alistair's life had been miserable, and yet he had hope.

Ava didn't want to let that hope die. Taking a deep breath, she opened her mouth, filling her lungs with as much air as she could.

And she sang.

The high-pitched sound cut through the thick air making Alistair cover his ears. Her own ears rang with the noise, but she kept on. Closing her eyes, she focused, pushing from her diaphragm, measuring the amount of air she had in her lungs as the sound went on and on. Her throat burned, but she continued until she had no breath left.

When her voice stopped, the silence was deafening. She inhaled huge amounts of air, grimacing as the pain in her stomach chastised her for working it so hard.

"Avalína?" Thorben's voice burst through the void, and Ava almost cried in relief. "Mé talé, is that you?"

"Thorben!" Ava's voice scratched, but she moved forward. His frame emerged from the blue ether, and she threw herself into his arms.

"I heard your voice." He breathed against her hair. "I've been looking for you."

Ava leaned back, pressing a kiss to his lips. "We need to get out of here and back to the ship. Can you help?"

Alistair took a step backward as Thorben's burning gaze found him. "You want to take him back?"

"Alistair is all that is left," Ava said. "He needs medical help. And he needs to get home, like I do."

"You need to send your spirit upward, not outward," he said. "Reach with your soul, Ava. Feel the level's surface far above you."

Ava reached out a hand to Alistair and turned to Thorben. "Can I take you with me?"

Something flickered across his face—hope, maybe, or the ghost of it. Then he shook his head and stepped back. "I thought you might be able to. I tried, last time—held your hand as long as I could." His mouth curved, sad and knowing. "But I only held you back."

"Thorben—"

"Go on." He lifted his chin, but his eyes were bright. "I'll still be here."

Ava pressed her lips together. She desperately wanted to find a way to help Thorben, but right now Alistair needed to return.

I'll come back for you, she thought fiercely. *I'll find a way.*

She stretched out her spirit, searching for the edge of the plane. When she thought she couldn't stretch anymore, the curtain between realms brushed against her soul. Breathing a sigh of relief, she grasped Alistair's hand and together, they passed through.

"Ava!" Dáhlia exclaimed as she suddenly appeared, Alistair beside her, both of them falling to the floor.

"I think he blacked out," Ava mumbled, pressing her hands to her face. The light here was blindingly bright compared to the dullness of the liminal plane.

"What happened?" Flip asked, keeping a wary eye on the commodore.

"Rey is gone," Ava said, "along with the other souls."

"So...who's in there then?" Flip lifted her chin.

"It's Alistair Van Alst," Ava replied. "He needs medical attention. He's not a threat."

Flip pursed her lips, but said nothing, glaring at the injured man.

Dáhlia glanced sideways at the blond woman. Her eyes went wide. "That is my dress! How did you—?"

"I was planning on returning it." Flip shrugged, mouth curving. "Eventually."

"Flip?"

"In the flesh, Lady Wynnstan." She winked.

Dáhlia's mouth opened. Closed. Opened again. "Oh, my souls. Wait until Toby hears about this."

"Where is Toby?" Ava asked.

"I don't know," Dáhlia said, her voice catching. "Mergen should be here any minute."

"Let's go," Ava headed for the door.

The three of them filed out and pressed against the railing as The Spirited Gent swept past. Mergen was at the helm, waving to them and shouting. Ava's gaze focused on her friend's lips, struggling to make out the words.

"Dáhlia," Ava turned to her friend. "Mergen said—"

"I know." Dáhlia's voice broke. "He's not on board. But he isn't dead—he isn't. I would feel it, Ava. I would know." Her fist pressed against her chest. "In here. I would know."

Ava hugged Dáhlia, and Flip reached around her other side. Together, they stood, looking out at the ships and the peach-colored sky, hoping and praying that Toby was out there somewhere, safe.

"We'll find him," Ava assured her with a gentle squeeze. "I promise." Dáhlia's hair rubbed against her bare shoulder as she nodded. Ava gave Flip a quick watch-over-her look before she turned toward the bow of the ship.

"Where are you going?" Dáhlia asked.

"I'm getting on my ship and going to look for Toby."

"I'm coming too." Dáhlia picked up her skirts and followed Ava, their shoes clicking loudly on the deck. Ava waved at Mergen, miming that they wanted to board.

A shadow fell across her path. Druid Priam stood before her, an antique box cradled in his hands like something precious. His smile didn't reach his eyes.

"Avalína. How fortuitous."

Ava's heart lurched into her throat, and she shoved Dáhlia behind her. "What do you want, Priam?"

"A moment, is all." Priam scanned Dáhlia, but quickly dismissed her. He took two steps closer, his cruel, dull brown eyes crinkling at the corners as he smiled.

"You masterfully moved Rey to the next life, so thank you for that. He was becoming difficult to deal with. However, I did agree with him on one thing."

"What is that?" Ava wedged herself further between Dáhlia and Priam, her hand gripping the ship's railing. Priam could do what he wanted to her, but Ava wouldn't let him touch Dáhlia.

"You are no longer needed." His palm connected with her chest—a sharp, brutal shove—and Ava went over the railing.

Chapter Forty-Four

T horben had been watching from the liminal plane, helpless, when Priam's palm connected with Ava's chest.

The shove. The railing. Her body tipping backward into nothing.

His mind went blank. Ten years of isolation, of careful planning and desperate hope—now, none of it mattered. Except the woman falling through the sky.

"No!" The scream tore from his throat.

Ava fell. Her ivory dress billowed around her like a surrendering flag, and her eyes that saw more than mere souls, were closed.

Thorben was already moving.

He didn't think about the curse. Didn't think about how his ghostly form had never been able to affect the Real, how jumping would change nothing, how he'd fall right through her like mist through fingers. He didn't think about any of it.

His feet hit the railing and he launched himself downward, arms pressed to his sides, willing his body to fall faster than physics should allow.

He bulleted toward her, the wind screaming past his ears. Ava's eyes were closed, her hair a dark halo whipping around her face. The few flowers left on her dress tore free and swept past him in a cascade of fragrance.

It felt like they fell forever.

Faster. Faster.

She was so close. Inches away. His hands reached for her, fingers straining—the silk of her dress fluttered against his fingertips.

Faster. He willed his cursed body to move.

The wind shoved a handful of silk into his palm and he grabbed—closed his fist around it like a drowning man clutching rope. He yanked her toward him, and then she was there, solid and real and warm against his chest, and his arms wrapped around her so tightly his muscles screamed.

I have you. I have you. I have you.

Her heartbeat pounded against his ribs. The warmth of her skin seeped through the ruined dress. And he was...

Crying. When had the tears started to fall?

Something caught his eye—a comet of light bursting from the horizon, sparks trailing behind it like a falling star in reverse. It was moving fast—and it was coming straight for them.

What—?

Thorben curled his body around Ava, shielding her. Whatever this was, it would hit him first. He braced for impact, for pain, for death—he didn't care anymore, if she was protected—

The light slammed into him.

The impact punched the air from his lungs and for a horrible moment he thought he'd been struck by lightning, that the sky itself was trying to tear him away from her.

Then the burning started.

It began in his chest—a hot pressure that spread like wildfyre through his veins. Thorben gasped, muscles spasming, and for a terrifying moment his grip on Ava loosened. No— He locked his arms tighter, refusing to let go even as fyre scorched him from the inside out.

A scream ripped from his throat.

The scorching spread to his arms. His legs. His fingers. It burned through ten years of numbness, ten years of existing as half a person, and in its wake left something he'd almost forgotten—

Feeling.

Not the muted echo of sensation he'd grown used to in the liminal plane. *Real* feeling. The kind that made his nerve endings sing and his skin prickle and his heart pound so hard he could hear it in his ears.

His soul. It was his soul.

It had found him.

Euphoric energy sang through his blood, his bones. Everything was *more*.

The wind wasn't just wind—it was a living thing tearing through his hair, cold and sharp and glorious. Ava's skin wasn't simply warm—it was velvet and silk and everything soft he'd been denied for a decade. The sky wasn't blue—it was a thousand shades of twilight he'd forgotten existed.

And then his magic woke up.

It shot through his veins like lightning, like joy, like coming home after years of exile. The remaining flowers on Ava's dress responded before he could stop them—bursting into bloom, unfurling petals, reaching toward him as if they'd been waiting for this very moment. They entwined themselves with each other, reproducing and curling around her frame and through her hair, hailing her like a falling flower goddess.

The forest below called to him.

He could *feel it*—every tree, every root, every blade of grass crying out in recognition. *You're back. You've finally returned.*

Thorben reached for them without thinking, and they answered.

Vines exploded from the ground, thick and green and impossibly fast. They wove together as they rose—knotting, twisting, building a net of living foliage that stretched toward them like arms reaching for a falling child. The vines caught him and Ava mid-air, cradling them, slowing their descent until they were lowered gently to the forest floor. His back felt the solidness of wet, fresh earth as Ava's form settled against his chest.

Thorben breathed. The smell of the forest hit him. Damp earth. Crisp leaves. The green scent of growing things and the mineral tang of recent rain. He lifted his face to the sky, filling his lungs until they ached, and the sob that escaped him was half laugh, half something he couldn't name.

Ten years. Ten years of muted existence, of watching life happen through fogged glass, of feeling like a sketch of a person instead of a real one.

His magic had never been this strong. Not even before the curse. And now—

Now he could smell the forest. Could feel the magic humming beneath his skin like a second heartbeat. Could feel the woman in his arms, warm and alive and *his*.

He turned his attention to Ava.

She was unconscious, her breathing shallow but steady. Thorben tucked his nose behind her ear and inhaled—flowers and spice, something warm beneath it that was just *her*. He'd caught hints of this scent before, in the liminal plane, but it had always been distant. Muffled. Now it filled his lungs and made his chest ache with how much he'd been missing.

Gently, he brushed the hair from her face. His fingertips traced the line of her jaw, her cheekbone, the soft curve of her shoulder where the ruined dress had slipped. Every touch was a revelation. Every inch of her skin a gift he'd never take for granted.

She sighed, and his heart cracked open a little more.

Carefully, he pressed his ear to her chest.

Thump. Thump. Thump.

Her heartbeat. Steady and strong and *real*.

A laugh bubbled up from somewhere deep in his chest—absurd and watery and slightly hysterical. Tears pricked his eyes and he let them fall. He'd spent ten years unable to truly cry, the liminal plane stealing even that from him.

Now he could cry and laugh and feel her pulse beneath his lips and know, with absolute certainty, that he was *alive*.

"Ava?" He pressed his lips to her cheek—velvet soft, impossibly warm. "Can you hear me?"

She moaned, her dark lashes fluttering. When her eyes opened and met his, Thorben's breath caught. He'd seen those eyes a hundred times in the liminal plane, but here—in light of the forest, in the Real—they were layers of blue and green and teal, flecked with gold he'd never noticed before.

"What happened?" Her voice was hoarse. "Where are we?"

"The forest beyond the city." He couldn't stop staring at her. Couldn't stop touching her face, her hair, her shoulders. "We're safe."

Ava's brow furrowed. Her hand lifted to his cheek, and he watched her expression shift from confusion to wonder.

"You look...different. You're—"

Thorben couldn't help it—he kissed her. Not the ghostly brush of lips they'd shared in the liminal plane—this was *real*. Her mouth opened for him, warm and willing, and she melted into his arms as he pulled her closer. She tasted like she smelled—flowers and spice and something underneath that was purely Ava.

When her tongue traced his lower lip, shivers cascaded down his spine. He groaned against her mouth, and she smiled into the kiss, and it was...*everything.*

This was what kissing was supposed to feel like. Not the shadow of sensation he'd grown used to, but heat and pressure and the fyre of certainty that burned through him—*she is mine and I am hers and nothing will ever take this from me again.*

Ava pulled back, taking a breath. "Why are you so warm? And your skin...it doesn't glitter anymore."

"The curse. It's...broken." Thorben's voice hitched. Speaking them aloud made them real.

"What? How?"

"When you fell, all I could think about was getting to you."

"Wait—did you jump?" Ava whispered.

"I couldn't have stayed on board if I tried," he said, his voice quiet. "Wherever you are, that's where I want to be."

Ava's fingers traced his jaw, his nose. The small callouses she had from sparring grazing the stubble on his cheeks. Her touch was familiar, but now, it was *more.* As if before today, her skin had been a whisper, a hint of something that he couldn't fully appreciate. "You did an act of utter selflessness. For me."

"I did." He grinned so wide, his skin stretched. His love for Ava was flowing through him, intertwining and binding with his magic. It raced through his veins ,delirious and bright.

"A *yah ageremé, mé inveni,*" she whispered. The ancient Ili words wrapped around him like a blessing.

"*Mé inveni?*" His voice came out rough.

"You have a name for me." Ava shrugged her shoulders, a smile playing at her lips. "I thought it fair I should give one to you."

He knew what *inveni* meant—but he wanted to hear her say it. "Remind me," he murmured, pressing a kiss on her bare shoulder. "What does *inveni* mean in Ili?"

Her fingers slid through his hair, nails scraping gently along his scalp, and he shivered from head to toe. "*Finder.*" Her voice was soft. "You found me, Thorben. And saved me. Twice now."

Thorben bent to kiss her again, but something caught his eye—a ring on her finger that hadn't been there before. "Is this Declan's ring?"

"*Seáh.*" Ava lifted her hand, studying the ring with a bittersweet smile. "His lost love. I caught her soul tonight—saved her from the machine."

Her smile faded. Her shoulders drooped.

"What is it?"

Ava's eyes went distant. Empty in a way that made his chest ache.

"All those souls," she whispered. "The ones I harbored. The ones I promised to protect." Her voice cracked. "Rey ripped them out of me and used them to destroy the purdahs. Thousands of them, Thorben. Gone. Because of me."

Thorben pulled her close, pressing his face into her hair. She smelled like home—or what he imagined home would smell like, after so long without one.

She'd stood against a thousand-year-old monster and won, ripping Rey from his stolen body with nothing but her voice and her will and the prince's song. She was magnificent—and she had no idea.

"You freed Van Alst," he said quietly. "You destroyed Rey. You saved Declan's love. That matters, Ava."

"And Priam..." Ava's eyes raised to his, alight in righteous anger. "That damn druid pushed me over the side of the ship."

Thorben clasped her shoulders. "We will fight back, *mé talé*," he said. A fiery, mad blaze of anger surged inside him, making his teeth grind together. That druid had tried to kill her. The next time he saw him, Thorben would make sure his soul was thoroughly destroyed.

Ava nodded, her fingers gripping her dress, her lips pressed together. He wanted to stay there forever, holding her, smelling her, learning her all over again. Ava had forced him to go beyond himself, to find what truly mattered, and it had saved his life. But he couldn't keep her here when the Realms—and her friends--needed her.

"Ava," Thorben murmured. "you broke a curse that has plagued me for a decade. You have unraveled me, *mé talé*, giving me hope when I had none. It is my turn to give you hope."

He tipped her chin, staring into those bottomless turquoise eyes. "I know you weren't able to save every soul tonight, but you saved me."

He kissed her again, the delicate skin on her lips smooth and pillowy beneath his. The intoxication of a simple kiss coursed through him, and it reminded him again of all he had been missing. When they had time, he planned on fully exploring Ava with his returned senses. But now, they needed to return. The forest's voice murmured against his soul. He stared into its depths, listening.

A shimmer in the shadows of the trees. A soul drifted toward them, cobalt blue streaked with orange and settled on Thorben's ankle like a cat seeking warmth.

He froze. "Can you see that?"

"Of course I can see it." Ava tipped her head, studying the soul with open curiosity. "The question is—how can you?"

Thorben stared at the soul. It should have avoided him. Souls always avoided him—or they had, when he was cursed. Now that he was free, shouldn't he be invisible to them again? Just another living person, unremarkable? "I spent ten years in the liminal plane," he said slowly. "Maybe some part of me still...understands its depths."

Ava's brow furrowed. "That shouldn't be possible. But neither should any of this."

"Let's get moving." Thorben stood and pulled her to her feet, marveling at how natural it felt—reaching for her, touching her, having her hand solid in his. "We have the rest of our lives to figure it out."

The rest of our lives.

The words settled into him like sunlight after a heavy storm. He had a life now. A *real* one. And he wanted to spend every moment of it with her.

Ava smiled—tired and sad and beautiful—and let him lead her into the forest. His magic picked up on a creek nearby, and he followed it until a dirt path emerged from the underbrush. The trees whispered of travelers, of a village not far ahead.

"This way," he said. "There's help nearby. The forest told me. I can't believe how much I've missed the trees." Being in the plane had been so...thickly quiet. Now, every chirp, groan of a branch, or rustle of a leaf in the wind filled his ears. Lingering raindrops dripped from leaf to leaf, and it was as if they touched his own skin. Flowers bowed in the breeze, and he heard them tittering in jealousy of Ava's beauty. Trees stretched for the sky, their branches itching to grasp one more drop of sunlight before the day turned over. "It's like having an entire army of living things at my fingertips."

Ava laughed—surprised and warm. "It's going to take a while to get used to that."

"Good." He grinned at her, and it felt strange on his face—his muscles remembered smiling, it had been so long. "I like surprising you."

Ava smiled, her eyes lighting. He squeezed her hand. "Ten years, Ava. Ten years of silence and shadow and existing without truly living. And now..."

He stopped walking. Turned to face her. Let himself look—*really look*—at the woman who had saved him.

"Now I have you. And my magic. A future." His voice cracked on the word, and he didn't care. "You gave me my life back, *mé talé*. I don't know how to thank you for that."

Ava reached up and cupped his face in her hands. Her thumbs brushed away tears he hadn't realized were falling.

"You jumped off a ship to catch me," she said. "I think we're even."

Thorben laughed—a real laugh, rusty from disuse but genuine. He pulled her close and kissed her forehead, her nose, the corner of her mouth.

They had a long walk ahead. A city to return to. Friends to find. Battles to fight.

But for now, in this moment, in this forest that sang with his returned magic—he was home.

Chapter Forty-Five

"No!" The scream tore from her throat as Priam's hands shoved Ava over the railing. Her childhood friend sank through the sky and there was nothing Dáhlia could do but watch her form shrink as she fell.

"Ava!" Flip's hands gripped the wood hard enough to whiten her knuckles. "You!" Flip spun on Priam. Before he could move, Flip's fist found his face. Priam's hands flew to his nose, the box he had been holding thudding to the deck.

"You worthless excuse for a druis—" Blood dripped from Priam's nose. He stepped forward but tripped over the box. Flip raised her fists. Priam glanced from her to his feet. Opting for the less painful, he grabbed the box and ran.

"That slimy, swale rat," Flip said. "I'm going to—"

"We don't have time—we need to—we have to—" Dáhlia's eyes couldn't leave Ava's form, now a billowing white cloud in the evening sky. She refused to blink, scanning the tree line for any flash of white fabric, any sign of—

"What in the Five..." A crew member at the port railing pointed toward the forest below. "The trees—look at the trees!"

Dáhlia spun. Below them, the forest was *moving*. Branches stretched and twisted like waking limbs. Vines spiraled upward, leaves unfurling in bursts of green so vivid they seemed to glow against the darkening sky. It was as if the entire woodland had suddenly remembered how to breathe.

Flip went rigid beside her, her face tilted toward something Dáhlia couldn't see.

"What is it?" Dáhlia demanded. "What are you looking at?"

"A light. Brighter than anything I've ever seen." Flip's voice was barely a whisper. "It's a spirit, but...souls, it's fast. I've never seen anything like—" She broke off, pressing a hand to her chest. "It just...it collided with..."

"With what?"

"A person?" Flip's gaze found hers. Dáhlia didn't understand what that meant, but she understood what she saw next: two figures in the heart of the forest's strange awakening. A woman in white, cradled in the arms of a man with dark hair. Vines wrapped and cocooned them as they were gently lowered to the forest floor, as if the trees themselves were protecting them.

"Oh, my souls." Relief crashed through her so hard her knees nearly buckled. "That's Ava. In my dress—I'd know it anywhere. But who is that with her? Is that her...ghost?"

Dáhlia stared at the man below—tall, broad-shouldered, very much solid. Very much *real*.

"I don't think he's a ghost anymore," Flip murmured, something like wonder in her voice.

For a long moment, they watched. The man cradled Ava in his arms. Even from this distance, Dáhlia could see them embrace, could see the forest continuing to bloom around them in impossible spirals of green until they were overtaken by the foliage and couldn't be seen any longer.

Ava was alive. Ava was *safe*. Which meant Dáhlia could focus on her brother. Her brief relief fell away. Where was he?

"Flip—Ava's zeppelin. Now!" Dáhlia's fingers worked at a rope, yanking it free from its cleat. Her chest tightened. What if he was gone?

No. She would feel it. Wouldn't she?

She waved frantically at Mergen, motioning for her to bring *The Spirited Gent* closer.

Mergen maneuvered to the side of the commodore's ship. She sent them a thumbs up when the decks were aligned.

"We're swingin', eh?" Flip took a rope. "I didn't take you for the swingin' type, D."

Dáhlia swallowed. She had seen other people swing from ship to ship. How hard could it be? Pressing her lips together, Dáhlia wrapped the rope around her forearm, took a steadying breath, and jumped.

The cool night air rushed into her open mouth. The scream she'd been holding back died somewhere in her throat. The rope jerked hard—her shoulder wrenched, fingers slipping—and then she was gliding, her blue, burnt dress fluttering in the wind, mahogany curls whipping across her face. Sulfurous smoke from the engine burned her nostrils, and the rope bit into her palms.

The deck quickly rose to meet her, and Dáhlia forced her fingers to let go. Her feet slammed into the wooden planks and pain burst through both her calves. She tumbled over, her dress tangling between her legs.

A few seconds later, boots thudded beside her. Flip released her rope and stood in one fluid motion, reaching up to smooth her blond hair as if she'd merely stepped off a carriage.

"What the hell?" Dáhlia muttered, tipping her head back from her position on the floor. "You do this a lot or something?"

Flip grinned at her. "You would be surprised at the things I know how to do."

Grasping Flip's offered hand, Dáhlia managed to stand, her feet aching from the hard impact.

"Souls, you had my stomach in knots," Mergen scolded, when they finally made their way to the control deck. "What is it with you people and swinging on ropes? And what happened to your dress?"

Dáhlia gave Flip a look. "Someone doused me with water."

"What?" Flip shrugged, but a smile played on her lips. "You were on fyre."

"Mage fyre. You should have known it wouldn't help." Dáhlia turned away from Flip. "Who else is swinging on ropes, Merg?"

"Tobias," Mergen clucked her tongue.

"Toby? Where is he? What happened to him?" The questions scraped out of her throat as she pulled a lever. She didn't want to ask. But she had to.

Mergen's hands tightened on the wheel. "I don't know. Dropped him off at the aircraft like he asked, then settled underneath to wait." A pause. "After a few minutes, the ship caught fyre. Started to sink. I tried to stay close, but with all the flying debris—" She shook her head. "*The Gent* would've gone up too. I'm sorry, Dáhlia."

The words landed like stones in Dáhlia's chest. She gripped the edge of the console, knuckles aching, and forced herself to breathe. To think.

"Toby is very creative." Dáhlia swallowed hard. "He would have figured out a way to survive."

Dáhlia turned back to scan the sky, searching for any sign of her twin, any hint of where he might have—

A gust of wind from above blew her hair back. Dáhlia threw an arm over her face and squinted into the wind—and froze.

A massive zeppelin hung in the air where moments ago there had been nothing but empty sky. Its wide ailerons blocked the last rays of sunset, casting the deck in sudden shadow.

"What in the souls—" Dáhlia's words died in her throat. She had seen a ship like this before. She had *been* on a ship like this before, years ago, in another life.

A rope ladder dropped onto the deck. Dáhlia stepped back, memories clawing at her chest—the smell of salt and gunpowder, rough laughter, kind eyes she'd trusted when she shouldn't have, a pair of hands she'd never stopped wanting to feel again.

A large man with wild red hair descended, his heavy form jostling the deck when he landed.

A knave. The word rattled through her like a bell struck too hard.

"Either of you lovelies lookin' fer a skinny lad with glasses?" He studied her face, then nodded slowly. "You look like 'im. Come aboard, then."

Toby. He had Toby.

"How—" Dáhlia's voice cracked. She cleared her throat and tried again. "How did your ship appear out of nowhere?"

The knave's weathered face creased into something like a smile. "Cap't's an illusionist mage. Keeps us hidden when we need hidin'. Apologizes for the sudden appearance—says it happens when he drops the cloak." He jerked his thumb toward the ladder. "You comin' or not?"

Dáhlia turned to Flip. "I'll be back," she said, her voice steadier than the tremor in her hands. If what she remembered was accurate, knaves wouldn't hurt anyone that didn't start a fight first. "Flip. Go back to the apartment and check on the girls. After everything that's happened tonight—" Her throat tightened. "I need to know that Aamina—and Gabrie—are safe."

"I'll take Flip back," Mergen offered. "Then I'll search for Ava on foot, make sure she gets home."

Flip nodded slowly. "Be careful, Dáhlia."

"Always am."

Dáhlia climbed. The rope ladder swayed with every rung. By the time Dáhlia hauled herself over the top, her arms trembled and her palms were raw.

A hand appeared in front of her face. She took it, and the man pulled her upright with easy strength.

"*Seáh llaéh*, welcome aboard the *Fairlight*." His grin was crooked, his black hair roguishly swept over his brow. A single earring glinted in his left ear, and when he smiled, a dimple appeared in his cheek. "I'm Declan, captain of this ship. And you are?"

"Dáhlia." She didn't add 'sir'. Something told her he'd laugh at her.

He did anyway—a warm, rolling sound that made the crew members nearby chuckle without pausing their work. "Dáhlia. Pretty name for a pretty face." His dark eyes swept over her, but not in a way that made her skin crawl. More like he was cataloging her, fitting her into some mental map. Noticing her dress, he raised an eyebrow. "Something happen to your, ah..." His hand motioned toward her.

Dáhlia felt heat rush to her face. "Oh." She brushed down the burnt remnants of her skirt. "Mage fyre...a fight...water..."

Declan smirked again, but didn't press. "Alright, then. Your brother's been asking for you."

"He has?" Relief rushed through her. "Where is he?"

Declan motioned for her to follow him. She observed the crew as she walked. The deck bustled with knaves—men and women from a dozen different realms, some climbing rigging, others hauling cargo. A massive man with diamonds embedded in his forehead caught her staring and winked, his teeth brilliant white against skin dark as midnight.

Dáhlia looked away quickly, but her eyes kept drifting to faces. Searching. She hated herself for it—for the flutter of hope every time she saw dark hair, broad shoulders. For the relief and disappointment that tangled together when the face was always wrong.

He's not here. He was never going to be here.

"Your brother suffered some bad burns," Declan said over his shoulder. "Mage fyre, from what my first mate said. Apparently what happens to one twin happens to the other, eh?"

He glanced back at her but when she didn't smile, he coughed lightly and continued. "He breathed some of it in, too. Needs an inyanga, and soon."

Mage fyre. Worse than regular flames—it burned deeper, longer, left scars that never fully healed. Dáhlia's throat tightened as she followed Declan into the captain's cabin. Her own skin was sore in places where the fyre had licked her, but it wasn't anything she was worried about.

Toby lay on a velvet couch, his skin an angry red latticed with blisters. Wet cloths covered his chest and arms, but even from the doorway she could see them steaming slightly, the fyre's residual heat fighting the cold. His breathing came in shallow, rattling gasps.

"Toby." She dropped to her knees beside him, her hand hovering over his face, afraid to touch. "Toby, I'm here. Can you hear me?"

His eyes fluttered but didn't open. A groan escaped his cracked lips.

"The device..." Toby's voice was a rasp, barely audible. "Destroyed with the ship. Didn't stop it in time."

"Shh." Dáhlia found a glass of water on a nearby table and helped him take a sip, her hand steady even as her insides shook. "The islands are still here. Nothing's drifted. You did enough."

"Ava?" The name came out cracked, desperate.

"She's safe." The words felt like a gift she could finally give. "I saw her. She's with—" Dáhlia hesitated, unsure how to explain a ghost who wasn't a ghost anymore. "She's not alone. Mergen will make sure she gets home."

Something in Toby's face eased. His eyes stayed closed, but the tension around his mouth softened.

He sighed. "Tell Ava I'm sorry. Please. I'm so sorry I failed."

"Like I said." Dáhlia gave him another sip of water. "Everything is fine. It doesn't matter."

"What was he trying to stop?" Declan asked, moving to the other side of the couch.

Dáhlia's exhaustion hit her all at once—the swinging, the fear, the relief, the fear again. She sank onto the arm of a nearby chair.

"Van Alst built a device. Transformed souls into energy." She watched Declan's face carefully. "He used it to destroy the purdahs."

The change in him was immediate. His easy charm vanished, replaced by something sharp and calculating. "The purdahs are...gone? You're certain?"

She nodded. "I felt the wave when they released."

Declan began to pace, his fingers snapping against his thigh in a restless rhythm. "So that's what that was." He spun to face her. "If the purdahs are gone, traveling between realms becomes effortless. No more boundaries. No more barriers."

"And no more anchors," Dáhlia finished quietly. "The islands could drift apart. Float into nothing. And we wouldn't know until it was too late."

The weight of it pressed down on her—not just fear, but the specific terror of a mother. Aamina. Her little girl, waiting at home, not knowing the world might be unraveling around her.

"Can you take us back to the city?" Dáhlia stood. "Quickly. Please."

Declan studied her for a moment—that cataloging look again, like he was filing her away for future reference. Then he nodded. "Need to get him to an inyanga anyway. We'll make good time."

He moved to the door and began issuing orders, his voice carrying across the deck with easy authority.

The *Fairlight* was too large for the city pier. They lowered Toby in a sling instead, the red-haired giant handling him as gently as if he were made of glass.

Dáhlia led them through the familiar streets to the apartment above the shop. Inside, Gabrie sat on the floor with Aamina, surrounded by scattered playing cards.

"Toby's room," Dáhlia said, pointing. "Please."

The giant carried her brother through the doorway like he weighed nothing. Flip was already there, changed from her dress back into pants and her dirty jacket. She caught Dáhlia's eye from the corner and gave a small nod.

Declan lingered in the common room, his dark eyes taking in the modest space with undisguised curiosity.

"Aamina." Her daughter's name on her lips was like balm to her heart. The little girl's head snapped up. Those dark blue eyes—*his* eyes—found Dáhlia's face, and then Aamina was running, her small body colliding with Dáhlia's legs before scrambling up into her arms.

Dáhlia held her tight. Breathed in the smell of her hair—soap and something sweet, probably whatever Gabrie had been feeding her. Aamina's small hands pressed against Dáhlia's back, holding on with the fierce grip of a child who wasn't often away from her mother.

"I'm here, mé veláh. Everything is fine." The tears came without permission, sliding hot down her cheeks. Aamina's little hands signed frantically, *What happened to Toby? What happened to your dress? Your face looks red.*

"I'll tell you in a minute," Dáhlia whispered back, kissing Aami's cheek. "But, he—and you and I—are going to be just fine." She wiped her face with one hand and settled Aamina on her hip. "Come meet the captain who saved your uncle."

She turned so Aamina could see Declan properly.

His easy smile froze mid-curve, then slid off his face entirely. He stared at Aamina's face like he was seeing a ghost—or worse, like he was seeing someone he knew very well.

"Is something wrong?" Dáhlia pulled Aamina closer, her arms tightening instinctively.

Declan stepped forward slowly, as if approaching something sacred. He held out his hand, palm up, waiting.

Aamina studied him with those deep, solemn eyes. Then, with the gravity of a queen receiving a suitor, she placed her small hand in his.

Declan lifted it to his lips. When he spoke, his voice had lost all its roguish charm.

"I know your face." He said to her. Then, his eyes met Dáhlia's over Aamina's head. "She's going to turn the Knave Guild upside down."

"The Guild?" Dáhlia's voice came out sharper than she intended. "What does my daughter have to do with the Knave Guild?"

But she already knew. Had known the moment Declan's face changed. Had spent four years dreading and hoping for this exact moment.

"She's his image," Declan said quietly. "Same eyes. Same jaw. Same way of looking at a person like she's deciding whether they're worth her time." A ghost of a smile. "He used to look at me like that when I was young and stupid and trying to impress him."

The room tilted. Dáhlia gripped Aamina tighter, anchoring herself.

"Where is he?" The words ripped out of her. "Tell me where he is."

Declan's expression shuttered. "If he hasn't told you himself, that's his choice. I don't interfere in the affairs of the Knave King."

Knave King.

The title hit her like a physical blow. All those years ago, he'd been no-body—a charming rogue with clever hands and a crooked smile, running small jobs for the Guild. Now he was their king?

And he'd never come back for her. Or for their daughter. Not even sent word.

Aamina squirmed, and Dáhlia realized she'd been gripping too hard. She loosened her hold, pressing a kiss to her daughter's temple in silent apology.

The red-haired giant appeared in the doorway and murmured something to Declan. The captain nodded.

"I have an appointment." He was already moving toward the door. "Your brother needs an inyanga. There's one in the South District who owes me a favor—tell her Declan sent you."

"Wait." Dáhlia stepped forward, Aamina still balanced on her hip. "You can't just leave. I need to know where he is. You have to—"

"I don't *have* to do anything." But Declan paused at the door, one hand on the frame. When he looked back, his expression softened slightly. "The Knave King keeps his own counsel. But if a mother and daughter showed up at a Guild gathering, asking questions?" He shrugged. "No one could stop them from asking. And no one could stop him from answering."

He winked at Aamina—who watched him with those grave eyes—and disappeared through the doorway.

The door clicked shut.

Dáhlia stood in the sudden silence, her daughter warm against her chest, her brother wounded in the next room, her best friend somewhere in the city with a man who used to be a ghost.

And somewhere out there, the Knave King ruled his empire, not caring that he had a daughter with his eyes.

Chapter Forty-Six

T horben kept touching things.

His free hand brushed against tree bark as they walked, fingers lingering on the rough texture. He tilted his face toward a patch of sunlight filtering through the canopy and closed his eyes, breathing deep. When a bird called overhead, he stopped walking entirely, head cocked, listening like he'd never heard birdsong before.

He hadn't. Not really. Not for ten years.

Ava watched him from the corner of her eye, cataloging the changes. His hand in hers was *warm*—not the faint echo of temperature she'd grown used to in the liminal plane, but actual heat, his pulse thrumming against her palm. She found herself wondering what that warmth would feel like elsewhere. Against her neck. Her waist. The small of her back.

He ran his fingers through his hair, and she followed the movement—the dark strands catching the evening light, falling in waves that looked soft as silk. Had his hair always been that thick? Had his shoulders always been that broad? In the liminal plane, he'd been beautiful. Here, in the Real, with his soul fully restored and his magic singing through him, he was something else entirely. Larger than life. More masculine, more vigorous, more *present*. The energy radiating off him made her skin prickle, magic and vitality tangled together in a way that was impossible to ignore.

He caught her staring and grinned—that crooked, devastating grin she loved. "What?"

"Nothing." She looked away quickly, heat rising to her cheeks. "Just... getting used to the new you."

"The new me." He lifted their joined hands and pressed a kiss to her knuckles. The sensation shot straight to her toes. "I could get used to this too."

They crested a small rise, and a town came into view—a cluster of buildings nestled in a valley, smoke curling from chimneys, the last rays of sunset painting the rooftops gold.

"Let's check in with the mail service." Ava pointed toward a small building with a brass tube system visible through the window. "They can tell us where we are, and we can find out when the next flight leaves for the city."

A bell tinkled as they pushed through the door. A young man worked behind the counter, sorting through message tubes, dressed in the typical mail garb of a blue pinstripe vest and matching pants. He looked up with a professional smile, dimples appearing as he tipped his dark blue aviator's hat.

"*Esprí meráh*, good evening." His smile faltered when he took in Ava's crushed and dirty dress, the leaves tangled in her hair. "Can I...help you?"

Heat crept up Ava's cheeks. She smoothed her hands down the ruined fabric, a stab of guilt slicing through her. She had ruined Dáhlia's beautiful dress. Combing her fingers through her disheveled hair, she tried to look like someone who hadn't recently been thrown off an airship and caught by a forest.

"Can you tell us when the next airbus to the city will be?" Her voice steadier than she expected.

"I'm sorry, *elehí*, but they are all are docked for the evening. Especially since tonight is the Gathering." He shrugged apologetically. "The next zep out will be first thing in the morning."

"Ask him what town we're in," Thorben said.

"You're in Wúrtere," the attendant answered, looking directly at Thorben.

Thorben went still. His eyes widened, then darted to Ava, then back to the attendant, who was now watching them both with polite confusion.

Ava pressed her lips together, trying—and failing—to suppress a laugh. "People can see you now," she whispered.

"Souls." Thorben's hand flew to his chest like he'd been startled. "I forgot. I actually forgot." He turned back to the worker, color rising in his cheeks. "Apologies. A *yah ageremé*. For the information."

"Quite welcome," the attendant said slowly, his eyebrows climbing toward his hairline.

Thorben cleared his throat. Shifted his weight. Looked at his hands like he wasn't sure what to do with them. For a man who had just recovered his soul and broken a decade-long curse, he suddenly looked like a boy who'd been caught talking to himself.

Ava bit her lip to keep from laughing harder.

Ava turned to leave, then stopped. "Actually—I'd like to send a tube, please."

"Of course." The attendant handed her a pen and paper.

She wrote quickly: *Dáhlia—safe. Thorben is with me. Will explain everything when I see you. Coming home tonight if we can find transport. Stop searching. —Ava*

She wanted to write more—about the curse breaking, about Thorben being real now, about the forest blooming around them like something out of a fairy tale—but there wasn't room. The story would have to wait.

She watched the attendant roll her note, seal it in a metal canister, and slot it into one of the conduits labeled Seráya City, Central District. The tube whooshed away with a satisfying thunk.

The attendant hesitated, his gaze drifting back to Ava's ruined dress. His brow furrowed.

"If you are truly desperate to get to the city tonight, I have a friend who is a tinker. She's been experimenting with a prototype that is supposed to travel at fast speeds."

"Where can we find her?" Thorben asked, his deep voice rumbling through Ava's chest.

"Down the lane, past the airbus station, and up the hill. She lives in a large windmill." He pointed. "You can't miss it."

The windmill stood proudly on the top of what Ava thought to be a small mountain instead of a hill. The silhouette of the sails against the sky reminded Ava of the ailerons on her ship. The golds and oranges of the evening light glinted off the stonework of the tower, making it sparkle.

"I guess that's it," Thorben mumbled. "Are you sure about this?"

"What harm is there in asking? Tinkers always have a solution." Ava grinned and tugged on his hand. "Let's go."

The windmill's massive wooden doors stood slightly ajar, releasing a symphony of banging, clanging, and creative profanity.

Without warning, both doors burst open. A plume of black smoke billowed out, followed by a short, white-haired woman in oversized goggles. She stumbled into the evening air, coughing violently and waving her hat at the smoke like she was fighting it personally.

"Half-arsed hydraulics should've worked," she snarled between coughs, smacking the hat against her thigh. "Pissant planetary gears are completely trashed, the flywheel shouldn't have fractured under that pressure differential, and if that camshaft throws another rod I'm going to melt the whole thing down and start from scratch—"

Ava and Thorben paused, unsure the best way to announce their arrival.

"Still think there is no harm in asking?" Thorben said out the side of his mouth. Ava hit him.

The motion got the woman's attention, and she stopped her rant, eyebrows lifting. Shoving her goggles on top of her soot-covered hair, she hobbled over to them, a pronounced limp in her gait.

"What do you want?" she asked, taking in Ava's elaborate, dirty dress and Thorben's tallness.

"The man at the mail service sent us this way." Ava stepped forward and gave her best smile. "I'm Ava, and this is Thorben. We were told you might be able to help us get to the city tonight."

"It's too late to see the Gathering," she shook her head. "I saw the souls on the horizon about an hour ago."

"That's not why," Ava said quietly. "We need to get there for other reasons."

The woman's amber eyes looked them over again, and she pursed her lips. She gave a curt nod. "I'm Emár. I'll show you what I have, but you might not like it."

She hobbled back inside, waving the last of the lingering smoke away with her hat. When Ava entered the workspace, her mouth dropped open.

It was four times as large as Toby's. Blueprints hung on one wall and shelves from floor to ceiling filled with books decorated another. The rest was covered in hundreds of hangers, buckets, and knobs with drawers haphazardly open showing gears, cogs, tools.

Emár plopped her hat on a large wooden workbench in the center of the room. An engine mounted to the side of the table still spewed a ribbon of smoke, the gears frozen in place.

"What are you working on?" Ava asked. Emár glanced over her shoulder and huffed. "An engine that will give zeppelins more speed and power, something to enable the airbuses to do more routes. This town needs to be able to travel better than it does."

Ava moved closer to the workbench, studying the seized engine. The configuration was ambitious—a hybrid system trying to marry steam power with pneumatic thrust. She could see where it had failed: the pressure had built unevenly, probably due to inadequate venting in the secondary chamber.

"Your problem isn't the planetary gears," Ava said. "They're a symptom, not the cause. The hydraulic fluid is contaminated—see the discoloration in the reservoir? That's causing inconsistent pressure in your actuators, which throws off the timing of the whole system." She traced the line of a pipe with her finger. "If you flushed the system and reconfigured the fyre box to contain a controlled burst of heat—something with a pressure release valve instead of traditional pistons—you'd get smoother combustion without the backfyre risk."

Emár had gone very still.

"Also," Ava added, "your flywheel cracked because the camshaft is slightly off-center. Probably happened during installation. It's creating micro-vibrations that compound over time."

Emár turned slowly, her amber eyes sharp behind the soot-smeared goggles. "Who in the Five are you?"

"I've been refurbishing a zeppelin." Ava shrugged. "I've learned things."

"You've learned things," Emár repeated flatly. She squinted at Ava for a long moment, then huffed—but it was a different kind of huff now. Impressed, maybe. Grudgingly respectful. She resumed her walk toward the back of the room.

Thorben had been watching her with an expression she couldn't quite read. When Emár turned away, he stepped close, his lips brushing the curve of her shoulder.

"I love it when you talk dirty," he murmured against her skin.

Heat flooded her face. She shoved him, but he was solid now—immovable—and her push only made him laugh, the sound rumbling through her like distant thunder.

"Behave," she hissed.

"I've been behaving for ten years." His grin was wicked. "I'm done behaving."

Emár stopped before a pair of massive double doors. She lifted the iron lock, her thin arms straining, and hauled them open.

Behind them stood a wolf.

No—not a wolf. A machine shaped like a wolf, forged from black iron and assembled from thousands of interlocking gears and cogs. It stood twice Ava's height, its body hollowed into a passenger cab with enough room for two. Its legs were frozen mid-prowl, paws the size of dinner plates. Its teeth were bared. Its hackles raised. Every line of it suggested motion, violence, hunger—even standing perfectly still.

"This is Micórse." Emár swept her hand over the beast with unmistakable pride. "Steam-powered, spellcast, and faster than anything else on the ground."

"He...hovers?" Ava managed.

"Hovers, gallops, flies if you push him hard enough." Emár patted the wolf's iron flank. "Micó can handle any terrain at speeds that would make a turbo prop jealous."

When Ava and Thorben didn't say anything, the old woman grinned. "I guess you've never seen anything like this, have you? Tell you what," Emár said, patting Micó's terrifying head. "I'll let you borrow him if you come back and help me with my engine."

Ava tore her gaze from the wolf's maniacal-looking eyes. "You'd let us borrow him? Really?"

"Why not?" she grinned. "Your questions surprised me but proves you know enough to appreciate his design."

Ava grinned back, glad to have made friends with another tinker. "It's a deal."

Emár turned out to be a mage as well as a tinker—which explained how she'd managed to create something as incredible as Micó.

She showed them how to secure the leather harnesses, pulling the straps tight across their chests and buckling them at the waist. Ava tested the give. There wasn't any. She was pinned to the seat like cargo.

"Is this really necessary?" she asked.

Emár just smiled. She produced an iron key from her pocket and whispered something Ava couldn't hear. The key blazed white-hot, and Emár slid it into a keyhole hidden beneath Micó's iron ear.

For a heartbeat, nothing happened.

Then the wolf moved. Not as in forward, but like a true animal as it stretched after a particularly long nap. The rigid iron rippled like fur, muscles shuddering beneath the metal skin. Micó stretched, shaking his massive head, gears clicking and grinding as he woke. When he turned to look at them, his eyes burned with fierce orange light—not painted, not mechanical, but *alive*.

Ava's breath caught. A thrill of fear and excitement raced down her spine.

Beside her, Thorben had gone absolutely rigid. His hands gripped the edges of the seat, knuckles white, his face pale.

"Thor?" she whispered. "Are you alright?"

"Fine," he said tightly. "Completely fine."

He did not look fine.

"The spell I cast will get you to the city," Emár explained, locking the door to the coach. "After he has delivered you, he will return."

Ava opened her mouth to thank Emár—

Micó growled. The sound vibrated through the cab, through Ava's bones, through her teeth. His legs lifted off the ground as jets beneath his belly roared to life, steam billowing in thick white clouds that sent Emár's hair flying.

Wings unfolded from his sides—Ava hadn't even noticed them—clicking open segment by segment like a mechanical fan. The wolf raised his iron snout to the sky and released a howl that shook the air itself.

And then he launched. The force slammed Ava back against the seat. The world blurred—trees whipping past, the ground dropping away, the wind screaming in her ears. She laughed, half-terror and half-delight, throwing her arms up in surrender as Micó tore through the forest at impossible speed.

Beside her, Thorben made a sound she'd never heard from him before.

It was somewhere between a groan and a whimper.

Micó was breathtakingly fast—not quite as swift as her zeppelin on black powder, but close. He wove through the forest with liquid grace, banking around trees, leaping over streams, his iron body moving like flesh and bone despite being neither.

Ava whooped as they crested a hill and went briefly airborne. The wolf seemed to feed on her joy, increasing his speed, taking sharper turns, showing off.

She glanced at Thorben.

His eyes were squeezed shut. His jaw was clenched so tight she could see the muscle jumping beneath his skin. Both hands gripped the harness straps like he was trying to strangle them. His complexion had gone from pale to faintly green.

"Thor!" She had to shout over the wind. "Are you alright?"

He shook his head once. A tiny, desperate movement.

"Do you need him to stop?"

His lips pressed into a thin line. He shook his head again—but this time it looked less like "no" and more like he was trying not to be sick.

Ava reached over and grabbed his hand. He seized it like a drowning man, his grip crushing.

Ten years in the liminal plane, she realized. Ten years of traveling without a body, without weight, without the physical sensations of motion. His first real experience of speed in a decade, and it was this—a mechanical wolf hurtling through the darkness at turbo-prop velocity.

She probably shouldn't find it as endearing as she did.

City lights appeared through the trees. Micó slowed and maneuvered toward a clearing at the forest's edge. Steam hissed as the jets cooled, and the wolf settled onto solid ground with surprising gentleness.

Ava's fingers fumbled with her harness buckle, her whole body still vibrating with adrenaline. She turned to Thorben, ready to share her exhilaration—

He hadn't moved.

His eyes were closed. His face was the color of old parchment. His hands still gripped the harness straps, and she wasn't entirely sure he knew they'd stopped.

"Thor." She touched his arm. The muscles beneath his sleeve were rigid, trembling slightly. "We're here. It's over."

His eyes opened slowly, unfocused. He swallowed hard—once, twice—his throat working.

"I need—" He fumbled with his buckle, hands shaking. "I need to—"

Ava helped him with the straps. The moment he was free, Thorben hauled himself out of the cab and stumbled a few steps away. He braced one hand against Micó's iron flank and bent over, taking deep, deliberate breaths through his nose.

"Are you going to be sick?" Ava asked, climbing down after him.

"No." A pause. Another breath. "Maybe." Another pause. "I'm fine."

After a few more moments, some color began returning to his face. He straightened slowly, wiping his forehead with the back of his hand.

"All this time," he said, his voice rough. "I've traveled through the liminal plane—no weight, no sensation, no...body. And my first experience back in the Real is a possessed wolf trying to shake my soul loose."

"He wasn't trying to—"

"He absolutely was." Thorben shot a dark look at Micó. The wolf's orange eyes gleamed with what Ava could swear was amusement. "He knew exactly what he was doing."

A laugh bubbled up before she could stop it. Thorben's gaze snapped to her, indignant.

"I'm sorry," she managed, pressing a hand over her mouth. "I'm sorry, it's just—you faced down Van Alst and Rey and the entire liminal plane, and you're undone by a coach ride."

"A coach ride." His voice was flat. "That was not a coach ride. That was assault."

She laughed harder. After a moment, the corner of his mouth twitched. Then curved. Then he was laughing too—shaky and breathless, but real.

"Come on." Ava took his hand, steadying him. "Let's get you somewhere that doesn't move."

Ava approached Micó's head, her boots sinking into the soft forest floor. The wolf's massive iron head swiveled toward her, those burning orange eyes meeting hers with an intelligence that made her breath catch.

She reached up—hesitantly—and touched the smooth metal between his ears.

A deep rumble vibrated through his frame. Not a growl. A purr.

"Thank you for the ride, Micó." She scratched gently, the way she might pet a real wolf—if real wolves were twice her height and made of gears. "I owe Emár a visit, so I'll be seeing you again soon."

The wolf dipped his head in what looked remarkably like a bow. Then he turned, his jets rumbling to life, and launched himself back into the sky. The gust of hot steam blew Ava's hair back, her ruined dress fluttering in his wake.

She watched until he disappeared over the tree line.

"Ready?" Thorben had come up beside her, looking steadier now, though still a bit pale.

Ava laced her fingers through his. "Ready."

The city lights glowed ahead of them. Somewhere in that sprawl was Dáhlia's apartment, and Toby, and explanations that Ava wasn't sure how to give. *By the way, this is Thorben. He was cursed and sort of a ghost, but he's not anymore. He jumped off an airship to catch me, and now the forest obeys him, and I'm fairly certain I'm going to spend the rest of my life with him, so please be nice.*

She squeezed his hand. One thing at a time.

Chapter Forty-Seven

T he climb up the stairs to the apartment felt longer than usual, Ava's legs heavy with exhaustion. But the moment Dáhlia opened the door, warmth flooded through her.

"Thank the souls." Dáhlia pulled her into a fierce embrace. "Mergen's been out searching for hours. We need to send word that you're safe before she combs through every street in the city—"

"Where's Rune?" Ava pulled back, scanning the room. "And Toby—is he—"

Dáhlia's gaze had drifted past her, frozen on something in the doorway.

"Ava!" Toby appeared from the hallway, shoving past Dáhlia to pull Ava into a fierce hug. His hair was mussed, his skin still flushed an angry red from the mage fyre—healing, but far from healed. She could feel the residual heat radiating off him even through his shirt.

"Souls, I'm glad you're alright," Ava breathed, returning his embrace. She could feel him trembling slightly—or maybe that was her. "I heard about the ship. Are you—"

"I failed." His voice cracked. "Ava, I'm so sorry. I tried, but there were two mages and the whole thing exploded before I could—"

He stopped mid-sentence. His arms loosened around her. His gaze had shifted to something over her shoulder, and his expression shuttered into something she couldn't read.

Ava turned.

Thorben stood in the doorway, filling it in a way she was still getting used to. His dark hair caught the lamplight, his broad shoulders nearly brushing the frame on either side. He wasn't doing anything—just standing there—but something about his presence made the room feel smaller.

"Oh." Ava stepped back from Toby, suddenly aware of the space between all three of them. "Toby, Dáhlia—this is Thorben."

Dáhlia's mouth opened. Closed. Opened again.

Thorben stepped forward and offered his hand—a normal greeting, nothing elaborate—but the smile he gave her was warm and genuine. "Thank you for being such a good friend to Ava. She speaks highly of you."

Dáhlia took his hand, and Ava watched the flush creep up her friend's neck, darkening her skin to a deep rose. "Thorben. It's...lovely to finally meet you." She cleared her throat. "In person. As a person. Who is...real."

"I am told that's a recent development," Thorben said, and Dáhlia laughed—a slightly breathy sound.

Toby hadn't moved. His jaw was tight, his hands shoved deep in his pockets. He was looking at Thorben the way one might look at a equation that refused to balance—like if he stared long enough, he could make it make sense.

Thorben met his gaze steadily. Something passed between them—Ava couldn't quite catch it, but she saw Thorben's posture shift almost imperceptibly. Shoulders squaring. Chin lifting. A subtle claiming of space.

Of her.

Then Toby turned on his heel and walked toward his rooms without a word.

"Toby—" Ava started, but he was already gone, his door clicking shut with a finality that made her stomach twist. She turned back to Thorben, confusion and something like guilt warring in her chest. "What was that about?"

Thorben's expression was carefully neutral, but there was a glint in his eye. "I have no idea."

"You're a terrible liar."

"I've been watching him for weeks, *mé talé*. Watching him watch you when he thought no one could see." Thorben's mouth curved. "This is going to be very interesting."

"Thorben."

"What? I'm simply observing that your friend seems...uncomfortable."

Ava wanted to press further, but Rune's voice cut through the moment.

"Is that my girl?" Rune emerged from Dáhlia's side of the apartment, Flip and Gabrie trailing behind her with little Aamina balanced on Flip's hip. She looked tired—there were shadows under her eyes that hadn't been there before—but she was whole. And alive.

"Rune." The word came out broken. Ava crossed the room in three steps and threw herself into her aunt's arms, a sob tearing loose from somewhere deep in her chest. "Where were you? I'm so glad you're safe."

"*Mé veláh.*" Rune stroked Ava's disheveled hair. Her aunt's floral scent encircled her, the comforting warmth of her voice filling Ava with a familiar peace, and she could breathe again. "It's alright. I'm here."

"What happened?" Ava sniffled, wiping away her tears.

"I could ask the same of you." Rune took in Ava's dirty dress and hair. Then she noticed Thorben. Rune lifted her eyebrows. Ava brought her aunt forward, and Thorben bowed his head, his dark hair sweeping along his sharp jaw.

"I am honored to finally meet you in person," he said, his left hand resting on his heart, his right extended in the traditional Ili greeting. Rune accepted his hand.

"I am equally honored."

"You'll never believe this," Flip said, wandering to the counter to investigate a bowl of snacks. She'd changed out of her borrowed dress into clean black pants, a loose shirt, and a red and black corset—still Flip, but a more polished version. "Van Alst brought Rune here himself."

"What?" Ava and Thorben spoke at the same time.

Flip popped a cracker into her mouth, clearly enjoying their shock. "*Seáh.* Showed up about an hour ago, Rune on his arm like she was royalty. Which, I suppose she technically is, being a thousand years old and all."

"He was very gentle," Rune added. "Kept apologizing the entire way. For everything—the kidnapping, the device, things I don't think were even his fault."

"It's like he was carrying the weight of ten lifetimes of guilt." Flip said around a mouthful of food.

"He is," Rune said quietly. "In a way, he was."

Dáhlia joined Flip at the counter. "He kissed Rune's hand before he left. Offered to double our pier space for free. Kept calling her 'honored elder' and bowing every time she spoke."

"Alistair," Ava murmured, remembering the man behind the commodore's mask. The young man who had never had magic of his own, who had been puppeted by his ancestors since childhood. Who had helped her escape the deep liminal plane with nothing but his knowledge and a desperate desire to finally do something good.

"His arm is in bad shape," Dáhlia continued, her tone sobering. "Completely black with frostbite. He can't move it at all. I think he may lose it."

The words landed like stones in Ava's chest. She looked at the floor, remembering the ice magic flooding through her, the savage satisfaction of freezing Van Alst's arm while Rey screamed inside him. Alistair had been in there too, trapped and helpless, and now he would carry the scars of her desperation for the rest of his life.

"I did that to him," she said quietly.

"You did what you had to," Thorben said, his hand finding the small of her back.

"So did he." Ava thought of Toby, somewhere in his room, carrying his own guilt over a device he'd built without knowing its purpose. How many of them were walking around wounded by choices that hadn't really been choices at all? "We all did things we wouldn't normally do. Because someone else was pulling the strings."

Rune's hand found hers and squeezed. "That's the nature of war, mé veláh. We survive it. And then we figure out how to live with what surviving cost us."

"Someone needs to tell Mergen to stop searching," Ava said suddenly, guilt pricking at her. "I sent you a tube, but I guess we arrived before it did."

"I'll ask Toby to find her," Dáhlia said. "Now, for the love of the Five, go change. Between Flip hijacking my best silks to play dress-up and you treating my ivory gown like a gardening apron, my expensive wardrobe is quickly becoming the go-to martyr for your adventures."

Ava looked down at the ruins of Dáhlia's beautiful dress—the creamy ivory fabric torn and soiled, the delicate flowers crushed beyond recognition. Dirt and blood had turned it into something unrecognizable. "I'm so sorry about your dress. I'll replace it, I promise."

"You'll do no such thing." Dáhlia's voice softened. "If you start taking care of my clothes, I'll never have a reason to go shopping. I'm just glad you're alive to ruin them, Ava."

She gave Dáhlia a quick hug, grateful beyond words for a friend who'd fought beside her without question and now joked about ruined dresses.

She released Dáhlia and looked for Thorben. He was examining one of Toby's mechanical projects on a shelf, giving her space—or pretending to. She slipped into Dáhlia's room to change.

When she emerged in the newly borrowed clothes, exhaustion settled into her bones like lead. Home. She needed to go home.

Toby had found Mergen and guided her back to his pier. After a quick hug, she took her own turbo prop home. Ava, Rune and Thorben piled into *The Spirited Gent*, Flip and Gabrie in the captain's cabin. The wheel beneath Ava's fingers felt like home. Her shoulders relaxed and she breathed deeply, the smell of grease, oil, and helium settling into her bones. She pulled the cord to flush heat into the balloon and set her coordinates for Dasírli Forest.

The kitchen was worse than she remembered.

A massive tree had crashed through the wall, its trunk lying diagonally across what remained of the worktable. Shattered jars littered the floor, their contents—herbs, dried flowers, things Ava couldn't identify—scattered across the debris. The hearth was cracked. One wall was simply.. .gone.

"Oh, Rune." Ava's chest ached. This had been her aunt's sanctuary for longer than Ava had could remember. Years of memories, and now it looked like a battlefield.

Rune said nothing, but her hand trembled slightly where it gripped Ava's arm.

"I can fix this."

They turned. Thorben stood surveying the damage, arms crossed over his chest. Ava caught herself staring at the way his forearms flexed, the solid breadth of his shoulders, and quickly looked away.

He walked to the hole in the wall, peered out at the forest beyond, and came back nodding. "Absolutely. I can work with this."

"Thorben, this is—" Ava gestured at the destruction. "This would take weeks to repair."

His grin was almost boyish. "For a normal person, maybe." He dropped a kiss on her forehead—quick, casual, and it still made her pulse stutter. "As I recall, you like surprises. Take Rune to the garden. I'll let you know when it's ready."

Ava wanted to argue. She also wanted to kiss him properly, but Rune was right there, and Flip was making a terrible job of pretending not to watch them.

"Fine," she said. "But if you need help—"

"I won't." He was already rolling up his sleeves, and the sight of his forearms really wasn't fair. "Go."

The garden was no better than the kitchen.

Scorched pathways cut through what had once been neat rows of herbs and flowers. The plants themselves were blackened and shriveled, leaves curled into ash. The air still smelled faintly of smoke and something bitter—burned magic, maybe.

But the gazebo still stood, and that felt like a small miracle.

"Our garden was so lovely," Rune said softly, grief threading through her voice.

Ava took her aunt's hand. "It will be again. I promise. We'll replant everything, and next season—"

"Ava."

She turned. Thorben stood at the edge of the garden, his smile stretching wide enough to show teeth. He was practically vibrating with barely contained energy.

"Already?" Ava stared at him. "It's been maybe twenty minutes."

"I had help." He bounced on the balls of his feet like a child waiting to show off a drawing. "The forest was very cooperative. Ready?"

He didn't wait for an answer, just grabbed her hand and pulled her toward the house with Rune following behind.

"I'm coming, you don't have to dislocate my shoulder—"

But she was laughing, and so was he, and when they reached the doorway to the kitchen, Ava's laughter died in her throat.

"Skyes."

The word left her in a breath.

A tree grew in the center of the kitchen. Not crashed through it—grew from it, as if it had always been there, as if the house had been built around it rather than the other way around. Its trunk rose from the stone floor, bark smooth and silver-gray, branches spreading outward in graceful arcs that curved into shelves, hooks, alcoves. Rune's jars lined the branches, organized by color and size. Her books nestled in natural nooks formed by the wood. Pots and pans hung from smaller branches, copper catching the light.

Above them, the canopy bloomed. Delicate flowers in shades of pink and fuchsia cascaded down like a living chandelier, their fragrance sweet and fresh—nothing like the smoke that had choked this room a day ago.

A massive stone hearth dominated one wall, large enough for Rune to stand inside. The opposite wall was a lattice of branches that arched together to form tall, elegant windows, letting the last of the evening light pour through.

"Thorben." Ava's voice cracked. "This is..."

"Do you like it?" He was watching her face with an intensity that made her chest tight. "Rune, what do you think?"

Rune walked slowly through the space, her fingers trailing over jar lids and book spines. When she turned back, her eyes were bright with unshed tears.

"It's the finest kitchen I've had in a thousand years," she said, and patted his arm gently. "You did well, young man."

A low whistle cut through the moment. Flip and Gabrie had appeared in the doorway, Gabrie's mouth hanging open.

"You did this?" Flip asked. "In twenty minutes?"

Thorben shrugged, a flush creeping up his neck.

"Ava." Flip turned to her with exaggerated solemnity. "Next time you find a ghost, you let me have him, alright?"

Thorben's flush deepened to crimson. Ava laughed—really laughed, for the first time in what felt like days—and the sound seemed to fill the beautiful new space like it belonged there.

"Is this how you built homes before?" Ava asked. "Before the curse?"

Thorben shook his head slowly, staring at his own hands like they belonged to someone else. "Before, my magic was...functional. I could coax a tree to bend, encourage growth, shape branches over time." He flexed his fingers. "This is different. It's like my magic spent ten years growing in the dark, building strength while I couldn't use it. Now it's..." He trailed off, searching for words. "The trees don't just respond to me. They want to help. They reach for me before I even ask."

"You feel it too," Rune said quietly. "The difference."

He met her eyes. "I feel alive. Truly alive."

Rune crossed to him and took both his hands in her weathered ones. "You have given an old woman a gift beyond measure, Thorben. This kitchen, this kindness—I will not forget it."

He bowed his head. "You raised her," he said simply. "You kept her safe for a thousand years. There is no gift great enough to repay that."

Ava's throat tightened. She watched them—her aunt, small and silver-haired, holding the hands of this man who had been a ghost and was now so achingly real—and something shifted in her chest.

This was what home could look like. This was what family could be.

"Ava." Thorben's hand found hers, his grip warm and solid. "I...need to visit Natalia. She doesn't know—" He stopped, swallowed. "She doesn't know my curse is broken. That I'm back. I need to see her."

Guilt flickered through Ava's chest. She'd been so wrapped up in her own exhaustion, her own relief at being home, that she hadn't thought about what Thorben needed. His sister had spent ten years unable to see him, hear him, touch him. And here Ava was, monopolizing his first hours of freedom.

"Of course." She squeezed his hand. "Go. Take as long as you need. Your nieces are going to lose their minds."

His smile was bright and nervous all at once. He kissed her cheek—quick, almost shy—and hurried out the door like he couldn't wait another second.

Ava watched him go, something warm and complicated blooming in her chest.

"That man is completely smitten with you, Avalina Rose."

She turned. Rune was watching her with knowing eyes, a small smile playing at her lips.

"He's alright, I guess." Ava tried for casual. Failed spectacularly.

"Mmhmm." Rune's smile widened. "Alright enough to build me a kitchen in twenty minutes."

Ava's face burned. She busied herself examining a jar of dried herbs, but she couldn't stop the grin spreading across her face.

Her smile lasted until Flip poked her head in and asked what was for breakfast.

Chapter Forty-Eight

T he walk back from Natalia's felt different than any walk he'd taken in the last decade.

His feet touched the ground. Actually touched it—not the muted, half-there sensation of the liminal plane, but real contact. Dirt and leaves and the occasional stone pressing through the soles of his boots. The evening air was cool against his skin, carrying the scent of pine and something floral he couldn't name.

He was here. *Real*. Part of him kept waiting for it to fade, for the curse to snap back into place and pull him under again.

But it didn't. And Natalia had held him for an hour, sobbing. The girls had climbed all over him like he was one of his own trees, their small hands grabbing at his hair and clothes, shrieking with delight at this uncle they'd only heard stories about.

Dellyn had watched from the doorway, arms crossed, face unreadable. That conversation would come later. Thorben didn't care how long it took—he would prove himself. He would be the brother Natalia deserved, the uncle those girls needed.

But right now, all he wanted was to get back to Ava.

The house came into view through the trees, and his pace quickened. He'd spent the walk back rehearsing what he would say, how he would show her what he'd built. What if she didn't like it? What if the essentiae idea was foolish? What if—

He knocked on the door before he could spiral further.

It swung open almost immediately, like she'd been waiting. The sight of her face—those turquoise eyes finding his—made something loosen in his chest.

"How is she?" Ava asked, pulling him inside.

"She cried." His voice came out rougher than he expected. "For about an hour. And then she hit me, which I probably deserved. And then she cried again while hitting me."

Ava's lips curved. "That sounds about right."

" The girls wouldn't let me go." He laughed, and the sound surprised him—easy, unguarded. "They're so beautiful, Ava. So smart and funny. They remind me of our mother."

"And Dellyn?"

The lightness dimmed. He looked away, studying a jar on a nearby shelf. "He wasn't pleased to see me. He remembers the man I was before the curse, and that man gave him plenty of reasons for distrust."

Her hand found his arm. "Thorben—"

"I'm not that man anymore." He met her eyes. "I'll prove it to him. However long it takes."

"If you need someone to vouch for you, I'll visit." Her fingers traced up to his face, her touch featherlight against his jaw. "You built half this house in an afternoon. What more proof does he need?"

He caught her hand and pressed a kiss to her palm, letting his lips linger. The warmth of her skin, the faint flutter of her pulse beneath his mouth—he would never tire of this. Never take it for granted.

"Speaking of building things," he said.

Her eyebrows rose. "What did you do?"

"Come with me."

He led her through the garden, his heart beating harder with every step. The scorched pathways still needed repair, the gazebo still stood sentinel over the ruined flowerbeds, but none of that mattered right now. What mattered was the wall of vines at the property's edge—and the doorway he'd coaxed into existence while she wasn't looking.

Ava stopped. Stared.

"Thorben. What is this?"

"Open it."

She reached for the curved handle, and he held his breath. The doors swung inward on silent hinges. He watched her face as she stepped inside. Watched her eyes travel upward to the canopy of woven branches, then down to the smooth stone floor, then across to the far wall where he'd arranged the shelves.

"I made it for you," he said, coming to stand beside her. His voice sounded strange in his own ears—too eager, too hopeful. "I know Flip and Gabrie have taken over your room, and I thought you might need a space of your own."

She turned, and something in her expression made his stomach flip.

"Only for myself?" One eyebrow arched.

Heat flooded his face. Years without a body, and now it betrayed him at every turn. "That depends entirely on you."

She walked deeper into the room, and he followed a few paces behind, watching her take in every detail. The canopy above. The smooth stones beneath her feet. The woven rugs he'd asked the forest to provide.

And then she saw the shelves.

He'd spent an hour on them—coaxing branches into alcoves and cubbies, arranging each item the trees had brought him. Porcelain cups and painted dishes. Toys worn soft with age. Jewelry tarnished by time. Hats and gears and glass figurines. Tiny treasure boxes with rusted hinges.

A thousand lost things. He'd hoped—prayed—that some of them might be more.

"Where did you get all of this?" Her voice was barely a whisper.

"I asked the forest." He stepped closer, near enough to see the wonder on her face. "I told the trees I needed treasures—things that had been lost, abandoned, forgotten. They passed them along their branches, root to root, until they reached me."

She stepped toward the shelves, her hand rising as if pulled by an invisible thread.

"Some of them are just objects," he continued, nerves making him talk too much. "But I thought...I hoped some of them might be more. That you could use them for bonding, when you needed vessels for essentiae."

Ava went still. Her fingers hovered over a chipped porcelain cup, painted yellow with a swirl of blue.

Then she reached for it, and he saw the change in her—the way her expression shifted, her breath catching, her whole body orienting toward something he couldn't see.

She moved along the shelves, gathering items into her arms. One, two, five, seven. She cradled them against her chest like they were infinitely precious. When she turned back to him, there were tears on her cheeks.

"Thorben." Her voice cracked. "These souls have been lost...some of them for decades, maybe longer. And you found them. You gave them another chance—so I could help them."

Relief crashed through him so hard his knees nearly buckled. He'd hoped. He hadn't been certain. But watching her now, watching the tears slide down her face as she held those lost souls close—he knew he'd gotten it right.

"You're a druis," he managed. "It's what you do. I just thought—"

"Thank you." She crossed to him, essentiae still cradled in her arms. "For seeing me. For knowing what this would mean."

He cupped her face in his hands, thumbs brushing away the tears. She was so beautiful like this—raw and open, her walls completely down. For him. Because of him.

"I will spend the rest of my life learning what matters to you, *mé talé*." The words came out like a vow, like a prayer. "And then I will fill every room with it."

Her eyes shimmered. For a moment, neither of them moved.

"I need to put these in my phylactery," she said finally, her voice thick. "They've waited long enough."

She turned to leave, then stopped. Her gaze had caught on the archway at the far end of the room—the one he'd woven with white flowers, the one that led somewhere more private.

"What's through there?"

His hand went to the back of his neck. His face was burning again. "The bedroom."

"Oh." The single syllable came out breathier than her usual voice, and the sound of it did something to his pulse.

She craned her neck, trying to see past the archway. He knew what she'd find—the large bed he'd grown from living branches, the soft glow of evening light filtering through gaps in the walls.

He stepped closer. Lifted his hand to cup her face, his thumb tracing the line of her jaw. Her skin was warm silk beneath his fingers, and he felt her pulse jump at the contact.

"I could show you now," he murmured. "If you want."

Her eyes met his. He could see the want there—the same want that had been building in him for weeks, months, longer than he cared to count.

The essentiae hummed softly against her chest, patient but present.

"When I come back," she said, and her voice was steadier than he expected, "you'd better be naked."

His eyebrows shot toward his hairline. A startled laugh escaped him before he could stop it.

Had she just—?

She held his gaze, refusing to look away, though he could see the flush creeping up her neck. She'd surprised herself with that, he realized. But she wasn't taking it back.

The shock melted into something hotter. Darker. He felt his body respond, felt the heat pooling low in his belly.

"Seáh, mé talé," he said softly. "As you wish."

She slipped out the door, essentiae clutched to her chest, and Thorben watched her go.

She had ordered him to get naked.

Thorben couldn't contain his grin as he stripped off that awful hunter green shirt and tossed it aside. Ten years in the same clothes. He never wanted to see them again.

His fingers found the buttons of his pants, then paused.

What would their future look like? Would she want to be his lovesoul? Would she want him the way he wanted her—completely? Permanently?

"I can't screw this up," he muttered to himself. "She's the one."

The bedroom door creaked open.

Ava stood in the archway, dark hair loose around her shoulders, turquoise eyes traveling slowly down his bare chest. The heat rose to his face. Had she heard him talking to himself like a fool?

"I thought you were supposed to be naked," she said, one corner of her mouth curving upward.

Skyes. She had heard him.

"I was getting to that."

"Well?" She raised an eyebrow, leaning against the doorframe. Waiting.

"You want me to undress while you watch?"

Her smile grew wider, and something about it made his blood warm. "Someone once told me they enjoyed watching."

He remembered saying those words in the liminal plane, half-teasing, half-desperate. He'd thought she hadn't understood.

Apparently, she had.

He stalked toward her, watching through his lashes, and stopped inches away—close enough to breathe in that intoxicating scent of fresh flowers and exotic spices.

His thumb hooked into his waistband, tugging just enough to reveal the sharp line of his hip.

"If you insist," he murmured.

Her eyes tracked his movements as he pushed the fabric down, letting it pool at his feet. He straightened, letting her look.

He'd always been confident in his body, but watching Ava's gaze rake over him was intoxicating. Her lips parted. Her eyes dropped to his cock—already thickening under her attention—and she inhaled sharply.

"I've wanted to make love to you since I saw you practicing with your laser whip in the garden," he said, stepping closer. "You didn't know I was watching. But I couldn't look away."

"You were watching me?" Her voice had gone slightly breathless.

"I wanted to make sure you were safe." He lifted a hand to her cheek, marveling at the velvet warmth of her skin. After years of muted sensation, touching her felt like pressing his palm against the sun. "You are the one my soul has longed for."

Her hair slipped through his fingers—silky, perfect. Such a simple thing. Such an exquisite pleasure.

"You are wearing too many clothes." His finger traced down her jaw, along her throat.

Through the thin fabric of her shirt, he could see the shadow of her nipples. He pulled it over her head in one smooth motion.

The sight of her nearly undid him. Full and round, tipped with dusky pink that puckered in the cool air. His cock twitched.

He untied her pants and let them fall, then sank to his knees, fingers trailing down the backs of her thighs. He lifted each foot to free her from the fabric, and when his fingers grazed the arch of her sole, she jerked away with a laugh.

"Does that tickle?"

"Yes!" She kicked at him, giggling.

"I'll remember that for later," he murmured, pressing his lips to her thigh. Then higher. Then higher still.

He nuzzled into the dark curls at the apex of her legs, and she bent her knees instinctively, her fingers threading into his hair. The scent of her arousal hit him—musky, sweet, devastatingly perfect—and his mouth watered.

He wanted to taste her. To devour her, worship her until she forgot her own name.

His tongue slipped along her center, and Ava gasped, her knees buckling.

"Give me time, *mé talé*," he whispered, catching her before she fell. He scooped her up and carried her to the bed, laying her down on the mattress of quilted petals. His lips found her jaw, her neck, the delicate hollow of her throat.

He wanted to go slow. To savor every sensation, every sound she made. Ten years of numbness, and now he could feel everything—the silk of her skin, the heat of her body, the desperate thrum of her pulse beneath his lips.

His thumbs drew slow circles on her ribcage as his mouth traveled lower. Her skin tasted of salt and honey, earth and sweetness. He wrapped his lips around one tight nipple and suckled, and the moan that escaped her shot straight to his groin.

She arched into him, and he moved to the other breast, his hands roaming—kneading her hips, her thighs, the curve of her waist. He wanted to memorize every inch of her. Wanted to map her body with his fingers and tongue until he knew it better than his own.

His mouth traced down her stomach, pausing to dip into her navel. She ran her hands through his hair, nails scraping his scalp, and the sensation sent sparks dancing down his spine. Had anything ever felt this good? Had he ever been *this* alive?

He rubbed his stubbled jaw against her inner thigh, and she squeaked—a sound so endearing he nearly laughed. The scent of her was dizzying. He teased, licking in slow circles, inching closer then retreating. She writhed, fingers twisting in his hair, trying to guide him.

"Thorben." Her voice was ragged. "Please."

That broke him. He dragged his tongue along her slit in one long, slow stroke.

She cried out, her hips bucking off the bed.

He spread her thighs with his hands, his tongue rough against silken heat. She was soaked, and the taste of her made him groan. His thumb circled her clit, slick with her arousal, while two fingers slipped inside.

She moaned, opening wider. Her slick walls gripped him, pulsing, as he pumped slowly—feeling her body respond to every movement.

He withdrew his fingers and brought them to his lips.

Her eyes, heavy-lidded and dark with want, tracked the movement. He held her gaze as he placed them on his tongue, licking her essence clean.

"More," she whispered, grabbing his wrist and pressing his hand back between her thighs.

He obliged.

His fingers slid into her again, faster, deeper. His thumb worked her clit while his mouth found her breast, teeth grazing the peak. She fisted the sheets, back arching.

He curled his fingers, searching for that spot. When he found it, she nearly screamed.

He lowered his mouth to her center, tongue replacing thumb, lapping while his fingers kept their relentless rhythm. She tasted like lightning, like salvation.

"Skyes, Thorben!" Her hips jerked wildly, her hands fisting his hair hard enough to hurt. He didn't care. He suckled her clit, flicking it with his tongue, and felt her entire body seize.

She came with a cry that echoed off the woven walls, her core clenching around his fingers, a rush of wetness flooding his mouth. He lapped at her greedily, drinking her in, prolonging her pleasure until she collapsed boneless against the bed.

For a long moment, he simply watched her. Her chest heaving. Her skin flushed and dewy. Strands of dark hair stuck to her damp face. She was magnificent—beautifully wrecked, trembling in the aftermath.

"Thorben." Her voice was barely a breath. "I need you."

His cock throbbed painfully. "Say it again."

Her turquoise eyes found his, liquid with desire. "Thorben. I need you inside me."

He moved over her, settling between her thighs. The head of his cock brushed against her slick heat, and he shuddered at the contact. A decade without sensation. Of wanting. And now—

Her legs wrapped around him, pulling him closer.

He rubbed himself along her entrance, coating his length in her arousal. The sensation was scorching and perfect, pleasure edged with pain.

"Look at me."

Her eyes locked onto his. He slid inside her in one slow, deep thrust.

The moan that escaped her was the most beautiful sound he'd ever heard. Hot and tight, gripping him like she'd never let go. He held still, buried to the hilt, giving them both time not to shatter.

"You feel incredible," he managed. "Like you were made for me."

She pulled him down and kissed him—deep and desperate, tasting herself on his lips. When she released him, her eyes were fierce.

"Move."

He obeyed. Thorben withdrew slowly, savoring the drag of her walls, then thrust back in. She gasped, nails biting into his shoulders. Again. And again. Building a rhythm that had her clawing at his back.

He shifted her legs over his shoulders, driving deeper. She cried out, her head falling back, and the sight of her throat bared in pleasure made something primal surge through him.

"Ava." Her name was a prayer. He was close—too close.

"Don't!" she gasped. "Not yet!"

He gritted his teeth. His thumb found her clit, stroking in time with his thrusts. She trembled, moans rising in pitch, body drawing tighter—

"Thorben!" Her nails raked down his back as she shattered, her core pulsing around him.

The sensation dragged him over the edge. His orgasm crashed through him—blinding, consuming—and he spilled into her, pleasure flooding every nerve until he thought he might dissolve entirely.

He collapsed beside her, pulling her close, refusing to break contact. Their legs tangled, slick with sweat, breathing ragged.

For a long moment, neither spoke.

Her honeyed skin was flushed, her lips swollen, her expression dazed and sated.

She was his rest after a dark storm. Hot embers chasing away a cold night. The embrace of a long-awaited home.

He pressed a kiss to her damp forehead.

"Mé talé," he whispered. "My treasure."

She smiled against his chest, and he felt it like sunlight breaking through clouds.

"Mé inveni," she murmured back. "My finder."

He held her tighter, listening to her breathing slow, feeling her body relax into sleep.

This was real. She was real. They were real.

And he would protect this—protect her—for as long as he existed.

Chapter Forty-Nine

I n the morning, Ava woke to an empty bed and the scent of lavender drifting through the open window. Her body ached in places she'd forgotten existed, a pleasant soreness that made her smile into the pillow.

She found Thorben in the garden below, coaxing a stubborn vine up the trellis with gentle encouragement. His magic rippled through the leaves, and the plant burst into bloom, winding its way toward the sky. When he caught her watching, his grin sent warmth spreading through her chest.

The morning felt impossibly bright, impossibly normal, like the world had decided to be kind for once.

It wasn't.

"A tube came for you." Rune said as Ava entered the kitchen. She handed Ava a slip of paper with a raised eyebrow. "Are you enjoying your new treehouse out there?"

Heat crawled up Ava's neck. The treehouse. The sounds they'd made. The way she'd shouted his name like a prayer and a curse combined.

She very deliberately did not look out the window. Rune muttered "hmph" and walked away.

"About as much as you love your tree kitchen," Ava shouted when she could swallow her embarrassment. Rune waved a hand, dismissing her remark, and disappeared beneath the arched doorway.

The door swung open, and Thorben stepped through with two colorful souls clinging to his wrists like living bracelets.

"They keep finding me." He held out his hands, bewildered.

A laugh bubbled up before Ava could stop it. She retrieved two essentiae from her belt, humming as she bonded the souls and tucked them into her phylactery.

"Well, but it makes my job significantly easier," Ava said, kissing him.

"What do you have there?" he asked, pointing to the scroll in her hand.

"Let's find out." Ava unrolled the parchment. Thorben inched closer, resting his chin on her shoulder and wrapping his hands around her waist.

"It's from Alistair," Ava said quietly. "Apparently, he's been talking with the Magisterium. Mage Clare has been getting reports from Star Fyre Realm. The Realms seem to be...shifting. He wants us to meet with them."

"That sounds like a stinky swale of a problem," Flip came in from the bedroom. Her blond hair fell clean and shining over one side of her face. While living with them, Flip had stopped trying to hide who she was. Something about that made Ava's chest ache in the good way.

"We should go, *mé veláh* ," Rune said from the kitchen as the scent of lavender oatcakes reached Ava's nose. The three of them followed Rune's voice--and the delicious smell--into the kitchen.

Gabrie was already seated at the high counter, downing breakfast. She was gaining weight, the color having returned to her cheeks. Her once tattered brown hair was now glossy, her bright blue eyes intelligent like Flip's, and equally cautious.

A tentative knock came at the door. Rune opened it to reveal a young girl with blond hair and large, blue eyes. She twisted her hands together, eyes darting to Thorben.

"Uncle Thorben." Her voice rang impertinent as a queen's. "You promised to help me plant my garden today. Mama said you'd probably be busy, but I told her you wouldn't dare break your promise."

The corner of Thorben's mouth quirked as he glanced at Ava. She raised her eyebrows. That little girl wasn't taking no for an answer. He crouched to her level. "I will never break my promises, little niece. I'll be right there."

The girl surveyed the room full of adults watching her, utterly unintimidated. She nodded at Thorben as if granting him permission to finish his business first.

Thorben straightened. "Uncle duty calls." Apology flickered across his face, but his eyes were bright with something Ava hadn't seen before—the quiet joy of being wanted by family.

"Go." Ava touched his arm. "I'll be fine. Rune will be with me. She needs you too."

He pulled her close, pressing his forehead to hers. "Be safe today, *mé talé*. I mean it."

He grabbed a few oatcakes, dropped a kiss on Rune's cheek—she swatted him but made him take one more—and left with one last lingering look at Ava.

"We can take the *Gent*," Ava said to Rune, accepting an oatcake.

"Let me gather my things." Rune untied her apron, and they headed out.

The trip to Seráya City felt like the longest flight Ava had ever taken. Dread sat heavy between her shoulders, pressing down with every mile. Ava piloted while Rune stood beside her, each lost in their own thoughts. If the islands were already drifting, she suspected they didn't have much time to figure out a solution.

When Alistair's private piers came into view, an aircraft marshal was there waiting for them. Ava docked, and she and Rune descended onto the walkway. A man wearing large, dark glasses and an oversized coat watched their approach.

"Avalína Llahenór?" he asked in an official voice, his accent lilting and melodic.

"Seáh," Ava answered. His black skin shimmered with bioluminescent tattoos of swirls, designs, and intricate, delicate patterns. He was walking art, and Ava couldn't tear her gaze away.

"I'm Hybel." He nodded satisfactorily. "I will take you to her majesty." He turned, expecting them to follow.

"I thought we were meeting with the Magisterium?" Ava asked.

"You are," he said, walking toward the pier doors. "Mage Clare is the Queen of Star Fyre Realm. Didn't you know that?"

"Of course, I did." Ava's cheeks heated slightly, and Rune touched her elbow in support. Hybel walked quickly, leaving Ava and Rune several paces behind. His large ears peeked out from beneath glossy dark curls, and Ava couldn't help whispering to Rune, "Why are his ears so big?"

"Because in the Star Fyre Realm," Hybel stopped and spun, pinning them with a stare from behind his large, dark lenses. "We need to hear every chirp of a bird and snap of a twig, or we might be eaten by an obsidian jackal."

"Oh. Why are you wearing glasses?" Ava asked, not being able to help herself.

Hybel froze. Ava supposed he was trying to see if she was truly curious or mocking him. He gave another slight nod and tapped the edge of his large black frames. "The brightness is too much for our eyes in this realm. We are used to very little amounts of light. Perhaps one day you will see." He shrugged. "Or perhaps not."

He motioned for them to follow. "Come, come. Mage Clare is waiting."

Hybel led them to a massive ship docked several piers from her own. The silver hull sparkled in the morning light. Stars and swirls had been painted in intricate detail, mapping patterns of what Ava supposed their night sky to look like. The main mast soared into the clouds, piercing the airspace above.

The group climbed several staircases ending at the highest room on the vessel. Large, white double doors filigreed with more star patterns dominated the landing. Alistair stood to the side, his eyes worried, his arm thickly bandaged and in a sling.

"I'm so glad you came," he approached them, and Ava's hand twitched toward her wired glove before she could stop it. Alistair stopped and lifted his uninjured arm.

"Druis Avalína, Inyanga Rune...I am so sorry for what my ancestors have done to you. I'm doing my best to right the wrongs, and it begins here. I came to welcome you and to apologize."

His icy blue eyes held hers steadily—no flinching, no calculating. When Ava reached out with her spirit, she found only stillness where the chaos had once churned.

"Alright, commodore," Ava sighed, shaking off her initial reaction. It was going to take time for Ava to acclimate to this new goodwill on the face she had only known as evil.

"Thank you. And please call me Alistair." He waved to the doors. "I have been in discussion with Mage Clare, but there are a few matters I need to attend to. She will brief you on what is happening."

Alistair left, and two guards wearing the same large glasses opened the doors. Hybel strutted inside, not looking back to see if they were following. The room was almost completely dark, and Hybel's back disappeared before they could take a step forward.

"Your majesty." Ava heard Hybel say from the darkness.

"I'll go first," Rune said, and led the way.

The space was sparsely lit by large glowing flowers placed evenly about the room. A sweetly scented breeze drifted across Ava's nose and her shoulders relaxed. The ceiling sparkled and shimmered, giving Ava the impression of what a true dark night might be like.

"Thank you, Hybel," a delicate feminine voice murmured. Hybel had taken the queen's hand, brushing it against his forehead in a respectful bow. She was a petite woman, wearing a long, pale lavender robe, and she turned when she saw Ava and Rune.

"Avalína Llahenór." The queen glided forward, her braided sable hair swinging with each step. Light seemed to cling to her. How was Ava supposed to address a queen? Unsure, she offered the only respectful greeting she knew, a traditional Ili greeting.

"Your majesty." Ava placed her left hand on her heart, extending her right for the queen to take.

Mage Clare paused, her oversized, hazel eyes taking in every detail. Delicately, she grasped Ava's wrist, allowing Ava to do the same. The queen's skin was even more intricately tattooed than Hybel's. Lines dipped and swayed over her arms, chest, and neck, coming to a point above her eyebrows.

"Thank you for your respectful greeting, Avalína," Mage Clare said, a slight smile on her face. "I adore how this tradition has stayed in the Realm of Souls. Not many do this in the Star Fyre Realm anymore. Who taught you?"

"My aunt," Ava said, gesturing to Rune. "She always told me it was the best way to show respect. Joining hands and touching our hearts acknowledges our respect for our souls and for the vessels to which we belong."

Mage Clare nodded solemnly. She turned to Rune and bowed, her hand over her heart. "I thank you also, for teaching the old ways. My grandmother's grandmother taught me, and now I am honored that I can return it."

Hybel appeared holding a tray of beverages, their contents slightly glowing. Ava accepted a glass but didn't drink. The liquid glowed invitingly, but her throat had closed around the dread she'd been swallowing since they left home.

"You probably know why I asked you to come." Mage Clare sipped, moving to a dark corner with four plush floor pillows. "I've had reports from the astral mages in my realm."

She looked at them with her huge eyes. "They say their views of the stars are changing. Which means the Realms are shifting."

Ava slumped onto a pillow, her greatest fear echoing in her ears. Rey had been successful in destroying the purdahs, and now everyone would pay the price for her failure to stop him.

"How are they measuring this?" Rune asked.

"In the Star Fyre Realm, we study the stars, charting their changes and movements to better understand the heavens. Most of the time the things we take note of are singular in nature. A single star shifting northeast by a degree, for example," Mage Clare explained. "However, since the barriers were dissolved, my mages report that the stars appear to be shifting as a unit, which means the world in which we measure them is moving."

"Oh no." Rune sunk back into her pillow, her eyes casting into her glass. "I had hoped it wouldn't matter. Part of me thought..."

"After all these years, perhaps we all thought nothing would change," Mage Clare said, nodding in agreement.

"How do we stop them?" Ava lifted her eyes to both women. "What can we do?"

"That's why I've asked you to come. Your family helped to create the purdahs. I thought perhaps you would know a way to fix them."

Rune's gaze drifted somewhere past Ava's shoulder, focusing on nothing visible. "Rubina, dear, you are going to need to come back. I know you don't want to, but it is necessary. I understand. Neo will need to come too. I know you don't..."

Rune rose and perused the room, muttering to herself.

"My aunt, she is...," Ava searched for a good explanation. "Sick. She frequently has hallucinations. I'm sorry. She won't be much help for a while."

"I understand what it is like to have an ill family member and not be able to help." Mage Clare took a sip and watched Rune with curiosity. "I will continue to meet with the Magisterium. I hope between us, and you, we can come to a solution."

"How much time do we have?" Ava asked.

Mage Clare set her drink aside. "At the rate the islands are drifting, my mages say four or five days before the islands are so high in the biosphere that the oxygen will be thin, and we will no longer be able to breathe."

Ava stared at her hands. The glass trembled between her fingers.

Four days. Maybe five.

She'd just found him. Just learned what it meant to wake up next to someone who saw her—all of her—and stayed anyway. Dáhlia had just found a clue to where Aamina's father was. The treehouse still smelled like fresh growth and possibility.

None of it would matter if they couldn't breathe.

"I know this is a large task I am asking of you," Mage Clare said, leaning forward. "But you and your aunt are the only ones with the knowledge of how the Realms were contained a thousand years ago. We need you to research what your family did, and replicate their solution, or devise a better one."

She reached out and pressed her delicate hand against Ava's own. "We will be doing the same. You are not alone. The next time we see each other, we must have a solution to save the Realms."

Ava set her glass aside. "I will do my best, Mage Clare." She placed her hand over her heart, farewelling the queen, and turned to gather Rune.

"Where are we going?" Rune asked as Ava steered her toward the door.

"Home." The word came out hollow. What made Mage Clare think she could fix this? Her aunt was barely lucid, and she had no idea what her family had done to save the Realms except for what the histories said.

"What am I going to do?" Ava whispered to herself as they stepped into the hall.

"We are going to see Zoya." Rune nodded firmly. "Rubi and Neo will be able to help."

"Rune, what are you saying?" Ava turned to her, huffing out a breath. "Rubi and Neo aren't here. They can't do anything for us."

Rune pulled three coins from her pocket. Silver, tarnished with age, warm from being held close for longer than Ava had been alive. Rune pressed her lips to them, murmuring something too soft to catch, then took Ava's hand and placed them on her palm.

The metal hummed against her skin. Not cold or inanimate.

Waiting.

"I have held onto these coins my entire life." A tear slipped down Rune's weathered cheek. "It's time for you to meet your family."

Chapter Fifty

The silver coins were decorated with ancient Ili symbols, each at the end of multiple lines crossing in the center. Ava ran her fingers over the ridges. Symbols of truth, love, desire, loathing, and foolishness slid beneath her fingertips. Could her family truly be bonded to these simple coins? She reached out with her spirit, excited to finally glimpse a bit of her mother or father. But she felt...nothing.

"They're sealed, remember?" Rune said. "Let's go to the temple. Zoya will know what to do. The temple keeps a mage for exactly this kind of work."

The swale stretched before them, familiar paths leading to the temple. Ava clutched the coins against her chest, terrified they might slip away. Her family was inside, waiting. Her fingers tightened around the coins until the edges bit into her palm.

They rushed through the greeting area and into the common space. Zoya entered from another room, pausing when she saw their concerned faces.

"Zoya, we need your help." The words tumbled out before Ava caught her breath. "These coins hold my family's souls, but they're sealed. And we need cadavers—two females and one male."

Zoya's expression shifted from curiosity to understanding. "Mage Oram is here today. I'll send for him." She gestured to a passing disciple, murmuring instructions. The girl hurried off. "Now, about the cadavers ...?"

Zoya looked at each of their grim faces. "I have a female and a male. That is all."

Ava's shoulders dropped. How would they choose who got the cadavers?

"What about in another district?" Rune asked, her eyes clear and focused.

Zoya considered for a moment. "I can send a messenger to Roxana in the South District. She may have some." Zoya motioned to a passing disciple. She quickly gave her instructions and the girl scurried off.

"We should know in about an hour," Zoya said. "I can show you the cadavers we do have."

Rune and Ava followed Zoya to the Passing Room, the scents of orange and ginger greeting them. Most of the stone benches were empty, but at the far end of the room were two bodies covered in white blankets.

The first was a large, middle-aged woman with deep bronze skin and wavy chestnut hair that flowed past colorful bangles at her wrists. Serene, even in death.

"She came to us last night," Zoya explained. "Ready to move on."

She led them to a stone bench on the other side. "This one might pose a problem—he said he was being hunted and wanted it done with."

He was striking. Shaved head, strong jaw, deep black skin. His muscular frame filled the entire platform, shoulders hanging over the edges.

"Black Sands?" Ava asked.

Zoya nodded. "From his accent, I'd imagine so."

"We don't have time to be picky," Rune reminded her. "Even if he is being hunted, it won't matter if we don't save the Realms."

Zoya nodded, lips pressed together. A moment later, a wiry man with silver-streaked hair entered—Mage Oram, Ava assumed. He moved with the quiet efficiency of someone who'd done this work a thousand times.

"The seals are old," he said, examining the coins Ava held out. "But intact. Well-crafted." His fingers traced patterns in the air above them, and Ava felt the magic shift—a lock clicking open that she hadn't known was there. "Done."

He nodded to Zoya and slipped out as quickly as he'd come.

Ava stared at the coins in her palm. Three small discs of silver, tarnished and ancient. Her family. She reached out with her spirit, tentative, afraid of what she might find—or worse, what she might not.

The first soul blazed against her senses like a bon fyre. Warmth, steadiness, a love so fierce it made her eyes sting. Beneath it, an ache—old grief worn smooth by time, but still present. *Father.* She knew it without knowing how.

The second burned hotter, sharper. Frustration coiled tight as a spring, impatience crackling at the edges. But underneath—loyalty. Protectiveness. A heart that loved fiercely even when it showed teeth instead of tenderness. *Sister.*

The third was cool and deep, like a lake at midnight. Calm surface, fathomless depths. Truth and righteousness woven together so tightly Ava couldn't tell where one ended and the other began. And love—quiet, certain, immovable as stone. *Mother.*

Her throat tightened. They'd been here all along. Waiting in Rune's pocket while Ava grew up wondering why she only had an aunt.

She blinked hard and chose two coins.

"This one will need the man's cadaver." She handed her father's coin to Zoya, the warmth of his soul still echoing through her fingers.

Ava hesitated over the remaining coins. Her mother's soul called to her—that deep, calm presence she'd been missing her whole life without knowing it. But the woman's cadaver before her had a warrior's build beneath the softness, a strength in the set of her jaw even in death.

Dorienne's fyre would fit here. Rubina's stillness would not.

She handed Zoya her sister's coin and prayed she was right.

Zoya waited for Ava to give her the other essentia. When Ava hesitated, she asked, "Would you like to perform the rituals?"

Ava loved reuniting souls with new forms, but to do it with her own family made her nervous. What if they didn't like the cadavers she had chosen? Or if she released them and they veered off into the liminal plane instead of bonding with the body? She wasn't sure she could face that.

"It will be alright," Rune assured her, seeing the hesitation on her face. "They won't leave you." Swallowing, Ava knelt next to the female cadaver, Zoya near the male.

When they were ready, Zoya requested quietly, "Avalína, please sing."

Ava closed her eyes. Her song formed, lilting and beautiful, the words cascading over her tongue in the beautiful language of Ili, as if her spirit knew she would need such a song for her family.

The soul within the coin burst outward in a flurry of scarlet and burnt umber. Woodsmoke filled the air, sharp and acrid. It swirled furiously, anxious and impatient. It hovered over the empty form, traveling from head to toe, inspecting it.

Ava's voice softened, the soul's turmoil overwhelming. It was angry, unsure if it wanted to live another life. Finally, she settled along the breastbone of the body, accepting the bond. Ava stopped singing, releasing her breath.

Out of the corner of her eye, Ava saw movement near Zoya. The large man was slowly rising into a sitting position, the white blanket falling off to reveal a strong, sculpted chest. It seemed his soul had bonded easily with his new form.

The woman's fingers twitched. Ava leaned over, gently placing her hand on the woman's shoulder. "Hello," Ava said quietly. "Take all the time you need. Bonding can be difficult."

The woman's eyes flew open, and she jerked upright, knocking Ava backward. "Where am I? How long has it been?"

"You're in the Temple of the Five." Ava gathered herself from where she had fallen on the stone floor. Dorienne's bright brownish gold eyes studied her, the piercing gaze carrying an accusatory glint that left Ava feeling exposed. She wrapped her arms around her middle.

"Who are you?"

"Avalína." Her sister's soul vibrated with irritation, anger, frustration. Ava resisted the urge to step back.

"Why am I here?"

"The Realms need you. The purdahs have been destroyed. The Magisterium requested you and..." It was too soon to speak out loud about her mother and father, the words tripping over her tongue.

"Of course," Dorienne sighed, irritated. "Always trying to help save the world, aren't we?"

"What?" Ava asked. She'd thought Dorienne had wanted to help the Magisterium—at least, that's how Rune's stories made it sound.

"Nothing." Dorienne rolled her eyes. "What kind of body is this anyway?"

"It's..." Ava blinked, still catching up. This was her sister? The hero from Rune's stories?

"Well, I can see it's going to need some work." Dorienne pinched her middle with a grimace. "I was never this out of shape."

"Dorienne." Zoya moved over, smiling. "I'm so pleased to finally meet you."

The large man followed Zoya, a white cloth tied around his middle. When he spoke, his voice was deep and rich. "Dori?"

"I'm here, *Decorimé*." Dorienne went to stand, her legs a bit shaky as she covered herself with the blanket. She motioned toward Ava. "This one brought me back."

Large, dark eyes swiveled to Ava, and he stared unblinkingly. He was intimidating, and Ava swallowed, trying to find her voice. "*Seáh ll-*"

"Bavjí?" He cut her off. "Is it really you?" The vibrations of his words flowed through her, settling in her chest. A single tear dripped down his dark face. "The last time I saw you, you had chubby hands that pulled everything out of my tinkering drawers." His voice faltered. "You used to hide my gears in your pockets and laugh when I couldn't find them."

Dorienne's eyes cut sideways, widening. "Bavjí?" Something flickered across her face—surprise, then something harder to read. She looked away quickly.

Avalína looked from one to the other. "I don't...My name is—"

"I would recognize your soul anywhere, *mé le dar*, my little one."

The soul Ava felt inside him was overflowing with love and adoration. She allowed him to wrap her in his arms. His embrace felt like a long-lost treasure, something she had cherished once but hadn't realized she was missing it. He stroked her hair and stepped back to study her face. "You are so beautiful."

Zoya lightly sniffed and Rune raised her eyebrows. Zoya waved her off and shook her head.

"Did you think I would let her be bonded with just anyone, Neo?" Rune asked him. "And her name is Avalína now."

Neo paused, turning the name over. "Avalína," he repeated softly. "One who guides the lost." His dark eyes glistened. "It suits you, *mé le dar*. You have always led souls home. Vivia, a *yah ageremé*. You chose well." Neo grabbed Rune and lifted her off her feet, squeezing her in his massive arms. She squealed and promptly hit him. "Put me down!"

His laugh rumbled through his chest as he released her. "I'm so glad to see you."

"Well. I didn't bring you back to reminisce," Rune sniffed, smoothing her clothes, but hiding a smile. "We have work to do."

"Work?" Neo raised an eyebrow.

"Neo?" Ava asked, turning to Rune. "You've been hallucinating about Neo and Rubi for years."

"I've held their secret for a long time." Rune brushed her pale hand against Neo's dark face. He kissed her palm. "I guess my wishes to talk to you manifested when I wasn't thinking clearly. It's so good to have you back, Neo."

"Where is Rubina?" he asked, looking around the room hopefully.

"We didn't have a cadaver for her," Zoya answered, apologetically. "But we asked another temple and are waiting for them to get back to us."

Ava held out the last coin. "Here she is." She carefully placed it in her father's massive dark hand. He touched the coin with reverence.

"Rubi," he whispered. A lump formed in Ava's throat. She'd never seen anyone look at a coin the way her father looked at that one.

"What disaster is the world in now?" Dorienne asked, brushing her hair away from her face.

"The purdahs are gone."

Dorienne's eyebrows hit her hairline. "Are you serious?"

"That isn't possible," Neo said firmly, looking up. "The purdahs were exceptionally made. No spell would be strong enough."

"Rey found a way," Avalína said.

"Rey?" Dorienne spat. "That black-hearted druid is still around? I'd thought he'd have gone to Tartarean by now."

"I pulled his soul from the cadaver he had been in and the prince collected him," Ava said.

Dorienne's lips tightened into a thin line, her nod barely perceptible. A flicker of disappointment settled in Ava's chest at Dorienne's muted response.

"He had been taking his descendants' bodies as cadavers, using their knowledge and magic. He had become quite powerful," Rune said.

"He bonded thousands of lost souls together and used their energy to take down the purdahs." The last bit Ava said quietly. Saying what had happened out loud brought a sadness to her heart all over again.

"How do you know they are gone?" Neo asked.

"Mage Clare has been getting reports from Star Fyre. The realms are floating away from each other. Soon, we will be so high in the atmosphere we won't be able to breathe. The Magisterium has asked us to recreate the purdahs."

"That's impossible," Dorienne huffed. "The sequence of events and combination of science magics was a once in a lifetime occurrence. You won't be able to repeat it."

"Dorienne's right." Neo's deep voice penetrated the room. "We were uniquely suited to the challenge back then. I'm not sure we will be the same people who can save the world a second time."

"We have no one else," Rune said quietly. "Rey is gone, but Ava needs you. Our family needs to be together for once without the world falling apart. Fix this and you will be able to have that time."

Dorienne looked at Neo and back to Rune.

"Fine," she sighed. "What do we have to work with?"

"Right now, not much," Ava said. "We don't know exactly what the biosphere is doing other than not holding the islands in place."

"If the purdahs are destroyed, we may need an entirely new solution," Dorienne said. "The barriers used opposing magnetic forces to hold the islands together. The original Five souls bonded with the Realms acted as glue. The higher the islands drift, the weaker that pull becomes."

"And the higher the islands drift—" Ava said.

"They'll disintegrate, releasing the Five's souls completely," Dorienne finished.

They were silent for a moment, the weight of an uncertain future settling in their minds.

Zoya suggested a time to reflect and led them through a corridor lined with alcoves—each with comfortable seating, a small hearth, tea service. Dorienne huffed off to one alone. Ava sat with Neo and Rune while Zoya left to check for Roxana's message.

Neo held the coin she had given him tenderly in his hand. She was trying to remember what he had been like before, but she couldn't recall.

Feeling her eyes on him, he looked at her. "You must have so many questions."

Ava moved her gaze to the fyre. She wanted to ask everything she never thought she would get an answer to. What had they been like as a family? Why did this have to happen to them? Were they...happy to be alive again?

"Dorienne was a little put off," Rune muttered.

"Don't worry about her," Neo said, waving a large dark hand. "You know what she can be like. Her reactions are always hot at first, but in the end, she knows what's important."

"Why is she so angry?" Ava asked. She saw her aunt exchange a look with Neo.

Neo sighed. "There is a lot of history between her, your mother, and I. She is hurt and it is partially my fault."

"Will she help us?" Ava asked, rubbing her arms. Without Dorienne's assistance they wouldn't be able to fix the biosphere.

"*Seáh.*" Neo's brow furrowed. "She will hold it over our heads for the next twenty years, but she will help."

Ava nodded, already dreading the next twenty years. She wondered what kind of relationship they had had as siblings. "What I was like...before?"

Neo smiled. "You were a beautiful little girl. Smart, spunky, and you spoke to the souls all the time. We knew then you would be a powerful druis." He paused, his face falling. "I'm sorry I wasn't fast enough to save us all."

He leaned forward and enclosed her hand in his. "I have wished for this moment many times. Being in the essentia was calm, but I remembered your little face, the way your skin smelled, the silkiness of your hair," he said, gazing at her with dark eyes. "You look different now, but you are still the same beautiful daughter I held and loved."

Ava gave him a small smile. "Rune told me how she brought my soul back from Empyrean. But—I remember being a child and growing up. The cadaver I received must have been someone very young."

"She was," Zoya entered, a small lantern in her hands. Ava turned, her mouth dropping open. Had Zoya known and never told her? Why?

"Please tell me," Neo requested. "I'd like to thank the family personally, if I could."

Zoya smiled. "They are no longer here, but know that you have been heard, Neo." Zoya hung the lantern on a hook and sat next to Rune.

"One night, Rune came to me asking for help. She needed a way to bring Ava back from Empyrean and the time was right for her return. The temple arranged a meeting with a young woman—pregnant, but the baby's soul had already decided to leave this world." Zoya sniffed and wiped her nose. "Together, we brought Ava back through the portal. She sought out the aching mother's heart instantly and did what she could to make her whole again. Claimed both the mother and the baby girl for herself."

Ava sat with the knowledge settling into her soul. Another mother. Somewhere out there, a woman who had carried her, loved her, let her go. The questions pressed against her heart—who was she? Where was she now?

Neo rose. "Thank you, Mother Zoya. For the services you have done for Viv—I mean, Rune, and Avalína all these years."

"It has been an honor," Zoya said quietly, bowing her head. "Also, they have brought a cadaver. Please come with me."

They followed Zoya to the Passing Room. A petite form lay waiting—milk-pale skin, platinum blond hair. Neo sucked in a breath.

"Will this do?" Zoya asked.

He nodded slowly. "She will accept this cadaver."

Zoya reached her hand out for the coin, and Neo gently placed it in her palm. Ava and Neo watched as Zoya's beautiful words brought her mother from within the coin. Her soul was a deep midnight blue with streaks of yellow and gold. The scent of fresh berries and lemons filled the air. Ava's spirit stirred, reaching toward the soul that had once created her. Rubina calmly flowed near Zoya, eventually settling into the waiting cadaver.

After a few moments, the cadaver's chest rose and fell, her breathing light and steady. Neo shuffled forward.

"Rubi?" he whispered.

The woman slowly opened her eyes—a prism of colors reflecting the light. Neo gasped. She lifted her hand, regal even in confusion, and he took it, helping her to stand.

"Where are we?" she asked in a soft voice. "What is this?" She lifted a petite hand to her face, studying the pale fingernails.

"Your soul has bonded with a new body," Neo explained.

Rubi barely reached Neo's shoulder, his frame twice as large as hers. She looked miniature and pale next to the largeness and darkness of her husband.

"That body is very large," she said pointedly.

"I suppose it is," he smiled at her. "It will take some getting used to. I have waited so long to see you again..."

"Rubi—" Neo placed his hand on Ava's back, urging her forward. "This is Bavjí. But she goes by Avalína now."

She reached both hands out to touch Ava's arms, her hair, her face.

"Avalína." Rubina tested the name on her tongue, her prismatic eyes studying her face, drinking in every detail. "My beautiful girl." Her voice caught. "You were barely walking when I last held you. I'm so sorry I wasn't there...."

"It's alright," Ava replied, her voice thick. "Rune was here. I know you did what you needed."

Rubina wrapped Ava in a hug. She was smaller than Ava, but the body she had bonded with was strong, and she held on like she was afraid Ava might disappear again. Tears spilled before Ava could stop them. She wanted to speak, to say something memorable, but her throat had closed around a thousand years of longing.

"Where is Dorienne?" Rubi asked Neo, releasing her hold on Ava.

"I'm here." Dorienne walked in, her hair now combed, swept into a crowning braid atop her head. She walked to Rubi and embraced her. "I've missed you so much, laurimé."

"I as well, adorimé," Rubi rubbed Dorienne's back in small circles, Dorienne physically relaxing under the touch.

"I'm here too," Rune piped up.

Rubi released Dorienne and turned to Rune, bringing her into a firm embrace. "Vivia, thank you for taking care of my girls."

"I said I would, didn't I?" Rune huffed.

"I wish this family moment could go on forever, but we've been told we have a crisis." Dorienne's voice carried its usual edge, but something underneath had softened. "Let's see what needs to be done."

Ava looked around the room—her father, her mother, and her sister. Family she'd never known existed but had felt that something—or rather *someone*—had always been missing.

And four days to save them all.

Chapter Fifty-One

When they arrived back at Rune's, Ava made introductions. Gabrie's eyes went round at the sight of Neo—this massive, dark-skinned stranger filling the doorway. She pressed herself against Flip's side.

Neo crouched to her level, his deep voice dropping to a rumble. Whatever he whispered made Gabrie's wariness dissolve into giggles.

Dorienne watched the exchange with flat eyes, then swept past without acknowledging anyone. Flip stiffened, positioning herself slightly between Dorienne and Gabrie. The two women's gazes met for a fraction of a second—mutual assessment, mutual dislike—before Dorienne disappeared into the kitchen.

Tubes had gone out to Toby and Mergen hours ago. Toby roared up on his skybyke before sundown. Mergen hadn't responded.

"This is magnificent." Neo's eyes widened as he entered Rune's kitchen. He touched a branched shelf, fingers tracing the living wood.

"Thorben made it," Rune said, heading to the fyreplace.

Neo turned to Thorben with a nod of genuine appreciation. "You have a gift."

"Thank you." Thorben's arm settled around Ava's waist—casual, possessive, unmistakable.

Toby's jaw tightened. He busied himself pulling out a chair, its legs scraping against the floor louder than necessary. "Where would you like to start?"

"We have four days, five max," Dorienne said, setting paper and writing material on the long wooden table. "Reports are that the Realms are drifting apart, moving away from the core. The purdahs are no longer holding them in place but the souls of the Five are still bound to each realm as far as we know, correct?" Dorienne asked, and there was a chorus of nods around the table.

"Ava," Rubina pressed her lips together. "Can you communicate with the spirits of the Five?"

"I...don't know," Ava said.

Rubina blinked her multicolored eyes at her. "Try. Please. Reach out with your soul," Rubina encouraged her. "Feel beneath our feet, to the very core of our world. They are ancient. Tired and weary, I'm sure."

Ava let her spirit unfold from within her, seeking an essence as regal and timeless as her mother. She pressed into the earth, stretching to the edges of the island, and out to the sky. Sweat beaded at her temples. Each small stretch cost her, but with every push, the world opened wider—souls brushing past like leaves in a current. Vaguely, she felt Thorben's fingers lace with hers. Steady. Grounding. Souls from the entire island brushed against her spirit, but she dismissed them. They weren't who she was looking for.

Finally, she gave up, the pressure against her temples too great. "I can't," Ava said, breathless. "I can only go so far."

Rubi dipped her head and nodded. "They are there, I assure you. Keep trying."

The group began discussing strategies and spells, but the words tumbled around Ava's numb ears. Her mother was right. She needed to be able to connect with the bonded souls if they were going to figure out a way to save the Realms. She gave Thorben's hand a small squeeze and quietly slipped out to the garden. She needed to be alone.

She sat beneath the gazebo and stared into the cold fyreplace. Her spirit unfurled again, pressing deep—through dirt, roots, crawling things. It spread through the forests, the city, and the mountains.

Finally, a spark of something caught her attention. A sensation drifted up from deep within the earth. An old soul gingerly reached out, its touch curious and cautious. Ava opened herself even more, her spirit flowing through the dirt beneath her feet.

"I feel you," Ava whispered. "Talk to me, tell me what's happening."

The spirit flowed and ebbed, dancing with her, getting familiar with her spirit. Ava smiled as they both recognized they were from the same time and place. An image hit Ava's mind and she gasped, eyes flying open.

Ava burst into the kitchen. "The souls of the Five are weaved into the liminal level."

"What?" Dorienne asked. "How do you know?"

"One of them showed me. Each of the five souls are not only bonded to their own realm but have been weaved into the fabric of the liminal level too. If they are torn from it, it will rip, and that will tear everything else from the inside out. We need to make sure they stay bonded to the liminal level *and* the Realms."

"Huh," Dorienne said. "My spell worked better than I thought."

"Thank you, Ava," Rubina said, casting an admonishing glance at Dorienne. Dorienne shrugged and went back to writing.

"What's the plan so far?" Ava moved toward her mother, but Dorienne shifted almost imperceptibly—a slight angling of her shoulders, a frost in her gaze that said, *not here.*

Ava swallowed the sting and rounded the table to Neo's side instead. Thorben shifted closer, his shoulder pressing against hers—warm where her sister's presence was cold.

"Dorienne and I are crafting a spell that will use the natural magnetic pull of the islands," Rubina said. "I can alter the atmospheric pressure, creating extremely dense air. If the compacted pressure is combined with the magnetic pull at the core, we can create a new sort of webbing. Now that we know the Five are already interwoven through the liminal level, we need to take that into consideration. Ava, can you connect with the souls again? We require any and all the information they can give us. The spell we use must be tailor made to fit the situation."

"Is there anything specific you want me to ask?"

"Find out..." Rubina paused. "How long before they will be released from their bonds."

"Until then," Neo said, "Toby and I will get to work on an enhancer that will magnify the spell you and Dorienne use. I'm suspicious that as the islands drift apart, the spell will need to be strong enough to pull them together again."

Toby nodded, already pulling tools from his pack. His movements were efficient, focused—the Toby she'd always known, most alive when his hands had something to build. He glanced up, caught her watching, and something flickered across his face before he looked away.

Ava frowned. What was he thinking? She scrubbed her face. It didn't matter. She needed space to think. She slipped out of the kitchen and headed toward the treehouse. Maybe the stillness would help. Thorben followed, silent on the grass behind her. His hand came to rest on the small of her back, and some of the tightness in her shoulders eased. The door closed behind them.

Ava spun. "Thor, what if...?" She couldn't finish, her unspoken fears echoing in the room. With the monumental task ahead of them, she questioned her own strength, her own resolve.

Thorben wrapped his arms around her, and Ava buried her nose in his neck, the smell of fresh rain and mint enveloping her. "We all feel a little overwhelmed at the moment," he said, rubbing her back. "But we can do this. I know we can. Look how far you've brought me, just by being who you are."

He leaned back, tipping Ava's chin up to meet his eyes. "I had no hope, and now, even though we may be facing the end, I wouldn't want to be anywhere else—with anyone else—other than you, right at this moment."

Thorben's rugged face became blurry as tears gathered in Ava's eyes, one dripping down her cheek. He kissed her, lingering to take the saltiness of the tears that had slid onto her lips.

"We can do this. You can do this," he whispered.

They settled on a sofa made of woven branches and soft pillows—one of the many things Thorben had grown for them in this strange, beautiful home. Ava tucked herself against his side, his heartbeat steady beneath her ear. For a moment, she let herself pretend this was just an ordinary evening. That they had time.

But they didn't.

She sighed, closed her eyes, and stretched out her spirit, seeking the other four souls. The first one she had met greeted her excitedly, and he branded his name on her mind.

"Imudír," Ava whispered. The weight of Thorben's body next to hers shifted, and she felt him lean closer. "How much time do we have?" Imudír's soul shifted, ebbed and flowed, touching her spirit but not able to bring her near enough. "Talk to me..." Ava scrunched up her face, trying desperately to connect with him. He kept coming forward, but then inching back, as if trying to draw her away.

Ava breathed out through her nose and opened her eyes. "I think he wants me to follow him somewhere. Almost like..."

"He wants you in the liminal level," Thorben said, dropping his gaze to his hands.

"Did you ever feel them—the Five—in the plane?" Ava asked.

Thorben shook his head. "Not specifically. But there was always this...pull." Thorben raised his head, thoughtful. "Like a grounding of sorts, but I could never figure out where it came from or how to get to it. It just...existed."

If Ava went into the liminal level, she was more confident now that she could return. But would she be able to connect with the Five?

"I'm going to try."

"I'll be here when you get back." He gave her hand a quick squeeze.

Ava took a deep breath and felt her way to the barrier between worlds, entering it easily. She dropped into the plane, the thick air surrounding her in a welcoming embrace.

A presence materialized beside her. She turned, expecting one of the Five.

"Thorben?" Ava's eyes widened. "How did you get here?"

"I..." Thorben looked around, an incredulous look on his face. "I don't know. One minute I was holding your hand and the next I felt the plane suck me in."

"It drew you back?"

Thorben shrugged. "Maybe it was because I was touching you?"

"That seems..." Ava frowned. "Not impossible I suppose."

Thorben shrugged, but grinned. "At least I can help you now."

Ava huffed a laugh. "I guess so."

Together, they wandered through the thick blue. "If I were a thousand-year-old soul, where would I be?" Ava muttered. Her soul reached out, seeking Imudír's familiar essence.

A moment later, the air shimmered, and a man materialized from the ether. He wore a druid's robes, his hair short and brown, his eyes kind.

"Are you the druis that found me earlier?"

"Y—yes. Are you Imudír?" Ava inched forward, her eyes straining to see through the mist. But he remained elusive, his form the same distance away no matter how much closer she crept.

"I am. You remind me of someone," he said, tapping his chin. "She had the same concerned look for everyone she knew."

"Who?"

"Her name was Vivia."

Ava's throat constricted, her eyes going wide.

"Ah, you must know her."

"She's my aunt," Ava said, her voice barely above a whisper. A thousand years, and he still remembered Rune. Still saw something of her in Ava. Something warm bloomed in her chest.

"You *are* the spirit I felt. I couldn't quite discern how your deep, ancient soul had a streak of youthfulness. Seeing you explains it."

"I'm Avalína." Ava placed a hand on her heart. "I am honored to meet you."

"Avalína?" he asked, his eyebrows raised. His image rippled as if wind blew across the surface of a reflection. "How intriguing. The honor is mine, Avalína," he replied, resting a hand to his heart. "I'm glad you are here. We have felt a disturbance and are wondering what has happened."

Ava recounted recent events, watching his mouth form a thin line at Rey's name.

"We felt the plane weaken, but we didn't know what had caused it. Rey never wanted to hear that his way was not the right way," he sighed. "The hold we have on the island is slipping as we are being torn away from each other. What is being done?"

"We are working on a plan," Ava said. "Can you tell me how much time we have before you lose all connection with the realm you are bonded with?"

"I cannot say for sure," he said. "Time is different here than it is there. But the bond is considerably weaker. I'm sure your friend can tell."

"Who?" Ava turned. "Thorben?"

"The plane recognizes those who have spent time here," Imudír commented. "We know you from your period of residence just like the plane does. It's only natural your soul would want to return to something it has been a part of for so long. Tell me, how does the plane feel to you?"

Thorben's eyes roamed the ether. "Now that you mention it, the air seems...thinner. Like it's spreading apart."

Imudír nodded slowly. "I wanted to be wrong, Avalína. I'm sorry."

"Thank you, Imudír." Ava offered him a touch to her heart as a farewell. "We better be getting back."

"I will tell the others to be patient," Imudír said. "They will be grateful a solution is coming."

Ava and Thorben rose out from the liminal plane, the warmth of the island air brushing against their skin. For a moment, they just breathed—readjusting to the solidity of the treehouse, the weight of their own bodies.

"The plane pulled you in," Ava said finally. "Just from touching me."

Thorben's expression was unreadable. "It remembered me."

Something in his voice made her chest tighten. A decade trapped there, and the plane still claimed him as its own. She cupped his face, waiting until his eyes met hers.

"You're here now. With me."

He turned his head to press a kiss to her palm. "Always."

"I need to tell Rubina—I mean, Laurimé—what we learned." She gave him a quick kiss. "I'll be right back."

Ava found her mother sitting on a bench in the garden, looking up at the clouds, her platinum blond hair swinging in the light breeze. Her eyes had a distant glow to them. Evening had fallen and dusky pinks, golds and peaches streaked across the sky.

"Are you alright?" Ava asked.

Rubina sighed. "I grew up in Star Fyre Realm. I have charted the lights of stars and planets my entire life. When your father brought me to his home, I continued. Back then, the night was truly dark. It was a habit, a reminder of home," she said. "It is strange for me to be in a place with no stars and no true darkness."

Ava sat next to her mother's slight frame, the coolness of the grass tickling her feet. "I'm sure this isn't what you wanted to wake up to."

"Neyá," Rubi said. "But I am glad I get to be here with you, if for only a moment."

"I spoke with Imudír," Ava said. Rubina's prism-colored eyes snapped to her. "He said the bond they have is weakening. The liminal plane is getting thinner."

"Imudír...He was always so kind. A very honest druid. I must tell Dorienne. We need to adjust our spellwork."

"Where is she?" Ava asked, looking around the garden.

"She said she needed space to think and went for a run. I don't think she likes that Flip girl very much," Rubina added, a note of weariness in her voice. "Dorienne doesn't like many people."

Ava smiled faintly. "She doesn't seem to like me either."

Rubina was silent for a long moment. "Your sister has...complicated feelings. About many things. Give her time."

Time. The one thing none of them had.

Ava let it go. She'd gained a deeper understanding of Flip these past weeks—the fierce protectiveness, the desperate choices made for family. She couldn't fault Dorienne for being wary of Flip. Hadn't Ava felt the same not long ago?

"I'll go find her," Rubina smiled. "Well done, Ava." She squeezed her hand and went back to the house.

After a quick meeting with the new information, they adjusted what they could. Rubina, Dorienne and Neo hadn't slept since their return, and Rune pointed out no one would be any good unless they had some sleep.

When Ava left the house, Thorben stood in the large tree-made doorway at the edge of the garden, hands in his pockets, the light from the house silhouetting his large, defined frame.

"We've decided to take a break," Ava said, stifling a yawn. Thorben pulled her into a strong, comforting embrace. She hadn't realized how much the liminal level had drained her. And her family—their presence was a gift and a weight she was still learning to carry.

Tomorrow, they'd save the world. Tonight, she just wanted to be held.

Chapter Fifty-Two

Thorben guided her into the bedroom, pulling her down onto the bed. Ava closed her eyes, willing sleep to come. It didn't. Her mind churned through spell components, atmospheric pressures, magnetic forces—none of which she fully understood. Would Dorienne and Rubina find something that worked? Would it be strong enough? Would Neo and Toby's design to maximize its output be effective? Maybe she should be helping them. She knew the intricacies of steam powered engines and how to communicate with the Five. If she could—

"What are you thinking about?" Thorben whispered, his hand lightly stroking her back. Ava took a breath to deny her worry, but Thorben said, "Don't tell me 'nothing'. I can feel your mind churning."

Ava sighed and propped her head on her hand, looking down at Thorben. "I can't sleep. I know I should, but—maybe I can help Neo and Toby? I know enough that I could offer some suggestions to the machine they're building."

"*Seáh*, if you wanted." He brushed her long, ebony waves over her shoulder. The shirt she was wearing slipped off and his finger traced along the edge of her skin, sending shivers through her. "But right now, everyone is sleeping. You'll think more clearly in the morning."

"I don't want to sleep. I *can't* sleep." Ava sat up and rubbed her face.

"What do you need?" Thorben asked. "I'll do anything in my power to help you."

"I don't know. I just need to...*do* something." She needed to move, to stretch and push against the restlessness in her bones.

Thorben's eyes darkened, a slow smile curving his lips. "I can think of something."

"Thor, I'm serious—"

"So am I." He sat up, and she felt the shift in him—from comforting to predatory. His voice dropped, words slipping into the ancient cadence of Ili. A vine crept across the blanket and encircled her wrist. Ava's breath caught.

"I could keep you busy," he murmured, and another vine slid around her other wrist, tugging gently. "Occupy that racing mind of yours."

Her pulse kicked. "What are you—"

"Let me distract you." His fingers traced up her arm, feather-light, while the vines tightened just enough to pin her hands to the bed. "Until all you can think about is me."

The restlessness in her bones shifted into something else entirely. Heat pooled low in her belly.

"Yes," Ava breathed. "Make me forget."

"No."

Ava paused. "N—No?"

Thorben placed a hand on each side of her face, caressing her cheeks with the pads of his thumbs, kissing her lightly. "I can't do that. I won't." Vines tickled her foot, wrapping themselves around her ankles. "I want you to remember this." His thumb traced her lower lip. "Why we're fighting. What we're fighting for."

He leaned close, his forehead pressing to hers. "A lifetime, Ava. With you. That's worth saving the world."

Vines trailed over her legs, their blossoming leaves kissing her skin with the faintest of touches, wrapping themselves around her ankles. Her heart hammered. She tugged against the bonds—testing, not fighting.

The vines held firm. She'd never seen him use his magic like this. Never imagined he would.

She should be afraid. She wasn't.

The vines seemed to sense her surrender. They loosened just enough to let her breathe deeper, then tightened again when her pulse spiked—responding to her body as if they were extensions of Thorben's own hands. He pulled her down, and she caught the look on his face—wonder and wicked delight mingled together. He had her bound and willing beneath his hands, his magic, his mouth.

He nuzzled between her breasts, breath whispering against her skin. When he nipped at her nipple through the thin fabric, her core clenched in response.

"Fight for this," he murmured, pulling her shirt low. One breast sprung free and he drew the pink nipple into his mouth, his other hand cupping her rear, squeezing. Ava arched into him, a whimper escaping her lips.

He released her with a soft pop, breath cool against her wet skin. "Remember what it feels like when I touch you here." His fingers trailed down her stomach, making her shiver.

"And here." His hand slid between her thighs, brushing against her folds. She gasped.

"Do you want to forget what it's like when I'm inside you?" He nipped at her earlobe. "When you come apart screaming my name?"

"No," she breathed. "I don't want to forget."

"Good." His voice was rough velvet. "Then remember. Every. Single. Moment."

His hands massaged her thighs, fingers curling into the fabric. The vines released her ankles before he even reached for them—anticipating his needs. He tugged her pants away slowly, savoring. The cool air tickled her skin, and she shuddered, heat flowing to her face.

The vines reclaimed her ankles as he plucked a delicate, cream-colored flower from it. He brushed it against her nose. "Do you like mint?"

"Seáh," Ava breathed. The flower's potent scent curled into her lungs, cool and sharp. Her shoulders loosened, tension unspooling with each inhale.

He dipped his fingers into the flower and brushed her nipples with the fluid, leaving a trail over her belly button, her inner thigh, behind her knee. Ava shuddered, the oils creating an icy heat over her skin.

He tipped the flower to his mouth, letting the nectar drip onto his tongue. Slowly, deliberately, he licked his lips until they glistened.

The way he looked at her—hungry, patient, certain—made her core clench.

One hand caressed her bottom while the other drifted to the curls at her apex, barely grazing. Before she could moan, his mouth captured hers. His tongue swept deep, painting nectar across her lips, her teeth, the soft inside of her cheeks. Cool fyre bloomed in her throat and spread through her lungs with every breath.

"Thor—" Ava squeaked. Her core throbbed, desperate for his touch. Her nipples were painfully tight.

"Not enough?" He asked. He picked two more flowers, coating his palms with the nectar. He pressed a thumb to her core, rubbing her small bud of pleasure, spreading the liquid over her folds. Every touch was searing frost, burning through her body, and she couldn't help the low moan that escaped her throat.

Ava raised her hips, inviting, asking, giving—she wasn't sure which. The vines read her need before she could voice it, tilting her pelvis higher, spreading her wider, offering her up to him like a gift. All she knew was that she needed *more*.

Thorben's mouth suddenly covered her center, hot and demanding. She jerked, his tongue lapping, stroking, and devouring. Ava cried out, her body wilting. The minty coolness of the plant's oils set fyre to her flesh making every movement of Thorben's mouth and tongue delicious agony. He stroked her, back and forth, massaging her rear, as his tongue invaded her innermost places.

His fingers parted her, and he blew against her hot flesh. Her hips bucked wildly, but the vines anticipated her—tightening where she pulled, loosening where she needed to move, holding her exactly where Thorben wanted her. Thorben's tongue flicked over her tight bud, and then his mouth descended.

Her body shuddered as the mixture of fyre, ice, and passion filled her to the brim, threatening to destroy her from the inside out. Blissful moans filled their forest den, and Thorben suckled harder making her shrieks louder, more desperate. A scream tore its way from her lungs, and exploded through her lips, her very being feeling everything and nothing.

Thorben discarded his clothing into a heap on the mossy floor. He snagged another flower, dumping the contents onto his shaft. Ava watched, the muscles in his chest twitching as he stroked along his length, distributing the nectar. His eyes bored into hers, lightning in a dark storm of desire.

Ava struggled to catch her breath. Her gaze was lazy as she watched her lover. Every muscle was defined, sculpted, hard. His black hair brushed his shoulders, and he knelt on the bed, still stroking himself. Without a word, the vines rotated her—gentle but firm—positioning her exactly how he wanted before his hands brought her close. He laid his palm on her back, fingers leaving a wet, hot trail along her spine.

"What do you want, Ava?" he asked, his voice deep with a slight tremor. She'd learned to read him well enough now to catch the smallest hint of doubt in his voice. Even after everything, part of him still wondered if he deserved this. Deserved her.

She knew the answer. How, in all the Realms, the curse had led him to her, a flicker of hope in his absolute darkness.

"You," Ava whispered. "Always you."

As if that admittance was all he needed, Thorben moved. He spread her from behind, his hands eager. He ran his cock along the seam of her ass, dipping, circling, teasing them both between her legs. Ava's breathing quickened as she waited, her body shuddering at the barely-there touch. She felt the tip of his cock nudge her opening. She pressed herself backward, inviting, begging—

Thorben suddenly thrust into her, and Ava groaned into the pillow, her face pushing against the soft fabric. His sex was cool fyre invading her warmth to the very core.

Thorben withdrew slowly then drove into her, steady and deliberate. She was throbbing, aching for every thrust. Again. And again. And *again*.

The sounds of their lovemaking filled the treehouse—skin against skin, breath against breath. Ava surrendered to the rhythm, letting the tension coil inside her. His hardness, the heat from the oils, the green scent of living things surrounding them... it brought her somewhere she hadn't been in longer than she could remember.

Peace.

The world could end right now and she'd be happy.

As if sensing her thought, Thorben stilled. The vines responded instantly—lifting her, turning her, raising her until they were face to face. He hadn't spoken a word. Hadn't needed to. His magic knew what he wanted before he did.

His stormy eyes searched hers. The vines tightened on her ankles and wrists, holding her suspended.

"Still with me?" he asked, his voice husky.

Ava's legs trembled, her whole body trembled, but she managed, "Always."

Grasping her hips, Thorben slid into her. Her sensitive opening enveloped him, squeezing every inch of his manhood. His fingers dug into her rear, bringing her legs on either side of him. The vines held her in the air, moving in tandem with Thorben's rhythm, making each penetration deep and fierce. He captured a nipple in his mouth, drawing hard, and a guttural cry tore from her throat.

The tension that had been building inside Ava exploded. She threw her head back, screaming into the forest canopy. A second later, Thorben erupted, Ava's name on his lips. He shuddered, his breath coming hard against her neck, but he kept moving, slow and deliberate, drawing out every last wave. Her fingers gripped his hair, holding on as she fought to catch her breath. One final thrust, the deepest yet, and Ava gasped at the finality of it.

For a long moment, neither of them moved. Just breath. And heartbeats. The vines cradled them both, their urgency spent.

Gradually, their breathing calmed, and the vines unwound from Ava of their own accord—releasing her as Thorben's body relaxed. Holding her rump with both of his hands, he carried her to the bed, his cock still inside her.

He laid her on the velvety sheets and let himself slip out. His member hung, hard and dripping. Thorben parted her legs, running his tongue along her wetness, licking at their combined orgasms and the minty nectar. Ava moaned. Her legs parted wider of their own volition, the side of her face buried in the softness of the bed. The heat of his mouth relaxed her and Thorben continued, devouring every last drop.

"Ava?" He whispered, dropping a kiss on her cheek, her lips.

"Mmm?" She was already drifting, boneless and warm.

"This." He pulled a blanket of fine-woven petals over them both, tucking her in. "Us. We are worth fighting for."

She meant to answer and tell him she agreed. She'd fight to the end of every realm to keep this. But sleep claimed her before the words could form.

Morning came too quickly. Ava dragged herself from the bed, her skin still slightly tingling from the nectar.

When she entered the cottage, she found everyone already gathered in the kitchen, papers spread across the table. Thorben caught her eye from across the room, a private smile flickering at the corner of his mouth.

"Dorienne and I have constructed a spell we think will work," Rubina said when Ava had grabbed a muffin and sat down, trying to hide the heat in her cheeks. "In order to create a stable biosphere, you will need to connect with the souls bonded to the islands and keep them anchored while we spellcast. We will adjust the atmosphere and pull the islands closer to stabilize them. Neo and Tobias will enhance our spell, making it stronger and extending its range. Between Ava connecting with the souls, our magic, and the magnification device, we should be able to bring the Realms back into balance."

"Are you going to create new purdahs?" Flip asked.

"We don't want to," Dorienne replied. "But we may have to depending on what happens when we get to the core."

"What's the core?" Gabrie asked in a quiet voice, her eyes wide.

"The core is where the center of our world used to be," Rune said. "Now it is the place of highest gravity, where the purdahs were connected and anchored before they were destroyed."

"As the islands drift from that apex, the wider the chasm gets and the further apart the souls bonded to the realms become," Rubina explained.

"When the islands get too far apart," Ava whispered, "the souls won't be able to communicate. They will be alone, unable to use the strength of the others to keep their realm complete. Everyone will die."

"Exactly." Dorienne looked down at her papers, frowning. "Applying magic from all sides is going to be the most strategic approach."

"We need to go to the core," Rubina said. "It's the only way to know if what we are doing is effective. If we do it here we may make things worse and not be able to adjust in time."

"I have a zeppelin we can use," Ava said. When she had almost fallen over the side of the island, the vast emptiness below had been terrifying, her feet dangling in the chilly air. She didn't know how far down the core was, but her ship was small and quick, and for a perilous journey like this one, she wanted something familiar beneath her feet.

Dorienne nodded, not meeting Ava's eyes. Every time Ava had tried to approach Dorienne she had done her best to avoid her, and Ava couldn't help but wonder if saving the realms would be enough to thaw the frost of Dorienne's attitude towards her.

"I can go," Thorben offered, and Ava's eyebrows shot up. "If there is a root system or plants of any kind, I can manipulate them in any way necessary. It could give you time."

"That's very thoughtful, thank you," Neo replied.

"We leave soon. Is everyone ready?" Dorienne looked around the table, collecting nods. Her piercing gaze landed on Ava last, heavy with judgment. Whatever Dorienne saw, she didn't share. She simply turned and walked out.

Chapter Fifty-Three

Ava grabbed a breakfast roll and went to help Neo and Toby install the magnifier on her airship. Every step sent a pleasant ache through her—remnants of last night that made her bite back a smile.

Ava met Flip in the hall and she paused, a knowing smile creeping onto her lips. "Well, someone enjoyed themselves last night."

Heat flooded Ava's cheeks, but she met Flip's gaze. "You have no idea." Flip snorted, and Ava laughed—then winced, which only made them both laugh harder. Worth it. Every twinge was a reminder of what they were fighting for.

Her smile slipped. She had barely gotten to know Flip, and already the thought of losing her— Flip's eyes went somber. She grabbed Ava's wrist before Ava could finish the thought.

"You have always been a light," Flip said, her voice dark and even. "I have faith in you. Gabrie does too. You do what you need to do, and I'll see you in a few hours."

Ava's throat tightened. She nodded. Flip released her, but before she left, Ava remembered she needed a favor. "Flip—can you send a tube for me? Tell Mage Clare what we are doing, alright?"

Flip nodded and went to gather Gabrie to head to the mail service station.

An engine's roar rattled the windows. Outside, Mergen's aircraft touched down, propellers flattening the garden flowers. Ava ran out, shielding her face from the grit.

"I'm so glad you made it." Ava squeezed Mergen in a brisk hug and quickly filled her in. "We're preparing to leave."

"I hope you kits are ready, because I only want to go once," Mergen said, clapping her gloved hands together.

"You aren't the only one," Ava muttered. They made their way to the *Gent*, filing in behind Neo and Toby. The spell magnifier dwarfed any device Ava had seen them build—a glass box housing a network of spinning gears, a golden orb churning at its center. She paused, drawn to the light pulsing inside like a heartbeat.

"Dorienne made the core," Toby said, awe softening his voice. "She wove particles together that latch onto magic and amplify it tenfold. I've never seen manipulation like hers. She could probably turn a tree into a skybyke."

"Only if you grovel," Dorienne said as she passed. Toby's cheeks went pink, and Ava squeezed his arm.

Ava took her place at the wheel. How many times had she stood here, dreaming of distant islands and unexplored skies? Never once had she imagined this—steering toward the end of everything, hoping to stop it.

Mergen moved behind the control panel, into the first mate's position. "Ready, Captain?"

Ava glanced back at her crew. Mergen in her blue aviatrix jumpsuit, wild curls escaping her helmet. Rune clutching a bag of tonics, insisting she go in case someone needed emergency medical help. Neo at the railing, his dark, broad frame taking up half the deck—and Rubina several careful steps away, small and pale, platinum hair streaming in the wind. Even at the end of the world, her mother kept her distance.

On the far side of the deck, Dorienne frowned over her papers, chestnut hair pulled severe at her nape. Toby adjusted his glasses, caught Ava's eye, and offered a crooked smile—but his fingers wouldn't stop moving, turning a small gear over and over. She'd teased him about that habit for years. Funny how he only seemed to do it when things mattered most.

Thorben stood apart, gaze fixed toward Natalia's home. He hadn't said goodbye. Neither of them had thought—no, she hadn't thought. He'd been so focused on her that she'd forgotten he had people to lose too. Ava's chest tightened. One more reason they had to come back.

"Everyone ready?' Ava asked. No one answered—but no one looked away either. If this was the end, at least she'd face it with them. She turned to the wheel. "Mergen, open the burners, please."

"Burners opening," Mergen murmured, her usual wicked grin replaced with a grim expression. She pulled the lever and flames plumed inside the balloon's skirt.

Ava guided the airship into the skyes. For a moment, they hovered on the airstreams—smooth, almost peaceful. Then they began to climb, and the air thinned with every foot of altitude.

"The oxygen—" Rubina's words came in labored breaths. "—it isn't stable."

Ava's vision spotted at the edges. She gripped the wheel tighter and focused on breathing. Just breathing.

"Douse burners," Ava said to Mergen quietly. "Activate ailerons and let's take him down nice and slow."

They descended past the island's edge, and Ava's stomach dropped into her boots. The void that had nearly swallowed her a week ago yawned beneath them—patient, waiting, as if it had known she'd return. Roots hung from the exposed earth like veins, water dripping from their tips into the nothing below. The ship lurched starboard, throwing everyone sideways.

"What—" Toby scrambled to the railing. A chunk of island the size of a house drifted past, shedding dirt and rocks across the deck. He and Rubi skittered out of the way.

"The islands are breaking apart," Rubi said grimly. "It'll only get worse the deeper we go."

"I'll go to the stern and let you know if I see anything," Toby said. "Keep going slow and steady."

Ava nodded. "Mergen, slow our descent."

Mergen adjusted the dials while Ava eased the pressure valves, letting the balloon deflate by fractions. If Toby spotted something, they'd need time to react.

The deeper they went, the easier it was to breathe—but cold crept in to replace the thin air. Ava's breath clouded white. She shivered, fingers stiffening on the wheel.

From the corner of her eye, she saw Toby glance up from the magnifier's dials, his gaze flicking to her pale hands gripping the wheel. He shifted his weight like he was about to move—but then warmth settled over her shoulders. She glanced backward to see Thorben, draping a jacket around her with a small smile.

When Ava returned her gaze to Toby, he had gone back to his readings, head bent low over the machine.

The airship sank in silence, broken only by the scrape of debris against the hull. Minutes stretched. Ava counted her breaths to keep from counting time.

"Slow now! Easy does it!" Toby shouted as he ran to stand beside her. "We're almost there. I can see the space between the Realms."

Ava turned the dials again and adjusted the wheel as another huge clod of dirt rocked the boat. "It's getting harder to navigate this far down," she said. "How much further?"

"Another few thousand feet," Toby reported, leaning over the side.

A presence brushed against her mind—*Imudir*. Ava gasped, so focused on steering she hadn't felt him approach. "I'm here," she whispered.

Then the others came. Not one by one, but all at once—heavy, demanding, deafening. The weight of five ancient souls slammed into her consciousness, and her knees buckled.

"Ava!" Mergen took a step toward her.

"Mergen," Ava gasped, putting out a hand. "Take the helm."

Mergen slid into position, one eye still on Ava. Pressure built behind Ava's eyes—she squeezed them shut, but it only made the presence louder.

"*Laurimé*," The endearing term slipped out. "I can feel them, the Five. They're...watching."

Thorben's arm circled her waist. She leaned into him, anchoring herself against the tide in her head.

"What are they saying?" Rubi asked.

Ava shook her head. "They're anxious...they want to know what we're doing."

Rubi motioned for Dorienne to join her and glanced at Toby. "Are we close enough?"

Toby cast a look at Ava—not just worried, but searching, like he was cataloging something. Checking her the way he checked his machines. "Just a few more minutes," he said, and something in his voice made it sound like an apology.

"Toby," Mergen said. "Take the first mate's position. We'll take him down together."

Neo knelt before the magnifier, adjusting knobs with surprising delicacy for hands so large. A dial began ticking. Inside the glass, gears spun faster, the golden orb pulsing in rhythm.

"Ready," he rumbled, his voice so deep Ava felt it in her chest.

Dorienne unrolled a long parchment covered in Ili script—the ancient language flowing in intricate patterns Ava had never seen outside of Rune's oldest texts. Her breath caught at the beauty of it.

"*Laurimé*, you go first," Dorienne instructed. "Stabilize the atmosphere. Then we can take the next step."

Rubina began to speak, and the words—Ava had no other way to describe them—sang. The ancient syllables rose and fell, beautiful and strange, and the air thickened in response. Pressure built in Ava's ears until they popped. Around her, the crew dropped to the deck or grabbed the railing, bracing against something they couldn't see.

Rubina's voice swelled, and Ava's vision shifted—she could see it somehow, particles spinning, compacting, the very air thickening around them. Each breath felt like inhaling syrup. Like the liminal plane, she realized. Like drowning in honey.

Rubina's voice faded. The machine's orb flared brilliant gold, drinking in the spell's power. Gears whirred frantically, and a sharp, acrid smell cut through the cold.

Dorienne picked up where Rubina left off, her voice quiet at first—almost tentative. Then it built. The syllables wove together, gaining power, gaining certainty, until her voice filled the deck like a living thing.

The pressure released like a cork from a bottle. Everyone gasped, gulping air that suddenly felt *normal*. Dorienne's spell had bought them a reprieve—but from her expression, not a long one. The machine hummed, steady now, storing power for what came next.

"Avalína." Her mother's voice was barely a breath. "It's time."

Ava reached for Thorben's hand—found it already waiting. She closed her eyes and let her spirit unspool, spiraling outward through the biosphere, reaching for the Five. *Stay with me*, she called to them. *Hold steady. I'm here.*

They watched. And waited.

"We're here to help," Ava whispered to them. "We still need you, ancient ones. You are the reason our world still exists...why we are living and breathing."

The connection snapped.

Ava's eyes flew open. The Five were gone—not distant, not fading, but *gone*, leaving a hollow ache where they'd been. She doubled over, bile rising in her throat.

"What happened?' Dorienne's voice was sharp as glass.

"I don't—" Ava pressed a hand to her mouth, swallowed hard. "They cut me off. I don't know why."

The airship lurched. Ava hit the deck hard, hearing the others cry out around her.

Thorben hauled her upright—and the Five came roaring back.

Not gently. Not carefully. They crashed into her mind like a wave against rocks, shoving her spirit between them. The pressure behind her eyes became blinding. Ava dropped to her hands and knees, fighting to keep her stomach down.

Another impact—a chunk of island grinding against the hull, shoving them sideways. Dirt and rocks pelted the deck. Mergen wrestled with the wheel, cursing. Through the chaos, Ava glimpsed Toby throwing himself over the magnifier, shielding it with his body as debris rained down. Always protecting what mattered most, keeping things running.

"No!" Ava screamed. Blood trickled out of her nose, and she swiped at it with her sleeve, leaving a smear on her cheek. She reached out again—and what she saw shattered everything she thought she understood.

The liminal plane wove through everything—the air, the islands, the very fabric of existence—and the Five were the threads holding it together. But the islands were pulling, straining against bonds grown fragile from the destruction of the purdahs. If they broke free, the liminal plane would unravel. Every realm would float away, and every soul in existence would dissolve into the ether.

Ava forced herself upright, planted her feet. "We're here to help," she called to them, blood dripping from her chin. "Stay with us. Please."

The wind answered. It seized her, lifting her off the deck, spinning her in a vortex of impossible force. The last thing she saw before her eyes rolled back was Thorben's face—reaching for her, too far away to catch.

Chapter Fifty-Four

"Ava!" The scream tore from Thorben's throat before he knew he was moving. The souls crashed into her—he felt it like a blade between his ribs, their ancient power threading through her spirit, claiming her. His heart forgot how to beat.

"What's happening?" Toby's voice broke. He stood frozen at the magnifier, knuckles white on the machine's frame, watching Ava float above them like something already lost.

"They're bonding with her." Thorben's voice came out hollow. "She will become part of the Realms."

"No!" Rubina's composure cracked. She grabbed Neo's arm, her small pale hands stark against his dark skin. "Turn it off! Turn off the device!"

"I can't." Neo's voice broke on the words—Thorben had never heard the man sound anything but steady. "If I stop the cycle, the magic will implode. It will kill everyone."

Dorienne stood apart, watching Ava's suspended body with curiosity. Not horror or grief. Something closer to calculation.

Thorben stumbled forward. Above, multicolored ribbons of light wove through Ava's body—golden and silver and colors that had no name—braiding themselves into a cord with her at its heart.

She began to glow. Terrible and beautiful, like watching a star be born and knowing it would burn everything you loved.

"Ava!" Thorben launched himself upward, snagging her wrist where it dangled in the light. Her skin burned cold beneath his fingers—alive and not alive, present and already fading. He wrapped both arms around her waist and pulled, hauling her back to the deck with every fragment of strength he possessed.

She didn't deserve this.

Ava was light wrapped in stubbornness, fierce love housed in exhausted bones. She had spent thirty years giving pieces of herself away and never once asked for anything back. If she gave herself now—all of herself, forever—it would hollow out everyone on this ship. Her mother and father, who had only known her as a toddler—two precious years before she was ripped away. A thousand years of waiting, and they'd barely had a week to learn the woman she'd become. Rune, who had just begun this lifetime with her. And Toby, still frozen at his machine, watching her with something raw and desperate in his eyes.

Himself? Thorben would simply cease to exist in any way that mattered. He knew it in his soul.

What did he have to lose? Only the life *she* had given him. The freedom he had begged for, and the future he had dared to imagine—all of it was hers. Had been since the moment she touched him and his carefully constructed walls came crashing down.

When he'd met her, he'd been calculating how to use her. Now he couldn't calculate a world without her in it.

The souls pressed against his spirit—curious, probing, ancient. Without thinking, Thorben shoved back. Hard.

The deck vanished. The cold vanished. Sound vanished.

He stood in the liminal plane's depths, the thickness he knew better than his own heartbeat wrapping around him like a homecoming he'd never wanted.

"You again." Imudír's form materialized from the murk, his ancient eyes holding something that might have been amusement. "You keep finding your way back, cursed one."

Thorben stepped forward, rage and terror warring in his chest. "Let her go."

"We require a nexus." Imudír's voice held no cruelty, only ancient pragmatism. "Someone to weave our souls back together, to anchor us to the fabric of existence. She offered herself."

"She never offered." Thorben's hands curled into fists. "I watched you take her. She was trying to help, and you took what you wanted."

"Is there a difference?" Imudír tilted his head. "She came to assist us. We accepted."

"Are you saying she wouldn't give her life for this?' Imudír's gesture encompassed everything—the plane, the Realms, the souls within them. "For her family? For you?"

Thorben's throat closed. He knew the answer. Had known it since the first night she'd talked to him, exhausted and grieving and still somehow reaching out to a stranger trapped in the dark.

Ava would give everything for people she'd never met. For the people she loved, she would give more than everything. She would give forever.

"Take me instead."

The words left him before thought could intervene. Before logic could remind him the cost of what he was offering, or the part of him that had spent ten years desperate for freedom could scream its protest.

Imudír went still. "You?"

"I know the liminal plane better than anyone living." Thorben stepped closer, forcing his voice steady. "You need someone to weave you together, to anchor you across the fabric of existence. Ava has visited this plane—I have *lived* it. Ten years, Imudír. I know every current, depth, and shadow. She would stumble in the dark. I could navigate it blind."

Imudír studied him with eyes that had seen civilizations rise and crumble. "You would trade your freedom? Your life? You only just reclaimed them."

"I would trade everything." Thorben held his gaze. "For her."

Silence stretched between them. Imudír's head tilted, listening to voices Thorben couldn't hear—the other four, deliberating his fate.

Finally, the ancient soul nodded. "We accept your offering, cursed one. You will be unmade and remade, everywhere and nowhere. Your spirit will hold us together until existence itself unravels."

"I understand."

"Do you?" Something flickered in Imudír's expression—pity, perhaps, or respect. "You will feel her live. And die. You will witness her grandchildren's grandchildren take their first breaths, and you will never be able to touch any of them."

The words carved him hollow. But he thought of Ava's laugh. Her stubbornness. The way she'd looked at him like he was worth saving.

"I understand," he repeated. "Take me."

The plane spat him out.

Thorben hit the deck gasping, the physical world slamming back into him—cold air, rough wood, the acrid smell of overworked machinery. For a moment he couldn't move or think. He simply lay there and feel his heart pound in a chest that wouldn't belong to him much longer.

Then he saw her.

Ava lay motionless, the glow having faded, her dark hair spilled across the deck like ink on parchment. He crawled to her, splinters biting his palms, and brushed his fingers against her cheek. Still warm. Here.

And his. For a few more minutes.

"Ava." Her name was a prayer on his lips. Her eyelids fluttered open. Her gaze found his, and she smiled—soft and relieved and utterly unaware of what he'd done.

He memorized that smile. Clutched it to his soul like a flower between pages.

He would never see it again.

"I need to stay." Ava's voice was thick with unshed grief, already mourning herself. She reached up and touched his face, and only then did Thorben realize tears were sliding down his cheeks. When had he started crying?

He turned his face into her palm, pressing his lips to the tender center. Let his stubble rasp against her skin. Let himself feel it, this last small touch.

"Neyá," he said. "You belong here."

"I can't. The Five—they need someone who understands the liminal plane." She pushed herself upright, her jaw set with terrible determination. "It has to be me, Thorben. This is my purpose. It's why I was brought back."

"Neyá." He caught her face in his hands, made her look at him. "Not anymore."

He watched understanding dawn—slow, then all at once. Her expression shifted from resigned acceptance to dawning horror.

"What did you do?" she breathed.

"You cannot—" Ava grabbed fistfuls of his shirt, yanking him closer. "Thorben, you can't go back there. You spent ten years in that darkness. *Alone.* You finally got free—"

"And I would spend ten thousand more." He covered her hands with his, felt them trembling against his chest. "To watch you live and breathe. Laugh and love—even if that love is never for me again—I would do it gladly."

Her shock was a physical thing, radiating through her grip, her gaze, the way her breath stuttered. This was the last time her touch would be something he could hold.

"Watching you sacrifice yourself would destroy me," he said, pressing his lips to her palm once more—tasting salt from her tears or his, he couldn't tell anymore. "But that's not why I'm doing this."

He lifted her chin, made her meet his eyes. Those impossible blue-green depths, spilling over, defiant even now.

"When I first saw you," he said quietly, "I thought you a means to an end. I cataloged everything about you." He watched her flinch but pressed on. "I wanted to use you to break my curse, Avalína. I was going to take everything you offered and give nothing back."

Her hands tightened in his shirt, but she didn't pull away.

"And then I touched you." He huffed a laugh. "Catching you from falling over the edge. And everything I'd planned fell apart. I stopped cataloging and started memorizing. Not as research, but as curiosity that turned into...love."

Ava's breath caught, but he continued. He had to get these words out if he was never going to speak with her again. She needed to know.

"I learned the way you laugh when you're surprised. The way you hum when you feel souls nearby. The way you look at people like they matter, even when they've done nothing to deserve it."

He tilted her chin up, thumb brushing her jaw. "You have unraveled me, *mé talé.* Taken apart every ugly, selfish piece and somehow—you knit me back together into a person who could do this." His thumb caught the wetness on her cheek. "Someone who could choose you over himself. You wove your grace into my wreckage, and this is who I became."

"Thorben—"

"You have people here who need you," he continued, his voice steady even as he shattered inside. "You are reunited with your family. Rune waited a thousand years for this." He paused and glanced toward Toby, still gripping the magnifier like it could save him. "And the tinker has loved you longer than I've known you existed. He might never say it—but somehow I know he won't ever leave you. He'll be here when I can't be."

Ava made a sound like something breaking.

"But this is *my* purpose!" She shoved at his chest, fury and grief tangled together. "I was brought back to save the Realms. Not you."

"Perhaps your purpose is to be more than a sacrifice." He caught her wrists, stilled them against his heart. "Maybe you were brought back to live, Avalína. To love and build something instead of burning yourself down for it." He touched his forehead to hers. "Let me give you the chance to find out."

"No." The word was a sob, a scream, a prayer. Her hands fisted in his shirt, shaking him, pulling him closer, pushing him away—all at once. "No, no, no—"

"The Five have accepted." He gentled his voice, even as his own tears fell freely now. "It's done, *mé talé*. My soul has been yours since the moment you saw me in the dark. Let me love you in the only way I have left. Let me love you from every corner of the Realms. Forever."

Thorben reached into his shirt and drew out a chain he'd kept hidden against his heart. He lifted it over his head and pressed it into Ava's trembling palm.

A silver flower hung from the delicate links. Small and perfect, with heart-shaped petals that caught the dim light.

"After my curse broke," he said, "and I could finally touch you—I knew. I went to Syldan and grew this. A mage turned it silver for me." His thumb traced the edge of a petal. "I was going to ask Rune's permission. I was going to do it properly—courting, and vows, and a lifetime of learning every single thing about you."

His voice broke.

"I was going to give you a lifetime."

The flower rested in her palm, catching the light—each flash a glimpse of the future he was surrendering. A home grown from living trees. A kitchen filled with her laughter. Children with her eyes and his magic, running through gardens he would never plant.

He lifted the chain and settled it around her neck. The silver flower rested against her chest, just above her heart.

"I can't serve you the way I wanted to," he said. "I can't wake beside you, or argue with you about dinner, or grow old watching you grow more beautiful." He touched the flower where it lay against her skin. "But I can hold the world together for you. I can be the ground beneath your feet and the air in your lungs and the space between islands. I can love you in ways that have no name."

His voice dropped to a whisper.

"I can be everywhere you are, *mé talé*. For as long as you exist."

"Thorben." His name came out ragged, barely a sound. "Please. There has to be another way. We can find—we can try—"

"*Mé talé.*" He smiled, and it was the saddest, most peaceful thing she'd ever seen. "There is no other way. And even if there were—I would still choose this. *You.* Every time. For eternity."

He pulled back just enough to look into her eyes.

"I give my spirit," he said clearly, so the Five would hear, "to the souls of the Realms."

"NO!" Ava's scream tore through the air. And through his heart. But he kept going.

"I give my spirit to the Realms."

She was sobbing now, clawing at him, trying to hold him here through sheer force of will.

"I give my forever, to hold the world together. So she can live in it."

Ava crashed into him.

Her mouth found his with desperate fury, kissing him like she could pull him back from the edge through sheer will. She tasted of salt and sweetness, grief and stubborn hope--everything he was about to lose and everything he was choosing to save.

He kissed her back filling the touch with ten years of loneliness, the handful of months he'd been allowed to love her properly, and all the decades he would never get to have.

His fingers threaded into her hair, drinking her in. He didn't care that her family was watching or that Toby had turned away, his shoulders rigid. He only wanted to memorize the taste and feel of her, the way she clung to him like he was the only solid thing in a dissolving world.

He was about to become the world. But he would never be solid again.

He pressed his lips to her forehead, her cheeks, the corners of her eyes where tears still fell.

"To be with you," he whispered against her skin, "in every breath you take."

He kissed her temple. "To be beneath you, holding you steady when the ground shakes."

He kissed the tears from her cheeks. "To surround you, in every flower that you smell and every ray of light that finds your hair."

He pulled her against his chest, her head tucked beneath his chin, her fists still buried in his shirt like she could anchor him here.

"For the rest of your life, Avalína. And whatever comes after."

Ava broke.

Not quietly, not gracefully—she shattered against him, her wails muffled in his chest, her whole body shaking with the force of a grief that had nowhere to go. He held her through it, stroking her hair, pressing kisses to the top of her head, giving her these last few moments of warmth.

Around them, the others stood in silence. Rubina weeping openly into Neo's chest—finally letting him hold her. Rune with tears streaming down her weathered face, one hand pressed to her heart. Mergen gripping the wheel with white knuckles, her expression carefully blank.

And Toby. His eyes moist behind his glasses.

Dorienne alone remained unmoved, watching with calculating eyes.

Finally, Thorben tilted Ava's face up. Brushed the tears from her cheeks one last time. Smiled at her with everything he had left.

"Guide my soul, *mé talé*," he whispered. "Sing for me. One last time."

Chapter Fifty-Five

The song rose defiantly in her chest. She fought it—shoved it down beneath her grief—but her magic had never answered to pain. And his choice wasn't something she could control.

She hated her gift in that moment, as the song rose, brazen and beautiful, against her will. Ava wept as the bittersweet words tumbled from her lips. Each note carved through her body, leaving her soul in shreds, her throat raw with magic she didn't want to give.

She cradled his face, thumbs tracing the lines she'd only just learned. His eyes held hers—storm-gray and steady, full of a love so fierce it undid her. This was the future she'd dared to imagine, slipping through her fingers like water.

"I love you, *mé talé*." His voice was fading, thinning like morning mist. "You are worth every moment I had. You are a treasure worth fighting for."

The Five claimed him. His body arched backward, wrenched from her grip. His hands slipped from her face as toes lifted off the ground.

Strands of lights streamed through the air and pierced his chest. Ava lunged for him, fingers closing on empty air. Her breath seized as she felt the souls overtake him, dragging him away.

The Realms groaned, ancient lands and biosphere shifting. Islands drifted closer as the soul-strands wove through the void, stitching the world back together. *The Spirited Gent* hung at the center of it all. The Realms narrowed around them and the smell of deep earth and wet loam pressed in.

The Five reached through him—she could see them now, straining from each realm toward the man who'd offered himself as their nexus. His body turned, suspended in air, and when his eyes found hers, the storm-gray was gone. In its place: cobalt, pearl, ember, gold. An eternal soulful light of ancient souls burned where the man she loved used to be.

Ava's song finished on her lips. Color poured down his face like luminous tears, painting rivers across his skin. He looked at her—one last moment of him behind those borrowed eyes—and let go.

His head fell back. His soul rose. Green and silver, twisting upward like smoke from sacred fyre. He smelled of rain-soaked forest and mint, of the morning after he'd held her through the night. Ava's eyes burned shut against it. Against him and the unbearable beauty of watching the man she loved become something eternal and untouchable.

His soul drifted to her. Not gone—not yet. He brushed against her cheek, cool where he'd once been warm. Threaded through her hair the way his fingers used to. Found her tears and took them, one by one, as if he could carry her grief with him into forever.

Then he wrapped himself around the silver flower at her throat. Poured something into it—a fragment of his essence, a piece of him she could keep. When he pulled away, the flower glowed soft and alive against her skin. A tiny piece of him she could grasp when she couldn't hold him anymore.

He drifted toward the prow, and the Five followed—drawn to him, weaving themselves into his essence. The chain of souls blazed against the dark, a lifeline stitching the Realms together.

Lightning split the air. Wind screamed across the deck. And Thorben—the man she had loved, the soul she never expected to find—became something *new*.

The atmospheric pressure lifted, a breath of air that felt as if it had been held too long. The Realms shuddered. But kept closing in, inch by inch, the earthen walls slowly tightening around their little ship.

"Ava," Mergen's voice, gentle but urgent. "We need to go."

"Not yet." Ava didn't want to tear her eyes from Thorben's spirit. She wasn't ready to let him go. She could still feel him, just a little, and she didn't want to lose that slim connection. It would destroy her.

'Go, *mé talé*,' a voice whispered inside her. '*I will protect you. But you must hurry.*'

"Ava," Mergen said more insistently.

"Not yet!" She ran to the prow, fingers white on the railing, watching the souls spiral away. Behind her, footsteps scrambled—the crew preparing to flee. Toby's voice calling out orders, steady despite everything. Doing what needed to be done while she stood frozen in her grief.

"The islands will crush us!" Mergen shouted.

Rubina appeared at Ava's side, small and steady. "I know you don't want to leave him, *adorimé*," she said. "But he is part of the Realms now. But you won't truly lose him. You'll see."

It wasn't comfort. Nothing would be. But it was enough to make Ava's feet move. Ava pressed a hand to her mouth, trembling. Toby's voice cut through the chaos—calm, competent, holding everyone together the way he always did. The way he would keep doing, she realized dimly, long after this day was over.

The *Gent* lurched upward, black powder roaring. Through her tears, Ava watched the web of souls—and Thorben—shrink until they were a distant glow in the dark.

The islands closed in faster, and the edge of the aircraft scraped against them, dirt and rocks flying everywhere. Rubi shielded Ava, covering her with her slight frame to protect against debris.

"Mergen!" Toby shouted. Two large pieces of land had moved into their path, suddenly closing off their route. Toby grabbed another black powder capsule. The motion jarred Ava from her pain. The ship slowly came into focus. Her chest tightened as the stark reality of their situation hit.

"You can't put in another shot!" Ava shouted, grabbing Toby's arm. "We're already going fast enough. It will blow the ship apart."

"We don't have a choice." Toby prepared the housing. "We will run out of thrust before we can get through. Doubling the combustion might make the ship a little shaky, but it's our only chance of getting out."

Ava searched the ship, desperate for a solution not involving blowing them to bits. Thorben was gone, her ship might explode in their attempt to escape, and she could lose her entire family.

Hot, angry tears rolled over her cheeks, blending with the dirt on her face. Indignant fury burned inside her. He'd taken her place when this was supposed to be *her* purpose. Made her love him and then left, even after clawing his way back to life. The dream of their future—gone. Because he had chosen her. And she had never asked for it.

She wiped them away and grabbed the black powder shell from Toby.

"It's my ship." Ava opened the housing and shoved in the capsule. "If anyone is going to blow it up, it's going to be me."

Ava prepped the hammer and waited for Toby's signal.

"Now!" Toby yelled. Ava slammed the hammer down, and a second later the ship jerked forward again. The zeppelin gained speed, the hull shuddering violently.

Mergen spun the wheel, the rudder flipping to the side. The balloon scraped against the earth, dirt and mud smearing along the edges of the zeppelin. Ava ground her teeth together. They had to make it through. She prayed to the Five—no, Six now—that they would.

They weren't going to make it. The gap was too narrow and closing too fast—

A root burst from the earth. Massive and alive with green-silver light. It wedged itself between the land masses, straining, holding, giving them just enough space to slip through.

Thorben.

Behind them, the islands crashed together with a sound like the world ending, a resounding crunch of earth meeting earth. But they were through. He'd saved her. One last time.

The *Spirited Gent* burst free, trailing black powder smoke like a scar across the sky.

No one spoke. The silence was heavy with what they'd lost and what they'd saved. Around them, the air softened. A gentle, cleansing mist began to fall. A breeze stirred, carrying the scent of rain and growing things.

The Realms were whole again. Closer than before.

And Ava had never felt so far from everything.

The Gent crested the island's edge, and sunlight spilled across the deck in golden steps. One beam found Thorben's body where it lay—empty now, still, his dark hair fanned around a face that would never smile at her again.

Ava sank to her knees beside him. One hand found the silver flower—still warm and glowing, the only part of him she could keep. The other pressed against his chest, searching for a heartbeat she knew she wouldn't find.

Angry, raw cries tore out of her throat in waves she couldn't stop.

Neo knelt beside her, his massive frame somehow gentle. "I didn't know him long," he said quietly. "But I saw the way he looked at you. Like you were the only light in his darkness. Would you like me to tend to his vessel, *mé le dar*? I will treat him with honor."

Ava laid her head on Thorben's silent chest. The mint-and-rain scent of him lingered—fading already, like everything else. She found his hand, laced her fingers through his. These hands had held her just last night. Had traced her skin, tangled in her hair, made her feel alive.

Now they were cold and still. Gone in every way that mattered.

Time passed. She didn't know how much.

Eventually, Neo helped her stand. Her legs didn't feel like her own. Nothing felt like her own anymore.

They were docked at Toby's workshop—she hadn't even noticed them landing. Toby stood at the gangplank, waiting. Just...there. Like he'd always been.

The mist had turned to soft rain, washing the dirt and grime from the deck. Somewhere in the distance, she heard noises—celebrations, she realized. People could dance, and sing, and live. They knew the Realms were saved.

But Ava stood in the rain and felt nothing.

Thorben was everywhere now, but she couldn't feel him. Not truly. He was in the air she breathed, the ground beneath her feet, the spaces between clouds. Everywhere.

And she had never been more alone.

Chapter Fifty-Six

Ava walked in, and Dáhlia stopped breathing.

Hollow eyes and skin the color of ash. Ava moved like her bones had been replaced with something fragile and sharp. Dáhlia knew that walk—the careful way you held yourself when everything inside had shattered and you were terrified the pieces would fall out if you went too fast.

Four years ago, she'd walked exactly like that.

She crossed the room and slid her arms around Ava, easing her away from Neo. "I've got her," she murmured against Ava's temple. "Come with me."

Dáhlia guided Ava to her side of the apartment, closing the door gently behind them.

"Ava, what happened?"

Ava didn't reply. Just stared at the floor, her hands in fists.

"Alright. We can talk about it later. Let's get you cleaned up, *seáh*?" Dáhlia's fingers brushed the silver chain at Ava's throat, and Ava's hand shot up—the first real movement she'd made. She clutched the flower pendant so hard her knuckles went white.

Dáhlia pulled back. "Okay. It stays."

The metal glowed faintly against Ava's palm. Warm, like it held a heartbeat.

Dáhlia didn't ask.

She turned her attention to what Ava was wearing. The clothes were ruined—stiff with salt and ash and something darker. How very typical of Ava to come back covered in grime. If the situation were less serious, Dáhlia would have teased her.

But not today.

Dáhlia peeled them away piece by piece, and Ava let her without protest. Ava made it two steps into the shower before her legs gave out.

The sound she made—Dáhlia would hear it in her nightmares. Not a scream. Not a wail. Something torn from deeper than that, ragged and unhinged, like her body was trying to expel a grief too big to hold.

Dáhlia kicked off her shoes and climbed in.

The water hit her fully clothed, plastering her dress to her skin, but she didn't care. She pulled Ava against her chest and held on while the sobs wracked through both of them. Her own tears came hot and silent, lost in the spray.

When the worst of it passed, Dáhlia reached for the soap. She worked it through Ava's hair with slow, careful fingers—the same way she'd done for Aamina a thousand times, with tender touches and gentle words meant to heal a seared soul. Down the back of her neck. Across her shoulders. Washing away the dirt and grime and traces of a world that had demanded too much from her.

She didn't speak. There was nothing to say that would help.

She got Ava to the bed somehow and pulled the blankets up to her chin, tucking them tight the way Aamina liked. Ava's eyes were already closing but tears still tracked down her temples into her wet hair.

Dáhlia wiped them away with her thumb. They kept coming.

Aamina had observed the whole thing from the doorway—quiet, watchful, old beyond her four years. She followed Dáhlia out and tugged her sleeve.

What's wrong with Ava? Her hands asked quickly.

Dáhlia crouched to her daughter's level. "I—" Dáhlia paused. She knew what that sort of loss looked like. But she wanted to hear it from someone who was there. "I'm not sure." Dáhlia pulled her close, breathing in the smell of her hair. "Let's go find out."

The common room was silent as a tomb.

Rune sat rigid in her chair. Neo stared at nothing. Dorienne's face was unreadable. And Toby—

Toby had taken off his glasses. His hand pressed against the bridge of his nose, a glass of boat-burned bourbon untouched in front of him.

That scared her more than Ava had. Her brother never stopped working, never sat still, never let himself just feel something without trying to fix it first. But here he was. Motionless.

"What happened?" Dáhlia tightened her grip on Aamina's hand. "Where's Thorben?"

The silence stretched.

"Gone," Dorienne said. Flat. Final.

Dáhlia's legs went unsteady. "What do you mean, *gone*?"

"The young man gave his soul to the Five." Neo's deep voice caught. "His spirit wove the others together, bringing the Realms back into place."

Dáhlia remembered. She and Aamina had been playing a game. She was trying desperately to keep her little girl occupied. To ignore the sudden shortness of breath, the thinness of the air. Then, the apartment had shuddered beneath her feet—she'd grabbed Aamina, ready to run. But when she'd looked out the window, over the city's skyline, she froze.

The shadows were moving.

Not the quick shift of clouds passing. Something slower. The angle of every shadow in the city began to crawl across the ground, as if the sun itself was being dragged to a new position. Buildings that had been in shade were suddenly lit gold. Streets that blazed with afternoon light dimmed to grey.

The Realms, she realized now. Shifting back into place. Pulling closer together.

And Thorben had been the one to hold them there.

Dáhlia's knees hit the floor before she realized she was falling. Aamina climbed into her lap immediately, small arms wrapping around her neck, and Dáhlia buried her face in her daughter's hair.

Thorben. That steady, patient man who looked at Ava like she'd saved every soul in every realm. Gone.

Aamina leaned back and moved her hands. *Ava needs love now.*

Dáhlia almost laughed—or sobbed, she wasn't sure which. Four years old and already wiser than half the adults in the room.

"*Seáh*, Aami. All the love we can give her."

Mergen offered to take everyone back to the cottage. Rune declined, insisting she needed to stay with Ava. Rubina, Dorienne, and Neo trudged up the stairs to the pier, their steps slow.

Toby threw back his bourbon in one swallow. Dáhlia grabbed an empty glass and held it out to him. He looked up, eyes red-rimmed behind the glasses he'd put back on and poured without asking why.

He knew. Of course he knew. He'd been there four years ago, pouring drinks for Dáhlia when her heart had been broken.

"I'll be back in a minute," she said quietly.

Toby nodded and poured another. He wasn't one to drink, and Dáhlia wondered if this was hitting him hard because of Thorben's sacrifice—or because he had to watch Ava suffer for it.

She knocked twice on the door and slipped inside. The room was dark, but she could hear Ava breathing—ragged, wet, the sound of someone who'd been crying so long their body had forgotten how to stop.

Dáhlia perched on the edge of the bed. "Drink this."

Not a question. Ava needed someone to tell her what to do right now.

Ava sat up, face swollen and blotched. She took the glass and downed it in one go. She handed it back, then collapsed against the pillows like the effort had emptied her.

"I'm so sorry." Dáhlia's throat tightened. "Thorben was—"

What? What word could possibly hold what he'd been to Ava?

"Everything." Ava's voice was muffled by the pillow. "He was everything."

Dáhlia opened her mouth, closed it. Tried again. "At least you're here."

The words tasted wrong the second they left her lips.

Ava sat up so fast Dáhlia flinched.

Those turquoise eyes—usually so warm—blazed like the center of a flame. In all their years of friendship, Dáhlia could count on one hand the times she'd seen Ava truly angry.

This was something beyond anger.

"He gave himself up." Ava's voice shook. "For *me*." She jabbed a finger into her own chest, hard enough to bruise. "I was supposed to do it. I was *ready*. And he—"

Her voice broke.

Dáhlia reached for her hand. Ava yanked it away.

"I know. I'm sorry—"

"He's gone," Ava sniffed, her entire body wilting. "I'm never going to see him again."

Dáhlia reached for her hand again—slower this time. Ava didn't pull away.

"Listen to me." Dáhlia waited until those red-rimmed eyes met hers. "He's part of the Realms now. Part of *everything*. You're a druis—you can reach him. Stretch out with your spirit and find him."

Ava's lips trembled. "What if I can't?"

The question hit Dáhlia like a fist to the chest. She knew that fear. Four years of searching for a man who didn't want to be found, four years of reaching into the dark and grasping nothing.

She shoved the thought down. This wasn't about her.

"You won't know until you try."

Ava nodded, and Dáhlia gave her hand one last squeeze. Her eyes caught on something she'd missed before—a thick silver band on Ava's middle finger, too large for her hand.

"Whose ring is that?"

Ava blinked down at it like she'd forgotten it existed. "Oh. Declan's. It holds a soul he was looking for." Her voice went distant. "I found her. I never got the chance to return it."

"Declan was here." Dáhlia's pulse quickened. "He brought Toby back after the ship caught fyre."

And he'd said something. Something that had lodged in her chest like a splinter and refused to come loose.

It's *not my place to mess in the affairs of the Knave King.*

"Dáhlia." Ava's voice sharpened. "What is it?"

"He knows." The words came out a whisper. "Declan knows where he is."

"Where who is?"

Dáhlia's throat closed, the words tight as they came out. "Aamina's father."

Ava went still. "What?"

"He recognized her." Dáhlia's hands had started shaking. She pressed them flat against her thighs. "He's never met Aamina. Which means—"

"He's seen her father." Ava finished.

Dáhlia nodded, not trusting her voice. Four years of dead ends and closed doors and people who'd never heard the name. And now, sitting in her apartment, a knave who knew exactly where to find him. Hopeful terror shivered through her.

"Oh, Dáhlia," Ava said, standing. "You need to find out what he knows."

Dáhlia pressed her lips together. Declan was going to tell her what he knew whether he liked it or not. She—and Aamina—deserved answers.

Ava pulled the ring from her finger and pressed it into Dáhlia's palm. The metal was warm.

"Take it. Pier two-fifty-six, docking station B—if they haven't left yet. Give him the soul, ask for answers in return." Her jaw tightened. "I don't need a cure for Rune anymore."

Dáhlia's chest ached. Even shattered and broken, Ava was still giving.

Dáhlia kissed her cheek, tasting salt. "Thank you," she whispered. The words weren't enough.

"You deserve to know." Ava grasped Dáhlia's shoulders, giving them a squeeze.

Dáhlia hugged Ava and took a shuddering breath. If she was going to find Declan before his ship left, she needed to hurry.

A knock. Rune's head appeared around the door. "Sorry to interrupt—there's a large red-haired man here. And another one, dark and..." she waggled her fingers vaguely, "mysterious?"

Dáhlia's heart stuttered.

"Look at that." Ava's voice held the ghost of something that might have been humor, once. "He came to you."

"I'm coming." Dáhlia gave Ava's hand one last squeeze. Rune took Dáhlia's place, her hand automatically going to Ava's forehead, words of concern fading as Dáhlia closed the door behind her.

Dáhlia squared her shoulders before she stepped into the common room. Knaves could smell weakness. She couldn't afford any.

"Declan." She kept her voice light, easy. "Wasn't expecting to see you again so soon."

"*Elehimé*. My lady." He dipped his head, all charm. The red-haired giant beside him stood like a wall of muscle and silence.

"What brings you back?" She already knew. But knave negotiations ran on information, and right now, she had it.

Declan's smile, his dimple peeking out from beneath the stubble on his cheek. "I'm looking for the druis. She has something of mine."

Dáhlia let the pause stretch. Then she raised her hand, the silver ring glinting between her fingers.

Declan went very still.

He reached for it—instinct, probably—and Dáhlia pulled it back, just out of range.

"She found her?" His voice had gone rough. His hand hovered in the empty air for a moment before he dropped it, running it over his mouth instead. "Her soul. She actually found her."

"*Seáh*." Dáhlia tilted her head. "Did you find the cure for her aunt?"

Declan's jaw flexed. "*Neyá*."

"Then Ava fulfilled her end. You didn't fulfill yours." He didn't know they no longer needed it. She played the game. Dáhlia spread her hands. "The deal's broken. You only get this ring if you deliver."

The red-haired giant shifted forward. Declan stopped him with a raised palm without looking.

"I can offer a boon." Declan's voice stayed even, but something flickered behind his eyes. Desperation, maybe. Or grief. "A boon for any service, whenever you need it."

"Ava gave the ring to me." Dáhlia met his gaze and held it. "Which means I decide what it's worth."

Declan's eyes narrowed. Good. Let him worry.

"I have a trade in mind."

"I'm listening."

"You recognized my daughter's face." Dáhlia's heart was pounding so hard she was surprised he couldn't hear it. She kept her voice steady through sheer force of will. "I want to meet the man whose face matches hers."

Declan's face shuttered. "I told you before. It's not my place—"

"To mess in the affairs of the Knave King." Dáhlia finished. "*Seáh*. You mentioned."

She saw the flicker of surprise that she'd remembered his exact words. "Pity." She shrugged, turning toward the door. "Thanks for stopping by."

A bluff. Her only lead in four years, and she was pretending she could walk away from it. But the naked want in his eyes when he'd looked at that ring said he needed what was inside it as badly as she needed answers.

"*Wait.*"

His hand slammed against the door before she could close it. Dáhlia allowed herself one heartbeat of relief—hidden behind the wood where he couldn't see her face.

When she turned back, her expression was perfectly composed. "Changed your mind?"

Declan's jaw worked. He glanced at his companion; the giant just shrugged, unhelpful.

"Fine." The word sounded like it cost him. "Information for the ring. Do we have an accord?"

"No."

His eyebrows shot up.

"Not information." Dáhlia's nails bit into her palms behind her back. "You take us to him. Tonight."

Declan's eyes widened. "You can't expect—"

"I can." She cut him off. "And I do. That's the deal. Take it or leave."

Silence stretched between them. Dáhlia counted her own heartbeats. One. Two. Three. Four—

Declan exhaled through his nose and extended his hand, his other pressed to his heart. "Agreed."

Dáhlia clasped his hand. Hers was trembling—she couldn't hide that—but her grip was firm. Her other hand found her own heart, the gesture completing the accord.

Then she placed the silver ring in his palm.

His fingers closed around the ring—reverent, careful. Something lost and found again. When he looked up, the knave's mask had slipped, just for a moment.

"Thank you," he said quietly.

Dáhlia nodded. She understood. Whoever was in that ring—he'd been waiting a long time too.

"Three hours." He tucked the essentia away carefully. "Be ready."

He swept out without another word. The red-haired giant followed, pausing just long enough to tip his head to her—respect, maybe, for someone who'd gone toe-to-toe with Declan and won.

The door closed behind them.

Dáhlia pressed her back against it and let herself breathe. Three hours. After four years of nothing, she had three hours.

And then she'd look him in the eye and ask where the icy hell he'd been while she raised their daughter alone.

Chapter Fifty-Seven

A va touched each object on the shelf—his comb, a brass button, the journal he'd started keeping. She reached out with her spirit, searching for any trace of him.

A week since he left her, and still...nothing.

The treehouse had gone wild without him. Vines crawled over the furniture and out the windows. Branches pushed through gaps in the walls. The trees themselves had shifted, leaning toward the changed angle of the sun—toward the Realms he now held in place.

Even the forest missed him.

Ava sank to the floor, her fingertips dragging through the dirt, catching on embedded stones.

"Why did you choose *them*?" she whispered.

The question had circled through her mind a thousand times this week. He should have let her do it. She'd been ready. And now he was back in the place he'd despised for ten years—the liminal plane, the biosphere, the nowhere.

It should have been her.

She inhaled—ragged, shaking—and let herself break.

The sound that came out of her wasn't crying. It was something older than that, something animal. Ugly, howling grief that echoed through the empty treehouse and out into the forest beyond. Her lungs burned. Her ribs ached like they'd been cracked open. Tears dripped off her lashes, splashing against the floor.

The wind stirred her hair against her wet cheeks, and she let it. Let the forest witness what losing him had done to her.

Through her blur of tears, something moved.

A small vine, lying on the floor in front of her. Trembling.

Ava wiped her eyes with her sleeve, blinking hard. The vine curled toward her—slow, deliberate, growing inch by inch. She reached out, fingers shaking, and touched it.

It wound around her finger like a greeting. A single leaf unfurled against her skin, soft as a whisper.

"What are you doing, little plant?" Ava sniffed and got to her knees. The vine kept growing, spiraling around her wrist, and tiny white flowers burst open along its length.

Ava stood. Her heart slammed against her ribs. All around her, the treehouse came alive. Vines crawled up the walls. Ferns unfurled from the floorboards. Moss crept across the windowsills. Everything green, everything growing, reaching toward her from every direction.

Don't cry, mé talé.

The voice came from everywhere—rustling leaves, creaking branches, whispers of petals against petals. Flowers exploded open. Pinks and purples. Golds and whites and blues she had no name for. They burst from every vine, every stem, filling the treehouse until she stood in the center of a living rainbow.

Sweetness flooded the air—nectar and pollen, the dark richness of turned earth, the sharp green of growing stems.

She pressed her hand to her chest, where the silver flower lay warm against her skin, and reached.

He was there. She could almost feel him—a shimmer just beyond her fingertips, a whisper she couldn't quite hear. She strained toward it, heart pounding, fingers splayed against the air—

Nothing.

Ava inhaled a shaky breath and scrubbed at her face. Why couldn't she feel him?

"Where are you?" she whispered, tracing the edges of a large purple and white flower. It fluttered its petals, as if in answer.

She turned to go.

A breeze caught her hair, soft against her cheek. She closed her eyes, breathing in—and there he was. Clean rain and fresh mint, wafting on the wind.

Seáh llaéh! Hello! I'm Myrenne Mae (pronounced MY-wren MAY) and I'm a transplant to the Northwest Arkansas area whose love for romance began when I swiped classic romance reads from my mom's bookshelf. I have always loved complex characters, high fantasy worlds, magic and, of course, heart-wrenching romances.

Three Coins from a Dead Man's Pocket is my debut novel in a new epic science fantasy romance series.

Scan the QR code to find my landing page. You can send me a tube, sign up for my awesome newsletters, and follow me on socials (because I love getting to know my readers!)

Maió yah aríla vylá efusar.

May your soul fly freely, friends.

~Myrenne